THE BEST
HORROR OF THE YEAR

VOLUME TWO

Also Edited by Ellen Datlow

A Whisper of Blood

Alien Sex

Black Heart, Ivory Bones (with Terri Windling)

Black Swan, White Raven (with Terri Windling)

Black Thorn, White Rose (with Terri Windling)

Blood is Not Enough: 17 Stories of Vampirism

Inferno: New Tales of Terror and the Supernatural

Lethal Kisses

Little Deaths

Lovecraft Unbound

Nebula Awards Showcase 2009

Off Limits: Tales of Alien Sex

Omni Best Science Fiction: Volumes one through three

Omni Books of Science Fiction: Volumes one through seven

Omni Visions one and two

Poe: 19 New Tales Inspired by Edgar Allan Poe

Ruby Slippers, Golden Tears (with Terri Windling)

Salon Fantastique: Fifteen Original Tales of Fantasy
    (with Terri Windling)

Silver Birch, Blood Moon (with Terri Windling)

Sirens and Other Daemon Lovers (with Terri Windling)

Snow White, Blood Red (with Terri Windling)

Swan Sister (with Terri Windling)

Tails of Wonder and Imagination

The Beastly Bride: And Other Tales of the Animal People
    (with Terri Windling)

The Best Horror of the Year, Volume One

The Coyote Road (with Terri Windling)

The Dark: New Ghost Stories

The Del Rey Book of Science Fiction and Fantasy

The Faery Reel: Tales from the Twilight Realm

The Green Man: Tales of the Mythic Forest (with Terri Windling)

Twists of the Tale

Vanishing Acts

Wild Justice

The Year's Best Fantasy and Horror (with Terri Windling, Gavin J.
    Grant, and Kelly Link)

THE BEST
HORROR OF THE YEAR

VOLUME TWO

EDITED BY ELLEN DATLOW

NIGHT SHADE BOOKS
SAN FRANCISCO

First Edition

ISBN: 978-1-59780-173-7

Printed in Canada

Night Shade Books
Please visit us on the web at
www.nightshadebooks.com

I'd like to dedicate this volume to all the horror readers out there.

ACKNOWLEDGMENTS

I'd like to thank Eugene Myers for his invaluable help throughout the year.

I'd like to acknowledge the following magazines and catalogs for invaluable information and descriptions of material I was unable to obtain: *Locus, All Hallows, Publishers Weekly,* and *Prism* (the quarterly journal of fantasy given with membership to the British Fantasy Society). I'd also like to thank all the editors who made sure I saw their magazines during the year, the webzine editors who provided printouts, and the book publishers who provided review copies in a timely manner. Also, the writers who sent me printouts of their stories when I was unable to acquire the magazine or book in which they appeared.

And thank you to Jeremy Lassen and Jason Williams for your support. And Ross Lockhart for your patience.

CONTENTS

SUMMATION 2009

The seventeen stories and novelettes chosen this year come from anthologies, magazines, single author chapbooks, and one was originally published in a webzine. The authors hail from the United States, Wales, England, Canada, and Australia. Eight stories are by writers whose stories I've never before chosen for a Best of the Year volume.

AWARDS

The Bram Stoker Awards for Achievement in Horror is given by the Horror Writers Association. The full membership may recommend in all categories but only active members can vote on the final ballot. The awards for material appearing during 2008 were presented at the organization's annual banquet held Saturday evening, June 13th 2009 in Burbank, California.

2008 Winners for Superior Achievement:

Novel: *Duma Key* by Stephen King; First Novel: *The Gentling Box* by Lisa Manetti; Long Fiction: "Miranda" by John R. Little; Short Fiction: "The Lost" by Sarah Langan; Fiction Collection: *Just After Sunset* by Stephen King; Anthology: *Unspeakable Horror*, edited by Vince A. Liaguno and Chad Helder; Nonfiction: *A Hallowe'en Anthology* by Lisa Morton; Poetry Collection: *The Nightmare Collection* by Bruce Boston; Lifetime Achievement Award: Chelsea Quinn Yarbro and F. Paul Wilson.

Richard Laymon, President's Award: John Little; Silver Hammer Award: Sèphera Girón; Specialty Press Award: Bloodletting Press.

The Shirley Jackson Award, recognizing the legacy of Jackson's writing, and with the permission of her estate, was established for outstanding achievement in the literature of psychological suspense, horror, and the dark fantastic. The second year's awards were announced at Readercon, held in Burlington, Massachusetts.

The winners for the best work in 2008:

Novel: *The Shadow Year* by Jeffrey Ford (William Morrow); Novella: *Disquiet* by Julia Leigh (Penguin/Hamish Hamilton); Novelette: "Pride and Prometheus" by John Kessel (*The Magazine of Fantasy & Science Fiction*); Short Story: "The Pile" by Michael Bishop (Subterranean Online, Winter 2008); Collection: *The Diving Pool* by Yoko Ogawa (Picador); Anthology: *The New Uncanny* edited by Sarah Eyre and Ra Page (Comma Press).

The World Fantasy Awards were announced November 1, 2009 at the World Fantasy Convention in Calgary, Alberta. Lifetime Achievement recipients were previously announced.

Winners for the best work in 2008:

Life Achievement: Ellen Asher and Jane Yolen; Novel: *The Shadow Year*, by Jeffrey Ford (William Morrow)and *Tender Morsels* by Margo Lanagan (Allen & Unwin; Knopf); Novella: "If Angels Fight", Richard Bowes (*F&SF* 2/08); Short Story: "26 Monkeys, Also the Abyss", Kij Johnson (*Asimov's* 7/08); Anthology: *Paper Cities: An Anthology of Urban Fantasy*, Ekaterina Sedia, ed. (Senses Five Press); Collection: *The Drowned Life*, Jeffrey Ford (HarperPerennial); Artist: Shaun Tan; Special Award Professional: Kelly Link & Gavin J. Grant (for Small Beer Press and Big Mouth House); Special Award Non-Professional: Michael J. Walsh (for Howard Waldrop collections from Old Earth Books).

NOTABLE NOVELS OF 2009

Midnight Picnic by Nick Antosca (Word Riot Press) is a lean novel that grabs the reader from the first line to the last, about a man drawn against his will to accompany the ghost of a murdered boy who wants to revenge himself on his murderer. No fireworks: just good writing, fine characterizations, a meditation on death—and a slowly mounting sense of menace.

The Domino Men by Jonathan Barnes (William Morrow) is a sequel to the entertaining *The Somnambulist*. If you liked that novel, you'll love this. If you didn't care for that one, I suspect you'll enjoy this one more. A secret war is being waged in contemporary London for the very soul of the city and its inhabitants. A mild-mannered file clerk is dragooned into the Directorate, the organization in which his grandfather played a great part. The terrifying, monstrous, and hilarious Hawker and Boon, two supernatural creatures of a destructive nature that appear as humans dressed as British schoolboys (think of them as the evil Tweedle Dee and Tweedle Dum) are more important in *The Domino Men* than in *The Somnambulist*. A few unexpected (and punch in the gut) twists and turns towards the end keep the plot moving towards its—just right—conclusion.

The Manual of Detection by Jedediah Berry (Penguin Press) is a charming first novel that brings to mind G.K. Chesterton's *The Man Who Was Thursday* and Franz Kafka. Despite superficial similarities to *The Domino Men*: a lowly clerk is promoted within a large organization whose job is to prevail against the chaos being created by evil personages, the protagonist comes of age while solving the dangerous mysterious around him. In *The Manual of Detection*, too, a clerk in a detective agency is promoted to detective when the detective he reported to disappears. But from there, the Berry veers into surreal territory.

The Little Sleep by Paul G. Tremblay (Henry Holt and Company) is an intriguing first novel that drags readers along with its narcoleptic detective protagonist through the pain, powerlessness, and humiliation of his medical condition while forcing us to accompany him on his search for truth no matter where it leads. Mark Genevich's car accident several years before the beginning of the novel has left him battered and odd looking and with narcolepsy—i.e. he falls asleep at the drop of a hat, as a result of stress or sometimes just living. He's a private eye whose biggest case falls into his lap while he's asleep. Compromising photos of a young woman who might be the DA's daughter are left by... someone—who hires him to... what? Mysteries abound and Mark's the only one who can (or wants) to solve them.

Handling the Undead by John Ajvide Lindqvist (Quercus) is by the Swedish author of the excellent novel *Let the Right One In*, adapted into an even better movie, so I had high hopes for his take on zombies. These are not teeth gnashing, brain eating George Romero zombies but dead-eyed empty vessels of their former owners remaining generally placid, unless they pick up strong emotions from those alive. The epidemic—which only lasts a fixed period of time and takes place exclusively in Sweden, seems to be triggered by mysterious falling caterpillars. The story is more concerned with the living than the unliving as the resurrected are dubbed and follows three recently bereaved families, and how they deal with the trauma of their loved ones' return, often in advanced states of decay.

Last Days by Brian Evenson (Underland Press) combines the novella "The Brotherhood of Mutilation," published in 2003, with a new section. A former undercover cop is lauded for not only surviving an attack that leaves him mutilated, but killing his attacker one-handed after he cauterizes the wound himself. His notoriety brings him to the attention of a cult that takes literally the biblical entreaty to cut off the hand that offends thee. The detective is abducted and brought to the religious compound to solve a mystery—or else—as he becomes involved in a power struggle between two warring groups within the cult. A scary and sometimes grisly well-written book about obsession.

Darling Jim by Christian Moerk (Henry Holt) opens with the discovery of the bodies of two sisters and their aunt in a suburb of Dublin and unfolds into even more horror, all radiating from a seductive traveling story teller who enchants every woman and girl within reach of his uncanny charms. Darling Jim, as he is dubbed by those he seduces, entrances the inhabitants of every pub he visits as he weaves his tale of two brothers, a wolf, a curse, and a princess. The mystery of the three deaths is painstakingly unraveled by a young mailman who *really* wants to be a graphic novelist as he doggedly searches for clues to the truth when he accidentally discovers the diary of one of the dead sisters.

The Mystic Arts of Erasing all Signs of Death by Charlie Huston (Ballantine

Books) is a macabre, moving, and darkly humorous novel about an emotionally damaged ex-teacher who's living off his oldest friend until he's offered the job of a lifetime—to work with Clean Team, a company that mops up after violent, or just messy, deaths. The plot careens from hilarity to tragedy, often in the same paragraph, as our protagonist meets a young lady "cute"— being hired to clean up after her rich dad, who blew his brains out with a 9mm. This is the first Huston novel I've read and it won't be the last.

The City & The City by China Miéville (Del Rey) is a dark, metaphysical police procedural that opens with the discovery of a body. The mystery is contingent on the unusual world Miéville creates, a world as bizarre in its way as any Miéville has previously envisioned: in an alternate reality from our own, two eastern European cities—Bes el and Ul Qoma—overlap in the same space, yet their citizens are forbidden to interact or acknowledge the existence of any person/event/physical location in the other, overlapping city. Breach is invoked for those caught breaking the law, and the guilty are taken away, never to be seen again. A detective from the Bes el Extreme Crime Squad is assigned to the murder and his life is utterly changed. It's a great read.

Finch by Jeff VanderMeer (Underland Press) is the culmination of the author's series about the imaginary city of Ambergris. Another reluctant detective, the eponymous protagonist, has a past that comes back to bite him in the ass, a girlfriend he doesn't trust, and a partner who is turning into something not human. Past wars among the various factions inhabiting Ambergris over the years are nothing compared to the enemy contemporary citizens face—the fungoid current rulers of their world. A great read that's not contingent on reading the earlier books.

Dark Places by Gillian Flynn (Shaye Areheart Books) is a disturbing, multi-stranded tale that begins one wintry January night in 1985, when most of a family are slaughtered, apparently by the fifteen year old son, in what is dubbed the "Satanic Sacrifice of Kinnakee, Kansas." A seven-year-old girl survives, and her testimony sends her brother to prison for life. The fallout from the crime and its aftermath haunt Libby Day for the next twenty-five years. Then, intruding into her depression, bitterness, anger, and unhappy solitude is a member of a club that studies and even celebrates the perpetrators of violent crimes. Some of the members think Ben is innocent and want to get Libby to recant. She's gradually forced to face the past and slowly becomes interested in discovering the truth of what actually happened that night.

Johannes Cabal the Necromancer by Jonathan L. Howard (Doubleday) is a darkly macabre and entertaining deal with the devil tale about a necromancer who realizes that without his soul (given up years before the novel begins) he cannot accomplish his best research. So Satan, a bit bored, makes a new deal in which Cabal must get one hundred suckers to sign their souls away in exchange for the return of his own. Satan helps Cabal along by giving him a traveling circus—all the necromancer's got to do is populate it with the animated dead.

Bad Things by Michael Marshall (William Morrow) is a fine, tense novel of supernatural and psychological horror. It begins with a four-year-old child dying—of nothing—after falling off the pier at the family home in a small town in Washington state. Three years later, the father—divorced and still grieving—is living in a summer resort town in Oregon and working as a waiter. A mysterious email he receives churns up the past, forcing him to return to Black Ridge, Washington and confront the dark practices of the founding family. It's more complex than it sounds and is a very good read.

The Forest of Hands and Teeth by Carrie Ryan (Delacorte) is a debut young adult zombie novel that while beautifully written, enjoyable and creepy, could have trimmed much of the (seemingly) never-ending teen angst. The set up is a good one. An isolated village is ruled by a strict religious order of Sisters and surrounded by hordes of the "unconsecrated" (zombies). The order inculcates the inhabitants with the dogma that they are the last enclave of humans on earth, although one family's females pass on stories of the "ocean." The protagonist is spunky and stubborn and adventurous and is forced throughout the story to make hard choices. This will probably appeal more to teenage girls than adults.

Slights by Kaaron Warren (Angry Robot) is the long and complex debut novel by a talented Australian teller of dark tales. At eighteen years old, Stevie (aka Stephanie) is responsible for the death of her mother in a car crash. Her beloved father, a cop, was killed in a shootout a few years before. The story follows the troubled eighteen year old Stevie through her mid-thirties. When not attempting suicide she works in a nursing home, keeps the front yard of the house she's inherited filled with manure, and spends hours sifting through the detritus of decades of her family's existence… including bones of all kinds.

The Little Stranger by Sarah Waters (Riverhead) is a terrific historical novel that slowly ratchets up the tension as it becomes a disturbing psychological puzzle and haunted house story. The story is told from the point of view of a middle-aged local doctor in a post World War II Britain still suffering shortages. Dr. Faraday becomes physician to the owners of Hundreds Hall, the now-dilapidated estate on which his mother worked as a maid years earlier. Are the members of the household becoming unhinged from stress or is there something at Hundreds that is actually trying to "get" them? Despite the house's fall into ruin, it becomes the focal point of Faraday's longed for acceptance by the local gentry, and his stubborn, extreme rationalization plus this fixation that has dominated his imagination since childhood prevents him from actually helping before it's too late.

The Sound of Building Coffins by Louis Maistros (Toby Press) is a nicely told novel about New Orleans in 1891. The one-year-old child of a lynched Sicilian immigrant has been possessed by a demon and after the doctor flees in terror, several other people attempt to save the child's life. The repercussions on those involved ripple over the years into a complex (sometimes too complex) tale of jazz, love, hate, betrayal, death, and redemption. Well worth reading for the way it brings New Orleans of that period alive.

The Lovers by John Connolly (Atria) is the eighth Charlie Parker book in the series. I've only read a couple, and not the immediate predecessor to this one, but the author provides enough back story for this hardboiled supernatural novel to stand on its own. Parker's private eye license has been pulled, and he works in a bar. Restless, he investigates events from when he was fifteen: his policeman father killed a pair of unarmed teenagers and then killed himself. As Parker probes deeper, he uncovers secrets that were meant to protect him from the mysterious, eponymous lovers.

Audrey's Door by Sarah Langan (HarperCollins) is a riveting novel of a promising but emotionally troubled architect who takes up residence in an infamous old building in New York. As in Jackson's *The Haunting of Hill House*, the Breviary—as a result of its mad creator, founder of the cult of Chaotic Naturalism—houses great evil that influences those who live there.

Therapy by Sebastian Fitzek, translated by Sally-Ann Spencer (St. Martin's Press) from German and published in the UK in 2008. A deft psychological thriller about a famous therapist who loses it when his twelve-year-old daughter goes missing. Four years later, his marriage is finished, he's quit his practice, and moved to the peaceful island where he and his family had a vacation home. Then things *really* go bad. This is the kind of book that three-fourths of the way through I was afraid to continue because I couldn't believe that the author would be able to pull off a believable, satisfying ending. I think he succeeded.

The Red Tree by Caitlín R. Kiernan (Roc) is a disturbing novel about a blocked writer who leaves Atlanta after a disastrous relationship for an isolated town in Rhode Island, hoping to find peace. Unfortunately, instead she finds an unfinished manuscript by a former tenant who committed suicide and her life goes downhill from there. Is the giant red oak that she can see from her kitchen window more than just a tree or is she overreacting in her fragile emotion state? The tale is told in diary entries, news reports, and excerpts from the abandoned manuscript but what really makes for a gripping read is the voice of the protagonist.

ALSO NOTED

This is not meant to be all inclusive but merely a sampling of dark fiction available during 2009.

When I wrote my summary of the 2008 year in horror, it looked like zombies were finally fading away, so I was surprised when the sub-genre made an overwhelming resurgence in 2009. Zombie zombies everywhere: anthologies, movies, novels, comic books.

Some of the notable zombie fiction: *Breathers: A Zombie's Lament* by S. G. Browne (Broadway) a black comedy about a newly risen zombie that just wants some love. *The Zombie Survival Guide: Recorded Attacks* by Max Brooks (Three Rivers) is a graphic novel history of zombie attacks beginning in 60,000 BC, Africa. The UK publisher Abaddon Books has a whole zombie line of novels dubbed "Tomes of the Dead" including *Way of the Barefoot Zombie* by Jasper Bark and *Tide of Souls* by Simon Bestwick. Then there's the first classic mash-up *Pride and Prejudice and Zombies* by Jane Austin and Seth Grahame-Smith (Quirk Books). *Jailbait Zombie* by Mario Acevedo (Eos) mixes vampires with zombies in this fourth of a series of novels featuring a vampire Private Eye. *Patient Zero* by Jonathan Maberry (St. Martin's Press) is about terrorists who have a weapon that can turn people into zombies.

Vampires never retreated—they can still be found in *23 Hours* by David Wellington (Three Rivers) fourth in his vampire series. Dacre Stoker (nephew of Bram) and co-author Ian Holt, wrote a sequel to the classic titled *Dracula The Un-Dead* (Dutton). Terence Taylor debuted with a vampire novel called *Bite Marks* (St Martin's) and *The Thirteenth* by L.A. Banks(St. Martin's), the twelfth and final novel in her vampire Huntress legend series was published. *Lord of Misrule*, (NAL) is book five in Rachel Caine's Morganville Vampires series. Guillermo del Toro tried his hand at prose, co-authoring *The Strain* with Chuck Hogan, the book is the first of a trilogy about a vampire plague. Charlaine Harris's Sookie Stackhouse series, bolstered by the hit TV adaptation, has a ninth entry with *Dead and Gone*, and Laurell K. Hamilton came out with *Skin Trade*, the seventeenth in the Anita Blake series.

Young adult vampire novels have exploded into the world as a result of the success of Stephenie Myers' *Twilight* series: *Night Life* is a young adult vampire novel by Nancy A. Collins (HarperTeen), sequel to *Vamps. Hunted* by P.C. Cast and Kristin Cast (St. Martin's), fourth in their House of Night series. *Eternal* by Cynthia Lietich Smith (Leisure), is a prequel to her novel *Tantalize*.

Plus a ton of paranormal romances featuring vampires. Paranormal romance in general continued to sell like crazy, but as I don't consider most of them horror, I won't mention any here.

Sandman Slim by Richard Kadrey (Eos) features the potent mix of noir, monsters and fallen angels. *Bestial* by Ray Garton (Dorchester) is a sequel to his werewolf novel, *Ravenous. Cold Black Hearts*, is a supernatural detective novel by Jeff Marriotte (Jove).

The Hound Hunters by Adam Niswander (Hippocampus) is a Lovecraftian novel, third in his Shaman Cycle series.

Adult literary writer Dale Peck turns his talents to horror with *Body Surfing* (Atria), about a demon-possessed teenager and a demon hunter. In the novella *The Show That Smells* (Akashic) by Derek McCormack the wife of a dying country western singer makes a deal with a vampire. In *Those Who Went Remain There Still* (Subterranean), Cherie Priest's short novel is about a winged monster in nineteenth-century-rural Kentucky. Her novel *Boneshaker* (Tor) got lots of buzz with its steampunk background and ravenous living dead.

Many of the field's regulars had new books out: Stephen King's *Under the Dome* (Scribner), is about a small New England town mysteriously trapped under a huge glass dome and how its inhabitants react. Dan Simmons followed up his brilliant *The Terror* with another historical novel with supernatural elements, *Drood*, (Little, Brown) about Charles Dickens and his unfinished novel, *The Mystery of Edward Drood*. L.A. Banks also had a werewolf novel out, *Undead on Arrival* (St. Martin's Press), third in the Crimson Moon series. Mike Carey's *Dead Man's Boots* (Grand Central) continued his excellent hardboiled series about an exorcist. *The Black Train* by Edward Lee (Leisure) is an historical novel about an evil train. Leisure also published Lee's *The Golem*, and *The Bone Factory* by Nate Kenyon, *Far Dark Fields* by Gary Braunbeck, and *The Shore* by Robert Dunbar.

Some horror novels were published as non-genre including *The Glister* by John Burnside (Doubleday/Nan Talese) about disappearances in the woods poisoned by a nearby chemical factory, *Fragment* by Warren Fahy (Delacorte) an sf horror novel about the discovery of a dangerous lost world, and *The Séance* by John Harwood (Houghton Mifflin/Harcourt) is the International Horror Guild Award-winning author's second novel and takes place in Victorian England.

And some promising debuts: *House of Windows* by John Langan (Night Shade Books) and *Twisted Ladder* by Rhodi Hawks (Forge).

ANTHOLOGIES

Phantom edited by Paul G. Tremblay and Sean Wallace (Prime Book) is a fine follow-up to their 2007 non-theme anthology *Bandersnatch*. This one, with fourteen new stories is more to my dark taste, with some very strong horror stories by Steve Rasnic Tem, Stephen Graham Jones, Steve Eller, Vylar Kaftan, Nick Mamatas, Steve Berman, and Lavie Tidhar. With an introduction by Tremblay. The Eller story is reprinted herein.

British Invasion edited by Christopher Golden, Tim Lebbon, and James A. Moore (Cemetery Dance) is a long overdue (the copyright page says 2008, but the book came out in early 2009), mixed bag of twenty-one stories intended to showcase contemporary horror from the United Kingdom. The stories range from ineffective and slight to powerful. The strongest are by Mark Morris, Adam L. G. Neville, Mark Chadbourne, Peter Crowther, Paul Finch, Phil Nutman, Tony Richards, Conrad Williams, and a collaboration by Steve Lockley and Paul Lewis. Steven Volk supplies an introduction, the three editors provide a preface, and Kim Newman wraps it all up with his afterword.

Shivers V edited by Richard Chizmar (Cemetery Dance) is the best of this non-theme series so far. Of the twenty-four stories, two, those by Stewart O'Nan and Steve Vernon, are reprints, and at least eight of the others are quite dark and very good. One other, by Chet Williamson, is also a winner but it's not very dark.

He is Legend: An Anthology Celebrating Richard Matheson edited by Christopher Conlon (Gauntlet) has an in interesting variety of sequels, prequels, and stories inspired by a fantastic writer who's written some of the most memorable pieces of horror in the genre's history. The book has fifteen stories and novellas, the best by Gary A. Braunbeck, Stephen King and Joe Hill, F. Paul Wilson, Joe R. Lansdale, and Richard Christian Matheson. The volume includes the previously unpublished 20,000 word screenplay of Fritz Leiber's novel *Conjure Wife*, adapted by Matheson and Charles Beaumont and later filmed as *Burn, Witch Burn*.

Poe: 19 New Tales Inspired by Edgar Allan Poe edited by Ellen Datlow (Solaris) was commissioned in honor of Poe's Bicentennial in 2009 and intends to showcase stories infused with Poe's themes while avoiding pastiches. Stories by Suzy McKee Charnas, Laird Barron, and John Lanagan are reprinted herein.

Return of the Raven: New Tales and Poetry Inspired by Edgar Allan Poe Master of the Macabre edited by Maria Grazia Cavicchioli (Horror Bound Magazine Publications) is another tribute volume, with twelve stories and poems that stay a bit closer to the originals.

Hellbound Hearts edited by Paul Kane and Marie O'Regan (Pocket Books) is an ambitious all original anthology of twenty-one stories inspired by images from Clive Barker's movie *Hellraiser*: the puzzle box that when opened brings forth the Cenobites, who promise extreme pain and pleasure. As in most cases, the stories that are the most interesting are those that use the theme as a starting rather than end point. The best stories are by Conrad Williams, Sarah Langan, Chaz Brenchley, Nancy Kilpatrick, Mark Morris, Kelley Armstrong, Peter Atkins, Simon Clark, a short graphic novel by Neil Gaiman and Dave McKean, and a collaboration by Gary A. Braunbeck and Lucy A. Snyder. Clive Barker provides a preface, Stephen Jones an introduction, and Doug Bradley (Pinhead in the movies) an afterword.

Strange Tales III edited by Rosalie Parker (Tartarus Press) is a strong follow up to the award-winning *Strange Tales II*, with seventeen odd, eerie, and outright strange stories. Not all of them are dark, but enough are to keep any horror reader happy. My favorites of the seventeen are those by Nina Allan, Gerard Houarner, Angela Slatter, and Adam Golaski. The Allan is reprinted herein.

Gaslight Grotesque edited by J.R Campbell and Charles Prepolec (Edge) is a Sherlock Holmes inspired anthology that's surprisingly fresh and entertaining, possibly because it's the rare volume that allows Holmes and Watson to be dumbfounded by matters (which is course, the antithesis of the ratiocination for which Holmes is known. There's much that's actually supernatural in here. The most interesting stories are by Neil Jackson, Robert Lauderdale, J. R. Campbell, and Barbara Roden.

American Fantastic Tales: Poe to Pulps and *American Fantastic Tales: 1940s to Now* edited by Peter Straub is a two-volume set of supernatural literature. The two books together are a treat to anyone interested in the evolution of the dark side of the fantastic in American literature.

Tesseracts Thirteen edited by Nancy Kilpatrick and David Morrell (Edge) is the first of Canada's *Tesseracts* series dedicated to horror fiction. Alas, the format—organizing the stories in three themed sections—lessens the impact of the whole book because it emphasizes the sameness of the stories in the first section (Youth) rather than showcasing their differences. The strongest stories in the book were by David Nickle, Suzanne Church, Daniel Sernine, and Michael Kelly.

Exotic Gothic 3: Strange Visitations edited by Danel Olson (Ash-Tree Press) is an all original anthology of nineteen stories set all over the world, with terrific ones by Simon Clark, Terry Dowling, Simon Kurt Unsworth, and Kaaron Warren and good ones by the other contributors. The Warren is reprinted herein.

Bare Bone 11 is the last volume of Kevin L. Donihe's (Raw Dog Screaming) anthology series that began life as a magazine, and it went out with a bang. Most of the eighteen stories were very strong.

The Eternal Kiss: 13 Vampire Tales of Blood and Desire edited by Trisha Telep (Running Press) is aimed at teens and was disappointing (conflict of interest alert—Terri Windling and I are co-editing one for the same market but with only a few sexy stories). The best are by Holly Black, Cecil Castellucci, Cassandra Clare, and Kelley Armstrong.

By Blood We Live edited by John Joseph Adams (Night Shade Books) boasts over 200,000 words of vampire fiction, all but two reprints by some of the biggest names around, including Anne Rice (with a much reprinted story), Stephen King, Kelley Armstrong, L. A. Banks, Garth Nix, Neil Gaiman, David Wellington, Tanith Lee, Caitlín R. Kiernan, and many others. The two originals, a story by Sergei Lukyanenko, Russian author of the vampire novels (adapted into films) *Night Watch* and *Day Watch* and a novella by John Langan, are extra special.

The Vampire Archives: The Most Complete Volume of Vampire Tales ever Published edited by Otto Penzler (Vintage Crime) is even bigger, with twice as many stories—but these include stories by some of the earliest authors of vampire fiction and poetry including Lovecraft, Poe, Keats, E. F. Benson, D. H. Lawrence, and M. E. Braddon up to 2001, with stories by Richard Layman, David J. Schow, Lisa Tuttle, Tanith Lee, and F. Paul Wilson.

Dark Jesters edited by Nick Cato and L.L. Soares (Novello Publishers) has ten humorous horror stories.

Half-Minute Horrors edited by Susan Rich (Harper) is an anthology of very short horror stories for kids, with contributors including Lemony Snicket, M.T. Anderson, Holly Black, Margaret Atwood, Neil Gaiman, Brian Selznick, Jonathan Lethem, Joyce Carol Oates, and Libba Bray, among many other well-known names.

Infernally Yours: A Descent into Edward Lee's Vision of Hell edited and illustrated by GAK (Necro) with all original stories by John Shirley, Charlee Jacob, John Everson, Bryan Smith, Brian Keene, Gerard Houarner, and the collaborative team of L.H. Maynard and M.P. N. Sims. Also included is a short novel by Lee, himself. A good-looking book for collectors and those who delight in Lee's type of horror.

Spook City edited by Angus Mackenzie (PS) features three Liverpudlian horror writers: Clive Barker, Peter Atkins, and Ramsey Campbell, showcasing stories by each of them that are meant to explore and illuminate their native city. The only original story in the book is by Peter Atkins, but it's a very good one. Doug Bradley, the actor who played Pinhead in Barker's *Hellraiser* movie series, wrote the introduction.

Eldritch Horrors: Dark Tales edited by Henrik Sandbeck Harksen (H. Harksen Productions) is volume one of a projected series of H.P. Lovecraft mythos anthologies. In this volume are nine original stories and five reprints. The best of the originals are by Linda Navroth, Gary Hill, Blake Wilson, and Paul Mackintosh.

Apparitions edited by Michael Kelly (Undertow Publications) is a very good anthology from a new imprint created by Kelly. While some of the thirteen original stories don't actually have enough *story* for my taste, there are some excellent tales by Simon Bestwick, Paul Finch, Gemma Files, Steve Duffy, and Gary McMahon.

Dark Delicacies III: Haunted edited by Del Howison and Jeff Gelb (Running Press) has nineteen new stories and a poem. The strongest stories in the book are by Marie Alexander, Michael Boatman, Simon Clark, Gary A. Braunbeck, John Connelly, Mick Garris, Richard Christian Matheson, and David Morrell (the latter, very moving but not horror).

Zombies: Encounters with the Hungry Dead edited by John Skipp (Black Dog & Leventhal) is a whopper of a zombie anthology (almost 700 pages) by the co-father of zombie anthologies. The book comes with an introduction and overview of the renewal of zombie fiction by the editor, an historical perspective of the zombie, and thirty-two stories, reprints, except for five originals. Most of the reprints will be overly familiar to zombie aficionados. The best of the originals are by Justine Musk, Eric Shapiro, Carlton Mellick III, Mehitobel Wilson, and Cody Goodfellow.

The Dead That Walk edited by Stephen Jones (Ulysses Press) is a mixed reprint and original zombie anthology of twenty-four stories. Most of the eleven originals are notable, particularly those by Robert Shearman, Stephen Woodworth, Nancy Holder, Gary McMahon, Lisa Morton, Scott Edelman, and Weston Ochse.

Cthulhu Unbound and *Cthulhu Unbound 2* are both edited by John Sunseri and Thomas Brannon (Permuted Press) and are entertaining volumes of fifteen original Lovecraftian stories each. The strongest from the first volume are by John Goodrich, John Claude Smith, Kim Paffenroth, Kevin Lauderdale, and C. J. Henderson and those from volume 2 are by Rhys Hughes, Joshua Reynolds, Brandon Alspaugh, William Meikle, and Inez Schaechterle.

Lovecraft Unbound edited by Ellen Datlow (Dark Horse) is intended to be Lovecraftian without ichor or tentacles. It features twenty stories, four of them reprints. A collaboration by Dale Bailey and Nathan Ballingrud is reprinted herein.

Leaves of Blood edited by Mike Brown (Altair Australia) may or may not be a themed anthology—hard to tell. Something about a "gothic reign" but there are spiders, bullies and ghouls, some mass and/or serial killings and vampiric critters. The best of the nine original stories is by Jean Claude Dunyach.

Campus Chills edited by Mark Leslie (Stark Publishing) has thirteen stories taking place on Canadian college campuses across the country. The strongest stories are by Steve Vernon and Brit Trogen.

Festive Fear edited by Stephen Clark (Tasmaniac Publications) has fourteen original Christmas stories by Australians. Few of the writers use the Australian landscape to differentiate these stories from those about any other English speaking country, most are unsubtle, and one is torture porn. Despite this, there *were* notable stories by Marty Young and Felicity Dowker.

Cinnabar's Gnosis: A Homage to Gustav Meyrink edited by D.T. Ghetu (Ex Occidente Press) has twenty-three original fantasy and dark fantasy stories, most a bit ornate for my taste. Meyrink was an Austrian who lived between 1868 and 1932 and is best known for his novel *The Golem*. My favorite stories in the book were by Michael Cisco, Steve Rasnic Tem, R.B. Russell, Reggie Oliver, and Adam Golaski.

Dead Souls edited by Mark Deniz (Morrigan Books) has twenty-five stories, sixteen of them published for the first time. The best originals are by Carole Johnstone and Sharon Irwin, (who has contributed a wonderful dark fantasy).

Monstrous: Twenty Tales of Giant Creature Terror edited by Ryan C. Thomas (Permuted Press) is exactly what it says, but only a few of the stories are a cut above the typical pulp tropes. The two best are by E. Anderson and Gregory L. Norris.

Midnight Walk edited by Lisa Morton (Darkhouse Publishing) showcases fourteen mostly new writers from the west coast or Midwest, many of them from southern California. The best story is by newcomer Joey O'Brian.

Buried Tales of Pinebox, Texas edited by Matt M. McElroy (12 to Midnight) is a loosely connected shared world anthology of a small town in eastern Texas with more than its share of haunts, monsters, and mysterious murders. Surprisingly, there's an original story by David Wellington, and perhaps unsurprisingly, it's the best in the book.

Vile Things: Extreme Deviations of Horror edited by Cheryl Mullenax (Comet Press) has fifteen stories by relatively new writers plus four reprints by Ramsey Campbell, Graham Masterton, Jeffrey Thomas, and C.J. Henderson.

Mighty Unclean edited by Bill Breedlove (DarkArts Books), has sixteen new and reprinted stories by four writers: Gemma Files, Gary A. Braunbeck, Cody Goodfellow, and Mort Castle. With an introduction by the editor.

The Fourth Black Book of Horror edited by Charles Black (Mortbury Press) is a disappointing lot of fifteen stories, with only a few standouts. The best were by Reggie Oliver, David Sutton, Daniel McGachey, and Gary McMahon. *The Fifth Black Book of Horror* with thirteen stories, was much better with notable stories by Craig Herbertson, David A. Riley, Ian C. Strachen, John Llewellyn Probert, and again, Reggie Oliver. The Oliver is reprinted herein.

Twilight Zone: 19 Original Stories on the 50ᵗʰ Anniversary edited by Carol Serling (Tor) is a, tepid tribute to the great original television series. Most of the stories have kind of predictable sting in the tail endings. The best dark ones are by Tad

Williams and Whitley Strieber.

New Dark Voices 2 edited by Brian Keene (Delirium Books) features novellas from three horror writers: Nick Mamatas and two relatively new writers Brett McBean and Ronald Damien Malfi.

Strange Brew edited by P. N. Elrod (St. Martin's Press) has nine urban tales of vampires and witches and werewolves, a few of them even scary. The best are by Rachel Caine and Faith Hunter.

Northern Haunts edited by Tim Deal (Shroud Publishing) presents 100 horror vignettes, all situated in New England.

Harvest Hill edited by Michael J. Hultquist and Douglas Hutcheson (Graveside Tales) present thirty-one interconnected tales about the town of Harvest Hill, Tennessee.

Deadly Dolls edited by Terrie Leigh Relf and David Byron (NVH Books) is possibly the only anthology I've ever seen titled to reflect the gender of contributors rather than the contents. It's an all woman contributor non-theme horror anthology of fourteen stories, including one by co-editor Relf. In addition, there are interviews with six female writers (only three of whom have stories in the anthology).

Twisted Legends features thirty three brief retellings of various urban legends. *The Middle of Nowhere: Horror in Rural America* has twenty-eight horror tales and are both edited by Jessy Marie Roberts (Pill Hill Press).

Butcher Shop Quartet II edited by Frank J. Hutton (Cutting Block Press) features four dark novellas by five new writers.

Cover of Darkness edited by Tyree Campbell (Sam's Dot) has twenty-one dark urban fantasy stories, all but one published for the first time.

The Ancestors by L. A. Banks, Tananarive Due, and Brandon Massey (Dafina) is comprised of three original horror novellas (no editor listed).

Fifty-Two Stitches: Horror Stories edited by Aaron Polson (Strange Publications) features fifty-two pieces of flash fiction.

Mammoth Book of Best New Horror 20 edited by Stephen Jones (Robinson) had twenty stories, and none overlapped with *The Best Horror of the Year, Volume One* although we both took different stories by some of the same authors.

MIXED-GENRE ANTHOLOGIES

This is the Summer of Love: A Postscripts New Writers Special Number 18, edited by Peter Crowther and Nick Gevers (PS) is the first volume in the quarterly anthology series replacing *Postscripts* Magazine. It's excellent, with most of the ten stories at least tinged with darkness if not outright horror. I very much enjoyed all of the stories, with Norman Prentiss's opener, the creepiest. It's reprinted herein. *Enemy of the Good* Number 19 edited by Peter Crowther and Nick Gevers (PS) has twelve stories about good vs. evil and the slippery demarcations between the two. The stories I liked the best were by M.K. Hobson, Daniel Abraham, Marly Youmans, and Justin Cartaginese. The third PS anthology of the year was *Edison's*

Frankenstein, Number 20/21, edited by Peter Crowther and Nick Gevers. Only a few of the stories in this volume were dark but the best of those were by Eric Schaller, Rjurik Davidson, and George-Oliver Châteaureynard. *Sideshow* edited by Deborah Noyes (Candlewick) is third in a series of young adult original anthologies. The first two *Gothic!* and *The Restless Dead* had some fine dark stories by a variety of writers known within the horror field. Alas, *Sideshow*, with its seven stories and three comic strips, has a minimal amount of dark fiction, with one strong story about tortured bread starter (really) by Cecil Castellucci. *Masques* edited by Gillian Polack and Scott Hopkins (CSFG Publications) is a mixed genre anthology featuring mostly new writers. Unfortunately, while some of the ideas and characterizations are good, the bulk of the stories are too short (thirty stories in 280 pages) and possibly for this reason they don't feel full finished. Despite this, there's good dark fiction by Cat Sparks, Chris Jones, Felicity Bloomfield, Marcus Olsson, Jason Fischer, and an intriguing mystery by Phillip Berrie. *Cern Zoo: Nemonymous Nine* edited by Des Lewis is an entertaining volume in this annual series of stories, not matching up the authors with the titles (until the next volume). A few of the stories are too fragmentary or oblique to be fully satisfying but others among the darker ones are quite effective, peculiarly those by Dominy Clements, Tim Nickels, Lee Hughes and Steve Duffy. The Duffy is reprinted herein. *The Stories Between* edited by Greg Schauer, Jeanne Benzel, and W.H. Horner (Fantasist Enterprises) celebrates the thirty year existence of the Delaware genre bookstore Between Books, with sixteen stories of sf/f/h, most original. One of the reprints is by Jonathan Carroll. The best new dark story is by Gregory Frost. *British Fantasy Society Yearbook 2009* edited by Guy Adams showcases twenty-one new stories by members of the organization, with fiction ranging from sword and sorcery, contemporary fantasy, supernatural and psychological horror. Some of the strongest darker stories are by Rob Shearman, Christopher Fowler, Tim Lebbon, Gary McMahon, Adam L. G. Nevill, Sarah Pinborough, Conrad Williams, and Stephen Volk. *The Death Panel: Murder, Mayhem, and Madness* edited by Cheryl Mullenax (Comet Press) has thirteen new hardboiled, dark, sometimes grotesque crime stories, many of them horror. The best are by Tim Curran, Kelly M. Hudson, David Tallerman, John Everson, and Tom Piccirilli. *The World is Dead* edited by Kim Paffenroth (Permuted Press) follows up on Paffenroth's 2007 zombie anthology *History is Dead*. In the new volume, living with zombies is the norm and the eighteen varied stories show how people do, with the best by William Bolen, Gary A. Braunbeck, Jack Ketchum, Carole Lanham, Ralph Robert Moore, and David Wellington. *Cinema Spec: Tales of Hollywood and Fantasy* edited by Karen A. Romanko (Raven Electrick Ink) has thirty-two poems and vignettes about Hollywood. The only notable dark pieces are by Sarah Brandel and Lisa Morton.

The Best American Mystery Stories 2009 edited by Jeffery Deaver (Mariner) has the best of the genre published in the year 2008 by Kristine Kathryn Rusch, James Lee Burke, Joyce Carol Oates, Michael Connelly, and others. Some of the stories are dark, half are taken from literary journals, others from venues ranging from *Ellery Queen's Mystery Magazine* and Akashic's Noir anthology series, to an sf anthology of alternative history. *Between the Dark and the Daylight and 27 More of the Best Crime and Mystery Stories of the Year* edited by Ed Gorman and Martin H. Greenberg (Tyrus Books) includes stories by Joyce Carol Oates, Norman Partridge, Kristine Kathryn Rusch, Jeremiah Healey, Bill Pronzini, and others. *Kaiki: Uncanny Tales From Japan volume 1: Tales of Old Edo* selected and introduced by Higashi Masao (Kurodahan Press) is the first volume of a three book series and is a wonderful introduction to the uncanny fiction of Japan. This book—with ten stories first published in Japan between 1898 and 1993—focuses on stories taking place in Old Edo (now known as Tokyo). With a preface by Robert Weinberg and an essay on the origins of Japanese weird fiction by Masao.

JOURNALS, NEWSLETTERS, MAGAZINES, AND WEBZINES

It's important to recognize the work of the talented artists working in the field of fantastic fiction, both dark and light. The following artists created art that I thought especially noteworthy during

2009: Mike Bohatch, Zach McCain, Daniel Merriam, Anita Zofia Siuda, Steven Archer, Russell Dickerson, Adam Tredowski, David Gentry, John Stanton, Andrew Hook, Dominic Harman, Derek Ford, Jason Van Hollander, Phil Fensterer, Cat Sparks, Adam Katsaros, Enaer, Saara Salmi, Sean Stone, Carrie Ann Baade, Jørgen Mahler Elbang, T. Davidson, Harry O. Morris, Bob Hobbs, Ben Baldwin, Laura Givens, Eric M. Turnmire, Hendrik Gericke, Allen Koszowski, Vance Kelly, David Prosser, Andrew Trabbold, Andrew Chase, Stephen Stanley, Shweta Narayan, Rhiannon Rasmussen-Silverstein, Vincent Chong, Danielle Serra, Julia Helen Jeffrey, Martin Bland, Mark Pexton, and Warwick Fraser-Coombe.

Because of the annual turnover in small-press magazines—most rarely last more than a year or two—it's difficult to recommend buying a subscription to those that haven't proven their longevity. But I urge readers to at least buy single issues of those that sound interesting. Most magazines have web sites with subscription information, eliminating the need to include it here. The following are, I thought, the best in 2009.

Some of the most important magazines/webzines are those specializing in news of the field, market reports, and reviews. *The Gila Queen's Guide to Markets*, edited by Kathryn Ptacek, emailed to subscribers on a regular basis, is an excellent fount of information for markets in and outside the horror field. *Market Maven*, edited by Cynthia Ward is a monthly email newsletter specializing in professional and semi-professional speculative fiction market news. Ralan.com is *the* web site for up-to-date market information. *Locus*, edited by Charles N. Brown (who died mid-2009), Liza Groen Trombi, and Amelia Beamer and *Locus Online*, edited by Mark Kelly specialize in news about the science fiction and fantasy fields, but include horror coverage as well.

The only major venues specializing in reviewing short genre fiction are the newly revived *Tangents* edited by David Truesdale and *Locus* but none of them specialize in horror. Of the two, only *Locus* publishes regularly.

There are, however, some important critical journals covering horror: *Dead Reckonings: A Review of Horror Literature* edited by S. T. Joshi and Jack M. Haringa and published by Hippocampus Press is a fine review journal that comes out twice a year. It focuses on contemporary work while also considering the classics. In addition to the reviews, it includes the regular column "Ramsey Campbell, Probably." Haringa is leaving the co-editorship with the next issue and Tony Fonseca will take his place. *Dissections* edited by Gina Wisker, David Sandner, Michael Arnzen, Al Wendland, and Lawrence Connolly is an online journal specializing in horror. The May issue focused on teaching horror. *Wormwood: Literature of the Fantastic, Supernatural and Decadent* edited by Mark Valentine and published by Tartarus Press, had two issues in '09 and they're as usual erudite and perfect for those interested in literature of "the fantastic, supernatural and decadent." *Studies in the Fantastic* edited by S. T. Joshi only published one issue in 2009 and unfortunately it was announced that it was to be its last.

Of the three nonfiction magazines I read that specialize in movies, my favorite is *Video Watchdog*, a bi-monthly edited by Tim Lucas. It specializes—some would say obsesses—over minute details of all kinds of movies, and is erudite yet entertaining. In addition to review of movies, it has a regular audio column by Douglas E. Winter and a regular column by Ramsey Campbell.

Fangoria, edited by Anthony Timpone, is the daddy of the existing magazines that cover horror movies of all types, and celebrated its thirtieth anniversary in 2009. It's superficial but entertaining, covering big budget and independent horror productions, the grislier the better. The magazine also features regular columns on news, DVD releases, video games, comics, and books. And lots of gore. A special anniversary issue had a Hall of Fame, featuring fifty top horror personalities as voted by the readers, and a new column by former "Raving and Drooling" columnist David J. Schow.

Rue Morgue, edited by Jovanka Vuckovic, is another monthly media magazine covering horror in all its bloody glory (with the still photos to prove it) but unlike *Fangoria*, in between the gore there are often thoughtful articles and columns. Probably the most intriguing article appearing in *Rue Morgue* in 2009 was *Graven Images: The Art of Japanese Bloody Ukiuo-E Woodcutting* by Jason Lapeyre, featuring full color illustrative examples of the art.

Black Static edited by Andy Cox is the most consistently excellent horror magazine published. Its mix of fiction, movie and book reviews, interviews, and regular columns creates a vibrant magazine that should be required reading for everyone interested in topnotch horror fiction. The six issues of 2009 had many fine stories. One, by Carole Johnstone, is reprinted herein.

Cemetery Dance edited by Brian Freeman has been trying its best to get back on a regular schedule. In 2008 there was only one issue published. In 2009 three came out, and they were chockfull of good fiction by Sarah Langan, Brian Keene, Darren Speegle, Lawrence C. Connolly, Bruce McAllister, Peter Straub, and Stephen Mark Rainey. During the year there were interviews with editor Stephen Jones and writers Thomas Tessier, Ray Garton, Jeff Strand, Tananarive Due, and Peter Straub. Starting with issue #61 I've been contributing a column called "The Last Ten Books I Read."

Supernatural Tales edited by David Longhorn, had two issues in 2009, both up to the magazine's usual high standards in writing quality. Despite this, too many stories in issue 15 telegraphed their endings within a few pages. The stories that most impressed me in both issues were by Huw Langridge, Jim Steel, Gary Fry, and Louis Marvick.

Not One of Us is the long running magazine edited by John Benson and the traditional annual one-off is *(Going Going) Gone* featuring some ghostly fare. The best darker pieces in 2009 are by Kent Cruse, Gemma Files, and Patricia Russo. There was a notable poem by J. C. Runolfson in the one-off.

Weird Tales edited by Ann VanderMeer had three issues out (one overlapping with '08) and they featured excellent stories by Kathe Koja, Eric Red, Jeffrey Ford, Eric Lis, Michael Phillips, Ben Thomas, Paul G. Tremblay, Robert Davies, Micaela Morrissette, and Felix Gilman. Included in the varied mix are reviews, columns on various subjects, and interviews. The Morrissette story is reprinted herein.

Necrotic Tissue edited by R. Scott McCoy moved from online to print with issue 7. There was good dark fiction in 2009 by Samantha Sterner and Bruce Cooper.

H. P. Lovecraft's Magazine edited by Marvin Kaye only lasted five issues and the last was only available as a free pdf file download. There were notable stories by Eugie Foster, Terry McGarry, Andrew J. Wilson, Park Godwin, and Ekaterina Sedia.

Midnight Street edited by Trevor Denyer brought out two issues in 2009 and announced that it would be leaving behind its print edition, instead being available for download from its website. In addition to the fiction there were book reviews plus interviews with Guy N. Smith, Gord Rollo, and self-proclaimed vampire and writer Michelle Belanger. The strongest stories in 2009 were by William Mitchell, Marion Arnott, Gary Couzens, and Tony Richards.

Arkham Tales: A Magazine of Weird Fiction edited by Nathan Shumate is a good online zine that I only discovered with its issue 4. There were strong stories by Maurissa Guibord, Paula R. Stiles, and Fraser Sherman.

Inhuman edited by Allen Koszowski published its first issue since 2006, with notable originals by Justin Gustainis, Joe, Nassise, Matt Cardin, Darren Speegle, Stephen Mark Rainey, and Kiel Stuart. There were also three classic reprints, an article on Stephen King by Bev Vincent, and illustrations by the editor throughout. All in all, it was a very good issue.

Dark Discoveries edited by James Beach published three issues in 2009, one celebrating the fiftieth anniversary of *Twilight Zone*. Throughout the year there were interviews with Steve Rasnic Tem, Dan O'Bannon, S. T. Joshi, Brian Lumley, and others. The strongest stories were by Cody Goodfellow, Glen Singer, W. H. Pugmire, David A. Riley, Steve Rasnic Tem, and Christopher Conlon.

The Digest of Philippine Genre Stories produced a special horror issue edited by Yvette Tan. Although some of the stories were good, I didn't find any of them especially dark.

MIXED-GENRE MAGAZINES

New Genre Issue six edited by Adam Golaski had only four stories. Two, those by Eric Schaller and Stephen Graham Jones were powerful horror stories. The Jones is reprinted herein. *Sybil's Garage* Issue six edited by Matthew Kressel had some fine darker stories by James B. Pepe, Genevieve Valentine, and Toiya Kristen Finley. *New Horizons* edited by Andrew Hook for members of the British Fantasy Society is tuned more toward fantasy than horror (their sister publication, *Dark Horizons*, takes care of that) but there were good dark tales by Paul Campbell and Eliza Chan. *On Spec* edited by members of the Copper Pig Society, including the fiction editors: Robin S. Carson, Barb Galler-Smith, Susan MacGregor, Ann Marston, and Diane L. Walton, is a Canadian quarterly that published sf/f/h. There was strong dark work in 2009 by Colleen Anderson, Sandra Glaze, Andrew Bryant, Amanda Downum, Dave Cherniak, and E. Catherine Tobler. Issue 78, the fall issue, celebrated the magazine's twentieth anniversary. *Borderlands*, an Australian magazine edited by Stephen Dedman is a mix of science fiction, fantasy, and horror. Number eleven, published in 2009 is the last issue of the digest-sized magazine and I'll be sorry to see it go. That issue had good dark stories by Madhvi Ramani, Durand Welsh, Bill Congreve, and Jason Fischer. *Aurealis*, the Australian mixed-genre magazine edited by Stuart Mayne brought out two issues in 2009. My favorites of the dark stories were by Jason Fischer, Brendan Carson, and Geoffrey Maloney. *Talebones* edited by Patrick Swenson published a good genre mix in 2009 and had notable dark stories by David Sakmyster, Marie Brennan, and Jason D. Wittman. Unfortunately, #39 was the magazine's last issue, after a run of fourteen years. Up until the last five issues Patrick and Honna Swenson co-edited the magazine, then Patrick took it over completely. *Albedo One* edited by John Kenny, Frank Ludlow, David Murphy, Roelof Goudriaan, and Robert Neilson published two issues in 2009. There was a scattering of dark stories during the year by Mike O'Driscoll, Sara Joan Berniker, and D.T. Neal plus the usual book reviews and interviews with Paul Di Filippo and Greg Egan. *Andromeda Spaceways Inflight Magazine* is an Australian bimonthly edited by a rotating co-op only sometimes publishes horror. The best dark stories in 2009 were by Anna Tambour, Grant Stone, Caroline M. Yoachim, and Jessica E. Kaiser. *Shimmer* edited by Beth Wodzinski is an attractive little zine that specializes in publishing newer writers and usually has at least some notable dark fiction. There were two issues out in 2009, with good dark stories by Nir Yanev, Alex Wilson, Sara Genge, and Claude Lalumière. *Electric Velocipede* edited by John Klima won the Hugo Award for Best Fanzine, (I think it's the first that a fiction magazine has ever won) and is a lovely little perfect bound digest sized zine that publishes a variety of material. There was more dark fiction than usual in its three 2009 issues, with notable stories and poetry by Matthew Kressel, Marly Youmans, Toiya Kristen Finley, A. C. Wise, and Barbara Krasnoff. *Paradox* edited by Christopher Cevasco, published its last issue in 2009 and had a strong piece of dark fiction by Maura McHugh. *Space and Time* edited by Hildy Silverman always publishes a mixed bag of fiction and poetry. In the three issues I saw in 2009 there were good dark stories by Ian R. Faulkner, Stephanie Burgess, and Rich Sampson. *The Magazine of Fantasy & Science Fiction* edited by Gordon Van Gelder always has a number of dark fantasy and horror stories and 2009 was no different. There were notable dark stories by Jim Aiken, Richard Bowes, Fred Chappell, Albert E. Cowdrey, Michael Meddor, Sarah Thomas, Geoff Ryman, and Matthew Hughes. *Realms of Fantasy* edited by Shawna McCarthy is a bi-monthly that focuses on fantasy but occasionally publishes dark fiction. The best dark stories in 2009 were by Tanith Lee, Dirk Strasser, and S. E. Ward. *Ellery Queen Mystery Magazine* edited by Janet Hutchings often has at least a few extremely dark stories during the year and in 2009 the strongest were by Kristine Kathryn Rusch, Charles Ardai, David Dean, R. T. Smith, Barbara Callahan, Trina Corey, Marjorie Eccles, Mick Herron, and David Raines. *Black Clock 10* edited by Steve Erickson, is a magazine published by California Institute of the Arts in association with the MFA Writing Program. While every issue has some interesting fiction, this one focuses on noir, and for me it was the best I've read in awhile. Interspersed with excellent dark fiction by Francesca Lia Block, Scott Bradfield, Brian Evenson, T. Towles, are recommendations of "essential noir" movies, characters, music, novels, performances, and even a poem. A highly recommended issue. *Lady Churchill's Rosebud Wristlet* edited by Gavin J. Grant and Kelly Link brought out issue 24 in 2009, in which there were notable dark stories by Alexander Lamb, Liz Williams, and Jasmine Hammer. *Probe* is the long running official publication of Science Fiction and Fantasy South Africa. In addition to publishing a few short stories every issue there are interviews and reviews and a letter column. It comes out quarterly.

COLLECTIONS

Northwest Passages by Barbara Roden (Prime) is an impressive debut collection of ten stories (two appearing for the first time). Four of the reprints were given honorable mentions in *The Year's Best Fantasy and Horror* series, and one was reprinted in #19. With an introduction by critic Michael Dirda. One of the best collections of the year.

Mindful of Phantoms by Gary Fry (Gray Friar Press) features eighteen ghostly stories, six of them original to the collection. In his introduction, he describes the genesis of the stories.

Madder Mysteries by Reggie Oliver (Ex Occidente Press) is a very attractive volume from a new press that has, in addition to eight stories (several published for the first time), several critical essays, and "curiosities"—a series of amusing vignettes, black and white illustrations by the author throughout, and a lovely frontispiece painting by Joanna Dunham. The stories are uniformly entertaining and most are extraordinarily creepy. Oliver introduces the volume.

Cold to the Touch by Simon Strantzas (Tartarus Press) is the second collection by the author, with thirteen stories, six of them new, all of them quite powerful and dark. With an afterword by the author. Tartarus also published Washington Irving's *The Legend of Sleepy Hollow and Other Stories*, the first to assemble all of Irving's supernatural fiction in one volume. Also *Tales of Terror* by Guy de Maupassant selected and translated by Arnold Kellett collecting thirty-two of the author's best tales of terror. *The Double Eye* by William Fryer Harvey brings together thirty of the author's uncanny tales, including "The Beast With Five Fingers," made into the classic horror movie with Peter Lorre.

Broken on the Wheel of Sex by Jack Ketchum (Overlook Connection Press) is an expanded and more reasonably priced edition of the collection published by Delirium in 2003. It has eighteen stories dubbed the "Stroup" stories written under a pseudonym early in Ketchum's career.

Got To Kill Them All and Other Stories by Dennis Etchison (CD Publications) contains eighteen reprints, some previously uncollected, spanning the author's forty year career. With an introduction by George Clayton Johnson.

Monstrous Affections by David Nickle (Chizine Publications) is this Canadian's first collection, although the stories in it were originally published between 1994 and 2009. That story from 1994, "The Sloan Men," was chosen for the *Year's Best Fantasy and Horror: Sixth Annual Collection*. Michael Rowe provides an introduction to a powerful collection.

Pictures of the Dark by Simon Bestwick (Gray Friar Press) is the author's second collection, following *A Hazy Shade of Winter* published in 2004. Of the twenty-three stories of supernatural and psychological horror, almost half appear for the first time. The originals are very strong and the collection is highly recommended.

The Darkly Splendid Realm by Richard Gavin (Dark Regions Press) is the author's third collection and showcases thirteen stories, eleven of them appearing for the first time. With an introduction by Laird Barron. The book is available in three editions, all signed by Gavin.

In the Closet, Under the Bed by Lee Thomas (Dark Scribe) features fifteen stories, nine original to this nicely varied and very readable collection. Some of the stories explore the intersecting guilt and confusion of men faced with their repressed desire for other men.

A Blood of Killers by Gerard Houarner (Necro Publications) collects thirteen reprints and twelve original dark, intense psychological horror stories, many about the brutal amoral hired assassin called Max and the Beast within him—a darkness that is even more depraved and brutal than he. Although a few of the stories about Max and his missions have story arcs that are a bit too similar, most of the stories are powerful and very readable.

The Catacombs of Fear by John Llewellyn Probert (Gray Friar Press) is the author's entertaining follow-up to his collection, *The Faculty of Terror*. Five macabre stories are tied together by linking interludes about a reverend given a tour of his new Cathedral post,. All the stories are original to the collection and they're sure to give the reader a chill.

Nachtmahr-Strange Tales by Hanns Heinz Ewers (Side Real Press) (1871–1943) wrote three (vaguely) autobiographical novels and several volumes of short stories. His novels and a few of his stories were translated and published in the 1920s but barring a volume by the Runa Raven press (published 2000) he is largely still unknown to the English speaking world not least because these volumes now command high prices on the second-hand market.

Blanket of White by Amy Grech is an expanded (by two new stories) edition of the author's first collection *Apple of My Eye*.

Men of the Otherworld by Kelley Armstrong (Bantam) collects four novellas, three of which originally were published on the author's website as e-serials, complementing her Otherworld werewolf novel series.

Shards by Australian writer Shane Jiraiya Cummings (Brimstone Press) and illustrated by Andrew J. McKiernan has over thirty pieces of flash fiction, eight published for the first time.

Midnight Grinding by Ronald Kelly (Cemetery Dance) is a first collection of thirty-two stories (two published for the first time) by a veteran writer of southern inflected horror, whose career boomed and busted back between the mid-eighties and the mid-nineties. Some of the reprints were originally published in small press magazines such as *2 AM*, *Deathrealm*, and *Eldritch Tales* starting in 1988, in *Cemetery Dance*, and in some high profiles original anthologies.

Putting the Pieces in Place by R. B. Russell (Ex Occidente Press) is an excellent and very satisfying debut collection of five stories of the supernatural, all published for the first time.

The Shadows of Kingston Mills by David B. Silva (Dark Regions Press) is the author's second collection and all but one of the twelve stories appear for the first time. The entertaining stories, a mixture of supernatural and psychological horror, all take place in the imaginary town of the title in Northern California.

Brief Encounters: Da Silva Tales by Chico Kidd is the fourth in a series of self-published chapbooks about the adventures of a Portuguese pirate captain with magical powers. In this volume there are four stories, two published for the first time.

Blood Will Have Its Season by Joseph S. Pulver, Sr. (Hippocampus Press) is an ambitious debut including thirty stories and one long poem, most published for the first time. Although obviously influenced by H. P. Lovecraft and Robert W. Chambers, for the most part Pulver uses their influences to create potent tales of his own. A writer to keep an eye on. S. T. Joshi provides an introduction.

Slices by James A. Moore (Earthling Publications) is the author's entertaining first collection, and includes nine reprints from 1998–2007 plus three new ones and individual story notes.

Taste of Tenderloin by Gene O'Neill(Apex) has eight stories, all taking place in San Francisco's tenderloin district. Three of the stories are published for the first time.

The Monster Within Idea by R. Thomas Riley (Apex) features eighteen stories, with more than half original to the collection.

Remove the Eyes by Ralph Robert Moore (Sentence Publishing) is the first collection by a fine writer, with nine stories, one reprinted in *The Year's Best Fantasy and Horror: Nineteenth Annual Collection*, and four new stories.

Aftershock and Others: 19 Oddities by F. Paul Wilson (Forge) is a great showcase for Wilson's storytelling, with a variety of supernatural and more naturalistic tales.

Feminine Wiles John Grover (Blu Ph'er Publishing) contains sixteen stories with females as the main characters.

Unhappy Endings by Brian Keene (Delirium) is the author's fourth collection. Some of the stories were originally published in limited editions so this is a boon for Keene fans. Other appear for the first time.

Dark to Be Scared 4: Thirteen More Tales of Terror by Robert D. San Souci (Cricket) are stories for kids. I've never found San Souci's work to be particularly scary or disturbing but perhaps eight-to twelve-year olds would.

Shades of Blood and Shadow by Angeline Hawkes (Dark Regions) has fourteen reprints published between 2002 and 2008 and three originals.

Copping Squid and Other Mythos Tales by Michael Shea (Perilous Press) features eight stories, four of them new. Shea's mythos tales are often shot with humor, despite the awful things happening to his characters, and always imaginative.

Mysteries of the Worm: Early Tales of the Cthulhu Mythos by Robert Bloch edited by Robert M. Price (Chaosium) contains twenty stories, an overall introduction and individual story introductions by Price, and an afterword by Bloch written in 1981.

The Day the Leash Gave Way by Trent Zelazny (Fantastic Books) is a first collection, with twenty-four horror stories by a young writer who has nice way with the vernacular but is a bit overly influenced by Joe R. Lansdale. Four of the stories appear for the first time.

Martyrs and Monsters by Robert Dunbar (DarkHart) has fourteen stories, running the gamut in subject matter from noir and urban legends to the origins of zombies and vampires. All are all reprints.

Broken Symmetries by Steve Redmond (Dog Horn Publishing) is the first collection by a writer of mostly satirical horror. Four of the twenty-six stories were originally published in 2009.

Fresh Blood: Tales From the Speculative Graveyard by Lawrence R. Dagstine (Sam's Dot) has thirteen stories, six original to the collection.

They That Dwell in Dark Places by Daniel McGachey (Ghost House/Dark Regions Press) is a collection of traditional and nicely creepy ghost stories by a Scottish writer new to me. Half the thirteen stories appear for the first time, one was published in an anthology in 2009, the rest were published in UK anthologies from 2006 to 2008. For those who enjoy M. R. James, McGachey's fiction might be your cup of tea. Included are story notes by the author.

Broken Skin by Nate Southard (Thunderstorm Books) is a beautiful looking limited edition hardcover of fifteen horror stories, nine published for the first time by a writer whose storytelling skills are growing by leaps and bounds.

Skeleton in the Closet and Other Stories by Robert Bloch (Subterranean Press) is a collection of sixteen previously uncollected stories and is edited by Stefan Dziemianowicz.

Dark Entities by David Dunwoody (Dark Regions Press) presents eleven stories, five of them published for the first time.

Slice of Life by Paul Haines (The Mayne Press) features seventeen of the award-winning Australian author's visceral, often profane stories. With one original.

Necroscope: Harry and the Pirates: And Other Tales from the Lost Years by Brian Lumley (Tor) has six Lovecraftian tales, three of them original novellas.

The Dream of X and Other Fantastic Visions by William Hope Hodgson (Night Shade) is the fifth and final volume of The Collected Fiction of William Hope Hodgson series. Edited by Douglas A. Anderson and with an introduction by Ross E. Lockhart.

Waking the Dead and Other Horror Stories by Yvette Tan (Anvil) feature ten stories in this debut collection by an award-winning Filipino writer.

The Edge of the County and Other Stories by Trevor Denyer (Immediate Directions) collects fourteen stories, four new.

Silent Weapons for Quiet Wars by Cody Goodfellow (Swallowdown Press) is an interesting mix of fifteen psychological, supernatural and sf/horror stories by a promising new horror writer.

MIXED-GENRE COLLECTIONS

Fugue State by Brian Evenson (Coffee House Press) features nineteen, surreal, strange, and sometimes extremely dark stories, a prolific short story writer under appreciated in the horror community. Several of the stories in the collection were given Honorable Mentions in *The Year's Best Fantasy and Horror*. *Returning My Sister's Face* by Eugie Foster (Norilana Books) features twelve stories published between 2005 and 2008 by a promising new fantasist. *The Haunted Heart and Other Tales* by Jameson Currier (Lethe Press) is the author's third collection. The twelve stories, six published for the first time are focused on the gay experience and most, despite being ghost stories, have only minimal elements of horror, or even fantasy. *You Might Sleep* by Nick Mamatas (Prime) is an intriguing mixed bag of twenty-two pieces of sf/f/horror/political/satirical fiction. Four stories are original to the volume. *Scenting the Dark* by Mary

Robinette Kowal (Subterranean) is a short collection of eight reprinted stories written by a winner of the John W. Campbell Award for Best New Writer, on the basis of her short fiction. Two of the eight stories are dark. *A Book of Endings* by Deborah Biancotti (Twelfth Planet Press) is the author's first collection and showcases twenty-one stories, six of them new. Some are horror, others not. But most are very fine. *Everland and Other Stories* by Paul Witcover (PS) has twelve stories of science fiction, fantasy, dark fantasy, and horror—five of them new and all are good. With an introduction by Elizabeth Hand. *The Nightfarers* by Mark Valentine (Ex Occidente Press) from an ambitious new publisher out of Romania, contains fourteen stories that are more in the weird and gothic tradition than outright horror but the collection is a very good example of its kind. Eight of the stories are published for the first time. *Ugly Man* by Dennis Cooper (Harper Perennial) has eighteen, mostly original, very brief stories about gay men. Some of the stories are as dark and powerful as his early novels, *Frisk* and *Closer*, both of which were obsessed with sex and death. *Horror Story and Other Horror Stories* by Robert Boyczuk (Chizine Publications) has nineteen short stories, five appearing for the first time in this debut mixing science fiction, surreal fiction, and dark fictions, most dealing with love and loss. *Scaring the Crows* by Gregory Miller (Stonegarden.net) features twenty-one stories and vignettes of fantasy and dark fantasy, all but two published for the first time. *The Sound of Dead Hands Clapping* by Mark Rich (Gothic Press) features six stories previously published in small press magazines between 1993 and 2000. *The Collected Stories of Roger Zelazny* (NESFAS) is a good-looking hardcover six volume series collected all Zelazny's short fiction and poetry. The series was edited by David G. Grubbs, Christopher S. Kovacs, and Ann Crimmins. It contains introductions and tributes by Robert Silverberg, Kristine Kathryn Rusch, Walter Jon Williams, Gardner Dozois, David G. Hartwell, Neil Gaiman, George R. R. Martin, and other sf/f luminaries. Although best known for his Amber series, much of his short fiction includes dark fantasy and sometimes horror. *Zoo* by Otsuichi translated by Terry Gallagher (Haika Sora) showcases eleven weird, fantastic, horrific, and just plain odd stories by the thirty-two-year old Japanese writer. *A Robe of Feathers and Other Stories* by Thersa Matsuura (Counterpoint) is a masterful debut collection of surreal, sometimes horrific but always richly Japanese stories. Eleven of the seventeen stories appear for the first time. *Pumpkin Teeth* by Tom Cardamone (Lethe Press) is a mixture of thirteen stories of fantasy, dark fantasy, and horror. Five of the stories appear for the first time. *Objects of Worship* by Claude Lalumière (Chizine Publications) features twelve strong stories of science fiction, fantasy, dark fantasy, and horror. Two stories appear for the first time. *The Best of Gene Wolfe: A Definitive Retrospective of His Finest Short Fiction* (Tor) features thirty-one of Wolfe's science fiction, fantasy, and horror stories published between 1970 and 1999, including many of my personal favorites, including two that were in the horror half of *Year's Best Fantasy and Horror*. *Collected Stories* by Lewis Shiner (Subterranean Press) is a gorgeous retrospective of forty-one stories by an underrated writer who has been writing stories of sf/f/h for over thirty years. With story notes by the author. *We'll Always Have Paris* by Ray Bradbury (William Morrow) has twenty-two new stories from the master of the fantastic. *Memories of the Future* by Sigizmund Krzhizhanovsky translated from the Russian by Joanne Trumbull (NYRB) has seven stories written in the Soviet Union in the 1920s, most satirical, some dark. *There Once Was a Woman Who Tried to Kill Her Neighbor's Baby: Scary Fairy Tales* by Ludmilla Petrushevskaya translated by Keith Gessen and Anna Summers (Penguin) is a very weird collection of nineteen stories by a writer who has won the Russian equivalent of the Booker Prize. *The Creepy Girl and Other Stories* by Janet Mitchell (Starcherone) features fifteen disturbing stories.

NONFICTION BOOKS

Horror 101: The A-list of Horror Films and Monster Movies edited by Aaron Christiansen (Midnight Marquee) is a collection of essays covering movies in detail, alphabetically, from all over the world. *Weird Words: A Lovecraft Lexicon* by Dan Clores (Hippocampus Press's) is a hefty trade paperback covering words/names from Abbadon to Zmargad, defining them, showing their derivation, and giving examples of their usage. *Bela Lugosi and Boris Karloff: The Expanded Story of a Haunted Collaboration* by Gregory William Mank (McFarland and Company) is a dual biography expanded by half from its original edition published in 1990. The new edition has more interviews, new photographs, and a revised filmography. *Twilight and Other Zones: the Dark Worlds of Richard Matheson* edited by Stanley Wiater and Matthew R. Bradley (Citadel) is a collection of essays, tributes, afterwords and introductions to Matheson's work, plus extensive bibliography. *Haunted Heart: The Life and Times of Stephen King* by Lisa Rogak (Thomas Dunne Books) is the first biography of the most famous practitioner of horror fiction alive today. *The Television Horrors of Dan Curtis* by Jeff Thompson (McFarland), about the director, producer, and writer of such classics as *The Night Stalker* and *Dark Shadows* TV series. *The Edogawa Rampo Reader* by Edogawa Rampo and translated by Seth Jacobowitz (Kurodahan Press) is an anthology of stories and essays by the grandmaster of Japanese crime and horror fiction. *In the Land of Long Fingernails: A Gravedigger in the Age of Aquarius* by Charles Wilkins (Skyhorse publishing) is a first person account of five months in the author's life during the summer of 1969, when he worked as a gravedigger in one of Toronto, Canada's largest cemeteries. *Zombie Holocaust: How the Living Dead Devoured Pop Culture* by David Flint (Plexus) is about the zombie in history, religion, and ultimately in movies. *The Zombie Handbook: How to Identify the Living Dead and Survive the Coming Zombie Apocalypse* by Rob Sacchetto (Ulysses Press) includes advice on everything zombie from feeding habits and favorite sexual positions to surviving and fighting the brain-eaters. *Phantom Variations* by Ann C. Hall (McFarland) examines the themes and variations evolving from the classic Gaston Leroux 1910 novel. Jack Hill: *The Exploitation and Blaxploitation Master, Film by Film* by Calum Waddell (McFarland) interviews Hill himself, Roger Corman, and others about the work of the man who wrote and directed such low budge movies as *Spider Baby*, *Foxy Brown*, and *Switchblade Sisters*, breaking racial and gender barriers. *Beyond Hammer: British Horror Cinema Since 1970* by James Rose (Auteur) provides new critical readings of several British horror films and contextualizes them vis-à-vis British themes and history. *Hollywood Monster: A Walk Down Elm Street With the Man of Your Dreams* by Robert Englund and Alan Goldsher (Pocket) is a memoir of the veteran actor who became a horror icon in 1984 by playing the villain in Wes Craven's *The Nightmare on Elm Street*. *Bite: A Vampire Handbook* by Kevin Jackson (Portobello Books Ltd) is a relatively brief history of vampires in history, literature, and the cinema. *The Pleasure and Pain of Cult Horror Films: An Historical Survey* by Bartłomie Paszylk (McFarland) is entertaining and informative, covering almost ninety movies from *The Phantom Carriage* (1921) to something called *William Winkler's Frankenstein vs. the Creature from Blood Cove* (2005). *Queens of Scream: The New Blood* edited by David Byron (BearManor) features a series of brief, lightweight interviews with contemporary scream queens, originally published in *NVF Magazine*. *Ghostly Tales of Route 66* by Connie Corcoran Wilson (Quixote Press) gives a taste of some of the weird stops along a road made famous by a song and a TV series. *Morbid Curiosity Cures the Blues* edited by Loren Rhodes (Scribner) compiles some of the best true stories from *Morbid Curiosity*, an underground magazine of the "unsavory, unwise, unorthodox, and unusual," published 1997–2006. *Inside the Dark Tower Series: Art, Evil and Intertexuality in the Stephen King Novels* by Patrick McAleer (McFarland) looks at questions of genre and art. *Stephen King Goes to the Movies* by Stephen King (Pocket) is a collection of five of the author's stories that were made into movies and his commentary about each. *The Complete Idiot's Guide to Vampires* by Jay Stevenson(Penguin/Alpha) is a general guide to vampire lore and popular media. *Stephen King: The Nonfiction* by Rocky Wood and Justin Brooks (CD Publications) is a guide to all of King's known nonfiction with synopses and criticism of over 560 published and twenty -four previously unpublished pieces. *They Bite: Endless Cravings of Supernatural Predators* by Jonathan Maberry and David F. Kramer (Citadel) is a compendium about various monsters. *Writers Workshop of Horror* edited by Michael Knost (Woodland Press) contains nuts and bolts and more general advice about writing horror, plus interviews with some horror notables such as Ramsey Campbell, Stephen Clive Barker, F. Paul Wilson, and Tom Piccirilli. *The Big Book of Necon* edited by Bob Booth (CD Publications) includes stories, poems, essays, and art most published in program books for Necon, the Northeast Regional Fantasy and Horror Convention. With an introduction by Douglas E. Winter, and many former guests' contributions. *The Unknown Lovecraft* by Kenneth W. Faig, Jr (Hippocampus) is a collection of thirteen essays about Lovecraft's family, life and others close to him and how they affected his work. *Classics & Contemporaries: Some Notes on Horror Fiction* by S. T. Joshi (Hippocampus) is a sampling of the reviews Joshi has published over thirty years. *On Monsters: An Unnatural History of Our Worst Fears* by Stephen T. Asma (Oxford University Press) is about the fascination of humans with monsters over the centuries. Asma studies the symbolic meaning of monsters and their psychological function. Illustrated by the author. *The New Horror Handbook* by A.S. Berman (BearManor) is a series of interviews with ten twenty-first century directors who have rebelled against the "cartoonish" character of '80s horror monsters like Freddy, Jason, and Michael Myers and moved on to more realistic and darker material.

POETRY

Star*Line, the Journal of the Science Fiction Poetry Society edited by Marge Simon, is a long-running bi-monthly poetry magazine. In 2009 there were notable dark poems in it by David Kopaska-Merkel and Marcie Lynn Tentchoff. *Mythic Delirium*, edited by Mike Allen, publishes two issues a year. In 2009 there was strong dark poem by J. C. Runolfson. *The Magazine of Speculative Poetry* edited by Roger Dutcher is published twice a year. In 2009 there was excellent dark poetry by Jennifer Crow and Spanish poet Alfredo Álamo. *Dreams and Nightmares*, edited by David C. Kopaska-Merkel, has been publishing two or three issues annually since January 1986. In 2009 there were notable dark poems by Marcie Lynn Tentchoff and Wade German. *Goblin Fruit* edited by Amal El-Mohtar, Jessica P. Wick, and Oliver Hunter is an excellent online quarterly for fantasy and dark fantasy poetry. There were notable poems by too many of the contributors to list here. Highly recommended.

The *2009 Rhysling Anthology* edited by Drew Morse (The Science Fiction Poetry Association in cooperation with Prime Books) collects the best science fiction, fantasy, and horror poetry of 2008. *Spores From Sharnoth and Other Madnesses* by Leigh Blackmore (P'rea Press) came out from an Australian Press in 2008 and contains over forty short poems, more than half published for the first time. Featuring a preface by S. T. Joshi. JoSelle Vanderhooft had two books of poetry published in 2009: *The Memory Palace*, (Norilana Books) is not really horror but the second *Fathers, Daughters, Ghosts, & Monsters* by JoSelle Vanderhooft (vanZeno Press), is far darker. The latter is illustrated by Marge Simon. *Barfodder: Poetry Written in Dark Bars and Questionable Cafes* by Rain Graves (Cemetery Dance) collects over one hundred new dark poems by the award-winning author. For anyone interested in dark poetry, this is the collection for you. *Chimeric Machines* by Lucy A. Snyder (Creative Guy Publishing) showcases thirty-six poetry of mixed-genres, some very personal.

CHAPBOOKS AND LIMITED EDITIONS

There was such an explosion of single author chapbooks in 2009 from small presses that I'm dismayed I didn't have the time to read most of them. But here are some:

The Harlequin and the Train by Paul G. Tremblay (Necropolitan Press) is an expansion of a story originally published in 2004. Surreal, complex, and extraordinarily creepy, it focuses on Rudy, a commuter train engineer, who after only a few months on the job, hits a harlequin clown standing on the tracks. The aftermath is shocking and unexpected and embroils Rudy in a web of despair and fear. There's some experimentation with structure that for me, neither enhances nor detracts from the powerful core of the tale.

The Witnesses are Gone by Joel Lane (PS) is a bleak novella about a man whose passive anger at contemporary politics and personal malaise combined with the discovery of a strange video tape draws him into a dark, Lovecraftian abyss. While this sort of story has been done before (indeed, Lane credits the anonymously written "The Vanishing Life and Films of Emmanuel Escobada" for the core idea) Lane's writing is compelling enough to make the idea his own. With an introduction by Conrad Williams.

Shrike by Quentin S. Crisp (PS) is about a bored, middle-aged Englishman who visits a widow with whom he's acquainted in a small Japanese town. The man is depressed about life in general and about a failed love affair in particular and becomes unhealthily interested in the bodies of lizards and toads that are displayed in the garden by an elusive shrike. Although the language is perfect, the introspection and lack of momentum is may not entice most readers of dark fiction. Introduction by Lisa Tuttle.

From Bad Moon: *The Hunger of Empty Vessels* by Scott Edelman is about a man whose bitter divorce has separated him from his adored emotionally disturbed son. Then one day while spying on his son at school he encounters a stranger who seems to get joy from the pain and upset that surrounds the boy; *The Lucid Dreaming* by Lisa Morton is a well-told story about a young violent paranoid schizophrenic who because of the medication she's on is one of the few people not affected by a plague of waking dreams and nightmares that wreaks havoc on society.

British writer Nicholas Royle has started publishing again with the imprint Nightjar Press. His last publishing venture was Egerton Press in the early1990s, which published the original anthologies *Darklands* and *Darklands 2* and Joel Lane's first collection *The Earth Wire*. Nightjar Press has been created to publish two fine chapbooks of the short stories: "The Safe Children" by newcomer Tom Fletcher about a desperate unemployed man who takes a job at a mysterious building as night watchman and *What Happens When You Wake Up in the Night* by Michael Marshall Smith, a deceptively simple tale about a child waking up in the night. The latter is reprinted herein.

Mama Fish by Rio Youers (Shroud) is a strong novella that begins in a such a way that seems predictable, but becomes anything but when a student at Harlequin High decides to befriend the class weirdo. The boy's determined curiosity to know more about his classmate totally changes his own life. Youers plays nicely with the reader, weaving a suspenseful and very satisfying tale.

Horn by Peter M. Ball (Twelfth Planet Press) is an entertaining fantasy/noir detective story taking place in a world in which magic abounds. A resurrected private eye is persuaded to investigate the ugly murder of a fourteen-year-old girl.

Roadkill by Robert Shearman and *Siren Beat* by Tansy Rayner Roberts (Twelfth Planet Press) are two excellent novellas in one chapbook. Shearman won the World Fantasy Award a couple of years ago for his first collection *Tiny Deaths*. *Roadkill* is as much a character study as a tale of an uneasy couple encounter with the strange during a dirty weekend. Roberts' story is more straightforward but just as entertaining as the wounded "Guardian" of Hobart, Tasmania must protect her people from two sirens on the prowl.

The Rolling Darkness Revue 2009: Bartlett: A Centenary Symposium is a lovely little chapbook purportedly honoring a little-known Edwardian writer of ghost tales, Thomas St. John Bartlett. It includes his biography and an introduction by Barbara Roden. Best of all though are three stories. One each by Glen Hirshberg and Peter Atkins, and a third by Bartlett (in actuality, by Hirshberg and Atkins). The Hirshberg is reprinted herein.

Cruel Summer by Matt Venne (Tasmaniac) is a coming of age story set against the backdrop of the series of killings committed by "The Night Stalker" in the summer of 1985. Introduction by Joe R. Lansdale.

Death Metal by Armand Rosamilia (Sam's Dot) is a fast-moving novella about a former writer/musician of "death metal" whose attempt to get out of the world he left behind is stymied by the kidnapping of his daughter.

A Pair of Little Things by John Little (Bad Moon Books) is made up of two stories—one barely published as a bonus by a publisher that went under and the other originally published in an anthology.

For You Faustine by Allyson Bird (Pendragon Press) was published to coincide with the British Fantasy Convention. A mother who lives in the sea goes to Coney Island to avenge her daughter's murder.

ODDS AND ENDS

It's Beginning to Look a Lot Like Zombies! A Book of Zombie Christmas Carols by Michael P. Spradlin (HarperCollins) is, surprise! very silly. With cheesy black and white illustrations throughout by Jeff Wiegel, over two dozen traditional carols are manhandled into songs for zombies, such as "I Saw Mommy Chewing Santa Claus" and "Deck the Halls with Parts of Wally." Need I say more? It's either your taste or not.

Dracula by Bram Stoker, pop-ups by David Hawcock, art by Anthony Williams, story by Claire Brompton (Universe) opens with an in your face pop-up of Dracula's castle plus fold-ins on the left and right page edges with the story and very small pop-ups of characters and creatures. Each subsequent paged is laid out similarly. The illustrations are richly gothic in the EC comics tradition, the paper engineering is ingenious, and the adaptation of the story does the job. It would make a great gift for kids or adults who enjoy pop-up books and horror.

The Late Fauna of Early North America: The Art of Scott Musgrove (Last Gasp) is a cornucopia of odd fantasy beasts some of which have a giant eyed cuteness that belies their utter creepiness. Think of surreal animal versions of the Keane children mixed with Japanese anime and you may have an idea of Musgrove's vision.

Amano: The Collected Art of Vampire Hunter D by Yoshitaka Amana (Dark Horse) is a four hundred page treasure of the full color art Amano created to accompany the series of novels by Hideyuki Kikuchi. The collection includes a story by Kikuchi.

A Time to Cast Away Stones by Tim Powers (Charnel House) is a beautiful, limited edition of a novella commissioned by the publisher to celebrate the house's twentieth anniversary. This imaginative dark fantasy was inspired by the discovery of the notebook with which Percy Bysshe Shelley drowned, and is related to Powers' novel *The Stress of Her Regard*, the first book Charnel House ever published.

Dissection: Photographs of a Rite of Passage 1880–1930 by John Harley Warner and James M. Edmonson (Blast Books) is a marvelous photographic exploration and social history of the education of American doctors. Many of the 138 photographs were taken by the students posing with the cadavers.

LOWLAND SEA
SUZY MCKEE CHARNAS

Suzy McKee Charnas is a born and raised New Yorker. After two years in Nigeria with the Peace Corps, she taught in private school in New York and then worked with a high school drug-abuse treatment program. In 1969 she married, and moved to New Mexico, where she began writing fiction full-time.

Her first novel, *Walk to the End of the World* (1974), was a Campbell award finalist. The cycle of four books that sprang from *Walk* ended in 1999 with *The Conqueror's Child*, which won the James P. Tiptree Award. Her SF and fantasy books and stories have also won the Hugo award, the Nebula award, and the Mythopoeic award for young-adult fantasy. Her play *Vampire Dreams* has been staged several times, and a collection of her stories and essays, *Stagestruck Vampires*, was published in 2004.

She lectures and teaches about SF, fantasy, and vampires whenever she gets the chance to, most recently in a writing workshop at the University of New Mexico. Her website is at www.suzymckeecharnas.com

Miriam had been to Cannes twice before. The rush and glamour of the film festival had not long held her attention (she did not care for movies and knew the real nature of the people who made them too well for that magic to work), but from the windows of their festival hotel she could look out over the sea and daydream about sailing home, one boat against the inbound tide from northern Africa.

This was a foolish dream; no one went to Africa now—no one could be paid enough to go, not while the Red Sweat raged there (the film festival itself had been postponed this year til the end of summer on account of the epidemic). She'd read that vessels wallowing in from the south laden with refugees were regularly shot apart well offshore by European military boats, and the beaches were not only still closed but were closely patrolled for lucky swimmers, who were also disposed of on the spot.

Just foolish, really, not even a dream that her imagination could support beyond its opening scene. Supposing that she could survive long enough to actually

31

make it home (and she knew she was a champion survivor), nothing would be left of her village, just as nothing, or very close to nothing, was left to her of her childhood self. It was eight years since she had been taken.

Bad years; until Victor had bought her. Her clan tattoos had caught his attention. Later, he had had them reproduced, in make-up, for his film, *Hearts of Light* (it was about African child-soldiers rallied by a brave, warm-hearted American adventurer—played by Victor himself—against Islamic terrorists).

She understood that he had been seduced by the righteous outlawry of buying a slave in the modern world—to free her, of course; it made him feel bold and virtuous. In fact, Victor was accustomed to buying people. Just since Miriam had known him, he had paid two Russian women to carry babies for him because his fourth wife was barren. He already had children but, edging toward sixty, he wanted new evidence of his potency.

Miriam was not surprised. Her own father had no doubt used the money he had been paid for her to buy yet another young wife to warm his cooling bed; that was a man's way. He was probably dead now or living in a refugee camp somewhere, along with all the sisters and brothers and aunties from his compound: wars, the Red Sweat, and fighting over the scraps would leave little behind.

She held no grudge: she had come to realize that her father had done her a favor by selling her. She had seen a young cousin driven away for witchcraft by his own father, after a newborn baby brother had sickened and died. A desperate family could thus be quickly rid of a mouth they could not feed.

Better still, Miriam had not yet undergone the ordeal of female circumcision when she was taken away. At first she had feared that it was for this reason that the men who bought her kept selling her on to others. But she had learned that this was just luck, in all its perverse strangeness, pressing her life into some sort of shape. Not a very good shape after her departure from home, but then good luck came again in the person of Victor, whose bed she had warmed til he grew tired of her. Then he hired her to care for his new babies, Kevin and Leif.

Twins were unlucky back home: there, one or both would immediately have been put out in the bush to die. But this, like so many other things, was different for all but the poorest of whites.

They were pretty babies; Kevin was a little fussy but full of lively energy and alertness that Miriam rejoiced to see. Victor's actress wife, Cameron, had no use for the boys (they were not hers, after all, not as these people reckoned such things). She had gladly left to Miriam the job of tending to them.

Not long afterward Victor had bought Krista, an Eastern European girl, who doted extravagantly on the two little boys and quickly took over their care. Victor hated to turn people out of his household (he thought of himself as a magnanimous man), so his chief assistant, Bulgarian Bob found a way to keep Miriam on. He gave her a neat little digital camera with which to keep a snapshot record of Victor's home life: she was to be a sort of documentarian of the domestic. It was Bulgarian Bob (as opposed to French Bob, Victor's head driver) who had noticed her interest in taking pictures during an early shoot of the twins.

B. Bob was like that: he noticed things, and he attended to them.

Miriam felt blessed. She knew herself to be plain next to the diet-sculpted, spa-pampered, surgery-perfected women in Victor's household, so she could hardly count on beauty to secure protection; nor had she any outstanding talent of the kind that these people valued. But with a camera like this Canon G9, you needed no special gift to take attractive family snapshots. It was certainly better than, say, becoming someone's lowly third wife, or being bonded for life to a wrinkled shrine-priest back home.

Krista said that B. Bob had been a gangster in Prague. This was certainly possible. Some men had a magic that could change them from any one thing into anything else: the magic was money. Victor's money had changed Miriam's status from that of an illegal slave to, of all wonderful things, that of a naturalized citizen of the U.S.A. (although whether her new papers could stand serious scrutiny she hoped never to have to find out). Thus she was cut off from her roots, floating in Victor's world.

Better not to think of that, though; better not to think painful thoughts.

Krista understood this (she understood a great deal without a lot of palaver). Yet Krista obstinately maintained a little shrine made of old photos, letters, and trinkets that she set up in a private corner wherever Victor's household went. Despite a grim period in Dutch and Belgian brothels, she retained a sweet naiveté. Miriam hoped that no bad luck would rub off on Krista from attending to the twins. Krista was an *east* European, which seemed to render a female person more than normally vulnerable to ill fortune.

Miriam had helped Krista to fit in with the others who surrounded Victor—the coaches, personal shoppers, arrangers, designers, bodyguards, publicists, therapists, drivers, cooks, secretaries, and hangers-on of all kinds. He was like a paramount chief with a great crowd of praise singers paid to flatter him, outshouting similar mobs attending everyone significant in the film world. This world was little different from the worlds of Africa and Arabia that Miriam had known, although at first it had seemed frighteningly strange—so shiny, so fast-moving and raucous! But when you came right down to it here were the same swaggering, self-indulgent older men fighting off their younger competitors, and the same pretty girls they all sniffed after; and the lesser court folk, of course, including almost-invisible functionaries like Krista and Miriam.

One day, Miriam planned to leave. Her carefully tended savings were nothing compared to the fortunes these shiny people hoarded, wasted, and squabbled over; but she had almost enough for a quiet, comfortable life in some quiet, comfortable place. She knew how to live modestly and thought she might even sell some of her photographs once she left Victor's orbit.

It wasn't as if she yearned to run to one of the handsome African men she saw selling knock-off designer handbags and watches on the sidewalks of great European cities. Sometimes, at the sound of a familiar language from home, she imagined joining them—but those were poor men, always on the run from the local law. She could not give such a man power over her and her savings.

Not that having money made the world perfect: Miriam was a realist, like any survivor. She found it funny that, even for Victor's followers with their light minds and heavy pockets, contentment was not to be bought. Success itself eluded them, since they continually redefined it as that which they had not yet achieved.

Victor, for instance: the one thing he longed for but could not attain was praise for his film—his first effort as an actor-director.

"They hate me!" he cried, crushing another bad review and flinging it across the front room of their hotel suite, "because I have the balls to tackle grim reality! All they want is sex, explosions, and the new Brad Pitt! Anything but truth, they can't stand truth!"

Of course they couldn't stand it. No one could. Truth was the desperate lives of most ordinary people, lives often too hard to be borne; mere images on a screen could not make that an attractive spectacle. Miriam had known boys back home who thought they were "Rambo". Some had become killers, some had been become the killed: doped-up boys, slung about with guns and bullet-belts like carved fetish figures draped in strings of shells. Their short lives were not in the movies or like the movies.

On this subject as many others, however, Miriam kept her opinions to herself.

Hearts of Light was scorned at Cannes. Victor's current wife, Cameron, fled in tears from his sulks and rages. She stayed away for days, drowning her unhappiness at parties and pools and receptions.

Wealth, however, did have certain indispensable uses. Some years before Miriam had joined his household, Victor had bought the one thing that turned out to be essential: a white-walled mansion called La Bastide, set high on the side of a French valley only a day's drive from Cannes. This was to be his retreat from the chaos and crushing boredom of the cinema world, a place where he could recharge his creative energies (so said B. Bob).

When news came that three Sudanese had been found dead in Calabria, their skins crusted with a cracked glaze of blood, Victor had his six rented Mercedes loaded up with petrol and provisions. They drove out of Cannes before the next dawn. It had been hot on the Mediterranean shore. Inland was worse. Stubby planes droned across the sky trailing plumes of retardant and water that they dropped on fires in the hills.

Victor stood in the sunny courtyard of La Bastide and told everyone how lucky they were to have gotten away to this refuge before the road from Cannes became clogged with people fleeing the unnerving proximity of the Red Sweat.

"There's room for all of us here," he said (Miriam snapped pictures of his confident stance and broad, chiefly gestures). "Better yet, we're prepared and we're *safe*. These walls are thick and strong. I've got a rack of guns downstairs, and we know how to use them. We have plenty of food, and all the water we could want: a spring in the bedrock underneath us feeds sweet, clean water into a well right here inside the walls. And since I didn't have to store water, we have lots more of everything else!"

Oh, the drama; already, Miriam told Krista, he was making the movie of all this in his head.

Nor was he the only one. As the others went off to the quarters B. Bob assigned them, trailing an excited hubbub through the cool, shadowed spaces of the house, those who had brought their camcorders dug them out and began filming on the spot. Victor encouraged them, saying that this adventure must be recorded, that it would be a triumph of photojournalism for the future.

Privately he told Miriam, "It's just to keep them busy. I depend on your stills to capture the reality of all this. We'll have an exhibition later, maybe even a book. You've got a good eye, Miriam; and you've had experience with crisis in your part of the world, right?"

"La Bastide" meant "the country house" but the place seemed more imposing than that, standing tall, pale, and alone on a crag above the valley. The outer walls were thick, with stout wooden doors and window-shutters as Victor had pointed out. He had had a wing added on to the back in matching stone. A small courtyard, the one containing the well, was enclosed by walls between the old and new buildings. Upstairs rooms had tall windows and sturdy iron balconies; those on the south side overlooked a French village three kilometers away down the valley.

Everyone had work to do—scripts to read, write, or revise, phone calls to make and take, deals to work out—but inevitably they drifted into the ground floor salon, the room with the biggest flat-screen TV. The TV stayed on. It showed raging wildfires. Any place could burn in summer, and it was summer most of the year now in southern Europe.

But most of the news was about the Red Sweat. Agitated people pointed and shouted, their expressions taut with urgency: "Looters came yesterday. Where are the police, the authorities?"

"We scour buildings for batteries, matches, canned goods."

"What can we do? They left us behind because we are old."

"We hear cats and dogs crying, shut in with no food or water. We let the cats out, but we are afraid of the dogs; packs already roam the streets."

Pictures showed bodies covered with crumpled sheets, curtains, bedspreads in many colors, laid out on sidewalks and in improvised morgues—the floors of school gyms, of churches, of automobile showrooms.

My God, they said, staring at the screen with wide eyes. Northern Italy now! So *close!*

Men carrying guns walked through deserted streets wearing bulky, outlandish protective clothing and face masks. Trucks loaded with relief supplies waited for roads to become passable; survivors mobbed the trucks when they arrived. Dead creatures washed up on shorelines, some human, some not. Men in robes, suits, turbans, military uniforms, talked and talked and talked into microphones, reassuring, begging, accusing, weeping.

All this had been building for months, of course, but everyone in Cannes had been too busy to pay much attention. Even now at La Bastide they seldom talked about the news. They talked about movies. It was easier.

Miriam watched TV a lot. Sometimes she took pictures of the screen images. The only thing that could make her look away was a shot of an uncovered body, dead or soon to be so, with a film of blood dulling the skin.

On Victor's orders, they all ate in the smaller salon, without a TV.

On the third night, Krista asked, "What will we eat when this is all gone?"

"I got boxes of that paté months ago." Bulgarian Bob smiled and stood back with his arms folded, like a waiter in a posh restaurant. "Don't worry, there's plenty more."

"My man," said Victor, digging into his smoked Norwegian salmon.

Next day, taking their breakfast coffee out on the terrace, they saw military vehicles grinding past on the roadway below. Relief convoys were being intercepted now, the news had said, attacked and looted.

"Don't worry, little Mi," B. Bob said, as she took snaps of the camouflage-painted trucks from the terrace. "Victor bought this place and fixed it up in the Iranian crisis. He thought we had more war coming. We're set for a year, two years."

Miriam grimaced. "Where food was stored in my country, that is where gunmen came to steal," she said.

B. Bob took her on a tour of the marvelous security at La Bastide, all controlled from a complicated computer console in the master suite: the heavy steel-mesh gates that could be slammed down, the metal window shutters, the ventilation ducts with their electrified outside grills.

"But if the electricity goes off?" she asked.

He smiled. "We have our own generators here."

After dinner that night Walter entertained them. Hired as Victor's Tae Kwan Do coach, he turned out to be a conservatory-trained baritone.

"No more opera," Victor said, waving away an aria. "Old country songs for an old country house. Give us some ballads, Walter!"

Walter sang "Parsley Sage", "Barbara Ellen", and "The Golden Vanity".

This last made Miriam's eyes smart. It told of a young cabin boy who volunteered to swim from an outgunned warship to the enemy vessel and sink it, single-handed, with an augur; but his Captain would not to let him back on board afterward. Rather than hole that ship too and so drown not just the evil Captain but his own innocent shipmates, the cabin boy drowned himself: "he sank into the lowland, low and lonesome, sank into the lowland sea."

Victor applauded. "Great, Walter, thanks! You're off the hook now, that's enough gloom and doom. Tragedy tomorrow—*comedy* tonight!"

They followed him into the library, which had been fitted out with a big movie screen and computers with game consoles. They settled down to watch Marx Brothers movies and old romantic comedies from the extensive film library of La Bastide. The bodyguards stayed up late, playing computer games full of mayhem. They grinned for Miriam's camera lens.

In the hot and hazy afternoon next day, a green mini-Hummer appeared on the highway. Miriam and Krista, bored by a general discussion about which gangster movie had the most swear words, were sitting on the terrace painting each other's toenails. The Hummer turned off the roadway, came up the hill, and stopped at La Bastide's front gates. A man in jeans, sandals, and a white shirt stepped out on the driver's side.

It was Paul, a writer hired to ghost Victor's autobiography. The hot, cindery wind billowed his sleeve as he raised a hand to shade his eyes.

"Hi, girls!" he called. "We made it! We actually had to go off-road, you wouldn't believe the traffic around the larger towns! Where's Victor?"

Bulgarian Bob came up beside them and stood looking down.

"Hey, Paul," he said. "Victor's sleeping; big party last night. What can we do for you?"

"Open the gates, of course! We've been driving for hours!"

"From Cannes?"

"Of course from Cannes!" cried Paul heartily. "Some Peruvian genius won the Palme D'Or, can you believe it? But maybe you haven't heard—the jury made a special prize for *Hearts of Light*. We have the trophy with us—Cammie's been holding it all the way from Cannes."

Cameron jumped out of the car and held up something bulky wrapped in a towel. She wore party clothes: a sparkly green dress and chunky sandals that laced high on her plump calves. Miriam's own thin, straight legs shook a little with the relief of being up here, on the terrace, and not down there at the gates.

Bulgarian Bob put his big hand gently over the lens of her camera. "Not this," he murmured.

Cameron waved energetically and called B. Bob's name, and Miriam's, and even Krista's (everyone knew that she hated Krista).

Paul stood quietly, staring up. Miriam had to look away.

B. Bob called, "Victor will be very happy about the prize."

Krista whispered, "He looks for blood on their skin; it's too far to see, though, from up here." To Bob she said, "I should go tell Victor?"

B. Bob shook his head. "He won't want to know."

He turned and went back inside without another word. Miriam and Krista took their bottles of polish and their tissues and followed.

Victor (and, therefore, everyone else) turned a deaf ear to the pleas, threats, and wails from out front for the next two days. A designated "security team" made up of bodyguards and mechanics went around making sure that La Bastide was locked up tight.

Victor sat rocking on a couch, eyes puffy. "My God, I hate this; but they were too slow. *They could be carrying the disease.* We have a responsibility to protect ourselves."

Next morning the Hummer and its two occupants had gone.

Television channels went to only a few hours a day, carrying reports of the Red Sweat in Paris, Istanbul, Barcelona. Nato troops herded people into make-shift "emergency" camps: schools, government buildings, and of course that trusty standby of imprisonment and death, sports arenas.

The radio and news sites on the web said more: refugees were on the move everywhere. The initial panicky convulsion of flight was over, but smaller groups were reported rushing this way and that all over the continent. In Eastern Europe, officials were holed up in mountain monasteries and castles, trying to subsist on wild game. Urbanites huddled in the underground malls of Canadian cities. When the Red Sweat made its lurid appearance in Montreal, it set off a stampede for the countryside.

They said monkeys carried it; marmots; stray dogs; stray people. Ravens, those eager devourers of corpses, must carry the disease on their claws and beaks, or they spread it in their droppings. So people shot at birds, dogs, rodents, and other people.

Krista prayed regularly to two little wooden icons she kept with her. Miriam had been raised pagan with a Christian gloss. She did not pray. God had never seemed further away.

After a screaming fight over the disappearance of somebody's stash of E, a sweep by the security squad netted a hoard of drugs. These were locked up, to be dispensed only by Bulgarian Bob at set times.

"We have plenty of food and water," Victor explained, "but not an endless supply of drugs. We don't want to run through it all before this ends, do we?" In compensation he was generous with alcohol, with which La Bastide's cellar was plentifully stocked. When his masseuse (she was diabetic) and one of the drivers insisted on leaving to fend for themselves and their personal requirements outside, Victor did not object.

Miriam had not expected a man who had only ever had to act like a leader onscreen to exercise authority so naturally in real life.

It helped that his people were not in a rebellious mood. They stayed in their rooms playing cards, sleeping, some even reading old novels from the shelves under the window seats downstairs. A running game of trivia went on in the games room ("Which actors have played which major roles in green body make-up?"). People used their cell phones to call each other in different parts of the building, since calls to the outside tended not to connect (when they did, conversations were not encouraging).

Nothing appeared on the television now except muay thai matches from Thailand, but the radio still worked: "Fires destroyed the main hospital in Marseilles; fire brigades did not respond. Refugees from the countryside who were sheltering inside are believed dead."

"Students and teachers at the university at Bologna broke into the city offices but found none of the food and supplies rumored to be stored there."

Electricity was failing now over many areas. Victor decreed that they must only turn on the modern security system at night. During daylight hours they used the heavy old locks and bolts on the thick outer doors. B. Bob posted armed lookouts on the terrace and on the roof of the back wing. Cell phones were collected, to stop them being recharged to no good purpose.

But the diesel fuel for Victor's vastly expensive, vastly efficient German generators suddenly ran out (it appeared that the caretaker of La Bastide had sold off much of it during the previous winter). The ground floor metal shutters that had been locked in place by electronic order at nightfall could not be reopened.

Unexpectedly, Victor's crew seemed glad to be shut in more securely. They moved most activities to the upper floor of the front wing, avoiding the shuttered darkness downstairs. They went to bed earlier to conserve candles. They partied in the dark.

The electric pumps had stopped, but an old hand-pump at the basement laundry tubs was rigged to draw water from the well into the pipes in the house. They tore up part of the well yard in the process, getting dust everywhere, but in the end they even got a battered old boiler working over a wood-fire in the basement. A bath rota was eagerly subscribed to, although Alicia, the wig-girl, was forbidden to use hot water to bathe her Yorkie any more.

Victor rallied his troops that evening. He was not a tall man but he was energetic and his big, handsome face radiated confidence and determination. "Look at us—we're movie people, spinners of dreams that ordinary people pay money to share! Who needs a screening room, computers, TV? We can entertain ourselves, or we shouldn't be here!"

Sickly grins all around, but they rose at once to his challenge.

They put on skits, plays, take-offs of popular TV shows. They even had concerts, since several people could play piano or guitar well and Walter was not the only one with a good singing voice. Someone found a violin in a display case downstairs, but no one knew how to play that. Krista and the youngest of the cooks told fortunes, using tea leaves and playing cards from the game room. The fortunes were all fabulous.

Miriam did not think about the future. She occupied herself taking pictures. One of the camera men reminded her that there would be no more recharging of batteries now; if she turned off the LCD screen on the Canon G9 its picture-taking capacity would last longer. Most of the camcorders were already dead from profligate over-use.

It was always noisy after sunset now; people fought back this way against the darkness outside the walls of La Bastide. Miriam made ear plugs out of candle wax and locked her bedroom door at night. On an evening of lively revels (it was Walter's birthday party) she quietly got hold of all the keys to her room that she knew of, including one from Bulgarian Bob's set. B. Bob was busy at the time with one of the drivers, as they groped each other urgently on the second floor landing.

There was more sex now, and more tension. Fistfights erupted over a card game, an edgy joke, the misplacement of someone's plastic water bottle. Victor had Security drag one pair of scuffling men apart and hustle them into the courtyard.

"What's this about?" he demanded.

Skip Reiker panted, "He was boasting about some Rachman al Haj concert he went to! That guy is a goddamn A-rab, a crazy damn Muslim!"

"Bullshit!" Sam Landry muttered, rubbing at a red patch on his cheek. "Music is music."

"Where did the god damned Sweat start, jerk? Africa!" Skip yelled. "The ragheads passed it around among themselves for years, and then they decided to share it. How do you think it spread to Europe? They brought it here on purpose, poisoning the food and water with their contaminated spit and blood. Who could do that better than musicians 'on tour'?"

"Asshole!" hissed Sam. "That's what they said about the Jews during the Black Plague, that they'd poisoned village wells! What are you, a Nazi?"

"Fucker!" Skip screamed.

Miriam guessed it was withdrawal that had him so raw; coke supplies were running low, and many people were having a bad time of it.

Victor ordered Bulgarian Bob to open the front gates.

"Quit it, right now, both of you," Victor said, "or take it outside."

Everyone stared out at the dusty row of cars, the rough lawn, and the trees shading the weedy driveway as it corkscrewed downhill toward the paved road below. The combatants slunk off, one to his bed and the other to the kitchen to get his bruises seen to.

Jill, Cameron's hair stylist, pouted as B. Bob pushed the heavy front gates shut again. "Bummer! We could have watched from the roof, like at a joust."

B. Bob said, "They wouldn't have gone out. They know Victor won't let them back in."

"Why not?" said the girl. "Who's even alive out there to catch the Sweat from anymore?"

"You never know." B. Bob slammed the big bolts home. Then he caught Jill around her pale midriff, made mock-growling noises, and swept her back into the house. B. Bob was good at smoothing ruffled feathers. He needed to be. Tensions escalated. It occurred to Miriam that someone at La Bastide might attack her, just for being from the continent on which the disease had first appeared. Mike Bellows, a black script doctor from Chicago, had vanished the weekend before; climbed the wall and ran away, they said.

Miriam saw how Skip Reiker, a film editor with no film to edit now, stared at her when he thought she wasn't looking. She had never liked Mike Bellows, who was an arrogant and impatient man; perhaps Skip had liked him even less, and had made him disappear.

What she needed, she thought, was to find some passage for herself, some unwatched door to the outside, that she could use to slip away if things turned bad here. That was how a survivor must think. So far, the ease of life at La Bastide—the plentiful food and sunshine, the wine from the cellars, the scavenger hunts and skits, the games in the big salon, the fancy-dress parties—had bled off the worst of people's edginess. Everyone, so far, accepted Victor's rules. They knew that he was their bulwark against anarchy.

But: Victor had only as much authority as he had willing obedience. Food rationing, always a dangerous move, was inevitable. The ultimate loyalty of these bought-and-paid-for friends and attendants would be to themselves (except maybe for Bulgarian Bob, who seemed to really love Victor).

Only Jeff, one of the drivers, went outside now, tinkering for hours with the engines of the row of parked cars. One morning Miriam and Krista sat on the front steps in the sun, watching him.

"Look," Krista whispered, tugging at Miriam's sleeve with anxious, pecking fingers. Down near the roadway a dozen dogs, some with chains or leads dragging from their collars, harried a running figure across a field of withered vines in a soundless pantomime of hunting.

They both stood up, exclaiming. Jeff looked where they were looking. He grabbed up his tools and herded them both back inside with him. The front gates stayed closed after that.

Next morning Miriam saw the dogs again, from her balcony. At the foot of the driveway they snarled and scuffled, pulling and tugging at something too mangled and filthy to identify. She did not tell Krista, but perhaps someone else saw too and spread the word (there was a shortage of news in La Bastide these days, as even radio signals had become rare).

Searching for toothpaste, Miriam found Krista crying in her room. "That was Tommy Mullroy," Krista sobbed, "that boy that wanted to make computer games from movies. He was the one with those dogs."

Tommy Mullroy, a minor hanger-on and a late riser by habit, hadn't made it to the cars on the morning of Victor's hasty retreat from Cannes. Miriam was doubtful that Tommy could have found his way across the plague stricken landscape to La Bastide on his own, and after so much time.

"How could you tell, from so far?" Miriam sat down beside her on the bed and stroked Krista's hand. "I didn't know you liked him."

"No, no, I hate that horrible monkey-boy!" Krista cried, shaking her head furiously. "Bad jokes, and pinching! But now he is dead." She buried her face in her pillow.

Miriam did not think the man chased by dogs had been Tommy Mullroy, but why argue? There was plenty to cry about in any case.

Winter had still not come; the cordwood stored to feed the building's six fire-places was still stacked high against the courtyard walls. Since they had plenty of water everyone used a lot of it, heated in the old boiler. Every day a load of wood ash had to be dumped out of the side gate.

Miriam and Krista their turns at this chore together.

They stood a while (in spite of the reeking garbage overflowing the alley outside, as no one came to take it away any more). The road below was empty today. Up close, Krista smelled of perspiration and liquor. Some in the house were becoming neglectful of themselves.

"My mother would use this ash for making soap," Krista said, "but you need also—what is it? Lime?"

Miriam said, "What will they do when all the soap is gone?"

Krista laughed. "Riots! Me, too. When I was kid, I thought luxury was to change the bedsheets every day for fresh." Then she turned to Miriam with wide eyes and whispered, "We must go away from here, Mimi. They have no Red Sweat in my country for sure! People are farmers, villagers, they live healthy, outside the cities! We can go there and be safe."

"More safe than in here?" Miriam shook her head. "Go in, Krista, Victor's little boys must be crying for you. I'll come with you and take some pictures."

The silence outside the walls was a heavy presence, bitter with drifting smoke that tasted harsh; some of the big new villas up the valley, built with expensive synthetic materials, smoldered slowly for days once they caught fire. Now and then thick smoke became visible much further away. Someone would say, "There's a fire to the west," and everyone would go out on the terrace to watch until the smoke died down or was drifted away out of sight on the wind. They saw no planes and no troop transports now. Dead bodies appeared on the road from time to time, their presence signaled by crows calling others to the feast.

Miriam noticed that the crows did not chase others of their kind away but announced good pickings far and wide. Maybe that worked well if you were a bird.

A day came when Krista confided in a panic that one of the twins was ill.

"You must tell Victor," Miriam said, holding the back of her hand to the forehead of Kevin, who whimpered. "This child has fever."

"I can't say anything! He is so scared of the Sweat, he'll throw the child outside!"

"His own little boy?" Miriam thought of the village man who drove out his son as a witch. "That's just foolishness," she told Krista; but she knew better, having known worse.

Neither of them said anything about it to Victor. Two days later, Krista jumped from the terrace with Kevin's small body clutched to her chest. Through tears, Miriam aimed her camera down and took a picture of the slack, twisted jumble of the two of them. They were left there on the driveway gravel with its fuzz of weeds and, soon after, its busy crows.

The days grew shorter. Victor's crowd partied every night, never mind about the candles. Bulgarian Bob slept on a cot in Victor's bedroom, with a gun in his hand: another thing that everyone knew but nobody talked about.

On a damp and cloudy morning Victor found Miriam in the nursery with little Leif, who was on the floor playing with a dozen empty medicine bottles. Leif played very quietly and did not look up. Victor touched the child's head briefly and then sat down across the table from Miriam, where Krista used to sit. He was so clean shaven that his cheeks gleamed. He was sweating.

"Miriam, my dear," he said, "I need a great favor. Walter saw lights last night in the village. The army must have arrived, at long last. They'll have medicine. They'll have news. Will you go down and speak with them? I'd go myself, but everyone depends on me here to keep up some discipline, some hope. We can't have more people giving up, like Krista."

"I'm taking care of Leif now—" Miriam began faintly.

"Oh, Cammie can do that."

Miriam quickly looked away from him, her heart beating hard. Did he really believe that he had taken his current wife into La Bastide after all, in her spangly green party dress?

"This is so important," he urged, leaning closer and blinking his large, blue eyes in the way that (B. Bob always said) the camera loved. "There's a very, very large bonus in it for you, Miriam, enough to set you up very well on your own when this is all over. I can't ask anyone else, I wouldn't trust them to come back safe and sound. But you, you're so level-headed and you've had experience of bad times, not like some of these spoiled, silly people here. Things must have gotten better outside, but how would we know, shut up in here? Everyone agrees: we need you to do this.

"The contagion must have died down by now," he coaxed. "We haven't seen movement outside in days. Everyone has gone, or holed up, like us. Soldiers wouldn't be in the village if it was still dangerous down there."

Just yesterday Miriam had seen a lone rider on a squeaky bicycle peddling down the highway. But she heard what Victor was *not* saying: that he needed to be able to convince others to go outside, convince them that it was safe, as the more crucial supplies (dope; toilet paper) dwindled; that he controlled those supplies; that he could, after all, have her put out by force.

Listening to the tink of the bottles in Leif's little hands, she realized that she could hardly wait to get away; in fact, she *had* to go. She would find amazing prizes, bring back news, and they would all be so grateful that she would be safe here forever. She would make up good news if she had to, to please them; to keep her place here, inside La Bastide.

But for now, go she must.

Bulgarian Bob found her sitting in dazed silence on the edge of her bed.

"Don't worry, Little Mi," he said. "I'm very sorry about Krista. I'll look out for your interest here."

"Thank you," she said, not looking him in the eyes. *Everyone agrees.* It was hard to think; her mind kept jumping.

"Take your camera with you," he said. "It's still working, yes? You've been sparing with it, smarter than some of these idiots. Here's a fresh card for it, just in case. We need to see how it is out there now. We can't print anything, of course, but we can look at your snaps on the LCD when you get back."

The evening's feast was dedicated to "our intrepid scout Miriam". Eyes glittering, the beautiful people of Victor's court toasted her (and, of course, their own good luck in not having been chosen to venture outside). Then they began a boisterous game: who could remember accurately the greatest number of deaths in the *Final Destination* movies, with details?

To Miriam, they looked like crazy witches, cannibals, in the candle-light. She could hardly wait to leave.

Victor himself came to see her off early in the morning. He gave her a bottle of water, a ham sandwich, and some dried apricots to put in her red ripstop knapsack. "I'll be worrying my head off until you get back!" he said.

She turned away from him and looked at the driveway, at the dust-coated cars squatting on their flattened tires, and the shrunken, darkened body of Krista.

"You know what to look for," Victor said. "Matches. Soldiers. Tools, candles; you know."

The likelihood of finding anything valuable was small (and she would go out of her way *not* to find soldiers). But when he gave her shoulder a propulsive pat, she started down the driveway like a wind-up toy.

Fat dogs dodged away when they saw her coming. She picked up some stones to throw but did not need them.

She walked past the abandoned farmhouses and vacation homes on the valley's upper reaches, and then the village buildings, some burned and some spared; the empty vehicles, dead as fossils; the remains of human beings. Being sold away, she had been spared such sights back home. She had not seen for herself the corpses in sun-faded shirts and dresses, the grass blades growing up into empty eye sockets, that others had photographed there. Now she paused to take her own carefully chosen, precious pictures.

There were only a few bodies in the streets. Most people had died indoors, hiding from death. Why had her life bothered to bring her such a long way round, only to arrive where she would have been anyway had she remained at home?

Breezes ruffled weeds and trash, lifted dusty hair and rags fluttering from grimy bones, and made the occasional loose shutter or door creak as it swung. A few cows—too skittish now to fall easily to roaming dog packs—grazed watchfully on the plantings around the village fountain, which still dribbled dispiritedly.

If there were ghosts, they did not show themselves to her.

She looked into deserted shops and houses, gathering stray bits of paper, candle stubs, tinned food, ball point pens. She took old magazines from a beauty salon, two paperback novels from a deserted coffee house. Venturing into a wine shop got her a cut on the ankle: the place had been smashed to smithereens. Others had come here before her, like that dead man curled up beside the till.

In a desk drawer she found a chocolate bar. She ate it as she headed back up the valley, walking through empty fields to skirt the village this time. The chocolate was crumbly and dry and dizzyingly delicious.

When she arrived at the gates of La Bastide, the men on watch sent word to Bulgarian Bob. He stood at the iron balustrade above her and called down questions: What had she seen, where exactly had she gone, had she entered the buildings, seen anyone alive?

"Where is Victor?" Miriam asked, her mouth suddenly very dry.

"I'll tell you what; you wait down there til morning," Bulgarian Bob said. "We must be sure you don't have the contagion, Miriam. You know."

Miriam, not Little Mi. Her heart drummed painfully. She felt injected into her own memory of Cammie and Paul standing here, pleading to come in. Only now she was looking up at the wall of La Bastide, not down from the terrace.

Sitting on the bonnet of one of one of the cars, she stirred her memory and dredged up old prayers to speak or sing softly into the dusk. Smells of food cooking and woodsmoke wafted down to her. Once, late, she heard squabbling voices at a second floor window. No doubt they were discussing who would be sent out the next time Victor wanted news of the world and one less mouth to feed.

In the morning, she held up her arms for inspection. She took off her blouse and showed them her bare back.

"I'm sorry, Miriam," Victor called down to her. His face was full of compassion. "I think I see a rash on your shoulders. It may be nothing, but you must understand—at least for now, we can't let you in. I really do want to see your pictures, though. You haven't used up all your camera's battery power, have you? We'll lower a basket for it."

"I haven't finished taking pictures," she said. She aimed the lens up at him. He quickly stepped back out of sight. Through the viewfinder she saw only the parapet of the terrace and the empty sky.

She flung the camera into the ravine, panting with rage and terror as she watched it spin on its way down, compact and clever and useless.

Then she sat down and thought.

Even if she found a way back in, if they thought she was infected they would drive her out again, maybe just shoot her. She imagined Skip Reiker throwing a carpet over her dead body, rolling her up in it, and heaving her outside the walls like rubbish. The rest of them would not approve, but anger and fear would enable their worst impulses ("See what you made us do!").

She should have thought more before, about how she was a supernumerary here, acquired but not really *needed*, not *talented* as these people reckoned such things; not important to the tribe.

"Have I have stopped being a survivor?" she asked Krista's withered back.

In the house Walter was singing. "Some Enchanted Evening!" Applause. Then, "The Golden Vanity".

Miriam sat with her back against the outside wall, burning with fear, confusion, and scalding self-reproach.

When the sun rose again she saw a rash of dark blisters on the backs of her hands. She felt more of them rising at her hairline, around her face. Her joints ached. She was stunned: Victor was right. It was the Red Sweat. But how had she caught it? Through something she had touched—a doorknob, a book, a slicing shard of glass? By merely breathing the infected air?

Maybe—the *chocolate*? The idea made her sob with laughter.

They wouldn't care one way or the other. She was already dead to them. She knew they would not even venture out to take her backpack, full of scavenged treasures, when she was dead (she threw its contents down the ravine after the camera, to make sure). She'd been foolish to have trusted Bulgarian Bob, or Victor either.

They had never intended to let the dove back into the ark.

She knelt beside Krista's corpse and made herself search the folds of reeking, sticky clothing until she found Krista's key to the rubbish gate, the key they had used to throw out the ashes. She sat on the ground beside Krista and rubbed the key bright on her own pant-leg.

Let them try to keep her out. Let them try.

Krista was my shipmate. Now I have no shipmates.

At moonrise she shrugged her aching arms through the straps of the empty pack and walked slowly around to the side alley gate. Krista's key clicked minutely in the lock. The door sprang outward, releasing more garbage that had been piled up inside. No one seemed to hear. They were roaring with song in the front wing and drumming on the furniture, to drown out the cries and pleadings they expected to hear from her.

Miriam stepped inside the well yard, swallowing bloody mucus. She felt the paving lurch a little under her.

A man was talking in the kitchen passageway, set into the ground floor of the back wing at an oblique angle across the well yard. She thought it was Edouard, a camera tech, pretending to speak on his cell as he sometimes did to keep himself company when he was on his own. Edouard, as part of Security, carried a gun.

Her head cleared suddenly. She found that she had shut the gate behind her, and had slid down against the inside wall, for she was sitting on the cool pavement. Perhaps she had passed out for a little. By the moon's light she saw the well's raised stone lip, only a short way along the wall to her left. She was thirsty, although she did not think she could force water down her swollen throat now.

The paving stones the men had pried up in their work on the plumbing had not been reset. They were still piled up out of the way, very near where she sat.

Stones; water. Her brain was so clogged with hot heaviness that she could barely hold her head up.

"Non, non!" Edouard shouted. "Ce n'est pas vrai, ils sont menteurs, tous!"

Yes, all of them; menteurs. She sympathized, briefly.

Her mind kept tilting and spilling all its thoughts into a turgid jumble, but there were constants: *stones. Water.* The exiled dove, the brave cabin boy. Krista and little Kevin. She made herself move, trusting to the existence of an actual plan somewhere in her mind. She crawled over to the stacked pavers. Slowly and with difficulty she took off her backpack and stuffed it with some of the smaller stones, one by one. Blood beaded black around her fingernails. She had no strength to pull the loaded pack onto her back again, so she hung it from her shoulder by one broad strap, and began making her painful way toward the well itself.

Edouard was deep in his imaginary quarrel. As she crept along the wall she heard his voice echo angrily in the vaulted passageway.

The thick wooden well-cover had been replaced with a lightweight metal sheet, back when they had had to haul water by hand before the old laundry pump was reconnected. She lifted the light metal sheet and set it aside. Dragging herself up, she leaned over the low parapet and peered down.

She could not make out the stone steps that descended into the water on the inside wall, left over from a time when the well had been used to hide contraband. Now… something. Her thoughts swam.

Focus.

Even without her camera there was a way to bring home to Victor all the reality he had sent her out to capture for him in pictures.

She could barely shift her legs over the edge, but at last she felt the cold roughness of the top step under her feet. She descended toward the water, using the friction of her spread hands, turning her torso flat against the curved wall like a figure in an Egyptian tomb painting. The water winked up at her, glossy with reflected moonlight. The backpack, painful with hard stone edges, dragged at her aching shoulder. She paused to raise one strap and put her head through it; she must not lose her anchor now.

The water's chill lapped at her skin, sucking away her last bit of strength. She sagged out from the wall and slipped under the surface. Her hands and feet scrabbled dreamily at the slippery wall and the steps, but down she sank anyway, pulled by the bag of stones strapped to her body.

Her chest was shot through with agony, but her mind clung with bitter pleasure to the fact that in the morning all of Victor's tribe would wash themselves and brush their teeth and swallow their pills down with the water Victor was so proud of, water pumped by willing hands from his own wonderful well.

Head craned back, she saw that dawn pallor had begun to flush the small circle of sky receding above her. Against that light, black curls of the blood that her body wept from every seam and pore feathered out in secret silence, into the cool, delicious water.

THE END OF EVERYTHNG
STEVE ELLER

Steve Eller lives in Seattle with his wife and their two feline children. His stories have appeared in a variety of magazines and anthologies. He won a Bram Stoker Award during his time editing fiction at The ChiZine (www.chizine. com). He edited the Stoker-nominated anthology *Brainbox: The Real Horror*, and *Brainbox II: Son of Brainbox*. He plays bass in the band Dread Effect (www.dreadeffect.com). For assistance in the creation of this story, he wishes to thank S, P, and DHL.

A priest, talking about *World Without End,* that's all I have left from a childhood of Sundays. Sweating in my miniature black suit, clip-on tie dangling from a starched collar. My family's voices, singing and testifying, were just background noise for those three words. Yanking my wayward mind back from daydreams of chasing goldbugs or sharpening knives, fixing me to the pew like cold metal through the heart. Just like the nails in the glistening Christ above the priest. I remember raising my hands, to see if I was dripping blood too.

If that priest was here with me now, I'd carve those words into his face, and see what dripped out of him. Not that it would do any good. Not for me, and certainly not for him.

When was the last time I saw glass that wasn't broken? It's nothing but spiderweb cracks now, or jagged shards like teeth. I wonder if there's one smooth pane left anywhere, to gleam like a sheet of fire in the sun. Or rim the world in frost.

The city street below me is empty. Unless there's some word beyond empty. Everything gleams a greasy grey. There's no sun peeking through the constant clouds, which isn't unusual for Ohio in wintertime. I'm just not sure it's still winter. It might be early morning or midnight. It could be tomorrow or yesterday.

I lean through the window frame, looking straight up. With so much grey I lose my perspective, slipping toward vertigo. It would be so easy to just let go, surrender my balance and tumble out. It's not the first time I've thought about it. But I'm afraid of what might happen. Almost as much as what might not.

Just like the rest of the world, the sky is dead. A fragment of a song pops into my head. Three words again. *Dead Ohio Sky*. I can't remember the rest.

Ninth Street runs straight to the lakefront, where the horizon is all water from my twentieth-story view. Lake Erie is choppy and frothed with white, though there's no wind. If not for the waves, there'd be nothing to distinguish water from sky. I used to stare out this window-hole, wondering when a ship would sail up, full of experts who'd climb on shore. Soldiers and scientists who knew what went wrong, people who could help me, in more ways than one. But they never came. And the world never got fixed.

This building used to be offices, and the walls are lined with roll-front book-cases. They were full of binders, some kind of financial records. I took them all out and threw them down the stairwell, replaced them with food and water. I grab a random can and pull the zip-top. Whatever's inside is orange as clown hair. It could be chili or soup, maybe dog food. The electricity is still on in the building and there's a microwave down the hall in a break-room, but that's too much trouble. It's just food, after all. Fake-colored chunks of slimy meat. Warmth won't make it taste good. I grab a plastic spoon.

When it all started ending, I stocked up on water and canned goods. Everyone else was busy panicking, getting their stupid selves killed. But I can't criticize them too much. They can't be as used to death as me. I've spent my life around it. So while they were screaming and running, I was looting stores and lugging crates up twenty flights, making myself a safe and secret place. I figured I'd be Vincent Price in that old movie. The last person on the planet, with all the monsters out to get me.

After a few tasteless mouthfuls, I shoulder the fire-door open. Can and spoon go down the stairwell. I don't hear them hit bottom. The meal sits in my belly like a stone, and I figure walking might grind it down to pebbles. The elevator in the hallway is open and waiting, since I'm the only one who uses it. I wish I had've known it was still working when I was carrying cases of water up the stairs. I tap the button for *Lobby* and the door shuts behind me. Machinery clanks and sputters inside the paneled walls, until the car jolts to a stop at the bottom. The elevator can't be safe to use, and may kill me one day. But some-how, I doubt it.

"Hey, mister," a soft voice said. "What's your hurry?"

Staying still was hard. The night wind was cold enough to bite through wool and skin. *Cold as God's heart*, I thought. There was a knife in my coat pocket, and I pricked my thumb. Penance, for thinking such a thing, no matter how true. Moving was the only way to keep warm. But the voice brought me to a stop.

A tangle of highway overhead, ramps and interchanges. Tires rumbled and whined. In the shadows beneath, people huddled around a trashcan fire. All scarves and hats, it was hard to tell them apart. Bits of metal and glass littered the ground, twinkling in firelight. The one who spoke stood away from the others.

A thin, hunched figure, rubbing ragged gloves together. There was enough light to see it was a young girl.

"It's cold out tonight," she said. "Take me home."

She had a knit cap pulled down to her eyebrows and the hood of her quilted coat was up. But I saw her face. She might've been born like that. Maybe she was burned, or her family threw her from a moving car like an unwanted pet. The ruined skin made her smile too beautiful, and I thanked Heaven for the strand of shadow she passed through. Her scent was unwashed flesh and the acid breath of an empty stomach, but her eyes were clear and hard like the icicles hanging from the guardrail.

I wondered what could've brought this child to Cleveland in the dead of winter. Her life story had to be a tragedy, like her face. But I didn't wonder why she called out to me, instead of the other dark shapes along the street. Fate is a story all its own.

"How old are you?" I asked.

"What are you, a cop?"

"No. I'd just like to know."

"Old enough to make it worth your while."

It touched my heart that such perfection could exist in the world. In this tiny creature, waiting in frigid darkness, willing to trade herself for warm air.

"So cruel," I whispered.

"Huh?"

"Creation without hope of redemption."

"Hey, look. Do you want to take me home, or not?"

I wrapped her in my arms, and she didn't resist. She raised her face, like offering me a kiss. One of my hands touched her cheek, so she didn't speak anymore. Her spoiled skin was rough as corduroy. My other hand left the knife in my pocket.

"You are home."

I've seen the lobby countless times, but it's still a sight. Like a war zone, where the battle's over but nobody's left to pick up the pieces. There's dry blood across the floor, ink-black. And more is sprayed on the walls. In places it's like a stencil, an outline of the person who bled there, or more burst than bled, maybe. I heard there were stencils like this in Japan after the atomic bomb. People burned so fast they left a human imprint scorched in stone. Bloodstains would take longer to set. There are piles of leaves and trash in every corner, but no bodies. They either got dragged away, or stood up and left on their own.

The revolving door is nothing but a metal frame. I turn it, though I could just as easily step right through. The city is silent. I never realized, before it all ended, how noisy the world used to be. Now there's no cars or buses, no airplanes humming overhead. No human voices chattering nonsense into cell phones. The silence was overwhelming at first, and I'd squeeze my head in my hands to keep it from splitting like a dropped pumpkin.

The lakefront is the only place worth going. Nothing happens there, but at least there's movement. The quiet of the world is broken by my boots smacking the sidewalk. Every storefront I pass has shattered windows, and I catch my reflection in the fragments. My hair is long now, breaking over my shoulders. It must take months, if not a year, for it to grow to this length. I stop for a better look, amazed at how much white is creeping into my beard. The little eye in my head still sees me as the same person, but somewhere along the line I've been getting old.

Two blocks from the lake, I hear them, stirring nearby. Who knows how many. A warning jangles down my spine. It's an instinct as old as time, rational mind giving in to the ways of meat and bone. There's nothing to be afraid of, but the ancient part of my brain, the lizard-jelly, will never be convinced.

Maybe it's because I'm not carrying a knife. That's something I haven't been able to say since kindergarten. Hiding a knife on me was part of getting ready to go out into the world. The sure weight of a switchblade in my pocket. The chill of an eight-inch carver up the sleeve of my overcoat. Before the world ended, I had it all worked out. A knife was part of me. Cold, hard metal was the perfect complement to soft, warm skin.

They don't make any sound. Not with their mouths or throats. But with the city so silent, I hear them coming closer. Feet dragging on asphalt, liquid spattering from their sodden clothes. With no wind, it's hard to smell them until they're near enough to touch. My skin tingles, the muscle underneath bunching to run, to save itself. But all I do is turn around and look.

The girl warmed herself by the radiator while I heated milk on the stove. She peeled off clothes as she lost her chill. First her gloves, then her coat. A flannel shirt, several sizes too big, fell onto the pile at her feet. It was a man's shirt, and I wondered how she bargained to get it.

"Do you like marshmallows with your cocoa?"

"Sure," she replied. "Whatever you got."

Her back was to me and I watched long, straight hair tumble down when she removed her cap. Too black to be anything but from a bottle. And recently dyed. Such a slice of the human heart, that she was capable of vanity while living under a highway.

I poured steaming milk into two mugs and stirred until brown powder dissolved. I couldn't find any marshmallows, but didn't think she'd care. I took the two mugs and carried them into the living room. She was down to a threadbare tank-top and jeans. Toes obvious through worn-out socks.

"Thanks," she said, cradling her mug in hands barely big enough to surround it. "This is a first."

"How so?"

"Usually somebody just hands me their…"

"We don't need to talk about that," I said.

She sipped, and I heard her stomach gurgle. It takes a while for a belly to get that empty. I couldn't tell which she liked more, the taste of the chocolate or the heat of the mug. I was barely started with my drink when she slurped the dregs of hers.

"That was good," she said, turning back to the radiator, still holding the mug.

I saw a ring of bruises around both her arms, the pattern like fingers. But there was no damage, like to her face. Her breathing was heavy and I wondered if there was a disease eating away her lungs. I could hear her heart. Or maybe it was just my own.

She was such a symbol of how callous God was. To make life and let it go its own way. Then let it end. But what does God know about dying? He leaves that to his children.

"So do you want to get started?" she asked.

"Like you said to me, what's your hurry?"

She turned around, locking her eyes to mine. Her shoulders were so thin, almost pointed. She seemed fragile, hollow-boned as a bird, like I could crush her in my bare hands. But life is never so easy to take.

"What are you," she asked, smiling gently, "one of those nice guys?"

"Far from it."

"You're not gonna try and help me, or save me?"

"I'll help you. Who knows if it'll save you."

"Not even gonna offer me a sermon?"

"Nope. Just a hot shower."

There's a line of them, maybe a dozen, coming out of an underground parking garage. I can't imagine what they were doing down there. At the head of the column is a young woman. She's coming straight at me, left hand raised, the other cradling her belly. Her eyes are gazing off toward the sky. It's unnerving, like interacting with a disabled person who uses senses in a different way.

She's in good shape. All her limbs attached, her clothes intact. Her skin is a pale grey, so she must've come back recently. The line behind her is a chronology. The further back, the older and more decayed they are. Maybe they move slower, or maybe they have less reason to approach me. On the shadowed ramp, the ones at the back are already turning and heading down again. They must've been through this before. Some of them look familiar. The girl must be new in more ways than one.

When she's an arm's-length away, she's the only one left. The others have all turned away, disappearing into the garage. This near, I see the cuts inside her arms. Long-ways, from wrist to elbow. She knew what she was doing. There's not even any blood on her T-shirt. Her wounds tell me all I need to know. She lived for a while, then ended her own life. She wasn't one of mine.

The girl stops, leans toward me. Her right arm, tight against her body, must be broken. There's nothing spilling out of her belly to hold inside. Maybe the arm was paralyzed while she lived. Her left hand comes close to my cheek and I feel the chill of her fingers. Mouth open, she tilts her head. Her gums are the color of dough. She has no breath, but her smell is old meat between teeth.

I've seen them kill so many times. The sudden burst of violence from their seemingly brittle bodies, fingers and mouths ripping chunks of meat they chew but never swallow. Driven by some strange instinct, or simple desire.

Her eyes could belong to a steamed fish, white and gelid. They roll down from the sky, meeting mine. But it's not sight, just coincidence. She doesn't move away, but her mouth shuts. I hear a sharp click where her jaw closes wrong. There's no blood in her, and her brain must be a puddle in her skull. But she's made her decision, and it's the same one all the others made.

"What am I to you?"

My voice doesn't keep her from turning away. They don't hear or see. No breath, so they don't know scents. I saw one of them without a tongue continue to eat, so they don't taste. But something draws them to people, and makes them walk away from me.

"What are you to me?"

When she's gone, I finish my walk to the waterfront. There are benches facing the lake and I pick one solely by proximity. The waves beat against the pier, moved by a power as mysterious as the dead girl's judgment. Sky and water, grey on grey, seem like one solid mass. I wonder if I stepped onto the waves, if I could walk across like Jesus. But even a messiah needs somewhere to go.

"I was wondering when you'd get here."

Her outline was a blur through the shower curtain, but her intent was clear. Steam billowed over the rod, clouding on the ceiling, smudging my reflection in the bathroom mirror. I figured she was enjoying the hot water. That's why she was gone so long. But she was waiting, certain I'd come in and join her. Like she needed to get this done now, so she could sleep under a ramp instead of in a warm bed.

When I slid the curtain back, she didn't so much as flinch. Her hair was soaked to a point at the small of her back. Her skin was pink as smoked pork. Eyes like gems in a stark desert of a face. Her starved body was flawless. Her only damage was to the thing all the world could see. Maybe that's why she was so eager to show the rest.

"Get your clothes off, already. And hop in. You're letting in a draft."

"I just want to look," I said. *At God's Work.*

"If you like to watch," she whispered, fingers moving over her skin.

My fingers moved, too. Into my pants pocket, around the handle of the knife. And it was over before she could raise a hand. She slumped and I caught her, helped her down into the tub. She curled like a child about to be born. I closed the curtain. The hot water would wash her blood clean, then away.

On my way back, I stop at the mouth of the parking garage. Staring down the dark ramp, listening. There's no sound of them moving, no sign of the dead girl. The rest must've followed her before. Now she's learned her lesson.

I take a few steps down the ramp, curious what could be below. Are they milling in the dark, waiting? Are they curled up, resting on the asphalt like sleepy babies? Do they need to save what remains of their rotten muscle for the next living thing to pass by? They could be sitting in cars for all I know, dreaming.

Relief sweeps through me as I walk back up the ramp, but it's only instinct. A basic need to be safe. My rational mind knows I could stop and sleep in the middle of the street. I wonder if I should look for someplace else to live. Closer to the water. Maybe I will, when the food is gone. That way, I won't have to carry it all back down. There's no reason for me to live in a hideaway, behind locked firedoors. I've never seen them climb stairs. And even if they could, they have no interest in me. Maybe I never needed to leave my ground-floor apartment.

Next time I walk to the lake I'll make a trip along the shoreline, and pick one of the abandoned mansions. There could be a comfy king-size bed to sleep on, instead of a carpeted office floor. There could be champagne and gourmet food. And a bucket and mop, in case the previous owners left a mess.

I spread plastic over the bathroom tile, the kind movers use. It clung to the floor and never curled at the corners. And it stuck to itself when it was time to ball it all up. I always kept a roll handy.

The air was cool, with no more steam. She must've used up all the hot water. My shoulder brushed the shower curtain as I unraveled more plastic, and it felt as cold as her breath, when I held her close under a highway. One more strip of plastic and there was enough to hold her. I trimmed it with my knife. A few red flecks dotted the seam, delicate as snowflakes. I thought I cleaned the blade better. Metal rings shrieked on the rod when I pushed the curtain open. It was freezing inside the shower and I shut off the water. I closed the knife and slid it back into my pocket.

She looked so small in death, like her miserable life made her larger. Bloodless pale, she could've been a porcelain statue. This was the gift I gave her. Something her creator could never imagine. Mercy.

I reached down to lift her out, and her eyes opened. I tumbled onto my back, and my wet fingers couldn't get any traction on the plastic. All I could do was watch as she stood, glaring down at me. There wasn't a hint of blood on her gaping throat. Her eyes kept going down, rolling to pure white. Her arms came up, hands curled like she was still holding her mug. She took a step, but couldn't lift her legs high enough to climb out of the tub. Instead, she toppled over, right toward me. On the way down, I saw her mouth open.

She was cold and wet, pale like some deep-sea thing. Heavier than I imagined, for a tiny girl with no blood in her. All her frigid weight was on me, and there was a wiry strength in her limbs. I couldn't get enough friction on soaked plastic to push her off. There was a clicking close to my ear, maybe fingernails on tile, maybe teeth on teeth. Her arms and legs pumped franticly, until she slid right off me.

I grabbed her hair, used her momentum to turn myself over. She was standing by the time I got to my knees. Pure reflex, I had the knife in my hand before I was on my feet. She wasn't moving, water pattering from her fingertips onto plastic. But I wasn't taking any chances. I jumped up. Two quick slashes, one to each side of her neck.

This had never happened before. Maybe I got careless. Or faithless.

She didn't weaken or fall. I opened her throat earlier in the shower, and the new neck-wounds completed a crooked letter *H*. But there was nothing left in her to seep from the cuts. She was dead, but not at peace. And there was nothing I could do.

She took a step toward me, and I lifted the knife again. I was running out of places to cut her, but it was all I can think to do. Her bare feet squeaked on plastic as she moved, but she bumped past me, out the bathroom door. I followed her, knife still in front of me. Naked, she walked to my front door. Breathless, I opened it for her.

They huddle around me. I'm only a few miles from the city, but I've never seen any of them. And obviously, they've never been near me. There must be twenty, all ages, rags of designer clothes hanging on their limbs. One woman still wears a diamond necklace. There's a man who must've been a sports star. Seven feet tall and broad as a wall, his clothes are still baggy. All the local heroes lived on the lake.

They each take a turn rushing up to me, then turning away. I stand still and wait for them to finish. Then I can get back to searching the mansion. It's got the largest deck I've ever seen, facing the water. I could live here, and pretend to watch the sunrise.

The crowd thins quickly, only a few stragglers coming up to me. Inside the house their smell is thick, clinging to my tongue like bacon-grease. After they're gone, I'll have to open up all the windows and let the place air out. But I'll keep the first floor windows shut, long-term, so newcomers don't tumble in. Actual, unbroken glass.

I make my way upstairs to the master bedroom, listening. There might be one of them up here. If so, I'll push them down the staircase. But it's deserted.

The scent of them, so many, has given me a headache. I search the master bath for aspirin. Inside the medicine cabinet, there's nothing but a bottle of sleeping pills. I turn on the cold water, splash my face and take a sip from my cupped palm. Another sip could wash the entire bottle of pills down my throat. But something tells me the only rest I'll be getting is on the master bed.

With so much chaos in the street, there was no need to hide my knife. Any blood I could spill would be lost in the flood. The girl I killed was obvious in the mob, white skin gleaming in streetlamp-light as she rode a struggling man down to the sidewalk. She wasn't the only killer, just the youngest. There were so many, most dressed in faded gowns or robes. And it made sense that if the dead rose, the first would come from hospitals and hospices. The crowd grew, but fewer clouds of breath rose from living mouths.

Something bumped my shoulder and I spun, knife ready. It was an elderly man in pajamas, a torn plastic tube taped to his nose. His teeth were bright red, the same as the throat of the girl in his hands. Two jabs and a slash from my knife, and his eyes were gone and his neck split open. But he kept chewing. The girl was limp, her breathing like bubbles through a straw. The bloody wad in his mouth fell out, and he went in for another bite.

I'd seen enough horror movies to know damaging the brain would stop the living dead. But my knife wasn't thick enough to go through skull-bone. So I searched the street for another weapon. A window suddenly shattered somewhere over my head, glass raining down. I lifted my arms as a shield, but nothing touched me. Huge shards crashed around me onto the sidewalk, and not a scratch. Along with the glass there was a piece of window-frame, long nails exposed. I grabbed it and hit the man on his head, three times. His skull was a soup-bowl, but he wouldn't stop. Not until the girl was dead, and he dropped her, walked away. A moment later, she got up.

She staggered up to me, palms open like begging. There was no way to kill her. No way to help her. I dropped the dripping wood, ready to accept my fate. At that moment, a pack of young boys, all in some kind of scout uniform, dashed by. They screamed, and the girl went after them. Heart hammering, I took the opportunity to run away.

Sitting on my deck, I watch the lake. The waves seem to form out of the colorless sky, vanishing as they hit the shore. Spreading more nothing on the world.

I found a collection of fancy knives in the kitchen, lined up on a magnetic strip. I would've loved to have them, back before everything ended. Now there's no more warm skin. The cold metal means nothing. Everything means nothing.

There's food in the cupboards, and there must be a store nearby. No need to go back for my supplies. I haven't checked the garage yet, but there could be a gassed-up car in there. Ready to take me out of the city. This might be an isolated thing, living people gathered in other places. But I doubt it. The tightness in my belly tells me that it's over. No matter where I go, I'll find the world the same.

I wonder if I stopped eating, if it would make any difference. The dead don't want to kill me. A hail of glass from the sky misses me. I'll bet the bottle of sleeping pills wouldn't make me yawn. And I can't give final peace to the afflicted.

Maybe the preacher was right. *World Without End*. And God gets the final laugh.

MRS. MIDNIGHT
REGGIE OLIVER

Reggie Oliver has been a professional playwright, actor, and theatre director since 1975. His biography of Stella Gibbons, *Out of the Woodshed*, was published by Bloomsbury in 1998. Besides plays, his publications include four volumes of stories: *The Dreams of Cardinal Vittorini*, *The Complete Symphonies of Adolf Hitler*, *Masques of Satan*, and *Madder Mysteries*, and a novel *Virtue in Danger* forthcoming from Ex Occidente Press in 2010. An omnibus edition of his stories entitled *Dramas from the Depths* is to be published by Centipede also in 2010. His stories have been republished in numerous anthologies. As an actor he is currently touring his one-man horror show *Stage Frights*.

What's the worst thing about being a celebrity? The intrusive press coverage? Forget it! I do. No. It's being roped into these charity projects, because nowadays you've got to be hands on, or they mark you down as a complete toe-rag. Oh, look at Lenny Henry, they say, look at Julie Walters: they weren't prepared just to swan around like celebs, they got their hands dirty, their feet wet: they endangered some extremity or other. And if you present a program like *I Can Make You A Star*, you're generally assumed to be someone who got where they are by being lucky, or sleeping with the right people, so you have to prove yourself all the more. Well, I got to be the presenter of *I Can Make You A Star* by sheer hard graft, and it tops the ratings because I am bloody good at my job. My qualifications: a first class honours degree in the University of Life, having passed my entrance exam from the School of Hard Knocks with straight A's in all subjects. That's the sort of bloke I am, as if anyone gives a flying fuck. Pardon my French. Anyway, that was why I was recruited to head up the Save The Old Essex Music Hall project.

The Old Essex: what can I say about the Old Essex? It's a glorious relic of those magical bygone days of Music Hall? No, it isn't. It's a filthy, rat-infested, dry-rotten, draughty, crumbling, mildewed dump that hasn't had anything to do with show business for well over a hundred years. Most recently it has been a hangout for winos and junkies; before that it was a warehouse and a motorcycle repair shop. Before that, God knows. The only reason it's survived is that some nutter slapped a preservation order on it. A few of its original features have remained intact, not that they're much to write home about. But I can't say all this, can I?

I have to say something like: "It's an amazing piece of living history which must be revived to serve the needs of the modern community." Call me a cynic, if you like. I prefer the word realist.

The Old Essex fronts onto Alie Street, Whitechapel, and it was in some god-forsaken courtyard round the back of it that Jack the Ripper did for one of his victims. Which one? Look it up for yourself. I have never understood why people should take the remotest interest in that squalid old monster, whoever he or she was. Eh? Well, why shouldn't it have been a *she*? I'm no sexist; I'm an equal opportunities sort of guy, me. I merely mention the fact, just to give you an impression of the kind of glorious, heritage-packed part of London we're talking about. As a matter of fact it was shortly after the Ripper murder that there had been a fire at the Old Essex, after which it stopped being a theatre, and embarked on its chequered history as a hangout for bikers and junkies. God knows how or why it escaped the Blitz: the Devil told Hitler to give it a miss, I reckon.

It was a mad March day when I first saw the Old Essex and the rain was blowing in great icy gusts across the East End. Even though it was eleven in the morning the sky was nearly black, and street lights were reflected fitfully in the water-lashed pavements. There were three of us who got out of the minicab outside the Old Essex, all kitted-out with yellow hard hats, Day-Glo jackets and torches. There was Jill, a bloke with the stupid name of Crispin de Hartong, and me, Danny Sheen, as if you didn't know. There was also supposed to be a camera crew, to film the whole thing for posterity, but their van had got lost—a likely story!—and they didn't show up till a lot later.

Jill was the reason I was in on the project, as a matter of fact. Her name is Jill Warburton and she has some sort of cultural adviser job in the Mayor's Office and had adopted this project as her baby. I hadn't much taken to her when she first rang me up because she had a posh accent, but at least she wasn't pushy so I invited her to come round to see me at my house in Primrose Hill. After a few minutes in her company I felt easier about her. I'm not saying she's a raving beauty or anything, but she looks nice. She's tall and quiet. She laughed at the jokes I made, and she wasn't faking it. That counts a lot with me. I know it sounds weird of me to say this, but she seemed to me like a good person. So I agreed to help the project, before almost instantly regretting it, and that was why I was here, about to inspect a derelict building in the pouring rain.

The other bloke tagging along, Crispin de Hartong, was there because he was an architectural expert. He was also a minor celeb who pronounces on that TV property makeover show, *Premises, Premises…* You remember: he's the poncy type who goes in for shoulder length blonde hair, bow ties and plum-coloured velvet jackets. I got the impression that he had his eye on Jill, and maybe that didn't exactly endear him to me.

The frontage of the Old Essex is mostly boarded up now to stop the druggies getting in. Jill undid a number of padlocks and we entered. At least we're out of the rain, I thought.

We shine our torches around and immediately Crispin starts raving about pilasters and spandrels and architraves. I don't want to hear all this rubbish, especially as I know he is just showing off to Jill. I only want to look.

We are in what I suppose was once the foyer. It is quite a narrow space and everything has been covered at some stage with a thick mud-coloured paint. The floor is covered in rubble and bits of plasterwork that have fallen from the ceiling, some of them quite recently, so I am glad we are wearing our hard hats. Our feet crackle and crunch on the floor. The most powerful thing in this area is the smell: it's a mixture of damp, decay, dust and death. You know when your cat has brought a dead rat or something into the house and has left its remains somewhere. Then you get that awful sweetish smell that seems to stick in your nostrils and as you haven't the nose of a dog and your cat can't tell you, you drive yourself mad trying to find out where it is coming from.

The other thing that I don't like is that there's a draught that feels like it's come straight from the Arctic, but, like the smell, I can't locate its source. I wet my finger and put it up to gauge the direction, but it's no use. Now I have a numb finger.

"Let's go into the auditorium, shall we?" Says Jill. She opens another temporarily padlocked door and we enter the Hall proper.

This is something of a shock. After the reeking claustrophobia of the foyer, it seems vast. The roof looks as high as a cathedral's and we can see a little without our torches because grey shafts of light come down at crazy angles from holes in the roof and from broken windows on either side high up. Through these shafts of light little sprinkles of rain fall down from outside like silver dust. We have come in under a gallery which curves in a great horseshoe around the auditorium supported by thin wrought iron columns. Facing us is the desert of an auditorium stripped of its original seating, and strewn about with all sorts of debris from its motorcycle and junkie days.

"Watch out for the odd used needle," said Jill. "As you can see we haven't even begun the clearing up operation.."

Beyond the auditorium is an oblong black hole which I assume to be the orchestra pit and then the remains of a raised stage, its floorboards cracked and rotten, with a dirty great hole in the middle. Part of the stage is thrust forward into the pit beyond a great rounded proscenium arch behind which hang a few tattered threadbare remnants of curtains and stage cloths. Close to the stage, at either side under the wings of the gallery I can just detect the remnants of two long bars where customers once drank as they watched the entertainment. I feel as if I am breathing an eternity of dust and decay. I don't think I would have liked the place even when it was alive. It would have been too much like a giant version of those Northern clubs where I once had a brief inglorious career as a comic.

"Get off! We want the bingo, not you, yer boring boogger!"

That voice from the past echoed in my head almost audibly. I look round at the others, half expecting them to have heard something, but they were just staring at it all. I was left to my own thoughts. The night I "got the bird" in that club all those years ago was the night I quit the show business for tabloid journalism. It was the best move of my life. And now I'm presenting *I Can Make You A Star*, and the man behind the "Get off… yer boring boogger"? Cancer, heart failure maybe: he had been a fat bloke with a face like a potato. I can see him now through a haze of booze fumes and cigarette smoke, and his voice still echoes. No, revenge is not sweet.

Meanwhile Crispin had said the thing that people always seem obliged to say when they enter some great cultural edifice: "What an incredible space!"

I was happy to be spared the necessity of saying this stupid, meaningless phrase myself. Anyway, Jill was paying no attention; she was on her mobile to the camera crew.

"Look, where the hell are you…? Hold on, you're breaking up… Look, just come now… The doors are unlocked… We'll be here for another… Fifteen minutes—"

I shivered and said: "Wouldn't it be better to cancel them and come back some other time when the weather's a bit better?"

"No, I'm sorry , Danny," said Jill. "I just can't afford to waste them. We're on this incredibly tight budget."

I thought of offering to pay for the camera crew to come back later, much later, but something prevented me. I thought it might lower me in Jill's estimation, but why should I care about that?

"You know," said Crispin, pausing after this introduction in that way people do when they feel they have something incredibly important to announce, "I have a theory that this could be a very early Frank Matcham." He looked at me. "Matcham you know was the great theatre architect of the late nineteenth, early twentieth centuries and—"

"I know who Frank Matcham was," I said. I caught Jill's eye and she smiled, but even this little victory didn't make me any happier. I was cold, I needed a drink; I was beginning to hate the Old Essex with a passion. The idea of waiting around here for another quarter of an hour for a poxy television crew made me livid. I strode away from the other two towards the bar on the left side of the auditorium.

"Careful how you go," said Jill. "The floor can be a bit treacherous."

As I crunched over to the bar, I heard her and Crispin having an earnest discussion about Matcham and architecture: "The Old Essex was thoroughly renovated in 1877 by the firm of Jethro T. Robinson who was Matcham's father-in-law, and so it could be…" I didn't want to leave those two together. After all, Crispin may have been a ponce but at least he was her age and her class; he wasn't a twice divorced forty-year-old father of three, as I was. But I felt so angry.

What was I doing here? I shone my torch. The bar was in surprisingly good condition with a fine marble top, cracked in two places and thickly overlaid with dust, but otherwise intact. I began to shift a lot of debris to get behind the bar. I had this vague idea, you see, that I might find some ancient bottle of

Scotch or Brandy, or something. A likely scenario! Even a bottle of Bass would have done.

I managed to squeeze behind the bar by shifting several wooden joists and a broken chair or two. It probably wasn't at all safe, but I didn't care. There were some shelves behind the bar into which I shone my torch. Their contents consisted mainly of rubble, the odd dead rat and, as Jill had predicted, a used needle or two, but at the back of one I thought I saw a wad of paper. I reached in a gloved hand and tentatively drew it out.

It was a sheaf of handbills from the Old Essex days. They were singed at the corners and buckled with damp but still legible. I was excited almost in spite of myself. The date on the top sheet was 1888, the year of the fire at the Old Essex, the year it closed down. The acts were listed and some of the names were familiar:

GUS ELEN
ALBERT CHEVALIER
MARIE LLOYD
DAN LENO
LITTLE TICH

Then there were others who were not known to me.

LITTLE Miss ELLEN TOZER
The Juvenile Prodigy
THE GREAT "HERCULE"
Astonishing Feats of Strength

And then, this:

Mrs. MIDNIGHT
And her Animal Comedians

I don't know why, but that name Mrs. Midnight struck a chord somewhere. Was her name really Midnight? It sounded too good to be true. And what, for God's sake were "animal comedians"?

I looked up from the bar where I had laid out the papers and across to the stage. I was not shining my torch in that direction, but I thought I caught sight of someone sitting just behind the proscenium arch in what legits call the "prompt corner". It looked like a great bulky old woman with a shawl over her head and shoulders, wearing a floor length dress, but I could barely see more than an outline in the gloom. The figure was leaning forward slightly and quite motionless. The face was completely obscured by the cowl of the shawl, but I had the impression that it was staring in my direction.

I flashed my torch towards the figure and saw at once that it had been an illusion. It was no more than a pile of furniture and junk covered by a tarpaulin. All the same it had been uncannily lifelike. I switched the torch off to recreate the effect, but the magic had gone. It just looked like a pile of junk covered with a tarpaulin.

"Are you okay, Danny?" Said Jill.

As a matter of fact I was shaking all over, but I said: "Come over here! Look what I've found."

Jill was very excited by the old music hall bills; even Crispin was reluctantly impressed. I don't know why—to please Jill I suppose—but I said I would do some research into the playbills and the history of the theatre. Then Crispin started offering me advice about how and where to research. I let him go on a bit; then I quietly reminded him that I had been quite a successful journalist for over a dozen years, so I did know a little about the techniques of research. Crispin shut up, and again I thought I saw Jill smile.

Finally the camera crew arrived and we did some fake shots of us arriving at the Old Essex and being amazed. Crispin repeated his line about it being an incredible space and his Matcham theory. He wanted me to ask him who Matcham was on camera, but I wasn't playing ball. We were about to film my "discovery" of the playbills when the crew started to get technical glitches: jams in the camera, gremlins in the sound system, erratic variations in the light levels. The sound technician was particularly jumpy. At one point he said he had got the noise of some animal crying out in pain, perhaps a cat, on his cans; but the rest of us had heard nothing.

I know camera crews: they can be very touchy and difficult when they want to be. Perhaps it's because they think they are doing all the work and us guys in front of the camera are taking all the credit. I could see they were getting into a state, so I tried to calm them down, but it was no good. The sound man said straight out that the place was giving him "the willies". At this Crispin started to be very sarcastic until I told him to shut the fuck up. It was all beginning to get a bit hairy so I made a cut-throat gesture at Jill to let her know that I thought we should wrap. She understood immediately, gave the word and we cleared out. I wasn't sorry to go.

For about a week or so I put the Old Essex out of my mind. I was heavily into meetings with some producers about hosting a new Reality TV show called *Celebrity Dog Kennel.* Apparently they were finding it hard to sign up even the B and C listers who were asking silly money anyway. In the end it was Jill who spurred me. She rang me up and asked me how the research was going. I was vague but invited her to have dinner with me in a couple of day's time when I would tell her all about it. The following morning I took myself off to newspaper library at Colindale.

I had already got the bare facts about the Old Essex from Mander and Mitchenson, that the theatre had suffered a very damaging fire on Saturday, December 1st, 1888 from which its fortunes had never recovered and it had been abandoned as a place of entertainment very soon after. So I began my researches by looking in the newspapers of that period for reports of the fire at the Old Essex.

Most of the national dailies contained little more than a few lines stating that the fire had been started shortly after the Saturday night performance and that there were no "human fatalities", but that one man, a Mr. Graham, had been severely injured. I did, however come across a passing reference to it in a letter to the Times on December 5th, stating that: "the recent riot and conflagration at the Old Essex provides further evidence of the extreme unrest among the denizens of Whitechapel following the appalling murders recently perpetrated in that district." I presumed that the writer meant the Ripper murders, the last of which had been committed in November 1888. Rather fatuously the letter ended by urging the Metropolitan Police to "redouble their efforts in hunting down the person responsible for these unspeakable atrocities."

Eventually I tracked down a more detailed account of the fire in a local paper called *The East London Gazette*. Monday, December 3rd, 1888. In it I read as follows:

"…the evening's entertainment at the Old Essex was proceeding as normal when, towards the end of the bill, there was introduced an act known as *Mrs. Midnight and her Animal Comedians*. In it a lady by the name of 'Mrs. Midnight', dressed as a gypsy vagrant (but in reality personated by a Mr. Simpson Graham) appears on stage with a number of animals, including a cat, a Learned Pig, a miniature bulldog, a cockerel and a Barbary Ape. These creatures under instructions from Mrs. Midnight performed a number of astonishing mental and physical feats. Especially notable we are told was the 'Learned Pig' Belphagor who was capable of solving elementary mathematical conundrums with the aid of numbered cards. On this particular evening, however, parts of the audience, especially those who had been drinking at the bars, became restive and took against Mrs. Midnight. These vulgar objections reached their height while the Barbary ape, called Bertram, was performing the act of rescuing the miniature bulldog, Mary from the top of a miniature tower of wood and canvas, designed to look like a castle keep. Coins and other small hard objects were thrown onto the stage, one of which hit Bertram, the ape. The animal was so provoked by this act that he became visibly agitated and having reached the top of the tower, in stead of rescuing the bulldog, Mary, he bit her head off.

"That disgusting incident, needless to say, only incensed the troublemakers further and a full scale riot ensued. The local constabulary was summoned and the theatre was cleared. The artists appearing on the bill, which included Mr. Dan Leno were led to safety, but Mr. Graham remained behind because he was fearful of being set upon by the mob who were indeed calling for him. It was at this point that smoke was seen to be coming from one of the dressing room windows at the back of the theatre, though precisely when and how the fire was started has been disputed. Our reporter who arrived on the scene with the fire brigade was told by one member of the crowd that the reason for the animus surrounding 'Mrs. Midnight' was that her impersonator Mr. Graham (formerly, we understand, a medical practitioner) was suspected by many to have some connection with the Whitechapel Murders, though quite why he should have fallen under suspicion we have been unable to ascertain. The gallant members of the Fire Service, under their leader Captain Shaw, soon had the fire under control and were able to spirit Mr. Graham away unseen by the crowd. However

Mr. Graham is understood to have sustained severe injuries from the blaze and his entire menagerie of 'animal comedians' has perished in the conflagration."

As I was coming out of Colindale with my photocopy of the article I had a brain wave. My last job before TV celebrity took me to its silicone-enhanced bosom was as Showbiz Editor of the *Daily Magnet*. There I got to know Bill Beasely, the head of crime news. We had worked together on the Spice Girl Shootings and rubbed along fairly well. He wasn't a bad bloke if you could put up with his smoker's cough, and the fact that he smelt of gin and peppermints at nine in the morning. One of his fads was his fascination with the Ripper Murders: he'd even come up with a theory of his own about it and done yet another Ripper book. I think his idea was that it was Gladstone and Queen Victoria in collaboration, which is loony of course, but not as loony as that daft American bint who thinks it was Sickert the painter. (I happen to own a Sickert. I'm not a complete muppet.) I thought Bill might know about this Graham bloke if he was a suspect.

I gave him a ring and he asks me over. I suggest meeting in a pub, but he insists I come to his flat. I don't want to go because Bill is a bachelor—well so am I at the moment, but you know what I mean—and a bit of a slob and lives at the wrong end of Islington.

My worst fears are confirmed. There is even some old gypsy tramp woman with a filthy plaid shawl over her head crouching on his doorstep. She holds out her hand, palm upwards for cash. Luckily Bill buzzes me up fairly quickly when I ring the doorbell.

His flat is on the top floor and is everything I had been dreading, and more. It is all ashtrays, booze bottles and books, plus a sofa and a couple of armchairs that, like Bill, were bulging in all the wrong directions. The books are everywhere. They look as if they'd spread out from the ceiling-high shelves like some sort of self-perpetuating fungus. It is ten in the morning and Bill offers me a Gin and Tonic. He's barely changed in five years: a bit more flab maybe, a more phlegm-filled cough. I ask if I could have a tea or coffee.

He looks at me as if I'd demanded quail sandwiches and an avocado pear, but wanders into the kitchen to light the gas for the kettle.

"Does that gypsy woman regularly camp out on your doorstep?" I asked.

"Who?"

I went to the window to point her out to him but she's gone.

Bill managed to make some proper coffee in one of those percolator things, but it was still filthy. When I mentioned what I was here about, Graham and the Ripper connection, he became all excited. What is it about Jack the Ripper and some people? He started pacing round the room, talking enthusiastically and pulling books out of the shelves.

"Ah, yes. Well of course Dr. Graham is known to ripperologists, but he comes fairly low down on the list of possible suspects, mainly because we don't know much about him. But this new stuff you've dug up is fascinating. Perhaps you and I could collaborate on a new Ripper book about it?"

Not wanting to put him off at this early stage, I merely shrugged. "You called him 'Doctor' Graham?" I said.

"Yes. He was a doctor. Struck off, if I remember rightly. Of course being a doctor is always a plus when it comes to Ripper suspects. Anatomical expertise, you see. Knowing how to cut up bodies." He is leafing through a rather squalid looking giant paperback entitled *The A to Z of Ripperology*. "Where are we? Ah, here we are! 'Graham, Dr. Simpson S. Date of birth unknown.' That ought to be easy enough to find out. 'Medical practitioner with eccentric theories. Devised a treatment known as *zoophagy* in which patients were treated by being fed organs from still living animals, by means of vivisection. Bloody hell, that's absolutely disgusting!" Bill, the ripperologist, seemed genuinely shocked. " 'Wrote a book on the subject: *A Treatise on Brain Food, Or the Benefits of Zoophagy Explained…*' Etcetera, etcetera. 'Struck off the register for misconduct towards a female patient. Thought to have been suffering from the early stages of tertiary syphilis….' Ah! Listen to this! 'Became an entertainer known as "Mrs. Midnight" who performed with a troupe of trained animals. The times and locations of his appearance at various East London music halls were said to have coincided with some of the Ripper murders, but this has not been confirmed. It is believed that he died in 1889 or 1890 in an institution for the insane, having been injured by fire in an accident.' He gets two bleeding daggers out of five on the Suspect Rating. Wait a minute, there's a book referred to here in the bibliography: *Quacks and Charlatans, Alternative Medicine in late Nineteenth Century England* by Harrison Bews. Might be worth a look."

He then asked me why I was so keen on the Old Essex project. I tried to sound genuinely enthusiastic, but I think he saw through it.

After a pause he said: "The thing these restoration nuts don't get is that some old things are best left buried and unrevived. Just because it's old doesn't mean it's good; quite the opposite sometimes. I come from down that way myself, and my old Dad wouldn't go near the Old Essex. He never really told me why, but he did say that just after the war they tried to turn it back into a theatre or something. I don't know what happened exactly, but he said it was a disaster."

That afternoon I rang Jill and proposed that we should meet for dinner in the evening at my local gastro-pub, *The Engineer* in Primrose Hill. I thought dinner at my house might seem a bit forward for her. She accepted.

Sometimes I'm a good judge, though that's not what people say about me in *I Can Make You A Star*, but I thought Jill would like *The Engineer* and she did. The food's well cooked and imaginative, all organic of course and that sort of rubbish; but it's classy and modern without being pretentious and overpriced. She seemed in her element there.

You know how when you meet someone and you go away and start fantasising about them; then when you meet them again it's a terrible let down? With Jill, it was the opposite. She was even better. I don't want to go on about it but everything about her was somehow clear: clear skin, clear eyes, clear laugh. She dressed nicely but obviously didn't worry much about her appearance. Her hair was mousy coloured, not dyed.

Immediately I wanted to start talking about her and me, but I knew this would be fatal, so I told her about my researches. She gave me her full attention and seemed thrilled by the information I gave.

I said: "You don't think it's all a bit sordid and sinister?"

"Good grief no! Fascinating stuff. It all helps to raise the profile. There's no such thing as bad publicity. You of all people should know that."

I could tell she was teasing me which I liked, but it was in the way you tease a favourite uncle, not a friend, or a lover. Still, I had done well, so I told her grandly that there were a couple of books I thought I would look out at the British Library which might help. She stretched out her hand and touched mine.

"You know, when somebody suggested you to help raise money for the Old Essex, I didn't like the idea. I thought you would be, well… I mean, your reputation, the kind of programs you do…."

"I know. A case of *Pride and Prejudice* on your part."

"Well, sort of. Not that I'd exactly describe you as Mr. Darcy."

"You wound me, Jill."

We both laughed, but she had wounded without knowing. Then we discussed the practicalities of fund-raising events, television air time, recruiting other "names" to support the cause, and all the rest of it. I realised that by now it was far too late for me to bow out of the Old Essex project, even if I wanted to, but I couldn't because it would mean losing her. Then at the coffee stage, she said something, though I can't remember how it came up. Mature people are supposed to take these things better than the young, but I don't think that's true.

She said: "By the way, you may as well know, I'm engaged to Crispin."

"Crispin de Hartong?"

"That's right."

"But you can't!" The words were out before I could stop myself. She seemed amused rather than shocked by my reaction.

"Why not?"

"Because he's a pretentious pillock."

"Actually, he's really rather sweet when you get to know him."

There was something very steely about the way she said that. I had offended her, so I apologised. Then I told her gently that in my very humble opinion I thought she deserved better.

"Thank you for your fatherly concern," she said coolly.

"I hope I'm more than a father to you."

"What do you mean by that?"

Quickly I said: "And what does *your* father think about it all?"

"My father is dead; my mother lives in Leamington Spa," she added, as if that explained the situation.

"I see." She giggled. I laughed. The rest of that evening would have been pleasant in a trivial sort of way if I hadn't felt this great weight on my chest, brought on by her announcement. It was only then, I think, that I admitted to myself how much I felt about Jill. It often happens that when you confess to yourself, your feelings come to be like a physical pain. Call it heart ache if you like; I won't. Since I stopped working for the tabloids I've tried to avoid clichés like the plague.

Shortly after eleven I put Jill into a taxi outside *The Engineer*, and kissed her chastely on the cheek. This was not like me at all. Then I walked slowly back to my house. I took a long way round so that I could think, but I didn't really think at all. My mind was too full of Jill, and what a pillock Crispin was.

I have a little Georgian terraced house in Princess Road. It was one of those ones with railings along the front and steps going up to the front door. I was quite some way off when I noticed that someone was sitting on my steps. It was no more than a squat black shadow in a long dress from this distance. A ridiculous hope that it might be Jill vanished almost as soon as it came. The figure was motionless. Perhaps someone had just dumped some black bin bags on my doorstep, but no; the form was too precise. It must be a tramp and I would have to give her or him something before they cleared off. The thought enraged me. Hadn't I enough problems already?

As I approached I could see more clearly what it was. It was dark of course but there was enough light from the street lamps for me to tell. It was a tramp of some kind, a bag lady, except that she had no bags. She was big bulky old woman in a rusty black dress. Over her head and shoulders was a plaid shawl, greenish in colour I thought, but so dirty I could barely make out the pattern. It was only when I had come right up to her that I could see the face under the shawl and even then half of it was in shadow.

It was an old face, jowelled and wrinkled with pale pendulous cheeks and a puckered, lipless, dog's bottom of a mouth. I could not see the eyes clearly as they were shadowed by the thick overhanging brow, but I sensed that they were looking at me fixedly. Something about the heaviness of the chin and the thickness of the nose was making me suspect that the figure in the dress was not a woman at all but a man. This was confirmed when it thrust out a hand, palm upwards, from the folds of the plaid shawl. It was a big, heavy, dirty man's hand and there were great scars on it like old burn marks.

He wanted money. Well, that was simple enough. I fished for pound coins in my pocket. Even so, the idea of coming close enough to this thing to give them filled me with loathing. I stretched out my hand to be able to drop the coins into his while remaining as far as possible from him, but just as I was about to let the money go he gripped my wrist.

It felt like a handcuff of ice. I screamed like a girl. I felt dizzy; I suppose I must have passed out; drink I suppose, but it had not been my imagination because when I came to I looked for the coins. They and the bloke in the dress had gone.

From that moment I became a driven man. The following morning I went to the British Library and ordered up *Quacks and Charlatans*, as well as *A Treatise on Brain Food*. In the B.L. catalogues I noticed that Simpson Graham M.D. was also credited with another book entitled *Mother Midnight's Chatechism*, so I ordered that as well.

Research is like fitting together the pieces of a jigsaw puzzle. *Quacks and Charlatans* had only a few pages about Graham, and was completely ignorant about his Music Hall career, but it gave me this:

"He had been a brilliant if erratic medical student and early showed an almost insatiable desire to make his mark in the world… Dr. Graham developed the idea that ingesting organs, in particular the brain, from a living animal was extraordinarily beneficial to human health. Several times he gave a demonstration before an interested and alarmed public in which he trepanned a fully conscious dog or cat, an operation which can, if skilfully done, be executed without much pain to the subject. He would then proceed to dip a spoon into the brain pan and devour the contents until the wretched animal finally lost consciousness. Many colleagues poured scorn on his unorthodox methods, but very few of them objected from an animal welfare point of view…. After his disgrace, he continued to give lectures and demonstrations on what he called *zoophagy* (the eating of a still living being), often doing so in female dress for no apparent reason. Doubts as to his sanity naturally grew and he was finally consigned to an asylum."

I only skimmed though *A Treatise on Brain Food, Or the Benefits of Zoophagy Explained* by Simpson Graham M.D. Something about the very act of reading it, even in the antiseptic surroundings of the B.L. seemed poisonous. I did gather from a cursory glance that Dr. Graham was no stylist and did a lot of boasting. All the same, I couldn't help noting down one passage which comes towards the end of this tedious little book.

"If we could only overcome the contemptible prejudice against using our fellow human beings in such experiments I am convinced that the benefits would be extraordinary. At present criminals, condemned by law and society, are either executed or left to languish in unhygienic conditions, an unconscionably wasteful practice. How much better for us, and indeed them, if their living, palpitating organs and brain cells were to be used to refresh and rejuvenate a select few. With the skills that I have perfected, the suffering of the reprobates in question could be kept to a minimum; or indeed prolonged and exacerbated, if required, to point a necessary moral lesson. By ingesting these living substances and fluids the health and sanity of our finest men (and women) of genius would not only be enhanced but also greatly prolonged. Through this use of 'living brain food' as I term it, human lives of two or three hundred years might in the future, I sincerely believe, become a commonplace."

The third book, *Mother Midnight's Chatechism* was subtitled *Zoophagy Explained to the Young*. Graham did not claim authorship on the title page, and I am not surprised. It is printed on cheap paper and decorated with crude, muddy woodcuts. Nearly all of it is in verse. It begins:

"How can you be big and strong?
Hear then Mother Midnight's song…"
Then there were a number of stories or anecdotes told in verse.
"Edward ate a living mouse
And he learned to build a house;
David downed a wriggling rat,
And so he grew big and fat…"
Concluding with the moral:
"Make your meal off breathing things
And become as great as kings."

The final set of verses tells the story of a boy called Alfred who catches his sister out in the act of cheating him at cards. Thereupon he ties her to a chair and proceeds to cut her open with his "trusty knife". It was all told in a light-hearted almost humorous way that was very difficult to gauge. How serious was the man being?

"Then he cut a slice of liver
While she still did quake and quiver…"
I wanted to be sick, so I started to skip this stuff, but I know it finished:
"When he'd eaten all his sister,
Do you think that Alfred missed her?
No, for all her wit and vigour
Had been used to make him bigger.
All his wants she could provide him
By being safely there inside him."

I'd had enough, and I left the British Library in a hurry, nearly tripping over an old bag lady in the courtyard outside. Then my mobile started to ring. It was Bill Beaseley. He seemed far away and his voice kept breaking up.

"Danny, I think I've found something which may…. I'll send you a…." The phone went dead. I tried calling him but the line was engaged. On an impulse I rang Jill and asked if she would like to come to the recording of the final of *I Can Make You A Star* the following night.

"Great!" She said. "Can I bring Crispin too? I'm sure he'd be fascinated."

I bit my lip and told her I would have two tickets biked round to her that afternoon. I could have sold them on eBay for silly money.

The following morning a rather grubby envelope arrived for me by first class post. It could only be Bill Beaseley. Sure enough, inside was a photocopy. (Bill was one of those Luddites who refuse to use PCs and e-mails.) On the back of it he had scrawled:

"Page from a book called *The Complete Ripper Letters*, containing all the letters that were sent to the Police about the Whitechapel murders in both facsimile and transcript. This just may be the clue that clinches it!!! But don't forget, we go 50/50 on any book deal. All right, mate? Bill."

The facsimile showed a few lines written in a big scrawly handwriting on a scrap of paper. I got the feeling that the writer was trying to make his handwriting look rather more primitive and uneducated than it actually was. The legend above the facsimile read:

"Note addressed to 'Inspector Frederick Abberline at Scotland Yard', which arrived 3rd October 1888, three days after the double murder of Stride and Eddowes. It was dismissed as a hoax at the time as, though the message had been written in blood, it was found to be the blood of a cat."

Here was the message:

"I have eaten some of the lights out of them girlies as you will see. I'd send you a morsel, Mr Abbaline [sic], only it'd be long dead and won't be no use. Still we may meat, some time, but you won't know me from midnight as I'm not wot I seam."

That night was the Big One. Well, you all saw the final of *I Can Make You A Star*, this year, didn't you? The tenor in the wheelchair won it because of the viewers' phone-in votes, even though the judges and I thought it should have been the blind juggler. Anyway the audience ratings went through the roof. Jill and Crispin came round afterwards for the champagne do with all the celebs. Jill was excited by it all and just thought it was a hoot, but Crispin was being very snotty and stand-offish, I'm glad to say. I kept my eye on them and, when I noticed that they seemed to be having a little argument, I came over. He was bored and wanted to go home apparently, but she wanted to stay. So I touched her bare arm and took her to meet some of my famous friends, purely because they might help out on the Save the Old Essex campaign, you understand. She loved that.

I was feeling pretty good the next morning, even when the doorbell rang shortly after seven-thirty. Those bloody tabloids, I thought, they'll be asking me to confirm some stupid rumour, or they want a picture of me looking rough in the altogether. I took care to dress carefully before I opened the door, but it wasn't the press, it was the police.

"Good morning, sir. Could we step inside for a moment....? Do you know a Mr. Bill Beasely of Flat C. 31 Congreve Street....? Well, the thing is, sir Mr Beaseley was found dead last night.... Murdered, sir.... There was a notebook on the desk and it was open at a page on which your name and address had been written... I wonder if you could possibly account for your movements last night...."

They actually asked me where I had been that night! I told them that my alibi was pretty impeccable as I had about twenty million witnesses to my whereabouts. Oh, says, the Inspector, all sophisticated, we thought those programs like *I Can Make You A Star* were pre-recorded. No, I said, you can check, it was all live, every fizzing second of it. I believe in live. If it isn't live it hasn't got that something.

I asked for details about poor Bill and they seemed happy to oblige. His skull had been split open with somethig like a meat cleaver and it looked as if part of his brain had been removed. That scared me, I must say, but I said nothing.

They asked me if Bill had had enemies. No, I could not think of any enemies, but Bill had been a crime reporter, you know.

The next day I let the press have it, and by the time the late editions of the *Evening Standard* were on the streets, there was a nice little spread on the inside pages:

I CAN MAKE YOU A STAR MAN CLAIMS:
"I HAVE SOLVED RIPPER MYSTERY"

Well, not exactly, but near enough by press standards. I had given them a pretty coherent run-down of the evidence, and they got most of it right. The one thing I'm afraid I hadn't told them about was old Bill's part in my discovery, but I thought what with his murder and everything, it would just make things too complicated. I did feel bad about that for a while.

I had rung Jill naturally, and she seemed delighted by the news coverage.

"I'm beginning to think you're a bit of a star too," she said.

"You are too kind, Miss Bennett."

"By no means, Mr. Darcy." That was progress.

I discussed with her the television feature on the Old Essex and the Ripper suspect that I was arranging for the Local London TV News and the possibility of a full-length documentary. Three days later Jill, Crispin and I were down at the Old Essex with a camera crew. I had specially asked Crispin to come along as our "architectural expert" which pleased Jill.

Once again it was raining, but not as heavily as the last time. We decided to film indoors first and wait for it to clear to do the establishing shots outside in the street. I did my stuff to camera about this wonderful old building and how it was steeped in the rich history of the East End, and then Crispin did his architecture bit. I wasn't going to tell him that his material was bound to end up on the cutting room floor. He wasn't bad, but he was too fond of his own voice.

Then there was a lightening in the rain so Jill and the crew went out to do the establishing shots. Crispin and I voted to stay indoors and drink the skinny lattes the P.A. had got us from the nearest Starbucks.

So there we were, the two of us, alone in the auditorium of that great dirty old Cathedral of Sin. It was so quiet; you could almost hear the dust falling through the shafts of grey light. Somewhere in the deep distance traffic rumbled in a twenty-first-century street, but it was miles and ages away. Crispin started to look at me very intently, so I looked back at him. He was not bad looking, I suppose, in a rather girly way, with his shoulder length blonde hair and his pretty mouth. The looks won't last, though, I thought. I'm dark with good cheekbones. I may be forty, but I'm built to last. I go to the gym.

"You really are a little shit," he said. I was astonished, but I said nothing. Crispin went on. "You may as well know; you haven't a chance with Jill. She is, as you would say, 'out of your league.' You do realise that, don't you?"

He was expecting me to react, to say something, but I didn't. I just went on staring at him. He reckoned without the fact that I didn't get where I am today without being a bit of a psychologist. After a pause, he started up again, but not quite as confident as before.

"I know all about your efforts to impress her. Visits to the British Library; dinners at gastro-pubs, tickets to that truly ghastly show of yours. It won't do you any good, you know. She isn't remotely interested in you, never will be, and shall I tell you why—? Good God, what's that?"

"What?"

"Didn't you see it? Some sort of flicker of light, there on stage, just behind the pros arch."

No. Nothing. Then, yes, there *was* something. By the proscenium arch, I saw a yellow light flicker, like a candle flame. Someone was holding a lighted candle on the stage of the Old Essex. Then it began to move and we saw the outline of the thing that carried it. It was a big old woman with a long dress and a shawl over her head. Her back was to us. She looked like a huge huddled heap of old clothes. Slowly she began to shuffle away from us upstage.

"Excuse me!" said Crispin, in his best public school prefect voice. He was talking loud and slow as if to an idiot child. "Excuse me, I don't know who you are, but I don't think you're supposed to be here. This is a listed building, you know! Excuse me!"

Then he started to move towards the stage.

"Christ, where are you going?" I said.

"I want to know what the hell's going on," he said. "Come on!" I couldn't stop him, so I just followed.

He climbed up onto the stage and I warned him about the floorboards. Dammit, there was a great hole in the middle of the stage; but he ignored me and I climbed up after him.

It was a funny thing. That great shambling lump of an old woman kept ahead of us the whole time as we threaded our way over piles of junk and rubble. We weren't able to catch up with her, but she was always in our sight. It was almost as if she were leading us somewhere. Crispin called out to her several times, but she simply did not react. She shambled on with her flickering candle.

When she got to the back of the stage she turned right and went through a narrow brick archway. There was now no light apart from the candle and our torches. Once through the archway we were in a backstage corridor. It was all brick, black with age or fire. To our right was a stone staircase up which we could see a flicker of candle and hear the heavy footsteps of the old woman ascending, accompanied by long groaning breaths.

Surely now we could catch up with her, so we plunged up the dirty, lightless stair, barely considering now what we were doing or why.

At the top of the steps we found ourselves in another dim, black brick corridor. And we were amazed to see that the old woman, now practically bent double and so headless to us, was halfway along it, about twenty yards ahead, hobbling away. We shouted at her, but on she went regardless.

The corridor smelt of something oily and old, and when I touched the wall by accident a black tarry substance stuck to my hand.

At last we were beginning to catch up with the woman when she suddenly stopped in a viscous looking puddle, turned and then started to climb yet another staircase to her right. When we arrived at the bottom of this flight we heard her steps cease and saw that she had halted ten steps up, her back to us. The groaning breaths were beginning to sound like some dreadful kind of singing. I thought I could recognise some words of the old Music Hall song:

"Why am I always the bridesmaid,
Never the blushing bride?
Ding dong, wedding bells,
Only ring for other gells…"

With little shuffles she was turning slowly round to face us, and I knew now that my worst fears would be confirmed. As she moved she let the plaid shawl slip from her head to reveal a greasy white cranium planted with wild tufts of white hair, sprouting like winter trees in frost on a barren landscape. Half of her face I had seen before. There was the heavy brow, the wild grey eye, the great blob nose, the thick mannish chin, but the other half was a mangled mess, an angry chaos of fiery scar tissue, utterly unrecognisable as a face at all. Mrs. Midnight lifted the candle to his head so that we could see it all.

"Why am I always the bridesmaid,
Never the blushing bride…?"

Then he hurled the candle down the stairs towards us. I thought it would extinguish itself in the oily pool at the bottom of the steps. But it did not. It guttered for a moment, then a great tongue of flame leapt up from the pool and began to lick at Crispin's jeans. There was a roar and the next minute he was engulfed in flame. I took off my jacket and tried to smother the fire, but he was screaming and fighting me off. The only thing to do was to hurry him back down the corridor which was now spitting little gobs of flame from every tarry crevice. Before we had reached the stairs leading down to the stage, Crispin collapsed. First I beat out the fire on his body with my jacket, then picking him up in a fireman's lift I carried him downstairs. Behind me the flames were roaring like an angry ghost.

I had got down onto the stage level with Crispin on my back. I thought we were home safe so I began to run across the stage, but I had forgotten how rotten the boards were. There was a crack and suddenly we were falling into a pit. Crispin broke my fall a little, but I felt a sharp pain in my shoulder and one leg appeared to be useless. We were in the dark. I could see nothing, but there was a reek of corpses all around us.

The Fire Brigade eventually heard our calls and we were rescued. They told me later that Crispin and I had tumbled into a cellar where they had also found a large number of dead cats in various stages of decomposition. What was odd, they told me, was that so many of the cats had suffered injuries to the head.

Some of them looked as if the tops of their skulls had been surgically removed. I did not want to know.

I had broken several bones in my body and needed a couple of operations, so I wasn't going to be pushed out of the hospital in a hurry as usually happens. I'm afraid Crispin was rather worse off. As well as other injuries, the fire had burned the beauty out of half his face. I genuinely feel bad about that.

I have a private room at the hospital, of course. In the evenings Jill, my angel, comes to see me with grapes or something else I don't really want, but I feel better for her coming. I want to say something to her so much, but I can't because I'm frightened of being turned down, rejected.

Get off! We want the bingo, not you, yer boring boogger!

And then, just recently, I have woken up in the early hours of the morning to find the great bulk of Mrs Midnight crouched by my bed. From the folds of the plaid shawl Mrs. Midnight will take a kitten, still alive and mewing, and out of its trepanned head Mrs. Midnight will scoop a quiver of grey jelly with a teaspoon.

"This is your brain food," says Mrs. Midnight. "Eat up!"

EACH THING I SHOW YOU IS A PIECE OF MY DEATH
GEMMA FILES AND STEPHEN J. BARRINGER

Born in England and raised in Toronto, Canada, Gemma Files has been a film critic, teacher and screenwriter, and is currently a wife and mother. She won the 1999 International Horror Guild Best Short Fiction award for her story "The Emperor's Old Bones", and the 2006 ChiZine/Leisure Books Short Story Contest for her story "Spectral Evidence". Her fiction has been published in two collections (*Kissing Carrion* and *The Worm in Every Heart*, both from Prime Books), and five of her stories were adapted into episodes of *The Hunger*, an anthology TV show produced by Ridley and Tony Scott's Scot Free Productions. She has also published two chapbooks of poetry. In 2010, her first novel—*A Book of Tongues*, Part One of the Hexslinger Series—will be released by CZP Publications.

Stephen J. Barringer's first publication was the short story "Restoration" in the Canadian SF magazine *On Spec*; he has since won first and second prizes in the long-running Toronto Trek/Polaris media convention's short story competition, and has written several gaming products for various RPG systems, as well as a radio-play adaptation of E.F. Benson's "The Room in the Tower" for Canada's Dark Echo Productions. A lifelong resident of Toronto, he is married to Gemma Files.

"There is nothing either good or bad, but thinking makes it so."
— *The Tragedy of Hamlet, Prince of Denmark*, William Shakespeare.

From a journal found in a New Jersey storage unit, entry date unknown:
Somewhere, out beyond the too-often unmapped intersection of known and forgotten, there's a hole through which the dead crawl back up to this world: A crack, a crevasse, a deep, dark cave. It splits the earth's crust like a canker, sore lips thrust wide to divulge some even sorer mouth beneath—tongueless, toothless, depthless.
The hole gapes, always open. It has no proper sense of proportion. It is rude and rough, rank and raw. When it breathes out it exhales nothing but poison, pure decay,

77

so awful that people can smell it for miles around, even in their dreams.

Especially there.

Through this hole, the dead come out face-first and down, crawling like worms. They grind their mouths into cold dirt, forcing a lifetime's unsaid words back inside again. As though the one thing their long, arduous journey home has taught them is that they have nothing left worth saying, after all.

Because the dead come up naked, they are always cold. Because they come up empty, they are always hungry. Because they come up lost, they are always angry. Because they come up blind, eyes shut tight against the light that hurts them so, they are difficult to see, unless sought by those who—for one reason, or another—already have a fairly good idea where to start looking.

To do so is a mistake, though, always—no matter how "good" our reasons, or intentions. It never leads to anything worth having. The dead are not meant to be seen or found, spoken with, or for. The dead are meant to be buried and forgotten, and everybody knows it—or should, if they think about it for more than a minute. If they're not some sort of Holy Fool marked from birth for sacrifice for the greater good of all around them, fore-doomed to grease entropy's wheels with their happy, clueless hearts' blood.

Everybody should, so everybody does, though nobody ever talks about it. Nobody. Everybody. Everybody…

…but them.

(The dead)

* * *

July 26/2009
FEATURE ARTICLE:
COMING SOON TO A DVD NEAR YOU?
"BACKGROUND MAN" JUMPS FROM 'NET
TO… EVERYWHERE
By Guillaume Lescroat, strangerthings.net/media

Moviegoers worldwide are still in an uproar over *Mother of Serpents*, Angelina Jolie's latest blockbuster, being pulled from theatres after only four days in wide release due to "unspecified technical problems." According to confidential studio sources, however, the real problem isn't "unspecified" at all—this megabudget Hollywood flick has apparently become the Internet-spawned "Background Man" hoax's latest victim.

For over a year now, urban legend has claimed that, with the aid of careful frame-by-frame searches, an unclothed Caucasian male (often said to be wearing a red necklace) can be spotted in the background of crowd scenes in various obscure films, usually partially concealed by distance, picture blur or the body-parts of other extras. Despite a proliferation of websites dedicated to tracking Background Man (over thirty at last count), most serious film buffs dismissed the legend as a snipe-hunt joke for newbies, or a challenge for bored and talented Photoshoppers.

But all that changed when the Living Rejects video "Plastic Heart" hit MTV in September last year, only to be yanked from the airwaves in a storm of FCC charges after thousands of viewers confirmed a "full-frontally naked" man "wearing a red necklace" was clearly visible in the concert audience... a man that everybody, from the band members to the director, would later testify under oath *hadn't been there* when the video was shot.

"You know the worst thing about looking for Background Man? While you're waiting for him you gotta sit through the crappiest movies on the planet! C'mon, guy, pick an Oscar contender for once, wouldja?!"
— Conan O'Brien, *Late Night with Conan O'Brien*, November 18, 2008

Background Man has since appeared in supporting web material for several TV shows (*House*, *Friday Night Lights* and *The Bill Engvall Show* have all been victims) and has been found in a number of direct-to-DVD releases as well, prompting even Conan O'Brien to work him into a monologue (see above). *Mother of Serpents* may not be the first major theatrical release to be affected, either; at least three other films this summer have pushed back their release dates already, though their studios remain cagey about the reasons. The current consensus is that Background Man is a prank by a gifted, highly-placed team of post-production professionals.

This theory, however, has problems, as producer Kevin Weir attests. "Anybody involved who got caught, their career, their entire life would be wrecked," says Weir. "Besides the fines and the criminal charges, it's just totally f---ing unprofessional—nobody I know who *could* do this *would* do it; it's like pissing all over your colleagues." Film editor Samantha Perry agrees, and notes another problem: "I've reviewed at least three different appearances, and I couldn't figure out how any of them were done, short of taking apart the raw footage. These guys have got tricks or machines I've never heard of."

Hoax or hysteria, the Background Man shows no signs of disappearing. However, our own investigation may have yielded some insights into the mysterious figure's origin—an origin intimately connected with the collapse last year of the Toronto-based "Wall of Love" film collective's Kerato-Oblation/Cadavre Exquis project, brainchild of experimental filmmakers Soraya Mousch and Max Holborn...

* * *

From: Soraya Mousch sor16muse@walloflove.ca
Date: Friday, June 20, 2008, 7:08 PM
To: Max Holborn mhb@ca.inter.net
Subject: FUNDRAISING PITCH DOC: "KERATO-OBLATION" (DRAFT 1)

To Whom it May Concern—

My name is Soraya Mousch, and I am an experimental filmmaker. Since 1999, when Max Holborn and I founded Toronto's Wall of Love Experimental Film Collective, it has been my very great pleasure both to collaborate on and present a series of not-for-profit projects specifically designed to push—or even, potentially, demolish—the accepted boundaries of visual storytelling as art.

Unfortunately, given that film remains the single most expensive artistic medium, this sort of thing continues to cost money… indeed, with each year we practice it, it seems to cost more and more. Thus the necessity, once government grants and personal finances run out, of fundraising.

- - - - - - -

(mhb): <yeah, say it exactly like that, that'll get us some money [/sarc]>

- - - - - - -

To this end, Mr Holborn and I have registered an internet domain and website (kerato-oblation.org), through which we intend to compile, edit and host our next collaborative project, with the help of filmmakers from every country which currently has ISP access (ie, all of them). The structure of this project will be an *exquisite corpse* game applied to the web-based cultural scene as a whole, one that anybody can play (and every participant will "win").

WHY KERATO-OBLATION?
Kerato-oblation: Physical reshaping of the cornea via scraping or cutting. With our own version—the aforementioned domain—how we plan to "reshape" our audience's perspectives would be by applying the exquisite corpse game to an experimental feature film assembled from entries filed over the Internet, with absolutely no boundaries set as to content or intent.

WHAT IS AN EXQUISITE CORPSE?
An "exquisite corpse" (*cadavre exquis*, in French) is a method by which a collection of words or images are assembled by many different people working at once alone, and in tandem. Each collaborator adds to a composition in sequence, either by following a rule (e.g. "The *adjective noun adverb verb* the *adjective noun*") or by being allowed to see, and either elaborate on or depart from, the end of what the previous person contributed. The technique was invented by Surrealists in 1925; the name is derived from a phrase that resulted when the game was first played ("Le cadavre exquis boira le vin nouveau."/"The exquisite corpse will drink the new wine."). It is similar to an old parlour game called Consequences in which players write in turn on a sheet of paper, fold it to conceal

part of the writing, then pass it to the next player for a further contribution.

Later, the game was adapted to <u>drawing</u> and <u>collage</u>, producing a result similar to classic "mix-and-match" children's books whose pages are cut into thirds, allowing children to assemble new chimeras from a selection of tripartite animals. It has also been played by mailing a drawing or collage—in progressive stages of completion—from one player to the next; this variation is known as "<u>mail art</u>." Other applications of the game have since included computer graphics, theatrical performance, musical composition, object assembly, even architectural design.

- - - - - - -

(mhb): <don't know if we need all this history, or the whole exquisite corpse thing—just call it "spontaneous collaboration" or something? keep it short>

- - - - - - -

Earlier experiments in applying the exquisite corpse to film include <u>Mysterious Object at Noon</u>, an experimental 2000 Thai feature directed by <u>Apichatpong Weerasethakul</u> which was shot on 16 mm over three years in various locations, and <u>Cadavre Exquis, Première Edition</u>, done for the 2006 Montreal World Film Festival, in which a group of ten film directors, scriptwriters and professional musicians fused filmmaking and songwriting to produce a musical based loosely on the legend of Faust.

- - - - - - -

(mhb): <the montreal things good, people might actually have seen that one—one more example?>

- - - - - - -

For your convenience, we've attached a PDF form outlining several support options, with recommended donation levels included. Standard non-profit release waivers ensure that all contributors consent to submit their material for credit only, not financial recompense. By funnelling profits in excess of industry-standard salaries for ourselves back into the festival, we qualify for various tax deductions under current Canadian law and can provide charitable receipts for any and all financial donations made. Copies of the relevant paperwork are also attached, as a separate PDF.

For more information, or to discuss other ways of getting involved, either reply to this e-mail or contact us directly at (416)-[REDACTED]. We look forward to discussing mutual opportunities.

With best regards,
Soraya Mousch and Maxim Holborn
The Wall of Love Toronto Film Collective

- - - - - - -

(mhb): <for crissakes soraya DON'T SIGN ME AS MAXIM—if I have to be there at all its just max, k?>

* * *

8/23/08 1847HRS
TRANSCRIPT SUSPECT INTERVIEW 51 DIVISION
CASEFILE #332
PRESIDING OFFICERS D. SUSAN CORREA 156232,
D. ERIC VALENS 324820
SUBJECT MAXIM HOLBORN

D.VALENS: All right. So you had this footage for what, better than six weeks—footage apparently showing somebody committing suicide—and you didn't ever think that maybe you should let the police know?
HOLBORN: People send us stuff like this all the time, man! The collective's been going since '98. Most of it's fake, half of it has a fake ID and half of the rest doesn't have any ID at all.
D.VALENS: Yeah, that's awful lucky for you, isn't it?
D.CORREA: Eric, any chance you could get us some coffee?
HOLBORN: I don't want coffee.
(D.VALENS LEFT INTERROGATION ROOM AT 1852 HRS)
D.CORREA: Max, I'm only telling you this because I really do think you don't know shit about this, but you need to do one of two things right now. You need to get yourself a lawyer, or you need to talk to us.
HOLBORN: What the fuck am I going to tell a lawyer that I didn't already tell you guys? What else do you want me to say?
D.CORREA: Max, you're our only connection to a dead body. This is not a good place to be. And your lawyer's going to tell you the same thing: the more you work with us, the better this is going to turn out for everyone.
HOLBORN: Yeah. Because that's an option.

* * *

From: 11235813@gmail.com
Date: Wednesday, June 25, 2008, 3:13 AM
To: submissions@kerato-oblation.org
Subject: Re: KERATO-OBLATION FILM PROJECT

To Whom It May Concern—
    Please accept my apologies for not fully completing your submission form. I think the attached file is suitable enough for your purposes that you will find the missing information unnecessary, and feel comfortable including it in your exhibition nevertheless. I realize this will render it ineligible for competition, but I hope you can show it as part of your line-up all the same.
    Thank you.

VIRTUAL CELLULOID (vcelluloid.blogspot.com)
Alec Christian: Pushing Indie Film Forward Since 2004

<- Rue Morgue Party | Main | Rumblings on the Turnpike ->

July 23, 2008
"Wall of Love" Big Ten Launch Party

Got to hang out with two of my favourite people from the Scene last night at the Bovine Sex Club: Soraya Mousch and Max Holborn, the head honchos behind the Wall of Love collective. The dedication these guys've put into keeping their festivals going is nothing short of awesome, and last night's launch party for the next one was actually their *tenth anniversary*. Most marriages I know don't last that long these days. (Doubly weird, given Max and Soraya are that rarest of things, totally platonic best opposite-sex straight friends.)

For those who've been under a rock re the local artsy-fart scene over each and every one of those ten years, meanwhile, here's a thumbnail sketch of the Odd Couple. First off, Soraya. Armenian, born in Beirut, World Vision supermodel-type glamorous. Does music videos to pay the bills, but her heart belongs to experimentalism. Thing to remember about Soraya is, she's not real big on rules: When a York film professor told her she'd have to shift mediums for her final assignment, she ended up shooting it all on her favorite anyways (8mm), then gluing it to 16mm stock for the screening. This is about as crazy as Stan Brakhage gluing actual dead-ass *moths* to the emulsion of his film *Mothlight*… and if you don't know what *that* is either, man, just go screw. I despair of ya.

Then there's Max: White as a sack of sheets, Canadian as a beaver made out of maple sugar. Meticulous and meta, uber-interpretive. Assembles narratives from found footage, laying in voiceovers to make it all make (a sort of) sense. Also a little OCD in the hands-on department, this dude tie-dyes his own films by swishing them around in food-color while they're still developing, then "bakes" them by running them through a low-heat dryer cycle, letting the emulsion blister and fragment. The result: Some pretty trippy shit, even if you're *not* watching it stoned.

Anyways. With fest season coming up fast, M. and S. are in the middle of assembling this huge film collage made from snippets people posted chain-letter-style. You might think this sounds like kind of a dog's breakfast, and any other self-proclaimed indie genius you'd be right. But S. took me in the back and showed me some of the files they hadn't got to yet, and man, there's some damn raw footage in there, if ya know what I mean; even freaked *her* out. So if you're looking for something a little less *Saw* and a little more *Chien Andalou*, check it out: October 10, the Speed of Pain…

* * *

From: Soraya Mousch sor16muse@walloflove.ca
Date: Wednesday, June 25, 3:22 PM
To: Max Holborn mhb@ca.inter.net
Subject: Check this file out!

Max—
Sorry about the size of this file, I'd normally send it to your edit suite but it's got some kind of weird formatting—missing some of the normal protocols—I don't have time to dick around with your firewalls. Anyway, YOU NEED TO SEE THIS. Get back in touch with me once you have!

From: Soraya Mousch *sor16muse@walloflove.ca*
Date: Wednesday, June 25, 3:24 PM
To: Max Holborn *mhb@ca.inter.net*
Subject: Apology followup

Max: Realized I might've come off a little bitchy in that last message, wanted to apologize. I know you've got a lot of shit on your plate with Liat (how'd the CAT-scan go, BTW?); last thing I want to do is make your life harder. You know how it goes when the deadline's coming down.
    Seriously, though, the sooner we can turn this one around, like ASAP, the better—I think this one could really break us wide open. If you could get back to me by five with something, anything, I'd be really grateful. Thanks in advance.
    See you Sunday, either way,
    Soraya.

From: Max Holborn mhb@ca.inter.net
Date: Wednesday, June 25, 4:10 PM
To: Soraya Mousch sor16muse@walloflove.ca
Subject: Re: Apology followup

s.—
cat-scan wasn't so great, tell you bout it later. got your file, i'm about to review. i'll im you when it's done.
 m.

* * *

TRANSCRIPT CHAT LOG
06/25/08 1626-1633

<max_hdb>: soraya? u there?
<sor16muse>: so whatd you think?
<max_hdb>: jesus soraya, w?t?f? who sent THIS in? even legal to show?
<max_hdb>: I didnt get into this to go to jail
<sor16muse>: message came in from a numbered gmail account, no sig—check out the file specs?
<sor16muse>: relax max—we didnt make it, no way anybody cn prove we did, got to be digital dupe of a tape loop
<max_hdb>: yeah, I lkd at specs—these guys know tricks I don't. u can mask creation datestamp in properties to make it LOOK blank, bt not supposed to be any way to actually wipe that data out without disabling file
<sor16muse>: my guess is the originals at least 50 yrs old
<sor16muse>: max, we cant NOT show this
<max_hdb>: gotta gt somebody to lk/@ it first—im not hanging my ass out in th/wind
<sor16muse>: why don't we meet @ laszlos? he can run it through his shit, see what pops
<max_hdb>: don't like him. his house smells like toilet mold, hes a freak
<sor16muse>: whatever, hes got the best film-to-flash download system in the city doesnt cost $500 daily rental, so just grow a fucking pair
<max_hdb>: you know he tapes every conversation goes on in there, right? wtf w/that?
<sor16muse>: (User sor16muse has disconnected)
<max_hdb>: and btw, next time you wanna show me shit like that try thinking about liat first
<max_hdb>: (User max_hdb has disconnected)

* * *

July 26/2009
"BACKGROUND MAN", Lescroat,
strangerthings.net/media
(cont'd)

"That original clip? Hands down, some of the scariest amateur shit I've ever seen in my life," says local indie critic/promoter Alec Christian, self-proclaimed popularizer of the "Toronto Weird" low-budget horror culture movement. "A little bit of *Blair Witch* to it, obviously, but a lot more of early Nine Inch Nails videos, Jorg Buttgereit and Elias Merhige. That moment when you realize the guy's body is rotting in front of you? Pure *Der Todesking* reference, and you don't get those a lot, 'cause most of the people doing real-time horror are total self-taught illiterates about their own history."

Asked if there's any way the clip might be genuine, rather than staged, Christian laughs almost wistfully. "Does it matter? Some people still think *Blair Witch* was real," he points out. "But seriously, think how hard it would be to shoot this using World War One technology and logistics, at the latest, which is what we'd be looking at if it was real—and if it was filmed later but aged to look older, then everything else could have been engineered as well. Sometimes you just have to go with common sense."

* * *

TRANSCRIPT EVIDENCE EXHIBIT #3 51 DIVISION
CASEFILE #332
RECOVERY LOCATION 42 TRINITY STREET BSMT
DATE 8/20/2008

Item: 89.2 MB .MPG file retrieved from hard drive of laptop SONY VAIO X372 s/n 10352835A, prop. M. Holborn, duration 15m07s.

0:00—(All images recorded in black-and-white monochrome.) Caucasian male subject (Subject A), 40s, est. 6'1", 165 lbs, dark hair, wearing black or brown suit appearing to be 1920s cut, shown sitting in upright wooden chair looking directly at camera. Room is a single chamber, est. 8' x 10', hardwood floor, one window behind subject, one door in right-hand wall at rear. No painting or other decoration visible on walls. Angle of light from window suggests filming began early morning; light traverses screen in right-to-left direction, suggesting southward facing of window and room. Unknown subject has no discernible expression.

0:01-4:55—Subject A rises and removes clothes, beginning with detachable celluloid collar. Each garment removed separately, folded and placed on floor. Care and placing of garment removal suggests ritual purpose. Subject is shown to be uncircumcised. Subject continues no discernible facial expression.

4:55-5:19—Subject A resumes seat and looks straight into camera without movement or speech. Enhanced magnification and review of subject's right hand reveals indeterminate object, most likely taken from clothing during removal.

5:20-5:23—Subject A opens object in hand, demonstrating it to be a straight razor. Subject cuts own throat in two angular incisions, transverse to one another. Strength and immediacy of blood flow indicates both carotid and jugular cut. Evenness and control of movement suggests anesthesia or psychosis. Review by F/X technicians confirms cuts too deep to have been staged without use of puppets or animatronics. Subject maintains lack of facial expression.

5:23-6:08—Subject A's self-exsanguination continues until consciousness appears lost. Subject collapses in chair, head draped over back.

6:09—Estimated time of death for Subject A.

6:11—Razor released from subject's fingers, drops to floor.

6:12—13:34—Clip switches from real-time pacing to timelapse speed, shown by rapidity of daylight movement and day-night transitions. Reconstruction analysis specifies 87 24-hour periods elapse during this segment. Subject's body shown decomposing at accelerated pace.

7:22—Primary liquefaction complete; dessication begins. Clothes left on floor have developed mold.

10:41—Dessication largely complete. Rust visible on blade of razor. Fungal infestation on clothes has spread to floorboards.

13:10—Subject's cranium detaches and falls to floor.

13:17—Subject's right hand detaches and falls to floor.

13:25—Subject's left arm detaches and falls to floor. Imbalance in weight causes remains of subject's body to fall off chair.

13:34—Decomposition process complete. Footage resumes normal real-time pacing.

14:41—Subject B walks into frame from behind camera P.O.V. Subject B's appearance 100% consistent in identity with initial Subject A, including lack of circumcision and identifiable body marks. Remains of Subject A still visible behind Subject B.

15:01—Subject B bends down in front of camera and looks into it. Subject B shows no discernible facial expression.

15:06—Subject B reaches above and behind camera viewpoint.

15:07—CLIP ENDS

* * *

TRANSCRIPT EVIDENCE EXHIBIT #2 51 DIVISION
CASEFILE #332
RECOVERY LOCATION 532 OSSINGTON AVENUE BSMT RESIDENCE
LASZLO P HURT DATE 8/19/2008
AUDIOTAPE PROPERTY OF LASZLO P HURT

(IDENTIFICATION RETROACTIVELY ASSIGNED TO VOICES FOLLOWING CONFIRMATION FROM M HOLBORN AND S MOUSCH OF CONTENT)

V1 (MOUSCH): (LOUD)… see, here it is. Never see it if you weren't looking for it.
V2 (HOLBORN): (LOUD) Shit. He really does have his own place bugged.

What's this for? Legal protection?

V1 (MOUSCH): (VOL. DECREASING) Maybe, but I think it's really just because he wants to. Like his whole life is a big cumulative performance art piece. Sort of like in that Robin Williams movie, where people have cameras in their heads, and Robin has to cut a little film together when they die to sum up fifty years of experience?

V2 (HOLBORN): Yeah. That really sucked.

V1 (MOUSCH): I know. Just… keep it in mind, that's all I'm saying.

(BG NOISE: TOILET FLUSH)

V3 (HURT): Sorry about that. I haven't got new filters put in on the tapwater yet.

V2 (HOLBORN): That's… okay, Laszlo.

V3 (HURT): Yeah, you want some helpful input? Try not patronizing me.

V1 (MOUSCH): Laz, come on.

V3 (HURT): Yeah, okay, okay. So I reviewed your file.

V2 (HOLBORN): And?

V3 (HURT): First thing comes to mind is a story I heard through the post grapevine, one of those boojum-type obscurities the really crazy collectors go nuts trying to find. Though this can't be that, obviously, the clip would be way older, not digitized—

V1 (MOUSCH): People digitize old stuff all the time!

V3 (HURT): Really? Yeah, Soraya, I get that, actually; do it for a living, right? Look, the upshot is that you do have some deliberate image degradation going on here, so—

V2 (HOLBORN): I knew it, I knew it was a fake. Thank Christ.

V3 (HURT): I'm not finished. There is image degradation, but it wasn't done through any of the major editing programs; I've run your file through all of them and tested for the relevant coding, and this thing's about as raw as digicam gets. I'm betting whoever sent this to you digitized it the old brute-force way, like a movie pirate: Physically projected the thing, recorded it with a digital camera, saved it as your .mpeg, and sent it to you as is. Whatever the distortions are, they're either from that projection, or they were in the source clip all along.

V1 (MOUSCH): So… this could be a direct copy of that original clip you were talking about. The urban legend boojum.

V3 (HURT): Yeah, if you wanna buy into that shit.

V2 (HOLBORN): And when Laszlo Hurt tells you something's too weird to believe…

V1 (MOUSCH): Max, don't be a dick; Laz's doing us a favour. Right?

V2 (HOLBORN): Yeah, okay. Sorry.

V3 (HURT): (PAUSE) Way I heard, it goes back to this turn-of-the-century murderess called Tess Jacopo…

* * *

8/23/08 1902HRS
TRANSCRIPT SUSPECT INTERVIEW 51 DIVISION
CASEFILE #332
PRESIDING OFFICERS D. SUSAN CORREA 156232,
D. ERIC VALENS 324820
SUBJECT MAXIM HOLBORN

D.VALENS: Jacopo. That was in Boston, in the 1900s—she was a Belle Gunness-type den mother killer, right? The female H.H. Holmes.
HOLBORN: Why am I not surprised you know this?
D.CORREA: Mr Holborn, please. Go on.
HOLBORN: The story isn't really about Jacopo herself. What happened was, this guy who'd been corresponding with Jacopo in prison, her stalker I guess he was, he managed to bribe a journalist who was on-site at her execution into stealing a copy of the official death-photo and selling it to him. Guess he wanted something to whack off with after she was gone. Anyway, a couple weeks later this guy's found in his flat, dead and swollen up, the Jacopo photo on his chest.
D.CORREA: How did he die?
HOLBORN: I don't think it matters. The point is, somebody there took a photo of the photo, and that became one of the biggest murder memorabilia items of the 20th century. You know these guys, right—kinda weirdos who buy John Wayne Gacy's clown pictures, shell out thousands to get Black Dahlia screen-test footage, 'cause they think they'll unearth some lost snuff movie they can show all their friends…
D.VALENS: I'm not seeing what this has to do with your film clip, Mr. Holborn.
HOLBORN: Okay. This is where the urban legend kicks in. See, Jacopo's mask slipped a bit during the hanging, so you can just barely see a sliver of her eyeball, and the story says if you blow up and enhance the photo like a hundred times original size, you're supposed to be able to see in the eyeball the reflection of what she was looking at when she died. Like an asphyx.
D.VALENS: Ass-what?
HOLBORN: It's the word the Greeks used for the last image that gets burned on a murdered person's retina, like a last little fragment of their soul or life-force getting trapped there.
D.CORREA: And under sufficient magnification, you're supposed to be able to see this?
HOLBORN: "Supposed to," yeah. Thing is, everyone who ever tried this, who actually tried blowing up their copy of the Jacopo photo? Went nuts or died. Unless they burned their photo before things got too bad. That's supposed to be why it's impossible to find any copies.
D.CORREA: Why? What did they see?
HOLBORN: How the fuck should I know? It's a spook story. Maybe they saw themselves looking back at themselves, whatever. The point is… it's not about

what those people saw, or didn't. It's about the kind of voyeuristic obsession you need to go that deep into this shit. And Laszlo said that was what the clip reminded him of. Somebody trying to make some kind of, of—"mind-bomb," was the term he used. An image that'd scar you so badly, the mere act of passing it on would be enough to always keep its power alive.

D.CORREA: Uh… why?

HOLBORN: Excellent question. Isn't it?

* * *

From: Liat Holborn <liath@ca.inter.net>
Date: Thursday, July 3, 10:25 AM
To: Soraya Mousch <sor16muse@walloflove.ca>
Subject: Max and me

Dear Soraya,

I was talking to Max last night about how we're going to try to handle the next few months, and it came out that for whatever reason, Max still hadn't filled you in completely on our situation. I think he finds it pretty tough to talk about, even to you. Upshot is, the last CAT-scan showed I have an advanced cranial tumor, and Dr. Lalwani thinks there's a very good chance it could be gliomal, which (skipping all the medico-babble) is about the least good news we could get. Apparently, it's too deep for surgery, so the only option we have is for me to go into a majorly heavy chemo program ASAP. So I'm going to be spending a lot of time in St. Michael's, starting real soon now.

My folks've volunteered to foot a lot of the bill, which is great, but poor Max is feeling kind of humiliated at needing the help—and of course he totally can't complain about it, which just makes it gall him even more. The reason I'm telling you all this is because (a) I want the pressure of keeping this a secret to be off Max, and (b) I know how much you depend on Max this time of year, and I don't want you to think he's bailing on you if he has to take time out for me, or that he's finally gotten fed up with you, the Wall of Love, or your work.

(Actually, I'm pretty sure the festival's the only thing that's kept him stable this past little while. I hope you know how much I appreciate the support you give him.)

Could you show this e-mail to Max when you get a chance, and apologize to him for me when he blows his top at my big mouth? :) He doesn't feel he can shout at me any more about anything, obviously. But I really think things'll be easier once all the cards are on the table.

Thanks so much for your help, Soraya. Come by and see me soon—I want you to get some photos of me before I have to ditch the hair.

Much love and God bless,

Liat

P.S.: BTW, I'm also totally fine with accidentally seeing that thing you sent Max, that file or whatever, so tell him that, okay? *Impress* it on him. He seems to think it "injured" me somehow—on top of everything else. Which is just ridiculous.

I have more than enough real things to worry about right now, you know?

— L.

* * *

8/23/08 1928HRS
TRANSCRIPT SUSPECT INTERVIEW 51 DIVISION
CASEFILE #332
PRESIDING OFFICERS D. SUSAN CORREA 156232,
D. ERIC VALENS 324820
SUBJECT MAXIM HOLBORN

HOLBORN: We were on about the third or fourth draft of the final mix when we started splicing in the clip—

D.VALENS: Splicing? I thought you said this was purely electronic.

HOLBORN: It is, it's just the standard term for—look, do you want me to explain or not?

D.CORREA: We do. Please. Go on.

HOLBORN: We broke the clip up into segments and spliced it in among the rest of the film in chunks; we were even going to try showing some shots on just the edge of subliminal, like three or four frames out of twenty-four. This was a few weeks ago, beginning of August. And then it started happening.

D.CORREA: What started, Max?

HOLBORN: The guy. From the clip. He started… appearing… in other parts of the film.

D.VALENS: Somebody spliced in more footage? Repeats?

HOLBORN: No, goddammit, he started popping up in pieces of footage that were already in the film! Stuff we'd gotten like weeks before, from people who never even saw the clip or knew about it. Like that performance art piece in Hyde Park? Guy walks by in the background a minute into the clip. Or the subway zombie ride, you look right at the far end of the car, there he is sitting down, and you know it's him 'cause he's the only one not wearing any clothes. This was stuff nobody ever shot, man! Changing in front of our fucking eyes! Christ, I saw him show up in one segment—I ran it to make sure it was clear, ran it again right away and he was just fucking there, like he'd always been in the frame. The extras were fucking walking around him…

(FIVE SECOND PAUSE)

D.CORREA: Could it have been some kind of computer virus? Something that came in with your original video file and reprogrammed the files it was spliced into?

HOLBORN: Are you shitting me?!

D.VALENS: Dial it back, Holborn. Right—now.

HOLBORN: Okay, sorry, but—no. CGI like that takes hours to render on a system ten times the size of mine, and that's for every single appearance. A virus carrying that kinda programming would be fifty times bigger than the file it rode in on and wouldn't run on my system anyway.

Besides, it kept getting worse. He didn't just show up in new segments, he'd take more and more prominent places in segments he'd already, corrupted, I guess?

Goes from five seconds in the background to two minutes in the medium frame. I'd get people to resend me their submissions, I'd splice 'em in to replace the old ones and inside of a minute he's back in the action. It was like the faster we tried to cut him out the harder he worked at—I don't know—entrenching himself.

* * *

ERROR MESSAGE
404 Not Found

The webpage you were trying to access ("http://www.kerato-oblation.org/cadavrexquis") is no longer available. It may have been removed by the user or suspended by administrators for terms-of-use violation. Contact your ISP for more information.

* * *

```
TRANSCRIPT CHAT LOG
08/07/08 0344-0346

<sor16muse>: max, wtf
<sor16muse>: the sites gone. like GONE
<sor16muse>: did u do that? ur only other one w/password
<sor16muse>: wtf max, were supposed 2 b live tomorrow
WHY
<sor16muse>: u there?
<sor16muse>: max, u there? need 2 talk.
<sor16muse>: laz sez he maybe has an idea who sent the file, and
why. need 2
<max_hdb>: im not going 2 b here, back
<max_hdb>: don't know when.
<max_hdb>: liat had episode. bad. in hosp. st mikes.
<max_hdb>: u ever want 2 talk in person, that's where ill b.
```

`<max_hdb>`: (User max_hdb has disconnected)
`<sor16muse>`: (User sor16muse has disconnected)

* * *

8/23/08 1937HRS
TRANSCRIPT SUSPECT INTERVIEW 51 DIVISION
CASEFILE #332
PRESIDING OFFICERS D. SUSAN CORREA 156232,
D. ERIC VALENS 324820
SUBJECT MAXIM HOLBORN

D.VALENS: So who was that guy? In the film?
HOLBORN: No idea. It's not like he—
D.CORREA: And what's it got to do with Tess Jacopo?
HOLBORN: Nothing, directly. But it's like Internet memes, man; Laszlo understood that. Stuff gets around. Maybe this guy heard about the thing with the photo, and thought: Oh hey, wonder how that'd work with a moving picture. Maybe he just stumbled across the concept all on his lonesome, or by accident: I don't know. But… he did it.
D.VALENS: Did what, Holborn?
HOLBORN: He put himself in there. Made himself an asphyx.
D.CORREA: So he could live forever.
HOLBORN: Yeah. Maybe. Or maybe just… so he could… not die. Maybe—
(TEN SECOND PAUSE)
HOLBORN: Maybe he was sick. Like, really sick. Or sick in the head. Or both. Maybe it just seemed like a good idea, given the alternative. At the time.
D.CORREA: So what did happen to the Wall of Love mainframe, Max?
HOLBORN: I crashed it. (BEAT) I mean—I told people there was a big Avid crash and the whole server got wiped… actually, I used a magnet. Like Dean Winchester in that "Ghostfacers!" 'Supernatural' episode.
D.VALENS: What?
HOLBORN: Doesn't matter. Ask me why.
D.CORREA: … why?
HOLBORN: Because I thought maybe I could trap him there, like he must have trapped himself inside that loop. Because he probably didn't think about that, right? When he was doing it. How it wasn't likely anybody was really going to watch that sort of shit, once they figured out what it was, let alone show it in public. How probably it would just end up left in the can, passed from collector to collector, never really watched at all, except by one person at a time. One… very disturbed… other person.

 I thought I could stop him from going any further, so I crashed my own mainframe, without telling Soraya. But…

D.VALENS: … it didn't work.

HOLBORN: Well. Would I even be here, if it did?

* * *

CYBER-CRIME OFFICE
TORONTO POLICE SERVICE 51 DIVISION
EXCERPTED REPORT
DETECTIVE LEWIS McMASTER (CYBERCRIME) SUPERVISING
DETECTIVES ERIC VALENS, SUSAN CORREA (HOMICIDE) CONTRIBUTING
Casefile #332: Notes

INITIAL CONTACT:

August 14 2008—CyberCrime received anonymous email sent from Hotmail account created that morning, with copy of "suicide guy" .mpg attached. Flagged as "harmful matter". Email noted .mpg was sent to kerato-oblation.org as experimental film clip submission; identified source of original message, webmail address 11235813@gmail.com.

[Hotmail account eventually traced through Internet café to Laszlo Hurt, known member of local Toronto "collector" circuit; Hurt now missing, presumed deceased based on evidence found in subject's apartment. —EV, SC]

INVESTIGATION:

August 15—Flagged file screened and sent for forensic analysis, results inconclusive. Source of original submission email traced to Google-owned server in Newark, New Jersey, United States of America.

August 16—Established contact with Detective Herschel Gohan of Newark CyberCrime Unit, who persuaded server admins to cooperate with investigation; message back-tracked and triangulated to establish physical location and address of originator machine. Address is confirmed as unit #B325 of E-Z-SHELF storage locker facility, 1400 South Woodward Lane, Newark. Facility manager, Mr. Silvio Galbi, provides name of renter ("John Smith"), confirms unit prepaid for six months with cash. Mr. Galbi refuses to cooperate with search request without a warrant.

August 18—Warrant issued for search and seizure operation at 1400 South Woodward, Unit #B325, by Judge Harriet Lindstrom. Operation executed under supervision of Detective Gohan. Contents of unit as follows:

1. Unclothed body of unidentified male, Caucasian, est. premortem age mid-20s, seated on floor in pool of waste.

2. One (1) empty film canister.

3. One (1) 35mm film projector, set up to project upon unit interior wall.

4. One (1) 35mm film reel mounted in projector, est. 15 minutes in length, confirmed on-site to be original of transmitted .mpg file.

5. One (1) white cotton sheet at base of same interior wall; tape on corners indicates sheet was hung on wall.

6. One (1) SONY video camera, with tripod, set up focused on same interior wall.

7. One (1) TV monitor, with built-in VCR and DVD player.

8. One (1) DELL laptop computer, with built-in wi-fi modem.

9. One (1) Coleman oil lantern, fuel supply depleted.

10. Pile of empty water bottles.

11. One (1) Black & Decker emergency brand power generator.

12. Fifty (50) gallon gasoline containers, empty.

13. Two (2) six-socket power bar outlets.

14. One (1) tube-gun of industrial caulking sealant.

15. One (1) journal with handwritten notes.

Galbi confirms he accepted illegal payment to lock unit on "Smith's" written instructions without confirming contents, in violation of state safety and insurance regulations. Galbi arrested and cited.

FORENSICS:

Examination of laptop hard drive reveals series of webcam captures which suggest basic chronology of events as follows:

1. Unidentified male (UM) arrives in unit roughly two weeks before email sent to kerato-oblation.org.

2. UM uses video camera to record digital copy of original film reel from wall projection (distortion visible in .mpg file caused by loose fabric in sheet).

3. UM uses laptop to program recorded file into continuous video loop on DVD.

4. UM arranges laptop and webcam to face DVD monitor, setting DVD on continuous play and webcam on indefinite record.

5. UM remains seated in front of monitor for majority of remaining time, urinating and defecating in place. Time-signatures confirm he created .mpg file, wrote submission email, then waited until death was imminent to send it, on date above.

6. Final action of UM on morning of death was to use sealant gun to caulk up door, rendering unit virtually airtight. This prevented odors from escaping unit, and retarded decomposition by hindering evaporation of fluids from the body.

AUTOPSY:

Body shows no sign of struggle or restraint. Autopsy reveals primary cause of death as oxygen deprivation, aggravated by starvation and dehydration. Probable date of death on or around June 25 2008 (date on which .mpg file was sent to kerato-oblation.org). Corneas of victim preserved by airtight environment, and found to be deformed on both exterior and interior surfaces, damage suggesting both physical and heat trauma to tissue. Computer reconstruction of deformation suggests artificial origin, as pattern appears to portray a fixed image: the face of suicide victim in original film, in close-up still frame. Pathologists unable to establish cause or method of corneal deformation.

RECOMMENDATIONS:

Unidentified male's selection of Holborn/Mousch as recipients suggests foreknowledge, possible contact. Recommend either Holborn or Mousch be brought in for further questioning.

* * *

From: Det. Herschel Gohan hgohan@newarkpolice.gov
Date: Thursday, August 21, 7:20 AM
To: Det. Lewis McMaster lewis.mcmaster@torpolservices.net
Subject: Notification: Evidence compromise

Lewis—

Bad news. We had a fire in our station evidence locker last night; looks like some meth really past its sell-by date may have spontaneously cooked off. Nobody hurt, but we lost some critical evidence on a number of cases, including, sorry to say, your film-nut-in-the-storage-unit material. The film reel's melted, the laptop motherboard is gone, and most of the other equipment's unusable now. I've attached .jpgs to document the losses; I'm hoping this'll be enough for your dept. to maintain provenance on your own stuff.

Sorry again; call me if you need to know anything not covered by the pictures.

—Herschel

* * *

8/23/08 1928HRS
TRANSCRIPT SUSPECT INTERVIEW 51 DIVISION
CASEFILE #332
PRESIDING OFFICERS D. SUSAN CORREA 156232,
D. ERIC VALENS 324820
SUBJECT MAXIM HOLBORN

HOLBORN: So I went home after crashing the mainframe, and I didn't go upstairs, because I thought my wife was asleep. And I wanted to let her sleep, because… she'd been in pretty bad shape, you know? She'd only just finished her chemo, she hadn't gotten a lot of… sleep…

But then I turned on TCM, to relax, and they were playing Richard Burton's adaptation of 'Dr. Faustus,' which was made the year before I was born, and—in the scene in the Vatican? Where Faustus is throwing pies at the Pope? I saw him. That guy.

Stuck around, kept watching; the next film was from 1944, and he was in it too. In the background, until—it was like—he notices me watching him. Turns and smiles at me, raises his eyebrow, starts—coming closer.

I swear to God, I jumped back. If Cagney hadn't been in the way—

And then it was Silent Sunday, some all-night Chaplin retrospective, and... yeah. There, too.

Everywhere.

So...

D.VALENS: Obviously not.

HOLBORN: Obviously.

[TEN SECOND PAUSE]

HOLBORN: My wife wasn't asleep, either, by the way. Just in case you were wondering.

D.VALENS: Aw, what the fuck—

D.CORREA: Shut up, Eric. [To HOLBORN] Look, you can't be serious, that's all. Are we supposed to believe—

HOLBORN: I don't give a fuck what you believe. Seriously.

D.CORREA: Okay. So what about the disappearance of Laszlo Hurt?

[FIFTEEN SECOND PAUSE]

HOLBORN: I don't know anything about that.

D.VALENS: And again: We should believe you on this... why?

[FIFTEEN SECOND PAUSE]

D.CORREA: Mister Holborn?

HOLBORN: ... you know, I don't know if you guys know this or not, but... my wife? Just died. So, in the immortal words of every 'Law And Order' episode ever filmed—charge me with something, or let me go. Or fuck the fuck off.

* * *

From: qmail@ca.geocities.mail.com
Date: Saturday, August 16, 9:45 PM
To: Soraya Mousch sor16muse@walloflove.ca
Subject: RE: LASZLO ANSWER ME

Hi. This is the administrator at qmail@geocities.com (00:15:32:A3)

Delivery of your message to {lazhurt@geocities.com} failed after <15> attempts. Address not recognized by system.

This is a permanent error; I've given up.

>Laszlo, it's Soraya, would you CALL ME PLEASE? I've left
>about twenty messages on your voicemail, Max and I have a big
>problem and we need your HELP! Where the fuck are you?
>Call me!
>S.

* * *

From: help@geocities.com
Date: Monday, August 18, 8:55 AM
To: Soraya Mousch sor16muse@walloflove.ca
Subject: RE: Account Tracking Request

Dear Ms. Mousch,

Sorry it took us so long to get back to you; we get a lot of backlog on weekends. I'm afraid I have to admit we're stumped on this one. I personally went through our server records day by day over the registration period you specified, and as far as I can tell, we have no record whatsoever of a "Laszlo Hurt" on our roster. I've checked under the "lazhurt", "laszloslabyrinth", and "hurtmedia" addresses and their variants, as well as with our billing department, and there's just no indication that this Mr. Hurt was ever a Geocities user.

I realize this may be an unwelcome explanation, but it sounds to me like you may have been a victim of an attempted phishing scam using dummy-mask addresses. I'd get your computer checked for viruses and malware right away.

Again, I'm sorry we couldn't be more help.
Best regards,

Jamil Chandrasekhar
Geocities.com Tech Support

* * *

From: Soraya Mousch sor16muse@walloflove.ca
Date: Saturday, August 23, 11:01 PM
To: Max Holborn mhb@ca.inter.net
Subject: Blank

Max, I'm just so sorry.
—S.

* * *

YOUR COMFORT SOUGHT
IN THIS TIME OF GRIEF

With sorrow we announce the passing of
Liat Allyson Meester-Holborn on August 23, 2008,
beloved daughter of Aaron and Rachel Meester and wife of Maxim Holborn.

Funeral service to be held at
St. Mary's Star of the Sea Catholic Church,
8 Elizabeth Avenue, Port Credit, Mississauga
Thursday, August 28, 11:00 A.M.

Commemorative reception
to be held at the Meester residence,
1132 Walden Road #744, 3:00 P.M.
Confirmations only

* * *

From: Max Holborn mhb@ca.inter.net
Date: Tuesday, September 2, 2:31 AM
To: Soraya Mousch sor16muse@walloflove.ca
Subject: look closer

s.—
    hospital released the file on liat to me today. was going over it. couldn't sleep.
found something.
    the attached .jpg's a scan of the last x-ray they took, just before she crashed
out. look at the upper right quarter, just up and right of where ribs meet breastbone. then do a b-w negative reverse on the image in your photoshop, and
look again.
    it's not a glitch. it's not me fucking with you. look at it. call me.
    —m.

* * *

SURVEILLANCE TRANSCRIPT 14952, CASEFILE #332
9/19/08 2259H-2302H 416-[REDACTED] TO 416-[REDACTED]
WARRANT AUTHORIZED HON. R. BORCHERT 9/9/08

(CONNECTION INITIATED)
MOUSCH: Hello?
HOLBORN: You never answered my e-mail.

MOUSCH: What did you want me to say? I read it, I looked at the scans you sent. That… could be anything, Max. A glitch in the machine, some lab tech sticking his hand on the negative—

HOLBORN: Soraya—

MOUSCH: —and even if it's not, what's it matter? What difference can it make? (PAUSE) I'm sorry, Max. I didn't—I'm sorry.

HOLBORN: Uh huh.

(PAUSE)

HOLBORN: So… I hear you put your stuff up on eBay. Going Luddite?

MOUSCH: Well, uh… no, I'm just switching disciplines. Going non-visual. Film's… all played out, y'know? I mean, you've noticed that.

HOLBORN: Yup. Good luck, I guess. (PAUSE) Everything just back to normal, huh?

MOUSCH: … hardly…

HOLBORN: You really think any of this is gonna help? Dropping anything with a lens like it's hot, cocooning?

MOUSCH: I don't…

HOLBORN: You remember what I told you, at the hospital?

(FIVE SECOND PAUSE)

MOUSCH: … I remember.

HOLBORN: That guy killed my wife, Soraya. Just because she saw him—over my shoulder, right? When she didn't even know what she was looking at. She's fucking dead.

MOUSCH: Liat's dead because she had a tumor, Max. Nothing we did made Liat die.

HOLBORN: What do you think he's going to end up doing to us, Soraya? After he's fucking well done with everybody else?

MOUSCH: Look… Look, Max, Christ. Liat, Laszlo, even that crazy fucking moron dude who made the clip in the first place, let alone sent it to us… (PAUSE) And why would he even do that, anyway? To, what… ?

HOLBORN: I don't know. Spread the disease, maybe. Like he got tired of watching it himself, thought everybody else should have a crack at it, too…

(FIVE SECOND PAUSE)

MOUSCH: I mean… it's not our fault, right? Any of it. We didn't ask for—

HOLBORN: —uh, no, Soraya. We did. Literally. We asked, threw it out into the ether: Send us your shit. Show us something. We asked… and he answered.

MOUSCH: Who, "he"? Clip-making dude?

HOLBORN: You know that's not who I'm talking about.

(TEN SECOND PAUSE)

HOLBORN: So, anyhow, 'bye. You're going dark, and I'm dropping off the map. I'd say "see you," but—

MOUSCH: Oh, Max, Goddamn…

HOLBORN: —I'm really hoping… not.

(CONNECTION TERMINATED)

* * *

OFFICE OF FORENSICS
TORONTO POLICE SERVICE 51 DIVISION
EXCERPTED REPORT
CASEFILE #332

Final analysis of X-ray images taken of Liat Holborn (dcsd) shows no known cause of observed photographic anomaly. Hand-digit comparison was conducted on all possible candidates, including Maxim Holborn, attending physician Dr. Raj Lalwani, attending nurse Yvonne Delacoeur, and X-ray technician John Li Cheng: no match found. Dr. Lalwani maintains statement that cause of death for Liat Holborn was gliomal tumor. Conclusion: Photographic anomaly is spontaneous malfunction, resemblance to intact human hand coincidental.

Following lack of forensic connection between Maxim Holborn and Site of Death 1, and failure to establish viable suspect, this office recommends suspension of Case #332 from active investigation at this time, pending further evidence.

* * *

July 26/2009
"BACKGROUND MAN", Lescroat,
strangerthings.net/media
(cont'd)

One year later, the crash which brought kerato-oblation.org/cadavrexquis down—melting the server and destroying a seventy-four-minute installation cobbled together from random .mpg snippets e-mailed in from contributors all over the world—has yet to be fully explained, by either Wall of Love founder. While Mousch cited simple overcrowding and editing program fatigue for the project's collapse, Holborn—already under stress when Kerato-Oblation got underway, due to his wife's battle with brain cancer—has been quoted on Alec Christian's blog as blaming a slightly more supernatural issue: a mysterious figure who first appeared in an anonymously-submitted piece of digital footage, then eventually began popping up in the backgrounds of other... completely unrelated... sections of the film. Background Man? Impossible to confirm or deny, without Holborn's help.

Still, sightings of a naked man wearing "red" around his neck wandering through the fore-, back- and midground of perfectly mainstream movies, TV shows and musics videos continue to abound. Recent internet surveys chart at least five major recent blockbusters (besides *Mother of Serpents*) and three primetime television series rumored to have inadvertently showcased the figure. At the moment, the (highly unlikely) possibility of pan-studio collaboration on a vast alternate-reality game remains unresolved, while at least three genuine missing persons reports are rumored to be connected with a purported Background Man personal encounter IRL. The meme, if meme it is, continues to spread.

Neither Mousch nor Holborn could be reached for comment on this article.

* * *

...and up they come—

(the dead)

Crawling through the hole with their pale hands bloody from digging, their blind eyes tight-shut and their wide-open mouths full of mud: Nameless, faceless, groping for anything that happens across their path. With no easy end to their numbers...

(For once such a door is opened, who will shut it again? Who is there—

—alive—

—that can?)

No end to their numbers, or their need: The dead, who are never satisfied. The dead, who cannot be assuaged.

The dead, who only want but no longer know what, or from who, or why. Or just how much, over just how long— here in their hole which goes on and down forever, where time itself slows so much it no longer has any real value—

—can ever be enough.

THE NIMBLE MEN
GLEN HIRSHBERG

Glen Hirshberg's novelette, "The Janus Tree," won the 2008 Shirley Jackson Award, and both of his collections, *American Morons* and *The Two Sams*, won the International Horror Guild Award. He is also the author of a novel, *The Snowman's Children*. His new novel, *The Book of Bunk*, is due out from Earthling in late 2010. He co-founded, with Dennis Etchison and Peter Atkins, the Rolling Darkness Revue, a traveling ghost story performance troupe that tours the west coast of the United States each October. His fiction has been published in numerous magazines and anthologies, including *Inferno, Dark Terrors 6, Trampoline,* and *Cemetery Dance,* and has appeared frequently in *The Year's Best Fantasy and Horror, The Mammoth Book of Best New Horror,* and *Best Horror of the Year.*

"But the air, out there, so wild, so white…"
—Thomas St. John Bartlett, in a letter to Robert Louis Stevenson
from the Orkney Islands in the winter of 1901

Ever notice how Satie, played in the dark at just the right volume, can tilt the whole world? That night, I had *Je te Veux* on the tinny cockpit stereo, and even before the snow, the pines at the edge of the great north woods just beyond the taxiway appeared to dip and lean, and the white lines disappearing beneath the wheels of our little commuter seemed to weave around and between each other like children at a wedding dance as we made our way to the de-icing station. Then the snow started, white and winking, a drizzle of starlight, and even the air traffic control tower looked ready to lift its arms and step off its foundations and sway.

And then Alex, my junior co-pilot of four months, opened his thermal lunch box. The reek flooded the cabin and set the panel lights wavering in my watering eyes. I swear to God, the iPod gagged. Alex just sat in the steam, eyes half-closed and grinning, as if he were taking a sauna.

"God, you Gorby, tell me that isn't poutine."

"Want some, Old Dude?" said Alex, and lifted the container from the cooler. Out the front of the plane, the world went on dancing, and the snow whirled through it. But I couldn't stop staring at the mess in Alex's container. A few limp, bloated French fries stuck out of the lava flow of industrial-colored sludge like petrified slugs. Congealed, gray lumps clung to their sides and leaked white pus.

"Is that meat?" I asked. "Cheese?"

Alex grinned wider. "It's your country. You tell me."

"Where'd you even find it? We had, what, three hours? Where does one even find poutine on a three-hour layover in Prince Willows Town, Ontario?"

"If you turn over control of the stereo, I'll put it away for a while."

We'd reached the de-icing station, and I pushed on the brakes and brought the coasting plane to a rolling stop. No matter how many times I did this, I was always surprised by the dark out here. At every other point within two miles of this tiny airport, manmade light flooded and mapped the world. But not here.

I peered through the windscreen and the wavering skeins of snow. It took a few moments, but eventually, my eyes adjusted to the point where I could just make out the de-icer truck parked a few meters off the taxiway in the flat, dead grass. Weirdly, it had its boom already hoisted, as though we were meant to make our way into the fields to get sprayed. I couldn't see either the driver of the truck or the guy on the enclosed platform at the top of the boom, because both were blanketed in shadow. But the platform looked tilted to me, almost chin-to-chest with the rotating metal stand that supported it. It reminded me of one of the dead Martians from *War of the Worlds*.

We sat and we waited. The truck didn't move.

"Peculiar," I murmured, and Alex passed his poutine container right under my nostrils. My eyes watered, and I turned on him. "What was that for?"

"You were muttering, Old Dude. Just making sure you were conscious. Now about control of that stereo. You ready to deal?"

For answer, I clicked on the intercom. "Ladies and gentlemen, this is your captain speaking. We hope all six of you have settled comfortably in your seats, that your luggage is crammed effectively between your knees and the seat in front of you—" Alex snorted at that—"and we look forward to having virtually no time to serve you during our brief skip-hop to Toronto. We will be cleared for takeoff shortly. In the meantime, sit back, relax, be happy this flight is *not* bound for Winterpeg, and please pay no attention to the gigantic, alien-shaped creature about to swoop down upon us. It comes in peace, to de-ice the wings. Also, we do apologize for the odor escaping into the cabin under the doors of our cockpit. It came with my co-pilot, and I'm afraid there's little we can do about it. If you need assistance of any kind, please don't hesitate to call on Jamie, our charismatic, experienced, and resourceful in-flight technician, at any time. We should be in the air shortly."

Alex laughed. "Come out with me tonight," he said. "Let's do Hogtown."

"Do it?"

"Paint it. Rock it. Suck it dry. Come on, Old Dude. You keep saying you'll let me show you *my* Toronto. I say it's time. You told me it's been three years, right? It's—*whoa*. What was that?"

He had his cap turned backward on his head, the container in his lap, and a gravy-soaked French fry halfway to his lips. For the thousandth time in the past four months—but the first tonight—I remembered how much I liked him.

"I think we just painted Prince Willows Town, Young Polyp. Milked it, licked it, whole works."

"You're babbling again, Old Dude."

"Northern lights, Alex. You've heard of them, maybe."

He shook his head. "Wrong time, right? Also too low."

As usual, he was correct on both counts. I turned back to the windscreen, peering down the tarmac toward the tops of the trees, where we'd both seen a spiraling flash of green, then aquamarine.

But there was nothing now except the snowflakes, settling in their millions onto the branches of the pines as though completing some massive, unmarked winter migration. We watched that a while, and then I glanced again toward the de-icing truck. It sat silent, and the snow shrouded the high platform's window glass.

"The Nimble Men," said Alex, savoring the words.

"What?"

"Is that the coolest name you've ever heard for the aurora, or what?"

"The Nimble Men?"

"It's catchy, no?"

"How many other names do you know, Alex?"

"Well, there's *chasmata*. That's from Ancient Rome. They thought the lights were cave mouths. For sky caves. Come on, Old Dude. Trump me. What you got?"

I would have smiled if not for the de-icer, hunkered in the dead grass like a junked car on a lawn.

"Well, there's one story…" I said.

"That's the Old Dude I know. Lay it on me."

"There are several versions. Usually, it goes that sometime during the Depression, a poor woodsman went out in those woods—"

"Those woods right there?"

"Whichever Ontario woods you happen to be closest to. Didn't anyone ever tell you a ghost story?"

Alex nodded. "Carry on."

"So the woodsman was out." This time I did smile. "Rockin' the forest."

That earned me a salute with a sludgy fry.

"And while he was out, he saw the lights."

"The Nimble Men," said Alex.

I held up a finger. "But not in the sky. In the trees. The woodsman had an inkling. He raced home. When he got there, his wife said their old, sick dog had got out, and their daughter had gotten frantic and gone after him. The dog came back. But the daughter didn't. She was never seen again. The woodsman went looking with his lantern every night for the rest of his life, but he never found so much as a trace. According to some, he's still looking, and those are his lights. Hey, Alex, I don't like this."

He'd been nodding and chewing, but now lowered the cardboard fry-boat back into his lunch box and wiped his hands on his uniform pants. "You're right, Old Dude. Why are we just sitting here?"

I flicked on the radio and called the tower. "This is Northwoods Air 2-8-4."

The response was immediate, the voice so clear it might have come from inside the cabin. "Northwoods 2-8-4, go ahead."

"Bill, that you?"

"What is it, Wayne?"

"We're at the de-icer. The de-icer isn't moving."

I don't know what I expected. *We'll wake him up*, maybe. Or, *How's that*? Or, since Bill had a little of Alex's puckishness, *Moon him*.

Instead, there was a long silence. I was about to repeat myself when Bill's voice came back.

"Sit tight," he said. "Don't move."

"What—" I started, and the link closed. Went off. I tried talking into the communicator again, but it was like yelling into a fist.

"Hey, another one," Alex said, but by the time I turned, there was just the faintest blue streak, a smear on the snow-curtain.

On normal nights, the de-icer springs awake the second a plane rolls to a stop. The truck maneuvers close, and the driver makes contact over the com-link. The pilot shuts down all systems and closes the vents so no fluid gets inside the cabin. Then the platform jockey swoops in with his pod, unfolds its nozzle-arms, and engulfs the wings in a blast of bright purple antifreeze. The whole process takes less than five minutes. Sometimes less than two.

But we'd already been here quite a while. I could make out the platform jockey now, or at least his shadow. He was hunched or slumped in his pod, fifteen meters off the ground. I couldn't see his face, because he had nothing illuminated. I couldn't hear his voice, because the truck hadn't plugged into us and made contact. As far as I could tell, the truck still wasn't running its engine. This time, the glimmer in the trees flashed red, and the redness hung a moment at the very edge of the forest before winking out.

"See, I don't get it," Alex said. "It doesn't make sense."

"That's what I'm—"

"Your story. I mean, what's the deal, Old Dude? The lights came to warn him? Or they're his daughter's soul at the moment of her death? Or a presentiment of his future as the Wood-Wandering Lantern Guy? You've got to get more specific, here."

The lack of movement on the taxiway was really starting to get to me. I almost clicked on the intercom and called Jamie in to take a look. But that would only have triggered a new round of Alex-hits-on-Jamie. Not that Jamie seemed to mind.

"It's not my story. And the lights were probably all of those things, depending on the telling," I said. "You know how those stories work."

"I know that one could work better."

"What does he mean, *sit tight, don't move?*"

"Let's go see," Alex said, unhooked himself from his belts and stood.

That at least drew my gaze from the taxiway to his face. "Go where?"

"Out. Tell me you've never wanted to go out there. You ever done it? We've got a perfect excuse."

"We can't go out there."

"Why not?"

I thought about that. "Aren't there regulations? There've got to be regulations."

"And yet there you are, already unhooking your belt." His grin was an eight year-old's, and lit him all the way to his moppy curls. And there I was, unhooking my belt. "Old Dude," he said approvingly. Then he threw open the cockpit door and marched into the tiny cabin of our commuter plane, chanting, "Oh, Jamie…"

By the time I emerged, he was standing as if onstage with his arm around our blond, too-thin flight attendant, who was without doubt closer to my age than his, and facing our six passengers. All of them were apparently traveling alone, since they'd each claimed their own row—we called them rows, though they were really only sets of single seats on either side of a narrow aisle—leaving only the front empty.

"What's going on?" called an exhausted-looking grad-school type in a green McGill sweatshirt from a couple rows back.

"Who's up for hide and seek? Come on, I'll count ten," Alex said, and Jamie dropped her head and shook it and laughed.

"Excuse him, ladies and gentlemen," I said. "He's American, he's just eaten his first poutine, and it's made him punchy."

"*Avez-vous poutine?*" said a white-haired woman three rows back, perking up as though she thought we might offer her a plateful with her complimentary ice water.

"*Je l'ai fini,*" Alex said, patting his non-existent gut. I couldn't see his face, but I was sure he'd winked.

I moved to the door, unlocked it, and Jamie swung toward me in surprise. "Wayne?"

I made a waving gesture, casual as I could make it. "We're just…"

"Checking something," Alex said. "Right back, y'all."

"Checking," I said quietly to Jamie. "It's not the plane. Not to worry."

Before she could ask, and before I had time to reconsider, Alex pushed the door outward. Frigid, resin-scented air gushed into the cabin, sweeping tendrils of snow around our ankles as the folding stair lowered itself to the ground.

Jamie took an immediate step back. Because of the cold, I realized, only the cold. But Alex hesitated, too, just momentarily. In thirty-one years as a pilot, I'd never once left my plane except at a gate. Certainly not on a taxiway or runway. I stared into the blackness, the snow cocooning the world. A high, industrial whine rode the air-currents, seeming to burrow uncomfortably into my ear canals.

I glanced over my shoulder. The only passenger not watching was the chubby, middle-aged guy in the seat closest to the open door. He had his head against the window, his tie still knotted tight at this throat, his eyes closed too tightly to be sleeping. At least, that's how it seemed to me. His skin looked pale and wet as the window-glass.

"He okay?" I murmured to Jamie.

She shrugged. "He's been like that since we boarded. I don't think he's having a heart attack or anything, if that's what you're asking. Are *you* okay, Wayne? This doesn't seem…"

"You're right," I said. "Hey, Alex, why don't we just go check in with Bill again."

"Because, Old Dude," he said. "We're the Nimble Men." And with his hands artfully tucked in the pockets of his ridiculous thrift-store bomber jacket, he strolled out of the plane, down the steps to the tarmac.

Why did I go? I've wondered that ever since. Because the lifeless de-icer bothered me, sure. Because Alex's enthusiasm for everything had stirred the embers of my own, dead not so long then. But there was something else. A *need*. Sudden. Overpowering. Was it mine? I still don't know.

I went down the steps. Behind me, I heard a single, saw-edged gasp or sigh from the not-sleeping guy. I heard another sound, too, or thought I did. That high, electrical whine, though we were the only plane out here.

When I reached Alex's side, he smiled. "One small step for Nimble Men…"

To my surprise, I smiled back. "See, now you're doing it."

"Doing what?"

"Are the lights the Nimble Men? Are we?"

"You know you're the coolest pilot I'm ever going to work with in my life, right, Old Dude? You know you've ruined cockpit chatter for me forever."

"Why, thank you, Alex. Sometimes, I feel the same."

"When we get back inside, could we at least put on a *Gymnopedie*? One of the *Gnossiennes*?"

Now I stared at him. "You know Satie, too?"

"I know *Je te Veux* makes you morose."

"For a punk kid, you know a hell of a lot of things, Alex."

"That's what things are for. Right?"

"Some things," I said, and immediately wished I hadn't.

"Hey, man," Alex said.

Ignoring him, trying to ignore myself, I looked across the tarmac at the de-icer. There really didn't seem to be anybody in the truck. There was someone on the platform up there, alright, but as far as I could make out, he still hadn't even noticed us. Unless the driver had left his keys in the ignition, or we could find a good stone to throw, we were going to have a hard time getting the platform jockey's attention. The whining was louder out here, too. Or, not louder. Closer. More shrill. If it hadn't been January, I'd have thought there were gnats in my ears.

Jamie's low-heeled shoes clicked on the folding staircase, and she appeared between us. Alex put his arm around her. Lights blossomed in the closest treetops, a scatter of turquoise and Kelly green and deep pink, as though someone had scattered a handful of marbles up there. The branches rippled with the color, then swallowed it.

"Jesus," said Jamie.

Alex put an arm around her waist. "Wacky north woods beautifulness. My favorite kind."

"Is that ice, do you think? Airport lights reflecting in the branches?"

Of course, that was right. Why hadn't I thought of it? I gestured back toward the plane. "Seriously, is that guy alright?" I asked. "The passenger in 2B?"

"I think mostly he's crying," said Jamie. "I've got my eye on him."

"I know you do."

"We shouldn't be out here, Wayne." She touched my hand.

"Go inside. We'll be right back."

More lights. A royal-blue flurry this time, concentrated in the pines nearest the taxiway, maybe thirty meters away. Up in the platform pod, I could see the jockey's shadow just a little more clearly through the snow. He was turned toward the forest. I still didn't think he'd seen us.

Unease flickered through me again. It felt almost good. It filled the emptiness, or at least colored it.

As if sensing that thought, Jamie squeezed my hand. I'd worked with her a long time. I squeezed back. "Go on inside. We're coming."

"You can offer White-hair in there the rest of my poutine," Alex said. "I didn't actually finish it all. Although it's kind of cold, now."

"Bleah," said Jamie, and turned for the plane. I saw her look backward at the woods as she climbed up. Maybe she was hoping for another light show. But I had the idea she was hoping the opposite. Maybe that was just me.

The whining swelled still more. Underneath the shrillness, I could hear another sound, now. A sort of low grinding. Then that faded. I lifted my hands over my head, waved them at the de-icer platform. Next, I tried jumping up and down.

"See?" said Alex. "You're still nimble. You know she digs you, right?"

I stopped jumping. "What?"

"Jamie. She's just waiting for you to say the word. She's been waiting a long time."

"What are you talking about? She told you this?"

"She didn't have to tell me. I know. It's one of those things Alex knows."

"Let's get that guy's attention and get out of here," I said.

"I'm just telling you. She's waiting for you to say you're ready. I say it's been three years, Old Dude. And no disrespect. But I say three years is plenty. I say you're ready. *Shit.*"

It came from nowhere, wasn't anything, vanished just as quickly. A flash of green-yellow right over our heads, like lightning stabbing into the ground. Or eyes blinking.

"Did you hear that?"

"Hear it? You have ears in your eyes, Old Dude?"

"Hey," I said. Our breath plumed in front of us. "He moved."

Both of us craned our necks back, trying to see. The guy up there *had* moved. I was sure of it. But he'd stopped now. And he was still staring straight at the woods. The whining was creeping deeper into my ears again. And there was yet another sound, this one more familiar. But several blank seconds passed before I realized what it was.

"That truck *is* on," I said.

"Well," said Alex, and for the first time, I heard doubt in his voice, too. Just a flicker. But that rattled me more than anything else out here. "If it won't come to us…I guess we just go get it."

He started that way, and I followed, and the driver in the cab finally sat up. He looked astonished to see us. Then he started flinging his hands wildly in front of his face, as though he had bees in there.

"What the fuck?" Alex mumbled, still moving, and I grabbed his wrist.

The driver was waving more wildly. But not at anything in the cabin. He was also shouting, but he had the windows rolled up tight, and all I could hear was that he *was* shouting. Not what he was saying.

And overhead, that sound had returned, not so much louder as higher, almost a shriek. The grinding was back, too. Alex and I were halfway between the de-icer truck and our open plane, right at the edge of the tarmac.

It didn't actually sound like grinding, I realized. It seemed too deeply lodged inside my own head for that. It sounded like teeth gnashing.

The lights didn't exactly erupt from the trees. They just slid from behind them, as though they'd been hiding there all along. They hovered at the edge of the forest, coagulating like snow-melt on a windowpane. Forming.

I didn't have to warn Alex. He was already running.

Of course he was decades younger, much faster. Maybe he didn't even see what the lights became, the thing with wings. Or the million smaller things, all of them shining.

They came like a blizzard on a glacier, all at once and from everywhere. I was flat-out sprinting, but knew I wouldn't make it. They were in my hair, ears, eyes, and they *ached*. It was useless to swipe at or fight them, but I was still running anyway, until the first blast from the de-icer blew me straight off my feet. The de-icer didn't stop. It went on pummeling me with fluid, and I started to scream, then shut my mouth tight for fear of what I'd swallow, liquid or light, and tried scrambling back upright. Then I gave that up and crawled.

The lights were screaming. Or I was. Or Alex and Jamie were from the doorway of the plane, both of them soaked, dripping, waving, shouting. I reached the steps, and the gnashing got louder, seemed to clamp down on my spine and chew straight through it, and I sagged bonelessly sideways, feeling light, so light. Then Alex yanked me inside and slammed the door tight.

For one long moment, there was only darkness and silence. Because I hadn't opened my eyes, I realized. Because I was too terrified to open my mouth. I felt a towel on my face, Jamie's gentle hand against the back of my neck. I opened my eyes to find Alex, dripping purple droplets everywhere like a freshly bathed poodle.

"Okay?" he said.

I nodded, trembling. "I think. You?"

He started to laugh. "Holy shit," he said. "Holy crazy Canadian shit."

It wasn't funny. But with Alex there, you couldn't help smiling anyway. Jamie was doing it, too, while pointlessly patting over and over at my face. I took her hand to stop her. Then I just held onto that.

We were back in our seats, our heads wrapped in scratchy airline towels, ears still ringing, hands still shaking but settled firmly on the controls that would guide us either safely back to the terminal or up in the air and as far from Prince Willows Town as this plane's pathetic fuel tanks could carry us, when the cockpit door opened. Alex was the one who turned. Then he said, "Wayne."

I turned, too. Jamie stood in the doorway, face waxy, eyes blank. "He's gone," she said.

"What?" I asked.

"The guy in 2B. The crying guy. He's not on the plane. He didn't go out past me either. He's nowhere."

I stood up, shaking my head. "That's ridiculous. He must have—"

"Wayne," Jamie said, and her eyes filled with tears. "He's gone."

It happened only occasionally, Bill told me once, years later, over one final round of Molsons, before both of us left the flying game for good. Only in the dead of winter, on the coldest nights. Mostly not even then. No one really knew when or how the realization had been made about the de-icing fluid. But that seemed to help. Sometimes. To keep them back. Sometimes.

"Always so sad," Bill had said. "Always, always, always."

At least, that's what I thought he'd said. It wasn't until that night, back in my hotel, pouring a drink, that my hands started to shake, and I realized I'd heard him wrong. Not *so* sad. *The* sad. Always the sad.

Was it grief that drew them? Or reacted with something else in that air, in those woods, and created them? Had *my* grief drawn or created them? If so, it wasn't the anti-freeze that saved me. It was the sobbing man. His was fresher.

Had they swallowed him? I like to think he was one of them, now, instead. Reunited, maybe, with what he'd lost. Or at least in company, with the Nimble Men. Sometimes, that thought comforts me.

You can't fly to Prince Willows Town, any more. Not long after that night, they closed the facility, redirecting all traffic to the bigger, better-serviced airport at Sudbury, where the light-towers are numerous and brighter, and the trees keep their distance.

WHAT HAPPENS WHEN YOU WAKE UP IN THE NIGHT
MICHAEL MARSHALL SMITH

Michael Marshall Smith is a bestselling novelist and screenwriter, writing under several different names. His first novel, *Only Forward*, won the August Derleth and Philip K. Dick awards. *Spares* and *One of Us* were optioned for film by DreamWorks and Warner Brothers, and the Straw Men trilogy—*The Straw Men*, *The Lonely Dead*, and *Blood of Angels*——were international bestsellers. His Steel Dagger-nominated novel *The Intruders* is currently in series development with the BBC. His most recent novels are *Bad Things* and *The Servants*, the latter, a short novel published under the new pseudonym M. M. Smith.

He is a three-time winner of the British Fantasy Award for short fiction, and his stories are collected in two volumes—*What You Make It* and *More Tomorrow and Other Stories* (which won the International Horror Guild Award).

The first thing I was unhappy about was the dark. I do not like the dark very much. It is not the worst thing in the world but it is also not the best thing in the world, either. When I was smaller I used to wake up sometimes in the middle of the night and be scared when I woke up, because it was so dark. I went to bed with my light on, the light that turns round and round, on the drawers by the side of my bed. It has animals on it and it turns around and it makes shapes and patterns on the ceiling and it is pretty and my Mummy's friend Jeanette gave it to me. It is not too bright but it is bright enough and you can see what is what. But then it started that when I woke up in the middle of the night, the light would not be on any more and it would be completely dark instead and it would make me sad. I didn't understand this but one night when I'd woken up and cried a lot my Mummy told me that she came in every night and turned off the light after I was asleep, so it didn't wake me up. But I said that wasn't any good, because if I *did* wake up in the night and the light wasn't on, then I might be scared, and cry. She said it seemed that I was waking every night, and she and Daddy had worked out that it might be the light that woke me, and after I was awake I'd get up and go into their room and see what was up with them, which meant she got no sleep any night ever and it was driving her completely nuts.

So we made a deal, and the deal said I could have the light on all night *but* I promised that I would not go into their room in the night unless it was really important, and it is a good deal and so I'm allowed to have my light on again now, which is why the first thing I noticed when I woke up was that it was dark.

Mummy had broken the deal.

I was cross about this but I was also very sleepy and so wasn't sure if I was going to shout about it or not.

Then I noticed it was cold.

Before I go to bed, Mummy puts a heater on while I am having my bath, and also I have two blankets on top of my duvet, and so I am a warm little bunny and it is fine. Sometimes if I wake in the middle of the night it feels a bit cold but if I snuggle down again it's okay.

But this felt really cold.

My light was not on and I was cold.

I put my hand out to put my light on, which was the first thing to do. There is a switch on a white wire that comes from the light and I can turn it on myself—I can even find it in the dark when there is no light.

I tried to do that but I could not find the wire with my hand.

So I sat up and tried again, but still I could not find it, and I wondered if Mummy had moved it, and I thought I might go and ask her. But I could not see the door. It had been so long since I had been in my room in the night without my light being on that I had forgotten how dark it gets. It's *really* dark. I knew it would be hard to find the door if I could not see it, so I did it a clever way.

I used my imagination.

I sat still for a moment and remembered what my bedroom is like. It is like a rectangle and has some drawers by the top of my bed where my head goes. My light is on the drawers, usually. My room also has a table where my colouring books go and some small toys, and two more sets of drawers, and windows down the other end. They have curtains so the street lights do not keep me awake, and because in summer it gets bright too early in the morning and so I wake everybody up when they should still be asleep because they have work to do and they need some sleep. And there is a big chair but it is always covered in toys and it is not important.

I turned to the side so my legs hung off the bed and down onto the floor. In my imagination I could see that if I stood up and walked straight in front of me, I would nearly be at my door, but that I would have to go a little way... left, too.

So I stood up and did this walking.

It was funny doing it in the dark. I stepped on something soft with one of my feet, I think it was a toy that had fallen off the chair. Then I touched one of the other drawers with my hand and I knew I was close to the door, so I turned left and walked that way a bit.

I reached out with my hands then and tried to find my dressing gown. I was trying to find it because I was cold, but also because it hangs off the back of my bedroom door on a little hook and so when I found the dressing gown I would know I had got to the right place to open the door.

But I could not find the dressing gown.

Sometimes my Mummy takes things downstairs and washes them in the washing machine in the kitchen and then dries them in another machine that makes them hot, so maybe that was where it was. I was quite awake now and very cold so I decided not to keep trying to find the gown and just go wake Mummy and Daddy and say to them that I was awake.

But I couldn't find my doorknob. I knew I must be where the door is, because it is in the corner where the two walls of my room come together. I reached out with my hands and could feel the two sides of the corner, but I could not find the doorknob, even though I moved my hands all over where it should be. When I was smaller the doorknob came off once, and Mummy was very scared because she thought if it happened again I would be trapped in my bedroom and I wouldn't be able to get out, so she shouted at Daddy until he fixed it with a different screw. But it had never come off again so I did not know where it could be now. I wondered if I had got off my bed in the wrong way because it was dark and I had got it mixed up in my imagination, and maybe I should go back to my bed and start again.

Then a voice said:

"Maddy, what are you *doing*?"

I was so surprised I made a scared sound, and jumped. I trod on something, and the same voice said "Ow!"

I heard someone moving and sitting up. Even though it was in the dark I knew it was my Mummy.

"Mummy?" I said. "Where are you?"

"Maddy, I've *told* you about coming into our room."

"I'm not."

"It's just not *fair*. Mummy has to go to work and Daddy has to go to work and you have to go to school and we *all* need our sleep. We made a *deal*, remember?"

"But *you* broke the deal. You took away my light."

"I haven't touched your light."

"You did!"

"Maddy, don't lie. We've talked about lying."

"You took my light!"

"I haven't taken your light and I didn't turn it off."

"But it's not turned on."

She made a sighing sound. "Maybe the bulb went."

"Went to where?"

"I mean, got broken."

"No, my whole *light* is not there."

"Maddy…"

"It's not! I put my hand out and I couldn't find it!"

My Mummy made a sound like she was very cross or very tired, I don't know which. Sometimes they sound the same. She didn't say anything for a little minute.

"Look," she said then, and she did not sound very cross now, just sleepy and as if she loved me but wished I was still asleep. "It's the middle of the night and everyone should be in bed. Their *own* bed."

"I'm sorry, Mummy."

"That's okay." I heard her standing up. "Come on. Let's go back to your room."

"What do you mean?" I said.

"Back to your room. Now. I'll tuck you in, and then we can all go back to sleep."

"I *am* in my room."

"Maddy—don't start."

"I *am* in my room!"

"Maddy, this is just silly. Why would you… Why is it so dark in here?"

"Because my light is off. I told you."

"Maddy, your light is in *your* room. Don't—"

She stopped talking suddenly. I heard her fingers moving against something, the wall, maybe. "What the hell?"

Her voice sounded different.

"'Hell' is a naughty word," I told her.

"Shush."

I heard her fingers swishing over the wall again. She had been asleep on the floor, right next to the wall. I heard her feet moving on the carpet and then there was a banging sound and she said a naughty word again, but she did not sound angry but like she did not understand something. It was like a question mark sound.

"For the love of *Christ*."

This was not my Mummy talking.

"Dan?"

"Who the hell else? Any chance you'll just take her back to bed? Or I can do it. I don't mind. But let's one of us do it. It's the middle of the fucking night."

"Dan!"

"'Fucking' is a *very* naughty—"

"Yes, yes, I'm terribly sorry," my Daddy said. He sounded as if he was only half not in a dream. "But we have *talked* about you coming into our room in the middle of the night, Maddy. Talked about it endlessly. And—"

"Dan," my Mummy said, starting to talk when he was still talking, which is not good and can be rude. "Where *are* you?"

"I'm right *here*," he said. "For god's sake. I'm… Did you put up new curtains or something?"

"No," Mummy said.

"It's not normally this dark in here, is it?"

"My light has gone,' I said. 'That's why it is so dark."

"Your light is in *your* room," Daddy said.

I could hear him sitting up. I could hear his hands, too. They were not right next to Mummy, but at the other end of my room. I could hear them moving around on the carpet.

"Am I on the floor?" he asked. "What the hell am I doing on the floor?"

I heard him stand up. I did not tell him "hell" is a naughty word. I did not think that he would like it. I heard him move around a little more, his hands knocking into things.

"Maddy," Mummy said, "where do you think you are?"

"I'm in my *room*," I said.

"Dan?" she said, to Daddy. My Daddy's other name is "Dan" It is like "Dad" but has a nuh-sound at the end instead of a duh-sound. "*Is* this Maddy's room?"

I heard him moving around again, as if he was checking things with his hands.

"What are we doing in here?" he said, sounding as if he was not certain. "*Is* this her room?"

"Yes, it's *my room*," I said.

I was beginning to think Daddy or Mummy could not hear properly, because I kept saying things over and over, but they did not listen. I told them again. "I woke up, and my light was off, and this is my room."

"Have you tried the switch by the door?" Daddy asked Mummy.

I heard Mummy move to the door, and her fingers swishing on the wall, swishing and patting. "It's not there."

"What do you mean it's not there?"

"What do you think I mean?"

"For Christ's sake."

I heard Daddy walking carefully across the room to where Mummy was. Mummy said: "Satisfied?"

"How *can* it not be there? Maddy—can you turn the light by your bed on, please?" Daddy sounded cross now.

"She says it isn't there."

"What do you mean, not there?"

"It's not *there*," I said. "I already told Mummy, fourteen times. I was coming into your room to tell you, and then Mummy woke up and she was on the floor."

"Are the street lamps out?"

This was Mummy asking. I heard Daddy go away from the door and go back to the other end of the room, where he had woken up from. He knocked into the table as he was moving and made a cross sound but kept on moving again.

"Dan? Is that why it's so dark? Is it a power cut?"

"I don't know," he said. "I... can't find the curtains."

"Can't find the gap, you mean?"

"No. Can't find the curtains. They're not here."

"You're sure you're in the right—"

"Of course I'm in the right place. They're not here. I can't feel them. It's just wall."

"It is just wall where my door is too," I said. I was happy that Daddy had found the same thing as me, because if he had found it too then it could not be wrong.

I heard Mummy check the wall near us with her hands. She was breathing a little quickly.

"She's right. It's just wall," she said, so we all knew the same thing.

But Mummy's voice sounded quiet and a bit scared and so it did not make me so happy when she said it.

"Okay, this is ridiculous," Daddy said. "Stay where you are. Don't move."

I could hear what he was doing. He was going along the sides of the room, with his fingers on the walls. He went around the drawers near the window, then past where my cloth calendar hangs, where I put what day it is in the mornings, then along my bed.

"She's right," he said. "The lamp isn't here."

"I'm really cold," Mummy said.

Daddy went past me and into the corner where Mummy had been sleeping, where I trod on her when I was trying to find the door. But he couldn't find it either.

He said the door had gone and the windows and all the walls felt like they were made of stone.

Mummy tried to find the curtains then too, but she couldn't. They tried to find the door and the window for a long time but they still couldn't find them and then my Mummy started crying.

Daddy said crying would not help, which he says to me sometimes, and he kept on looking in the dark for some more time.

But in the end he stopped, and he came and sat down with us. I don't now how long ago that was. It's hard to remember in the dark.

Sometimes we sleep but later we wake up and everything is the same. I do not get hungry but it is always dark and very cold. Mummy and Daddy had ideas and used their imaginations. Mummy thought there was a fire and it burned all our house down. Daddy says we think we are in my room because I woke up first, but really we are in a small place made of stone near a church. I don't know but we have been here a very long time now and still it is not morning yet. It is quiet and I do not like it.

Mummy and Daddy do not talk much any more, and this is why, if you wake up in the night, you should never ever get up out of bed.

WENDIGO
MICAELA MORRISSETTE

Micaela Morrissette's fiction has been published in *Conjunctions*, where she is a senior editor; in *Paul Revere's Horse*, where she is a contributing editor; in *Best American Fantasy 2*, and Heide Hatry's anthology *Heads and Tales*. Her reviews and other nonfiction can be found in *Rain Taxi*, *LIT*, and *Jacket*. She is the recipient of a 2009 Pushcart Prize, and an MFA candidate at Brown University.

"Wendigo" was written to illustrate a bust by artist Heide Hatry (mixed media, including untreated pig skin, raw pig lips, and pig eyes). Originally published in *Weird Tales*, "Wendigo" also appears in Hatry's anthology *Heads and Tales*, together with a photograph of the generative sculpture.

Dinner was special. The candles were miraculous, emanating a light that went oozing into pores, piercing into strands of hair, that found its way inside the thin glass of the champagne flutes, the rough, quartzy crystal of the punch bowl. Nothing glittered, nothing sparkled, nothing shone. Everything glowed, everything throbbed. The other guests did not smile, but they radiated pulses of tender heat in her direction, until her cheeks were mottled red. Each course in the banquet had an aura that hung heavily over the platter, like steam weighed down with globules of grease, thick particles of oily light.

She swallowed the wine that paused in her mouth, clung there, spreading itself. She swallowed the black soup: thin, sour broth swimming with clots that trailed delicate filaments. She swallowed the tempura of cobra lily, and, inside its cup, the pale, limp moth that seemed to sigh and dissolve on her tongue. When the songbirds were served, her gracious companion, sensing her confusion, placed a steadying hand on the back of her neck and guided her head under the starched napkin. She ate the scorching meat, needled with tiny bones her teeth had splintered. She felt little ruptures where they scratched her throat. Her companion was missing the fifth and second fingertips of his right hand, the entire middle finger of his left. Bluntly, blindly, fondly, the stubs knocked against her skin. The manservant brought the baby octopi in shallow bowls filled with, her host informed the company, vibrio fischeri, which sent a faint gold-green luminescence throughout the water. She dipped an octopus in the spicy sauce and trapped it lightly between her teeth. Its small heavings and sucks brushed against the pads of her cheeks like tiny kisses.

The main course was a roast: mild, slightly stringy. Sweet bursts of fat jetted from the sinews as she chewed. The light in the room was so dense it oppressed her; she could barely see through it. Food filled her stomach like air in a balloon; the heavier she grew, the higher above her chair she seemed to float. Her solicitous companion murmured an inquiry; it was decided they would leave before the dessert. She deposited her hand in that of her host. Rivulets of sweat trickled through the plump seams in his palm. He twinkled and beamed at her with his eye; the side of his face where the eye patch adhered remained stolid. In the car, she sniffed at her fingers, still slick from her host's farewell; they smelled like earth newly turned over: fresh, rich, heady. The smell seemed to cleanse her palate: her eyelids spasmed in the bottomless night; her stomach wrenched in sudden appetite.

In the morning she woke with a head that felt stuffed with cement, cracking and crumbling against the inside of her skull in jagged pressure. Her bedroom was narrow and spare, the walls shrunk tight around the heat that came shrieking and spitting from the iron radiator. She scrabbled frantically at the window; it screeched open in a flurry of dirty paint chips, and the air shoved in, knocking her aside, gnashing at her shrinking skin. She sank down, flinching at the grit that bit her legs and hands, and entered her stretches. Inflexible, she tore tentatively at her muscles, lunging forward with shallow gasps. Compelling her forehead to the floor, she felt frustration lash up her spine and stab the back of her neck like a handcuff snickering tight around her straining.

The bathroom smelled strongly of the new plastic shower curtain. She brushed with her lips pursed around the handle of the toothbrush, preventing the froth from running out over her chin. Her skin was getting worse. Her face, which at sixteen had been so pure and watertight, was at thirty-three beginning to boil and leak. Her virginity, which had been withered, dry, and hard, was beginning to rot and extrude. Like a 1,000-year-old egg, it had softened, become pungent, delicious, disgusting. She tapped against her pubis with one finger. She flattened her palm against her stomach. "Somewhere in there," she said, "like a little dead baby."

She hobbled out in her matted pink robe, cleared the table of its ketchup-caked refuse, cooked three strips of bacon, which she ate with the fat still gelatinous and slightly cool. Her professional wardrobe was consistent: slacks, with leggings underneath to intervene against the scratch of the wool; a cardigan; another cardigan.

On the bus she leaned her head against the window so the jolts of the motor and the road chattered her teeth together. She tried to give up her seat to an expecting mother, but the woman didn't want to sit there. When she entered her cubicle there was an unfamiliar odor: creamy, sweet, powdery. Later in the day she could only smell it by whirling her head suddenly to the side. Her new colleague across the aisle caught her doing it and laughed. He had laughed the day before, too, at her dispersal of pillows: one on the seat of her folding chair, one at her back, two under her feet, one on her desk for her elbow to rest on. He had a gaping laugh, this new colleague, she could see the hole at the back of his mouth, he opened that wide. It was delightful. She thought of smiling at him, but resisted. Her smile, she knew, was crooked: it had a forced quality. Nonetheless, pleasure rocked through her in slow waves at the trust implicit in her new colleague's exposed gullet. She settled for beaming at him with quiet kindliness. When she swung around, she checked her beam in her little round mirror. There was a grimness to it, in the set of the jaw, but something in the eyes, she thought, that was accurate.

Her elegant companion invited her to accompany him to the grocery store, and she accepted. "Dress warmly," he counseled. He drove for hours in the dark, the headlights spinning uncertainly off the broken curbs, the sharp teeth of the stoops, the strobing telephone poles. The supermarket was in a bad neighborhood, but vast, swallowing several city blocks. Homeless were encamped at the intersections of the aisles. They each took a cart and moved quickly to the meat department, looking neither left nor right. The meat department was a gargantuan walk-in refrigerator: the space so enormous and the cold mist so dense that she could not see from one wall to the opposite. They did not leave each other's sides. They did not speak or touch. They filled their carts: chicken, goat, bear, salmon, pork, lamb, conch, squab, rabbit, shark, beef, veal, turkey, eel, venison, duck, mussels, ostrich, frogs, pheasant, squirrel, seal. Tripe, kidneys, liver, tongue, and brains. She suggested the purchase of some lemons and marinade; he reproved her cordially.

She helped him load the boxes into the service elevator of his building; then he drove her home. Outside the door of her apartment, probing her bag for her key, she discovered he had slipped in a small package of pancreas sweetbreads: a token. She tucked it beneath her pillow and dreamt all night of the beating of her heart.

The new colleague sat at her table in the company cafeteria. She had a Ziploc bag of cold shrimps, while he had brought a Tupperware of deviled eggs, each half in its own hollow of molded plastic, which he ate by forking out the middles, then peeling off cool white wedges of the whites.

The new colleague had been transferred from a branch of the firm located in another state. He described himself as "corn-fed." Moving to the city had not been as difficult as he had anticipated. There were lots of ways to meet people. He had joined a church choir and was taking a photography course. The first half had dealt with still lifes; the second was on snapshots. He produced a picture he had taken of her in her cubicle. She looked as if the flash of the camera had struck her across the face. It was flattering. She wished she had known it was happening. "It's out of focus," she said. He smiled. He said, "That's artistic."

"Are you a good singer?" she asked. He used to be incredible, he said, before his voice changed. It had been his whole life. It had given him a kind of spiritual mission, as a kid. He was a very mature child. He felt he had been charged with something. After his voice changed, he felt neither release nor despondency. At that point, he stopped considering things like blessings and missions. He became childlike; he lost the habit of thinking much about himself or the things that happened to him. "What about now?" she said. "Do you wish you had become a castrato?" Behind his tongue, his throat was roseate, and the flesh there jerked with his laughter.

When at the conclusion of the meal she folded her Ziploc bag, sealing in the salty film of pink water, and began to rise, he forestalled her, and took her garbage with his to the trash receptacle. She did not reflect on the contact their hands had made during the exchange until, late that afternoon, she noticed him scratching feverishly at a rash that had swollen across the range of his knuckles. She wished she had remembered beforehand to think of it.

The door of her apartment shuddered with the force of the knocking of her illustrious companion. When she flung it open, he staggered in, holding up his right hand. The tip of his index finger was flapping there on a strap of skin. In his left hand was a plastic grocery bag. "Take it off!" he said, in a voice admirably controlled, if keen in pitch. She got him into a chair at the kitchen table, and placing a skillet under his hand to catch the blood, snipped off the fingertip with her nail scissors. She swathed the stump in toilet paper and tied dental floss tightly around the base of the finger to stop the bleeding. He whistled in relief, and pulled a rueful face. He lit a cigarette, picked up the grocery bag from the floor beside his chair, and jiggled it merrily in the air. "Would you care to dine with me this evening?" he inquired.

She set the table while he busied himself at the stove. He had removed his tuxedo jacket and tucked a dishtowel into his collar to protect the pique bib of his shirt. While his back was to her, she glanced covertly around the apartment. But everything seemed to be in place: the sag of the couch springs had a decadent grace, like a courtesan in the half-swoon that succeeds a debauch; the buzz of the fluorescents was textured and complex, a Gregorian plainchant heard from across a great distance. Water stains undulated across the ceiling, like tentacles of a translucent sea-monster half glimpsed through immense currents. The smell from the cooking wove an intricate web from wall to wall; she felt it smothering against her nose and mouth, rich with the scents of ingredients that surely were absent: zedoary, fenugreek, frankincense.

He brought the skillet to the table to ladle the meal, still bubbling, into their bowls. Without ceremony, but gravely, he maneuvered the digit into her portion.

Her genteel companion had extracted the nail, or it had dissolved. She speared the tines of her fork through the nailbed, and ran her tongue across the pattern of lines on the pad of the finger. She inserted the portion into her mouth and sucked off the dark, congealing stew. Her companion's breaths were audible and steady. She removed the part and considered its form, then inserted it again and began, with small strokes of her incisors, to shuck the nugget of flesh from the bone. There was not much meat there, but once she had it all behind her lips, it seemed to fill the space of her mouth. It tasted like her tongue, her gums, her cheeks. She was nervous to chew; she was afraid to bite down on her own tissue. She swallowed it whole. The rest of the stew had the taste that had been drained from the finger: savory, ripe, and plummy.

Her companion, always immaculate, kissed her hand at the door. "Your hospitality," he purred, "such a gift." She said, "Thank you for dinner." "Leftovers are in the fridge," he smiled, and backed out into the oblivion of the unlit hallway.

In the middle of the night she woke and stumbled clumsily toward the kitchen. The smoke from the cooking still curtained the windows, gagging the weak light of the streetlamps. She forgot in her haste the jut of the walls, the menacing corner of her bookcase. She poured the remains of their supper into a half dozen mugs and bore them on a tray into her bedroom. She drank them off in the dark, propped on her pillows, then dreamed she was inside the stomach of a whale.

Her skin was much worse: abraded, blistered, mucid, rubicund. Her eyelids were swollen and tears of pus welled up in the depths of the sockets. Her chest was hot as if sunburned; when she pushed her hand against the breastbone the imprint did not fade away for some minutes. During her stretches, bending over at the waist, she could feel the satiny slithering of her organs over each other, the horrible pappy give of them. The putrification of her virginity shocked her with its rapacity and virulence. Her hair was broken and thin. It floated in the air, repelled by the electric charge of her damp scalp.

The fever was constant and she fed on the extra degrees. She was bright and alert and vibrating. She took measures. She packed the bathtub with ice and slept in there one night. When she awoke, the swelling around her eyes had shrunken, her face and chest were pale, she was hard and smooth and cold inside and out. She was tremulous with gratitude. But the thawing nearly crippled her. She had to leave work early, as much so that her new colleague across the aisle would not actually hear the sharp cracking and rending in the marrows of her bones, as because of the savagery with which the molten brimstone of her decay attacked the frozen blocks of her limbs.

She began swimming, trusting that she was not infectious, visiting the heavily chlorinated YWCA pool at senior citizens' hour, in enormous goggles and a latex swim cap. The chemicals in the water helped her face. She submerged and held still, and could see the bubbles race up from her cheeks and chin, hear the hypochlorous acid hissing against her skin. Her complexion lost its rawness, though it was still pitted, and the skin now flaked away in fragile, dusty layers. Inside, however, she continued to rot.

At last she began swimming in the city bay at night, naked. The water was syrupy, warm, stinking, and crowded with objects she did not identify, which nudged her meekly, skimmed along the side of her body, and were dragged on and out by the slow, mild movements of the sea. She floated face down or up, legs and arms open, and felt the sludge of the bay flush in and out of her. She rocked calmly in the wake of garbage tugs or police speedboats. She didn't know if the high toxicity of the bay really had killed her virginity once and for all, or if the organic soup of the water, crowded with things living and dead, had simply calmed its hunger, given it to feed. Whatever the case, her fever dropped, her blood thickened and slowed, her organs grew leathery and dense, her pustules shrank into her pores. The only stain the water left on her was a distinctive smell, salty and dark, that plucked constantly at her hunger; and a dull, muddy smear, like a skin, that covered the orbs of her eyes.

Her charming companion invited her to a gathering of intimates, something special and private, he said. She was to wash her hands and wear old clothes. He drove. The headlights poured out like floodwaters submerging a condemned city. They arrived at their destination in no time at all.

She was happy to revisit the home of her amiable host, though the dining hall was not suffused with radiance on this occasion, and the atmosphere did not bewilder her with scents that choked the air. Nonetheless, she was struck anew by the welcome implicit in the cavernous chambers, which never threw her footsteps back at her in repulsing echo, but muffled sound in their embrace, opening gladly to her ingress and to that of her astonishing companion. The smell of her host—storm-soaked sediment, shrinking fungi, nacreous gastropods—trembled shyly in her nostrils.

In neat array around the empty banquet table, the other guests awaited her arrival. They too were dressed shabbily, in torn jerseys, paint-stained singlets. Again they did not smile, but she felt their geniality drift warmly over her, tickling her hair. She took a seat beside her magnificent companion, and on that cue the great doors opened for the manservant, wheeling in his late employer on a gurney sumptuously draped.

Her host was thickly glazed with pomegranate sauce, and flushed livid from the boiler, and legless, but otherwise was all she had remembered—massive, calm, beatific. An affectionate drone, a deep, low appreciation, rose from the company. A tall, angular woman, drenched in hair, stood to speak. "Loving," the woman pronounced. "Inspired, messianic, but gentle. Always with us," said the woman, "a comfort and a rare delight." The guests touched each other's wrists and shoulders with whispering care. The manservant, reverential, slid his employer's corpse from the gurney to the table. The bounteousness of the body of her host brought a part of him within easy reach of each pair of tender hands.

The guest to her left noted her hesitation and leaned in, sharp, wry, and twinkling. "Don't hold back," the guest advised. "It's our gift to him." She asked, "And his gift to us?" "Oh, particularly that," crooned the guest. "When I knew that I was going to lose my baby before term, I came straight here. You can't imagine what it did for me, all my dear friends taking in the little half-body, holding him in the warmth of their mouths, giving him sanctuary. My role in it was an act of necessity, of course. Getting him back where he belonged. He was always part of me. But our friends, our host. Ah, our host," sighed the guest. "He wasn't tasty, you know, my baby boy. He was raw, immature, flaccid, an inharmonic composition. But now I think I can taste him in our host, completed, ripened. A small fresh note, like a little pocket of lavender snuggled in among the fat of the flank here. Can't you taste it? Ah, our host. He gives and gives."

She reached out and, digging her nails into the crease of her host's breast, tore a tendril from the body. "Be sure to chew," the guest prompted anxiously. She chewed. Her host smiled inside her mouth. "He's delicious," she said.

"Ah, he's delicious," hummed the guest. With a hurried flick of the tongue, the guest caught a rivulet of their host where he was racing from wrist to elbow. "He always ate for this moment," said the guest. "He primed himself for us. Such munificence!" said the guest. "Such benevolence!"

When the funeral was complete, the host was a tattered thing, and the guests were smeared with sauce and peppered with black flakes of charring from the skin. Sated, exhausted, elated, and mournful, they reflectively sucked the fibers of flesh caught between their teeth.

This time her regal companion had the honor of taking her into the parlor for coffee and dessert. A Black Forest cake was served, the host's favorite confection.

Coming late into the company cafeteria, she joined the new colleague for lunch. She had just purchased a stout block of shrink-wrapped foie gras; he had arranged the ingredients of his meal on an unfolded square of butcher paper, and was spreading tuna salad on crackers, crowned with thin wafers he cut off a radish. He drew her attention to the sores on her mouth. A new nervous habit, she explained. Her lips were shredded and mangled with teeth marks. It must happen during sleep, her colleague suggested. He had never seen her do it at her desk.

His photography course was proceeding well; he spread out on the table the latest additions to his series of portraits of her. Undoubtedly, she was losing weight. The hinge of her jaw protruded with a truculent insistence; her shoulders were mean, angry splinters that snagged at her sweater. Her posture was impeccable: paralyzed. "Missing—Have You Seen This Woman?" she said.

Her new colleague sputtered with glee and cut cleanly through his radish and into the ball of his hand. He coughed in surprise. The blood beaded and hopped on the waxed paper, like spit on a griddle. She moved quickly over to his bench, and secured his wrist in an efficient grip, and sucked at the cut.

"Oh, my god!" said her new colleague. "Please stop that!"

"What?" she said. "I just thought, the radish juice, I thought it might sting."

"Well," said her colleague, "that's thoughtful, but I really can't ask you to do that. You're too kind!" he said, laughing and shaking his head.

"It's okay," she said. "I would want someone to do it, to help me, in a similar situation. Look," she said, picking up his paring knife and drawing it cleanly down. She held her palm up to the ceiling and tilted her arm so the flow ran neatly into her sleeve. "You can make it up to me," she said. She maneuvered awkwardly to bring her hand to mouth-level without dripping blood on the tan slacks of her colleague.

"No!" he said. " I'm getting the first-aid kit. Just hang on!" he said. "Keep your hand elevated."

Sadly, she considered the wastage of her blood, soaking through the acrylic of her cardigan onto the tile floor. Her colleague wasn't returning with first aid, and finally she sealed her lips over her palm and began nursing the wound. Her blood was better than his: strong, fermented, with a bitter, gritty strength and a distant note of figs and honey. His was sour, with a pickled sharpness like cut grass; a stale dustiness, like a glass of water left all night on the bedside table; and a slick coolness, like broken glass. Hers numbed the flat of the tongue, like strong tea; it stroked the inside of the esophagus, like horehound syrup; it moved in the stomach, she could feel it stroking the walls, coaxing her hunger. She took the afternoon off and went home to eat.

She returned repeatedly to the supermarket in search of her distinguished companion. At last he strolled in, urbane, guiding his shopping cart with the tips of his fingers, light, tasteful intimations of pressure. At the sight of her his face broke apart in amazed enchantment. Beside him was a young girl, still plump, with stippled indigo circles sagging ponderous under her eyes. "Am I interrupting?" she said. "My dear," replied her companion, throatily, "what a question." He leaned forward to kiss her cheek; she felt his busy sniffing at her neck. He retracted from her, his profile pivoting this way and that as he searched the air. "Child," said her courtly companion, "have you been plundering your harvest? You have been dining in?"

"Once," she said, "twice, three times. I wanted to see if I was tasty. I am," she said, "ambrosial. I wanted to know if it would be an insult to offer—"

"This?" said her lustrous companion, running his fingernail across the zipper of her handbag. She scrabbled briefly, it was wedged between her change purse and her date book, but at last she produced it without embarrassment, with a cold dignity, the item crumpled in cling wrap, a pasty purple, bruised and browning at the edges. "Hymenaeus," said her companion, warming it between his hands. "The son of Aphrodite." His smile tumbled over her, eager and youthful; she had to brace herself against the weight of it. "You have made your decision?"

asked her devoted companion. "This is something that would never have been asked of you."

She put it to him: wasn't it true that her rapacious and unremitting hunger was fueled by her feeding? Was it not the case that, having been devoured, she would be full? "Little wendigo," said her refulgent companion, "it is so. For a time, indeed."

Her companion had counseled her to eat, but she would not eat. He came to her apartment bearing gifts: a shapely thigh, a breast fulsome with milk, a smoky, musky phallus; but she merely measured off frugal doses of her blood with a syringe and dispensed them gingerly into the plastic tops of cough syrup bottles, marked off in tablespoons. In the gray, silken evenings they sat comfortably on her couch and sipped in companionable silence. She asked whether her blood did not give him the hungers, but that, he said, was what he liked it for. Disrobing with supple tact, her considerate companion displayed the sliced planes of his buttocks, the half-moons where his torso had been spooned out like a melon. She inquired why it was their fellows had so far declined with gratitude the offering of her own parts. "You're still such a virgin, little one," said her loyal companion. She pinned him with sharp eyes. "The flesh eaten still on the living body," he told her, "there is the union." "Your finger, our host, my hymen?" she asked. "Fellatios, my sweet," lisped her companion. She eyed the swell of his forearm with avarice, the muscles coiled in knots under his slippery shirt. "Not me, my darling," he said, and lifted his remaining finger to tick-tock through the air in drowsy admonishment. "You make your own way; then you come home."

She turned and looked full into the stutter of the camera of her colleague. He berated her. "That's not spontaneous!" He insisted that the project set for the class was for the photographer to be the hunter, and the subject the prey. That made it edgy. "Oh," she said, "you're not hunting; you're farming. Picking off creatures grazing at pasture, dull in contemplation." She struck a candid pose, lips slightly agape, eyes askew, her expression garbled, transparent and opaque, like a muddy pond. He was discontent. If she stalked the camera, he reasoned, if she had him in her sights, while he had her in his, that skewed the terms of the assignment. "True," she conceded, "that's not hunting," she said; "that's war." He snapped her picture. "Caught you!" her new colleague crowed. "Let's eat," she proposed. She had forgotten to pack a meal, so he accompanied her through the lunch line, selecting a Charlotte of Bavarian creme and ladyfingers, while she consumed a Manwich.

She escorted her exquisite companion to the city bay where they sat on the dock, shoes off and pants rolled to the knees, smiling at the disparity of their feet in the water, hers crumpled and dented and damp from her pumps, his slender, prosthetic, dove-gray. The bats in the twilight were reckless and extraordinary;

the seagulls had hidden themselves but called out fierce and lonesome, like the whistles of locomotives on the track of the tremulous far horizon. They had purchased small waxed envelopes of sweet, crispy nuts. She swallowed hers nearly whole, while he chewed his bites minutely and spat them out in neat piles on the gravel shore.

Her companion was wistful. The fine engraving of his face looked stony and the quizzical glances and debonair moues by which she knew him seemed painful to execute. She reached in experiment to probe the softness of his cheek and he winced, a tremor of delectable fineness and subtlety.

"Melancholy," her companion apologized, "a disease not commonly recognized as having its origins in exposure to freshness of air. I am so little accustomed to the pathos of the junction of the land and the sea."

He was sorrowful, wondering, his chin tucked into the refuge of his collar, his cowlick sprouting in the salt spray like that of a small boy.

"Don't," he chastised her, "feel maternal. You can't imagine the monsters in those deeps. That is so much more dangerous."

"More dangerous than this?"

"There's little danger here."

"Is our safety so assured?"

"Au contraire." He was amused again, his mouth twisting and curling to savor the joke. "It's our downfall that's reliable."

She was comforted. She wedged herself against him, and he allowed this, though she could feel the warmth on her shoulder where a suture on his breast had wrenched open with the nesting of her weight. The bats were sucked upward into the sky, caught by the magnetic pull of the stars, and the mosquitoes rushed in, enveloping the happy couple, and falling in quivering piles to the dock, all around them.

She woke at the first stain of sunlight on the face of the sky and slithered to the floor to enter her stretches. They came more easily now that her muscles were drained and limp and she laid her cheek between her legs against the floorboards and sniffed the old gasoline smell of the paint; the gamy traces of her footsteps; a cloying, pulpy odor of breakfast in the apartment below. In the bathroom, she brushed her teeth, tilting her chin back to cup the toothpaste in her mouth, staring down her nose at the mirror. This gave her an accusing look. She made a kind, understanding face that returned to her as a nauseous leer. She giggled. In the shower she ran the water so hot it nearly melted the glue that held her skin to her substructure. Her flesh slipped dangerously over its ligaments. "Oops," she said.

She had recently treated herself to a French press and, swaddled luxuriously in her old pink robe, she tipped in the beans she'd ground the night before, and punished them with water at a rapid boil. Setting the egg timer to four-and-a-half minutes, she dressed for work: leggings, slacks, two cardigans. She relaxed at the table with granola and berries, slapping back the unfurled and flapping wings of the newspaper. A merry little robin perched on her windowsill, stabbing with its beak at its reflection in the pane.

At work she attacked the keys of her calculator with especial vivacity, tapping her rhythm into the brain of her new colleague. She broke a light sweat, and several pencil leads. The chalky scent of her perspiration, buoyed on a cloud of lily-pale eau de toilette, made its way across the aisle. Her hair was hectic with static. She kept her best three-quarters profile toward the door of her cubicle, and never looked round.

Her colleague invited her to an after-work aperitif. He had a Bloody Mary; she enjoyed a Cinzano. His photography course was finished; he would move on to sculpture in just a few weeks. He displayed the final array of photographs on the tabletop. There she was, blinking, flinching in all her poses. "You see," he chortled, "it was better when you didn't know I was taking them. You came at the camera," he said, gesticulating, "in a flurry of fear. It was kinder, after all, to take you unaware." She concurred with her new colleague.

He fell asleep with the lights on. If the patchwork of her body, the scars of old decay, the faint sifting and rattling sounds of shriveled things within her, had worried him, he hadn't shown it, and she would now require the illumination for precision. She had discovered that the area least sensitive to touch was likely to be the back of the shoulders. She inserted the point just above his scapula, turning the flat of the blade parallel to his skin, and cut two sides of a small triangle. Without completing the figure, she lifted the flap, hovering above him in an unwieldy posture, propped on her knuckles, and chewed the skin. She was careful not to sever it, as she did not want to have to cut another piece. The living, she noted, did not have as much taste as the dead. He was tough and elastic. And she could feel the muscles shrinking away from the grind of her teeth. When she had at last reduced the flesh to a small, spongy lump, sticky but bloodless, she yanked it off—he snorted slightly—dropped it in the trash can, wrapped in a tissue; drank a glass of water in the crackling light of the bathroom; dabbed on a touch of lipstick; and locked the door behind her as she went.

She had never eaten so well in her life. They brought her sweet, sticky rice; curried cauliflower delirious with coconut milk; jungles of spaghetti, mired in Alfredo sauce; pinto-bean chili black with molasses. For a long time she would not touch meat, not trusting the source, but then they began to carry in animals roasted whole: a suckling pig, turned on a spit; an infant lamb in a roasting pan, its hooves tucked in trustingly; turkeys spilling out oysters; crabs crusted in ethereal salt; and these she felt safe in consuming. She promised she would sit very still, so they cuffed her only by one foot; and she kept her word, burrowed in somnolent complacence in her featherbed, in an endless drowse, basting herself for her banquet. She was stupefied, seduced, but she knew herself to be tempting, was confident their mouths would water for her. She waited, and every day she grew more ardent.

She had little idea of the passage of time, and when the temperature in her cell began to rise she wondered if summer was finally upon them and if they were saving her, perhaps, for a midsummer feast. The intensification of the heat was, however, accompanied by great commotion in the hall, by the repeated jostling of doors and the thumping of wheels over uneven ground, by the smell of outdoors, lichen and bark and wood sap, and finally, it came to her, a far-away rushing sound, a flickering, hissing, panting growl, like the anger of the surf.

To her beautiful companion, who came every day to see her, she said, "Something is not right."

Her companion asked if she was weary of waiting. He had lost his nose, and his face, always a ravishment, was now even more moving to her, a stately ruin sliding down the cliff of his skull to the sea beneath. She denied his imputation. She was eager, she said, but not weary. She would do whatever was necessary to be most pleasing to the company. "Only," she said, "they have built a fire."

Her faithful companion assented to this conjecture. "A very large one," he said, "they began it in the dining hall, with the banquet-table, and they have been piling wood on for days."

"I thought," she faltered, "that I was not to have been slaughtered first."

Her companion considered the suave line of his shoe. He tugged sadly at the scraps of his earlobe. At last he said, "You are not held to be quite delicious enough for that."

"No?" she said.

"Lamentably not," said her doting companion. "I consider it a piece of great foolishness."

"You would have eaten me alive?" she beseeched him.

"Oh," said her companion, "I fear it must be acknowledged that I would not have been able to eat you at all."

Blackout curtains covered the windows, but she could hear the hammering of the rain against the glass, like a mob of useless fists. "Please help me," she said.

Her loving companion held her hands between the butts of his wrists. He smiled down at her. "I can't help you," he said, "but I won't hinder you." And then he took his leave.

She heaved her body from the bed to the floor. The manacle, she discovered, could slide some distance up her leg, but could not be made by any contortion to allow her foot to slip through. Bending her leg at the knee, she grasped her toes with both hands, and stretched forward. The skin at her ankle was tender, and she was not prepared for the juice that shot out and battered the back of her throat in an insistent stream. After her long recumbence, the muscle was creamy and fine. She nibbled all around, using her nails to tear at the meat on the far opposite side of the limb, and flexed her jaw for the bone. But this shattered in her mouth, releasing a puff of powder that mingled unpleasantly with the red paste of the marrow. With the elimination of the foot, the manacle clanked to the ground. Staunching the bleeding took time, however, and she endured this impatiently. At last she was able to lurch to the door of her cell, and propping her body against the wall, to heave it open.

The guests were garlanding the dining-hall fire with armfuls of flowers; burning petals drifted in the air. The thin crystal flutes they held glowed with the champagne inside them, like pale coals. The long limbs of the women waved gracefully in greeting; the men bobbed their heads at her with rough affection. Her own companion was not among them. Across the room, beside the door, the eyes of the manservant were black in the black smoke. She hobbled in his direction. At this movement, a cry went up, and the guests began applauding. The champagne slapped the sides of the flutes in cheerful chimes and the celebration lashed across the room, and all the company danced in a great spiral, like a whirlpool sucking through the house. The eyes of the guests were brilliant, adoring; their faces were tilted up, innocent, anticipatory, as if to be kissed. Their delirium raised a dazzling bright wind in the hall: she breathed it in: odorless; swallowed it: tasteless; trapped it in her lungs, where it disappeared, weightless. She stood on her leg and observed the guests as, fingers interlaced, hair tangled together, their breaths muddling in each other's mouths, their exultant cries in each other's ears, they danced and danced. She saw that in an instant the floor would collapse beneath the force of their joy and their affection for her.

IN THE PORCHES OF MY EARS
NORMAN PRENTISS

Norman Prentiss lives in Baltimore, Maryland, and works as a high school English teacher. Since the summer of 2006, he has served as Associate Editor for *Cemetery Dance* magazine. His fiction has appeared in *Tales from the Gorezone*, *Damned Nation*, *Postscripts*, and the *Shivers* anthology series, and at the Horror Drive-In website. His first book, *Invisible Fences*, is forthcoming in the Cemetery Dance novella series.

Helen and I should have paid more attention to the couple we followed into the movie theater: his stiff, halting walk, and the way the woman clung to him, arm around his waist and her body pressed tight to his side. I read love into their close posture, an older couple exchanging long-held decorum for the sort of public display more common among today's younger people. I felt embarrassed for them and looked away. I regret that neither my wife nor I noticed a crucial detail in time, but real life doesn't always inspire the interpretative urgency of images projected on a screen, and it's not as if a prop department provided the obvious clues: sunglasses worn indoors, or a thin white cane tapping the ground, sweeping the air.

Helen went ahead to get us seats, while I stood in line at concessions to buy bottled waters. We disliked popcorn for its metallic, fake butter smell and, more importantly, because we chose not to contribute to the surrounding crunch—a sound like feet stomping through dead leaves, intruding over a film's quieter moments. For similar reasons, we avoided candy, with its noisome wrappers, and the worst abomination of recent years, the plastic tray of corn chips and hot cheese dip. Fortunately, the Midtowne Cinema didn't serve the latter, making it one of our preferred neighborhood theaters. That, and the slightly older clientele who behaved according to that lost era, back before people trained themselves to shout over rented movies in their living rooms.

The Midtowne wasn't quite an art house, rarely showing films with subtitles or excessive nudity. Instead, it tended towards Shakespeare or Dickens or E. M. Forster adaptations, the big-screen, bigger-budget equivalents to television's *Masterpiece Theatre*, which I tended to prefer; or, closer to Helen's taste, romantic comedies more palatably delivered through British accents.

Helen had chosen the afternoon's entertainment, so we'd once again see that short, slightly goofy actor who survived an embarrassing sex scandal a few years back and still, *still* managed onscreen to charm the sandy-haired, long-legged actress (who was actually American-born, but approximated the preferred accent well enough for most, and smiled brightly enough to provoke the rest to forgive her). I brought the water bottles into the auditorium—two dollars each, unfortunately, but we broke even by saving as much on matinee admission—and searched for Helen in the flickering dark.

We were later than I expected. Previews had already started, and the semi-dark auditorium was mostly full. I knew Helen's preference for an aisle seat, on the right side of the main section, but the crowd had forced her to sit farther back than usual. I walked past her before a whispered "Psst, Steve," called me to the correct row.

She turned sideways, legs in the aisle so I could scoot past easily. I handed her a water bottle before I sat down.

"Is this okay?" she asked.

"Fine." I responded without really thinking. It was her movie choice, so it wouldn't bother *me* to sit too far back from the picture.

Helen gestured toward the man in front of me, then forked her middle- and forefinger to point at her eyes. I recognized the man from the couple I'd half-noticed on the way inside. He sat tall in his seat: his shoulders and gangly gray-fuzzed head, from my vantage, cut a dark notch into the bottom of the screen like the interlocking edge of a missing jigsaw piece. His companion was a good bit shorter, granting my wife a clear view of the film.

I knew Helen felt guilty because she liked the aisle, actually thought she *needed* it because she typically left to use the restroom at least twice during a ninety-minute film. The water bottle didn't help, obviously.

Music swelled from the preview's soundtrack, and a glossy country manor montage shimmered onscreen. Like a sequel to *Age of Innocence,* or maybe *A Room with a* Different *View.* "I can see fine," I assured her. Besides, the slight obstruction was better than having Helen climb over my legs several times once the film was in progress. "As long as there's no subtitles," I joked.

Helen pointed to her eyes again, and her fingertips nearly touched the lenses of her glasses. I could tell she wanted to say more, but she stopped herself.

"What *is* it?"

I spoke normally, just loud enough so she'd hear over the trailer's quoted blurb from *The New Yorker,* but from Helen's expression you would think I'd shouted "Fire!"

"Never mind," she said, especially quiet, but her message clear.

Then the man in front of me turned his head. It was a quick motion, almost like a muscle spasm, and he held the angle for a long, awkward profile. His shoulder pressed into the chair cushion, and he twisted his head further around toward me. From a trick of the projection light, I assumed, his eyes appeared fogged, the irises lined like veined gray marble.

His companion tapped him. "The movie's about to start." As if she'd activated a button on the man's shoulder, his head snapped quickly around, face front.

"Strange," I said, barely audible, but still Helen winced. I couldn't understand her agitation. In our shared interpretation of moviegoer etiquette, it was perfectly acceptable to speak quietly during the "coming attractions" portion of the show.

The exit lights dimmed completely, and the studio logo appeared on the screen. Then before the credits, a pan over Trafalgar Square, then Big Ben, then a red double-decker bus. Quick establishing shots so any idiot would know—

"We're in England."

The woman in front of us spoke with a conspirator's whisper, a quiet, urgent tone far less musical than the lover's lilt she'd expressed earlier when she tapped his shoulder.

Jeez. Thanks for stating the obvious, lady.

The credits began, yellow lettering over a long shot of the Thames river and the London skyline. The two main actors' names appeared first, then the film title.

In that same strident whisper, the woman read aloud to her companion. The stars, the costars, the "Special Appearance by Sir James So-and-so." The screenwriter, editor, for-God's-sake the music composer, and finally the director.

He can see for himself, I thought. He's not…

But of course, he *was,* and I'd been a fool for not realizing sooner. For a moment I held out a glimmer of hope that the man was simply illiterate. Once the credits ended, she'd grow silent and they'd watch the movie in peace. Wishful thinking, however, because I recalled how she'd held him close coming inside the building. Guiding him.

And I knew she'd be talking over the entire movie.

If we'd figured it out sooner, we could have moved. Dark as it was, I barely distinguished a few unoccupied seats scattered around the theater—including an empty to my left—but no pairs together. Helen and I always had to sit together. If the movie ended up being ruined for us, at least it would be a shared experience.

The commentary began in earnest. "She's trying to lock the door, but she's got too much in her arms. A purse, an accordion briefcase, a grocery sack, and a Styrofoam coffee cup. The lid's loose on the coffee."

Onscreen, the Emma- or Judi- or Gwyneth-person—possibly I've conflated the actor's name with the character's—juggled the coffee cup, the lid flew up and the liquid slipped out and over her work clothes. "Damn, damn, damn," she said in a delightful accent, and the audience roared with laughter.

"She spilled it," the man's companion told him. "A huge coffee stain on her blouse."

I hadn't laughed. The woman's commentary—I assumed she was the blind man's wife—had telegraphed the spill. Had the lid really been loose? Enough for any of us to see the clue?

"I can't believe this," I whispered to Helen, and she half-winced again. Finally, I realized the source of her tension: the commonplace wisdom that a person lacking in one physical sense gained extra ability in another—in this case, hearing.

Sure. His loud-mouth wife can ruin the whole film for us, but God forbid we whisper anything that might hurt the guy's feelings.

Helen risked a quick whisper of her own: "I'm sorry."

It wasn't her fault, of course—not really. But we'd been married almost fifteen years, and familiar intimacy brought its own yardstick for blame. The woman, her husband, the *situation itself* created the problem, and we could share disapproval of the couple's imposition, or shake fists skyward in synchronized dismay at Fates who brought us together at the same showing. And yet, Helen had eaten her lunch slowly this afternoon, had misremembered the show's start time, which in turn limited her seating options (and she *must* have the aisle seat, and *must* see these British comedies the first weekend of their release). So I blamed her a bit, then—the type of blame saved for those you love deeply, blame you savored as you indulged a spouse's habits and peculiar tastes.

Helen did the same for me. When she disliked one of my film choices—the somber violence of the latest *King Lear* adaptation, or any Thomas Hardy depression-fest other than *Under the Greenwood Tree*—I could sense her unspoken discomfort beside me, all while the film flickered toward an inevitable, tragic end. In an odd way, her discomfort often improved the experience for me, magnifying the tension of the film. Making it more authentic.

The tension was all wrong here, though, since nothing spoiled a comedy like an explanation. As the Rupert- or Ian- or Trevor-character blustered through confident proclamations, and Emma/Judi/Gwyneth mugged a sour expression, the blind man's wife stated the obvious: "His arrogance offends her. He's so self-centered, he doesn't yet realize he's in love with her."

Oh, really? Do tell.

It was easy enough to infer the same conclusions from the dialogue. I could have closed my eyes and done fine without the woman's incessant whispers. Score myself a hundred on the quiz. Besides, these romantic comedies all followed the same formula: the guy would Darcy her for a bit, she'd come around just when it seemed too late, there'd be a misunderstanding on one or both sides, until a ridiculous coincidence threw them awkwardly and then blissfully together, the end.

"Now she puts her Chinese take-out cartons in the trash, aware she's eaten too much, but also aware it doesn't matter, because she's alone."

A slight bit of interpretation there, against the whimsical Supremes song hurrying love on the soundtrack, but probably accurate. At that moment, I wondered exactly how many others in the theater could hear the woman's commentary. The people in front of them, surely, were in the same position as Helen and I: close enough to overhear, but too close to make a show of offence. Nobody else seemed to react to the voice: no grunts of disapproval, no agitated shiftings in the seats. There wasn't that ripple of cold scorn that chills the orchestra seats when a cell phone goes off during the first aria. Perhaps her whisper was one of those trained, *directed* voices, sharp in proximity but dropping off quickly with distance—as if an invisible bubble cushioned the sound into a tight circumference.

Lucky us.

I actually tried to control my indignation, for Helen's sake. We were both hyper-sensitive to extraneous chatter during a film, but this was her type of movie (though not, as was already evident, the pinnacle of the art form), and I was determined not to spoil her experience further by huffing my disapproval throughout. Instead, I touched the top of Helen's hand on our shared armrest. Our secret signal in the dark: three quick taps, for *I-love-you.*

It was a slight film, stupidly titled *Casting a Romance*: a reference to the Darcy character's job as a casting director for movies, then a pun on casting a *fishing* line, since he joins the girl and her father at a summer cottage, only to lose his stuffy demeanor amid hooks and slipping into lakes, and her getting a massive rainbow trout next to his emasculating tadpole. Somewhere along the way— about half-way between Helen's first and second trips to the Ladies' Room—I'd settled into the film, and into the commentary. I grudgingly appreciated it after a while—the woman's skill at selecting the right details, firing the narration rapidly into her husband's hungry ear. To keep myself amused, I played around a bit, closing my eyes for short stretches and letting the woman's words weave images around the dialogue. When Helen returned from the restroom, I didn't have the burden of summarizing what she missed: the woman's commentary easily filled the gaps.

After a while, I didn't mind being in the bubble with them. The shape of the blind man's head became familiar to me, atop his thin neck and leaning perpetu- ally to one side to catch his wife's every word. That sharp underlying whisper became part of the film, like the experts' comments during a televised sporting event. I half-toyed with the idea she was an expert herself. For example, she whispered how the man left his jacket draped over the chair, and she warned, correctly, that the plane tickets would spill out. She also predicted the moment when he realized his embarrassing connection to the heroine's brother—the cad who'd tried to blackmail him into an acting job during the first reel. Her delivery was so good, that I suspected she'd seen the film before—perhaps even practiced with a notepad and a stopwatch, to pinpoint the precise moments to whisper crucial details or hiss clues that inattentive viewers might miss.

So, I'd grudgingly grown to admire her skill, almost to rely on it for my full appreciation of the movie. And then she did that malicious thing during the final scene.

She changed the ending. It was almost elegant how she did it, an interplay between the silences and the openness of the characters' final words. Onscreen, the man said "I still love you," and there was a faint rise in his voice, maybe the actor's insecurity rather than the character's, but the woman twisted a question mark over his declaration.

"They say they are in love," she whispered, "but they don't mean it. He reaches out to hug her—" and on the screen they *are* hugging, "but she pulls away. It is too little, too late."

I realized, then, how precarious this type of movie was: a teasing, near-romance, suspended over ninety brittle minutes. The main characters' relationship is simultaneously inevitable and fragile—a happy ending endlessly deferred, the threat of ruin always beneath the comic surface.

The actress laughed onscreen, a clear display of relief and joy, and the woman said: "She's bitter. It is a dry, empty laugh. Her face is full of scorn."

I reached again for Helen's hand beside me. We didn't speak; our touch expressed the outrage well enough. This horrible woman at once betrayed the movie, *and* her blind husband.

I felt certain now that she'd rehearsed the commentary. How else could she best deliver her poison into his ear—at what time, and at how strong a dose—certain no additional dialogue would provide an antidote?

Thinking back, I realized something more sinister. The woman's descriptions of the lead actor had made him taller than the visual reality, gave him a thin neck and wobbled head that tilted awkwardly to the side, very much like… the head in front of me, a shadow rising above the seat to darken the bottom edge of the movie frame. She'd transformed the hero into a younger version of her husband, making the character fit how the blind man—for lack of a better word—*saw* himself. For him, the disappointed ending would be particularly cruel.

The camera pulled back from the onscreen couple's happy, final embrace, and a song blared from the soundtrack. The song was allegedly a cheerful choice, with an upbeat tempo and optimistic lyrics. Most people in the audience probably tried not to dwell on how the lead singer died of a drug overdose, just as the group verged on the brink of stardom.

The blind man's shoulders shook in uneven rhythm. His head, formerly tilted toward his wife, now drooped forward. I couldn't hear over the joyful soundtrack, but clearly, the man was crying.

Still, neither Helen nor I said anything—to them, or to each other. The woman had done an awful, unforgivable thing to her husband, but we decided it wasn't our place to comment. An overheard whisper is sacred, like the bond of a confessional. We needn't involve ourselves in another couples' private drama—even if its language had been forced upon us, even if (and I knew Helen felt this more than I did) the whispered words had spoiled our afternoon's entertainment.

My wife and I didn't need to voice this decision. It was communicated though a strange telepathy, refined over many years in darkened movie houses: a released breath after an exciting chase scene; an imperceptible shift in posture to convey boredom; a barely audible sigh at a beautifully framed landscape. We felt from each other what we couldn't hear or see. Helen's soft gasp had told me, "It's not worth it." I tapped my foot on the floor, as if to say, "You're right. I'll let it go."

Like many patrons of the Midtowne Cinema, we were "credit sitters." We wouldn't stay to the very end, necessarily—even the greatest film buff has little interest in what stylist coiffed the extras' hair, or who catered lunches for the crew—but it was always worth sitting through the list of characters, to recognize an actor's name and think, "Ah, I thought I'd seen him before. Wasn't he the one in… ?"

But the blind man and his companion began to leave right away. The woman seemed to lift him from his seat. Together, they moved slowly into the aisle. Instead of guiding him, as she had upon entering the theater, it now seemed more like she was *carrying* him out, her arm around his back and supporting slumped, defeated shoulders. The house lights were raised slightly to help people exit, and I'd caught a brief glimpse of his sad expression. I wished his wife had given him more time to collect himself, before exposing his raw emotions to the bright, sighted world of the lobby.

In a bizarre, random thought, I wondered if she'd purposely ushered him out before the rapid scroll of names and obscure job titles made a mockery of her remarkable skill. She would have short-circuited trying to keep up, like an early computer instructed to divide by zero.

Helen and I waited through the rest of the cast list, maintaining our silence even as the real-life names of "Florist" and "Waiter #4" floated toward the ceiling. About a third of the seats were still occupied when we stood to leave. After we pushed through the double doors into the lobby, my wife took a detour to the side: another trip to the ladies' room.

I dropped our empty water bottles into the recycle bin, then stood aside near the front doors. A line stretched outside, people buying tickets for the next show, and a steady trickle emerged from the auditorium doors on either side of the concessions counter. They blinked their eyes against fresh light, and all of them had pleasant expressions on their faces. Some people, at least, had been allowed to enjoy the film.

Beside an archway to the side hallway, I spotted the blind man. He stood by himself, slouched slightly against the wall. His head bobbled indecisively on the thin neck, as if longing to lean toward his wife's voice.

The opportunity presented itself. Despite what Helen and I tacitly agreed to, I moved toward him, my tennis shoes soundless—to me, at least—over the lobby's worn beige carpet.

"Excuse me," I said, but before I got the words out, his face turned toward me. He looked older than I'd imagined, overhead lamps etching shadows under the wrinkles in his skin. Although he was dressed in casual clothes—a light blue short-sleeve shirt and twill pants—he stiffened into a formal posture which, sadly, made him seem more foolish than dignified. His eyes were expectant and vacant and puffy red.

"Excuse me," I repeated, stalling for time even as I feared one of our wives would return from the ladies' room. My voice was loud, but I couldn't control it—as if I needed to pierce the fog of his blank stare. "I just, um, I just wanted to say…"

"Yes." It was the first time I'd heard him speak. His voice sounded weakened by his bout of tears, with barely strength to encourage me to continue.

People walked past us, oblivious. I squinted down the hallway toward the rest rooms. No sign yet of Helen, or the awful, whispering woman.

"The movie didn't end the way she described it to you." I blurted out the rest, before I lost my nerve. "The couple was happy at the end. Still in love. I thought you should know."

The blind man didn't react at first. Then I saw something like relief: his body relaxing, the tight line of his mouth loosening as if he sought permission to smile.

He swung his left arm to the side with a flourish, cupped his right arm over his stomach and bent his torso forward in a deep, exaggerated bow. He straightened, then spoke with a firmness I hadn't expected: "Oh, thank you. Thank you *so* much. I don't know what I would have done without your help."

It was a parody of gratefulness. The sarcasm settled into his face, an expression of scorn that immediately dismissed me from his presence.

Luckily, I spotted Helen approaching. I crossed to meet her in the archway, and I steered her across the lobby, keeping her distant from the blind man. As we reached the sidewalk outside, before the theater door swung shut with a rusty squeak, I thought I heard the blind man thank me again.

At dinner, we didn't discuss the film as we normally would. No revisiting favorite lines of dialogue, seeking subtleties in the script; no ranking of the performances or nuanced comparisons to films of similar type. Instead, we tore small pieces off store-bought rolls or rearranged silk flowers, their petals dusty in a white ceramic vase. We took turns saying we were hungry, wondering aloud when the minestrone soup would arrive.

Finally, Helen broached the subject. "I don't know what I was thinking. I wish I hadn't sat there."

"No need to blame yourself," I said. "I hadn't even noticed the guy was blind. And who'd ever expect his wife to describe the whole film for him?"

"I wish I hadn't sat there," Helen repeated.

That was pretty much all we needed to say about the matter. After the main course, though, when we decided *not* to stay for dessert or coffee, the waitress took too long to bring our check. In the awkward silence, I weakened and decided to confess. I told her about my curious encounter with the blind man in the lobby.

Helen shivered, like it was the most frightening story she'd ever heard.

Let me tell you about a different movie. It's another romantic comedy, this time about a long-married couple who stop everything so they can take a month to travel the world together. The man is reluctant at first, afraid to fall behind on his work accounts, and it's not their anniversary or either of their birthdays, and he's never been that spontaneous anyway. But she convinces him, and she's already booked the flights, the hotels, the cruise ship, and she's bought books and brochures and printed off pages and pages of advice from travel websites: little restaurants tourists didn't visit; special tours given only Sunday afternoons, *if* you know who to ask; "must see" lists for each city, itineraries to fill each day.

Before they leave, she surprises him with a wrapped package, and it's a digital camera with lots of storage space, so they can take as many pictures as they want. He'd never believed in photographs, thought taking them distracted from the experience of travel. On previous trips, other tourists were a nuisance with cameras, blocking his view or popping a flash to interrupt the soft calm of natural light. But it's a thoughtful gift, and he finds out he enjoys it: framing a waterfall or mountain or monument, with her in the foreground, and the fun of checking through the pictures that night in the hotel.

He had agreed to the trip just to please her, but soon her enthusiasm wins him over, and he ends up loving it. To be a better comedy, though, things need to go wrong: missed connections, bungled hotel reservations; a random "I'll have that" finger pointed at a menu, and lamb brains arrive at the table, or a five-pound exotic fish with bubble eyes staring up from the plate; or ill-pronounced words to a French street juggler—*fou* instead of *feu*, for instance, ("You called him crazy, m'sieu!")—and hilarious misunderstandings ensue.

But there's none of that. Similar things occur, but not often, nothing major. A forgotten toothbrush, rather than a lost passport. She's a fantastic tour guide, and he loves her more than ever. The trip is unforgettable, revitalizing. Okay, it's not that great a film: no conflict, no complications. But it's sweet.

After the trip, he has the memories, and the pictures. The woman smiles in all of them—leaning against the ship rail during their Hawaii cruise, the Nepali coast in the background; tiny in one corner, hair windswept, with the Grand Canyon vast behind her; at a table outside a Venice cafe, a glass of local vintage raised for the camera, and for him.

He's printed all the photos, hundreds of them. He fans a stack, like a cartoon flip-book, and the world rushes behind his wife's constant, smiling image. The heavy paper stock creates a gust of air, almost like a whisper.

Bladder cancer, it says. *Inoperable.*

Everything had seemed like one of Helen's fluffy, happy-ending movies. She kept it that way as long as she could.

The specialists call it bladder cancer, if that's where the tumor originates, even if the disease spreads to other parts of the body. Helen's frequent visits to the bathroom were a symptom, but the change happened gradually, and neither of us had noticed. By the time she got the diagnosis, things had progressed too far. Even with radical treatment, the prognosis wasn't good. When she found out, she decided not to tell me. Instead, she announced, "Let's take a trip!"

If this were really a movie, that omission makes for a more significant story. We were always a happy couple, but I was especially happy during that month-long vacation. *I* was happy. I can only imagine what really went on in Helen's mind, despite those ever-present smiles. Thoughts of aggressive therapy when she returned home; dread of long hospital days, pain still sharp through medicated fog. If she was lucky, maybe, a swift decline.

The trip wasn't for her benefit, but for mine. A beautiful, poignant farewell gift. And always, beneath the sweet surface of her romantic comedy, an awful, unnarrated tragedy.

I hate myself for not noticing it. Helen spared me the knowledge, as long as she could.

One day near the end, from the intensive care bed that she'd dreaded in silence, she revealed something very strange. I almost wish she hadn't told me—though I can understand why she needed to. Something else happened that day at the theater, after we sat behind the blind man and his talkative companion. In the ladies' room, when the film was over, Helen heard that whispered voice again, from the adjoining stall. The voice was clear and *directed*; Helen knew she was the only one who could hear it. The whisper began at the precise moment when my wife strained and began to empty her bladder. Helen remembered exactly what the voice had said: "It doesn't hurt. It's just a minor inconvenience, so you put it off. By the time you get to a doctor, it will be too late." As she repeated the words, Helen's voice, weakened by the cancer and the treatments, achieved a perfect, uncanny duplication of the woman's urgent whisper.

The hospital seemed instantly more sterile and hopeless and cold. Helen passed away that night, while I was home asleep.

And now, all my movies are sad. I go to them alone. I want to feel Helen's presence in the empty seat next to me, embrace those half-conscious signals we always shared in the dark. I want to tap the top of her hand gently, three times.

Instead, I lean my head slightly to the side. A whispered voice distorts the context of the film, makes the story all about me and my loss. It changes the ending, twists it into something horrible.

LONEGAN'S LUCK
BY STEPHEN GRAHAM JONES

Stephen Graham Jones has published six novels, including *Demon Theory* and the Shirley Jackson Award finalist *The Long Trial of Nolan Dugatti*, one collection, *Bleed Into Me: A Book of Stories* with another, *The Ones That Almost Got Away* forthcoming from Prime Books. His short fiction has been published in *Cemetery Dance*, *Asimov's Science Fiction Magazine*, *Brutarian*, *Juked*, and almost one hundred other magazines. He teaches in the MFA program at The University of Colorado at Boulder. More at http://demontheory.net.

Like every month, the horse was new. A mare, pushing fifteen years old. Given his druthers, Lonegan would have picked a mule, of course, one that had had its balls cut late, so there was still some fight in it, but, when it came down to it, it had either been the mare or yoking himself up to the buckboard, leaning forward until his fingertips touched the ground.

Twenty years ago, he would have tried it, just to make a girl laugh.

Now, he took what was available, made do.

And anyway, from the way the mare kept trying to swing wide, head back into the shade of town, this wasn't going to be her first trip across the Arizona Territories. Maybe she'd even know where the water was, if it came down to that. Where the Apache weren't.

Lonegan brushed the traces across her flank and she pulled ahead, the wagon creaking, all his crates shifting around behind him, the jars and bottles inside touching shoulders. The straw they were packed in was going to be the mare's forage, if all the red baked earth ahead of them was as empty as it looked.

As they picked their way through it, Lonegan explained to the mare that he never meant for it to be this way. That this was the last time. But then he trailed off. Up ahead a black column was coming into view.

Buzzards.

Lonegan nodded, smiled.

What was dead there was pungent enough to be drawing them in for miles.

"What do you think, old girl?" he said to the mare. She didn't answer. Lonegan nodded to himself again, checked the scattergun under his seat, and pulled the mare's head towards the swirling buzzards. "Professional curiosity," he told her, then laughed because it was a joke.

The town he'd left that morning wasn't going on any map.

The one ahead of him, as far as he knew, probably wasn't on any map either. But it would be there. They always were.

When the mare tried shying away from the smell of death, Lonegan got down, talked into her ear, and tied his handkerchief across her eyes. The last little bit, he led her by the bridle, then hobbled her upwind.

The buzzards were a greasy black coat, moved like old men walking barefoot on the hot ground.

Instead of watching them, Lonegan traced the ridges of rock all around.

"Well," he finally said, and leaned into the washed-out little hollow.

The buzzards lifted their wings in something like menace, but Lonegan knew better. He slung rocks at the few that wouldn't take to the sky. They just backed off, their dirty mouths open in challenge.

Lonegan held his palm out to them, explained that this wasn't going to take long.

He was right: the dead guy was the one Lonegan had figured it would be. The thin deputy with the three-pocketed vest. He still had the vest on, had been able to crawl maybe twenty paces from where his horse had died. The horse was a gelding, a long-legged bay with a white diamond on its forehead, three white socks. Lonegan distinctly remembered having appreciated that horse. But now it had been run to death, had died with white foam on its flanks, blood blowing from its nostrils, eyes wheeling around, the deputy spurring him on, deeper into the heat, to warn the next town over.

Lonegan looked from the horse to the deputy. The buzzards were going after the gelding, of course.

It made Lonegan sick.

He walked up to the deputy, facedown in the dirt, already rotting, and rolled him over.

"Not quite as fast as you thought you were, eh deputy?" he said, then shot him in the mouth. Twice.

It was a courtesy.

Nine days later, all the straw in his crates handfed to the mare, his jars and bottles tied to each other with twine to keep them from shattering, Lonegan looked into the distance and nodded: a town was rising up from the dirt. A perfect little town.

He snubbed the mare to a shuffling stop, turned his head to the side to make sure they weren't pulling any dust in. That would give them away.

Then he just stared at the town.

Finally the mare snorted a breath of hot air in, blew it back out.

"I know," Lonegan said. "I know."

According to the scrap of paper he'd been marking, it was only Friday.

"One more night," he told the mare, and angled her over to some scrub, a ring of blackened stones in the packed ground.

He had to get there on a Saturday.

It wasn't like one more night was going to kill him, anyway. Or the mare.

He parked the buckboard on the town side of the ring of stones, so they wouldn't see his light, find him before he was ready.

Before unhooking the mare, he hobbled her. Four nights ago, she wouldn't have tried running. But now there was the smell of other horses in the air. Hay, maybe. Water.

And then there was the missing slice of meat Lonegan had cut from her haunch three nights ago.

It had been shallow, and he'd packed it with a medley of poultices from his crates, folded the skin back over, but still, he was pretty sure she'd been more than slightly offended.

Lonegan smiled at her, shook his head no, that she didn't need to worry. He could wait one more day for solid food, for water that wasn't briny and didn't taste like rust.

Or—no: he was going to get a *cake*, this time. All for himself. A big white one, slathered in whatever kind of frosting they had.

And all the water he could drink.

Lonegan nodded to himself about this, leaned back into his bedroll, and watched the sparks from the fire swirl up past his battered coffee pot.

When it was hot enough, he offered a cup to the mare.

She flared her nostrils, stared at him.

Before turning in, Lonegan emptied the grains from his cup into her open wound and patted it down, told her it was an old medicine man trick. That he knew them all.

He fell asleep thinking of the cake.

The mare slept standing up.

By noon the next day, he was set up on the only street in town. Not in front of the saloon but the mercantile. Because the men bellied up to the bar would walk any distance for the show. The people just in town for flour or salt though, you had to step into their path some. Make them aware of you.

Lonegan had polished his boots, shaved his jaw, pulled the hair on his chin down into a waxy point.

He waited until twenty or so people had gathered before reaching up under the side of the buckboard, for the secret handle.

He pulled it, stepped away with a flourish, and the panel on the buckboard opened up like a staircase, all the bottles and jars and felt bags of medicine already tied into place.

One person in the crowd clapped twice.

Lonegan didn't look around, just started talking about how the blue oil in the clear jar—he'd pilfered it from a barber shop in Missouri—how, if rubbed into the scalp twice daily and let cook in the sun, it would make a head of hair grow back, if you happened to be missing one. Full, black, Indian hair. But you had to be careful not to use too much, especially in these parts.

Now somebody in the crowd laughed.

Inside, Lonegan smiled, then went on.

The other stuff, fox urine he called it, though assured them it wasn't, it was for the women specifically. He couldn't go into the particulars in mixed company though, of course. This was a Christian settlement, right?

He looked around when no one answered.

"Amen," a man near the front finally said.

Lonegan nodded.

"Thought so," he said. "Some towns I come across… well. Mining towns, y'know?"

Five, maybe six people nodded, kept their lips pursed.

The fox urine was going to be sold out by supper, Lonegan knew. Not to any of the women, either.

Facing the crowd now, the buckboard framed by the mercantile, like it was just an extension of the mercantile, Lonegan cycled through his other bottles, the rest of his jars, the creams and powders and rare leaves. Twice a man in the crowd raised his hand to stop the show, make a purchase, but Lonegan held his palm up. Not yet, not yet.

But then, towards mid-afternoon, the white-haired preacher finally showed up, the good book held in both hands before him like a shield.

Lonegan resisted acknowledging him. But just barely.

They were in the same profession, after all.

And the preacher was the key to all this, too.

So Lonegan went on hawking, selling, testifying, the sweat running down the back of his neck to wet his shirt. He took his hat off, wiped his forehead with the back of his sleeve, and eyed the crowd now, shrugged.

"If you'll excuse me a brief moment," he said, and stepped halfway behind the ass-end of the buckboard, swigged from a tall, clear bottle of nearly-amber liquid.

He swallowed, lifted the bottle again, and drew deep on it, nodded as he screwed the cap back on.

"What is that?" a woman asked.

Lonegan looked up as if caught, said, "Nothing, ma'am. Something of my own making."

"We—" another man started, stepping forward.

Lonegan shook his head no, cut him off: "It's not *that* kind of my own making, sir. Any man drinks whiskey in the heat like this is asking for trouble, am I right?"

The man stepped back without ever breaking eye contact.

"Then what is it?" a boy asked.

Lonegan looked down to him, smiled.

"Just something an old—a man from the Old Country taught this to me on his deathbed. It's kind of like… you know how a strip of dried meat, it's like the whole steak twisted into a couple of bites?"

The boy nodded.

Lonegan lifted the bottle up, let it catch the sunlight. Said, "This is like that. Except it's the good part of water. The cold part."

A man in the crowd muttered a curse. The dismissal cycled through, all around Lonegan. He waited for it to abate, then shrugged, tucked the bottle back into the buckboard. "It's not for sale anyway," he said, stepping back around to the bottles and jars.

"Why not?" a man in a thick leather vest asked.

By the man's bearing, Lonegan assumed he was law of some kind.

"Personal stock," Lonegan explained. "And—anyway. There's not enough. It takes about fourteen months to get even a few bottles distilled the right way."

"Then I take that to mean you'd be averse to sampling it out?" the man said.

Lonegan nodded, tried to look apologetic.

The man shook his head, scratched deep in his matted beard, and stepped forward, shouldered Lonegan out of the way.

A moment later, he'd grubbed the bottle up from the bedclothes Lonegan had stuffed it in.

With everybody watching, he unscrewed the cap, wiped his lips clean, and took a long pull off the bottle.

What it was was water with a green juniper leaf at the bottom. The inside of the bottle cap dabbed with honey. A couple drops of laudanum, for the soft headrush, and a peppermint candy ground up, to hide the laudanum.

The man lowered the bottle, swallowed what was left in his mouth, and smiled.

Grudgingly, Lonegan agreed to take two dollars for what was left in the bottle. And then everybody was calling for it.

"I don't—" he started, stepping up onto the hub of his wheel to try to reach everybody, "I don't have—" but they were surging forward.

"*Okay*," he said, for the benefit of the people up front, and stepped down, hauled a half-case of the water up over the side of the buckboard.

Which was when the preacher spoke up.

The crowd fell silent like church.

"I can't let you do this to these good people," the preacher said.

"I think—" Lonegan said, his stutter a practiced thing, "I think you have me confused with the k-kind of gentlemen who—"

"I'm not confused at all, sir," the preacher said, both his hands still clasping the Bible.

Lonegan stared at him, stared at him, then took a respectful step forward.

"What could convince you then, Brother?" he said. "Take my mare there. See that wound on her haunch? Would you believe that four days ago that was done by an old blunderbuss, fired on accident?"

"By you?"

"I was cleaning it."

The preacher nodded, waiting.

Lonegan went on. "You could reach your hand into the hole, I'm saying."

"And your medicine fixed it?" the preacher anticipated, his voice rising.

Lonegan palmed a smoky jar from the shelves, said, "This poultice, yes sir. A man named Running Bear showed me how to take the caul around the heart of a dog and grind—"

The preacher blew air out his nose.

"He was Oglala Sioux," Lonegan added, and let that settle.

The preacher just stared.

Lonegan looked around at the faces in the crowd, starting to side with the preacher. More out of habit than argument. But still.

Lonegan nodded, backed off, hands raised. Was quiet long enough to let them know he was just thinking of this: "These—these snake oil men you've taken me for, Brother. People. A despicable breed. What would you say characterizes them?"

When the preacher didn't answer, a man in the crowd did: "They sell things."

"I sell things," Lonegan agreed.

"Medicine," a woman clarified.

"Remedies," Lonegan corrected, nodding to her to show he meant no insult. She held his eyes.

"What else?" Lonegan said, to all.

It was the preacher who answered: "You'll be gone tomorrow."

"—before any of our hair can get grown in," an old man added, sweeping his hat off to show his bald head.

Lonegan smiled wide, nodded. Cupped a small bottle of the blue oil from its place on the panel, twirled it to the man.

He caught it, stared at Lonegan.

"I'm not leaving," Lonegan said.

"Yeah, well—" a man started.

"I'm *not*," Lonegan said, some insult in his voice now. "And, you know what? To prove it, today and today only, I'll be accepting checks, or notes. Just write your name and how much you owe me on any scrap of paper—here, I've got paper myself, I'll even supply that. I won't come to collect until you're satisfied."

As one, a grin spread across the crowd's face.

"How long this take to work?" the bald man asked, holding his bottle of blue up.

"I've seen it take as long as six days, to be honest."

The old man raised his eyebrows. They were bushy, white.

People were already pushing forward again.

Lonegan stepped up onto his hub, waved his arms for them to slow down, slow down. That he wanted to make a gift first.

It was a tightly-woven cloth bag the size of a man's head.

He handed it to the preacher, said, "Brother."

The preacher took it, looked from Lonegan to the string tying the bag closed.

"Traveling like I do," Lonegan said, "I make my tithe where I can. With what I can."

The preacher opened it.

"The sacrament?" he said.

"Just wafers for now," Lonegan said. "You'll have to bless them, of course."

Slowly at first, then altogether, the crowd started clapping.

The preacher tied the bag shut, extended his hand to Lonegan.

By dinner, there wasn't a drop of fox urine in his possession.

When the two women came to collect him for church the next morning, Lonegan held his finger up, told them he'd be right there. He liked to say a few prayers beforehand.

The woman lowered their bonneted heads that they understood, then one of them added that his mare had run off in the night, it looked like.

"She does that," Lonegan said with a smile, and closed the door, held it there.

Just what he needed: a goddamn prophetic horse.

Instead of praying then, or going to the service, Lonegan packed his spare clothes tight in his bedroll, shoved it under the bed then made the bed so nobody would have any call to look under it. Before he ever figured this whole thing out, he'd lost two good suits just because he'd failed to stretch a sheet across a mattress.

But now, now his bedroll was still going to be there Monday, or Tuesday, or whenever he came for it.

Next, he angled the one chair in the room over to the window, waited for the congregation to shuffle back out into the streets in their Sunday best.

Today, the congregation was going to be the whole town. Because they felt guilty about the money they'd spent yesterday, and because they knew this morning there was going to be a communion.

In a Baptist church, that happened little enough that it was an event.

With luck, nobody would even have noticed Lonegan's absence, come looking for him.

With luck, they'd all be guilty enough to palm an extra wafer, let it go soft against the roofs of their mouths.

After a lifetime of eating coarse hunks of bread, the wafer would be candy to them. So white it had to be pure.

Lonegan smiled, propped his boots up on the windowsill, and tipped back the bottle of rotgut until his eyes watered. If he'd been drinking just to feel good, it would have been sipping bourbon. For this, though, he needed to be drunk, and smell like it.

Scattered on the wood-plank floor all around him, fallen like leaves, were the promissory notes for yesterday's sales.

He wasn't going to need them to collect.

It was a funny thing.

Right about what he figured was the middle of lunch for most of the town—he didn't even know its name, he laughed to himself—he pulled the old Colt up from his lap, laid the bottom of the barrel across the back of his left wrist, and aimed in turn at each of the six panes in his window, blew them out into the street.

Ten minutes and two reloads later, he was fast in jail.

"Don't get too comfortable in there now," the bearded man Lonegan had made for the law said. He was wearing a stiff collar from church, a tin star on his chest.

Lonegan smiled, leaned back on his cot, and shook his head no, he wouldn't.

"When's dinner?" he slurred out, having to bite back a smile, the cake a definite thing in his mind again.

The Sheriff didn't respond, just walked out.

Behind him, Lonegan nodded.

Sewed into the lining of his right boot were all the tools he would need to pick the simple lock of the cell.

Sewed into his belt, as back-up, was a few thimblefuls of gunpowder wrapped in thin oilcloth, in case the lock was jammed. In Lonegan's teeth, a sulfurhead match that the burly man had never even questioned.

Lonegan balanced it in one of the cracks of the wall.

He was in the best room in town, now.

That afternoon he woke to a woman staring at him. She was sideways—*he* was sideways, on the cot.

He pushed the heel of his right hand into one eye then the other, sat up.

"Ma'am," he said, having to turn his head sideways to swallow.

She was slight but tall, her face lined by the weather it looked like. A hard woman to get a read on.

"I came to pay," she said.

Lonegan lowered his head to smile, had to grip the edge of his cot with both hands to keep from spilling down onto the floor.

"My father," the woman went on, finding her voice, "he—I don't know why. He's rubbing that blue stuff onto his head. He smells like a barbershop."

Lonegan looked up to this woman, wasn't sure if he should smile or not.

She was, anyway.

"You don't see its efficacy," he said, "you don't got to pay. Ma'am."

She stared at him about this, finally said, "Can you even spell that?"

"What?"

"Efficacy."

Now it was Logan's turn to just stare.

"Got a first name?" she said.

"Lonegan," Lonegan shrugged.

"The rest of it?"

"Just Lonegan."

"That's how it is then?"

"Alone, again…" he went on, breaking his name down into words for her.

"I get it," she told him.

"Regular-like, you mean?"

She caught his meaning about this as well, set her teeth, but then shook her head no, smiled instead.

"I don't know what kind of—what kind of affair you're trying to pull off here, Mister Alone Again."

"My horse ran off," Lonegan said, standing, pulling his face close to the bars now. "Think I'm apt to make a fast getaway in these?"

For illustration, he lifted his right boot. It was down at heel. Shiny on top, bare underneath.

"You meant to get thrown in here, I mean," she said. "Shooting up Molly's best room like that."

"Who are you, you don't mind my asking?"

"I'm the daughter of the man you swindled yesterday afternoon. I'm just here to complete the transaction."

"I told you—"

"And I'm telling you. I'm not going to be indebted to a man like you. Not again."

Lonegan cocked his head over to her, narrowed his eyes. "Again?" he said.

"How much it going to cost me?"

"Say my name."

"How much?"

Lonegan tongued his lower lip out, was falling in love just a little bit, he thought. Wishing he wasn't on this side of the bars, anyway.

"You like the service this morning?" he asked.

"I don't go to church with my father anymore," the woman said. "Who do you think swindled us the first time?"

Lonegan smiled, liked it.

"Anyway," the woman went on. "My father tends to bring enough church home with him each Sunday to last us the week through. And then some."

"What's your name?" Lonegan said, watching her.

"That supposed to give you some power over me, if you know?"

"So you think I'm real then?"

Lonegan shrugged, waiting for her to try to back out of the corner she'd wedged herself into.

"You can call me Mary," she said, lifting her chin at the end.

"I like Jezebel better," he said. "Girl who didn't go to church."

"Do you even know the bible?" she asked.

"I know I'm glad you didn't go to church this morning."

"How much, Mister *Lonegan*?"

He nodded thanks, said, "For you, Jezebel. For you—"

"I don't want a deal."

"Two dollars."

"They sold for two bits, I heard."

"Special deal for a special lady."

She held his stare for a moment longer then slammed her coin purse down on the only desk in the room, started counting out coins.

Two dollars was a full week's work, Lonegan figured.

"What do you do?" he said, watching her.

"Give money to fools, it would seem," she muttered.

Lonegan hissed a laugh, was holding the bars on each side of his face, all his weight there.

She stood with the money in her hand.

"I *bake*," she said—spit, really.

Lonegan felt everything calming inside him.

"Confectionary stuff?" he said.

"Why?" she said, stepping forward. "You come here for a matrimony?"

"...Mary Lonegan," Lonegan sung out, like trying it out some.

She held the money out, her palm down so she'd just have to open her fingers.

Lonegan worked it into a brush of skin anyway, said at the last moment, "Or you could just—you could stay and talk. In the next cell, maybe."

"It cost me two more dollars not to?" she said back, her hand to her coin purse again, then stared at Lonegan until he had to look away. To the heavy oak door that opened onto the street.

The Sheriff was stepping through, fumbling for the peg on the wall, to hang his holster on.

"Annie," he said to the woman.

Her top lip rose in what Lonegan took for anger, disgust. Not directed at the lawman, but at her own name spoken aloud.

"'Annie,'" Lonegan repeated.

"You know this character?" the man said, cutting his eyes to Lonegan.

"We go back a long ways, Sheriff," Lonegan said.

Annie laughed through her nose, pushed past the lawman, stepped out into the sunlight.

Lonegan watched the door until it was closed all the way, then studied the floor.

Finally he nodded, slipped his belt off with one hand, ferreted the slender oilcloth of gunpowder out.

"For obvious reasons, she didn't bake it into a cake," he said, holding the oil-cloth up for the lawman to see.

"Annie?" the lawman said, incredulous.

"If that's the name you know her by," Lonegan said, then dropped the oilcloth bag onto the stone floor.

The lawman approached, fingered the black powder up to his nose. Looked to the door as well.

By nightfall, Annie Jorgensson was in the cell next to Lonegan's.

"Was hoping you'd bring some of those pastries you've been making," he said to her, nodding down to the apron she was still wearing, the flour dusting her forearms.

"Was hoping you'd be dead by now, maybe," she said back, brushing her arms clean.

"You could have brought something, I mean."

"That why you lied about me?"

"What I said, I said to save your life. A little courtesy might be in order."

"You think talking to you's going to save me?" she said. "Rather be dead, thanks."

Lonegan leaned back on his cot, closed his eyes.

All dinner had been was some hardtack the Sheriff had had in his saddlebag for what tasted like weeks.

Lonegan had made himself eat all of it, though, every bite.

Not for strength, but out of spite. Because he knew what was coming.

"You're sure you didn't go to church this morning?" he said to Annie Jorgensson.

She didn't answer. It didn't matter much if she had though, he guessed, and was just lying to him about it, like she had with her name. Either way there was still a wall of bars between them. And he didn't know what he was going to do with her anyway, after. Lead her by the hand into the saloon, pour her a drink?

No, it was better if she was lying, really. If she was a closet Baptist.

It would keep him from having to hold her down with his knee, shoot her in the face.

Ten minutes after a light Lonegan couldn't see the source of was doused, the horses at the livery took to screaming.

Lonegan nodded, watched for Annie's reaction.

She just sat there.

"You alive?" he called over.

Her eyes flicked up to him, but that was all.

Yes.

Soon enough the horses kicked down a gate or a wall, started crashing through the town. One of them ran up onto the boardwalk it sounded like, then, afraid of the sound of its own hooves, shied away, into a window. After that, Lonegan couldn't tell. There was gunfire, for the horse maybe. Or not.

The whole time he watched Annie.

"Mary," he said to her once, in play.

"Jezebel to you," she hissed back.

He smiled.

"What's happening out there?" she asked, finally.

"I'm in here," Lonegan shrugged back to her. "You saying this doesn't happen every night?"

She stood, leaned against the bars at the front of her cell.

One time before, Lonegan had made it through with a cellmate. Or, in the next cell, like this.

He'd left that one there, though. Not turned, like the rest of the town, but starved inside of four days anyway. Five if he ate the stuffing from his mattress.

It had been interesting, though, the man's reactions—how his back stiffened with each scream. The line of saliva that descended from his lip to the ground.

"I've got to piss," Lonegan said.

Annie didn't turn around.

Lonegan aimed it at the trap under the window, was just shaking off when a face appeared, nearly level with his own.

It was one of the men from the crowd.

His eyes were wild, roving, his cheeks already shrunken, making his teeth look larger. Around his mouth, blood.

He pulled at the bars of the window like the animal he was.

"You're already dead," Lonegan said to him, then raised his finger in the shape of a pistol, shot the man between the eyes.

The man grunted, shuffled off.

"That was Sid Masterson," Annie said from behind him. "If you're wondering, I mean."

"Think he was past the point where an introduction would have done any good," Lonegan said, turning to catch her eye.

"This is supposed to impress me?" Annie said, suddenly standing at the wall of bars between them.

"You're alive," Lonegan told her.

"What are they?" she said, lifting her chin to take in the whole town.

Lonegan shrugged, rubbed the side of his nose with the side of his finger.

"Some people just get caught up when they're dying, I guess," he said. "Takes them longer."

"How long?"

Lonegan smiled, said, "A day. They don't last so long in the sun. I don't know why."

"But you can't have got everybody."

"They'll get who I didn't."

"You've done this before."

"Once or twice, I suppose. My oxen gets in the ditch like everybody else's…"

For a long time, Annie just stared at him. Finally she said, "We would have given you whatever, y'know?"

"A good Christian town," Lonegan recited.

"You didn't have to do this, I mean."

"They were asking for it," Lonegan said, shrugging it true. "They paid me, even, if I recall correctly."

"It was that poppy water."

Lonegan raised his eyebrows to her.

"I know the taste," she said. "What was it masking?"

In reply, Lonegan pursed his lips, pointed with them out to the town: that.

"My father?" Annie said, then.

Lonegan kept looking at the front door.

Her father. That was definitely going to be a complication. There was a reason he usually passed the night alone, he told himself.

But she was a *baker*.

Back in her kitchen there was probably all manner of frosting and sugar.

Lonegan opened his mouth to ask her where she lived, but then thought better of it. He'd find her place anyway. After tonight, he'd have all week to scavenge through town. Every house, every building.

Towards the end of the week, even, the horses would come back, from downwind. They'd be skittish like the mare had been—skittish that he was dead like the others had been, just not lying down yet—but then he'd have oats in a sack, and, even if they had been smart enough to run away, they were still just horses.

Or, he hoped—this time—a *mule*.

Something with personality.

They usually tasted better anyway.

He came to again some time before dawn. He could tell by the quality of light sifting in through the bars of his window. There were no birds singing, though. And the smell. He was used to the smell by now.

Miles east of town, he knew, a tree was coated with buzzards.

Soon they would rise into an oily black mass, ride the heat into town, drift down onto the bodies that would be in the street by now.

Like with the deputy Lonegan had found, though, the buzzards would know better than to eat. Even to them, this kind of dead tasted wrong.

With luck, maybe one of the horses would have run its lungs bloody for them, collapsed in a heap of meat.

With luck, it'd be that onery damn mare.

They'd start on her haunch, of course, finish what Lonegan had started.

He nodded, pulled a sharp hank of air up his nose, and realized what had woke him: the oak door. It was moving, creaking.

In the next cell, Annie was already at the bars of her cell, holding her breath.

"They can't get in," Lonegan told her.

She didn't look away from the door.

"What were you dreaming about there?" she said, her voice flat and low.

Lonegan narrowed his eyes at her.

Dream?

He looked at his hands as if they might have been involved, then touched his face.

It was wet.

He shook his head no, stood, and the oak door swung open.

Standing in the space it had been was the Sheriff.

He'd seen better days.

Annie fell back to her cot, pulled the green blanket up to her mouth.

Lonegan didn't move, just inspected. It wasn't often he got to see one of the shufflers when they were still shuffling. This one, he surmised, he'd fallen down in some open place. While he was turning, too, another had fed on him, it looked like. His face on the right side was down to the bone, one of his arms gone, just a ragged sleeve now.

Not that he was in a state to care about any of that.

This was probably the time he usually came into work on Monday.

It was all he knew anymore.

"Hey," Lonegan called out to it, to be sure.

The thing had to look around for the source of the sound.

When he found it, Lonegan nodded.

"No… " Annie was saying through her blanket.

"He can't get through," Lonegan said again. "They can't—keys, tools, guns."

For a long time, then—it could sense the sun coming, Lonegan thought—the thing just stood there, rasping air in and out.

Annie was hysterical in a quiet way, pushing on the floor with her feet over and over, like trying to back herself out of this.

Lonegan watched like she was a new thing to him.

Maybe if he was just seeing his first one too, though. But… no. Even then—it had been a goat—even then he'd known what was happening. It was the goat he'd been trying all his mixtures out on first, because it would eat anything. And because it couldn't aim a pistol.

When it had died, Lonegan had nodded, looked at the syrup in the wooden tube, already drying into a floury paste, and been about to sling it out into the creek with all the other bad mixes when the goat had kicked, its one good eye rolling in its skull, a sound clawing from its throat that had pushed Lonegan up onto his buckboard.

Finally, when the horse he'd had then wouldn't calm down, Lonegan had had to shoot the goat.

The goat had looked up to the barrel like a child, too.

It was the same look the thing in the doorway had now. Like it didn't understand just how it had got to be where it was.

The front of its pants were wet, from the first time it had relaxed into death.

Lonegan watched it.

In its other hand—and this he'd never seen—was one of the bottles of what Annie had called poppy water.

The thing was holding it by the neck like it knew what it was.

When it lifted it to its mouth, Annie forgot how to breathe a little.

Lonegan turned to her, then to the thing, and got it: she knew what that water tasted like, still thought it *was* the water, doing all this to her town.

He smiled to himself, came back to the thing, the shuffler.

It was making its way across the floor, one of its ankles at a bad angle.

Now Annie was screaming, stuffing the blanket into her mouth. The thing noticed, came to her cell.

"You don't want to—" Lonegan started, but it was too late.

Make them take an interest in you, he was going to say.

Like anything with an appetite, jerky motions drew its attention.

Annie was practically convulsing.

Lonegan came to the wall of bars between them, reached for her hand, just to let her know she was alive, but, at the touch she cringed away, her eyes wild, breath shallow.

"You should have gone to church," Lonegan said, out loud he guessed, because she looked over, a question on her face, but by then the thing was at the bars. It wasn't strong enough to come through them of course, but it didn't understand things the way a man would either.

Slowly, as if *trying* to, it wedged its head between two of the bars—leading with its mouth—and started to push and pull through.

The first thing to go was its one good eye. It ran down its cheek.

Next was its jaw, then its skull, and still it kept coming, got halfway through before it didn't have anything left.

Annie had never been in danger. Not from the thing, anyway.

She wasn't so much conscious anymore either, though.

For a long time, Lonegan sat on the edge of his cot, his head leaned down into his hands, the thing in the bars still breathing somehow, even when the sunlight spilled through, started turning its skin to leather.

It was time.

Lonegan worked his pantsleg up, slid the two picks out, had the door to his cell open almost as fast as if he'd had the key.

The first thing he did was take the shotgun off the wall, hold the barrel to the base of the thing's skull. But then Annie started to stir. Lonegan focused in on her, nodded, and turned the gun around, slammed the butt into the thing until its head lolled forward, the skin at the back of the neck tearing into a mouth of sorts, that smiled with a ripping sound.

When the thing fell, it gave Lonegan a clear line on Annie.

She was dotted with black blood now.

He might as well have just shot the thing, he figured.

"Well," he said to her.

She was crying, hiding inside herself.

"You don't catch it from the blood," he told her, "don't worry," but she wasn't listening anymore.

Lonegan pulled the keys up from the thing's belt, and unlocked her cell, let the door swing wide.

"But—but—" she said.

Lonegan shrugged, disgusted with her.

"*What?*" he said, finally. "I saved your life, Mary, Jezebel. Annie Jorgensson."

She shook her head no, more of a jerk than a gesture.

Lonegan twirled the shotgun by the trigger guard, held it down along his leg.

The easy thing to do now would be to point it at her, get this over with.

Except she was the cake lady.

For the first time in years, he wasn't sure if he'd be able to stomach the cake, later, if he did this to her now.

"What's the name of this town?" he said to her.

She looked up, the muscles in her face dancing.

"Name?"

"This place."

For a long time she didn't understand the question, then she nodded, said it: "Gultree."

Lonegan nodded, said, "I don't think I'll be staying in Gultree much longer, Miss Jorgensson. Not to be rude."

She shook her head no, no, he wasn't being rude.

"I'm sorry about your father," he said then. It even surprised him.

Annie just stared at him, her mouth working around a word: "… why?"

"The world," he said to her, "it's a—it's a hard place. I didn't make it. It just is."

"Somebody told you that," she said weakly, shaking her head no. "You don't… you don't believe it."

"Would I do this if I didn't?"

She laughed, leaned back. "You're trying to convince yourself, Mister Alone Again," she told him.

And then she didn't stop laughing.

Lonegan stared hard at her, hated Gultree. Everything about it. He was glad he'd killed it, wiped it off the map.

"Goodbye then," he said to her, lifting the fingers of his free hand to the hat he'd left... where?

He looked around for it, finally just took a sweated-through brown one off the peg by the door.

It fit. Close enough, anyway.

For a moment longer than he meant to, he stood in the doorway, waiting for Annie to come up behind him, but she didn't. Even after the door of her cell made its rusty moan.

Lonegan had to look back.

Annie was on her knees behind the thing the Sheriff had become.

She'd worked his revolver up from his holster, was holding it backwards, the barrel in her mouth, so deep she was gagging.

Lonegan closed his eyes, heard her saying it again, from a few minutes ago: "But—but—"

But she'd drank the poppy water too. Thought she was already dead like the rest of them.

She only had to shoot herself once.

Lonegan narrowed his lips, made himself look at what was left of her, then turned, pulled the door shut.

Usually he took his time picking through town, filling saddlebags and feedsacks with jewelry and guns and whatever else would sell.

This time was different, though.

This time he just walked straight down main street to his buckboard, folded the side panel back into itself, and looked around for a horse.

When there wasn't one, he started walking the way he'd come in. Soon enough a horse whinnied.

Lonegan slowed, filled his stolen hat with pebbles and sand, started shaking it, shaking it.

Minutes later, the mare rose from the heat.

"Not you," he said.

She was briny with salt, from running. Had already been coming back to town for the water trough.

Lonegan narrowed his eyes at the distance behind her, for another horse. There was just her, though. He dumped the hat, turned back around.

Twenty minutes later, her nose to the ground like a dog, she trotted into town.

Lonegan slipped a rope over her head and she slumped into it, kept drinking.

All around them were the dead and the nearly dead, littering the streets, coming half out of windows.

Ahead of him, in the straight line from the last town to this one, there'd be another town, he knew. And another, and another. Right now, even, there was probably a runner out there from *this* town, trying to warn everybody of the snake oil man.

Lonegan would find him like he'd found the last, though. Because anybody good enough to leave his own family to ride all night, warn people twenty miles away, anybody from that stock would have been at the service Sunday morning too, done a little partaking.

Which meant he was dead in the saddle already, his tongue swelling in his mouth, a thirst rising from deeper than any thirst he'd ever had before.

Lonegan fixed the yoke on the mare, smeared more poultice into her wound.

If things got bad enough out there this time, he could do what he'd always thought would work: crush one of the wafers up, rub it into her nostrils, make her breathe it in.

She'd die, yeah, but she'd come back too. If she was already in the harness when she did, then he could get a few more miles out of her, he figured.

But it would spoil her meat.

Lonegan looked ahead, trying to figure how far it was going to be this time. How many days. Whether there was some mixture or compound or extract he hadn't found yet, one that could make him forget Gultree altogether. And Annie. Himself.

They'd been asking for it though, he told himself, again.

If it hadn't been him, it would have been somebody else, and that other person might not have known how to administer it, then it would have been one half of the town—the *live* half—against the other.

And that just plain took too long.

No, it was better this way.

Lonegan leaned over to spit, then climbed up onto the seat of the buckboard. The mare pulled ahead, picking around the bodies on her own. The one time one of them jerked, raising its arm to her, Lonegan put it down with the scattergun.

In the silence afterwards, there wasn't a sound in Gultree.

Lonegan shook his head, blew his disgust out his nose.

At the far edge of town was what he'd been counting on: a house with a word gold-lettered onto the back of one of the windows: *Wm. Jorgensson*. It was where Annie lived, where she cooked, where she'd *been* cooking, until the Sheriff came for her.

Lonegan tied the mare to a post, stepped into Annie's living room, found himself with his hat in his hands for some reason, the scattergun in the buckboard.

They were all dead, though.

"Cake," he said aloud, trying to make it real.

It worked.

In the kitchen, not even cut, was a white cake. It was smeared with lard, it looked like. Lard thick with sugar.

Lonegan ran his finger along the edge, tasted it, breathed out for what felt like the first time in days.

Yes.

He took the cake and the dish it was on too, stepped back into the living room.

The father was waiting for him, a felt bowler hat clamped down over his skull. He was dead, clutching a Bible the same way the Sheriff had been carrying the bottle.

The old man was working his mouth and tongue like he was going to say something.

Lonegan waited, waited, had no idea what one of these could say if it took a mind to.

Finally he had to say it for the old man, though, answer the only question that mattered: Annie.

"I got her out before," he said. "You don't need to worry about her none, sir."

The old man just creaked, deep in his throat.

Walking across his left eyeball was a wasp.

Lonegan took a step back, angled his head for another door then came back to the old man.

If—if the buzzards knew better than to eat these things, shouldn't a wasp too?

Lonegan narrowed his eyes at the old man, walked around to see him from the side.

He was dead, a shuffler, but—but not *as* dead.

It hadn't been a bad mixture, either. Lonegan had made it like every other time. No, it was something else, something…

Lonegan shook his head no, then did it anyway: tipped the old man's bowler hat off.

What spilled out was a new head of hair. It was white, silky, dripping blue.

The old man straightened his back, like trying to stand from the hair touching his neck now, for the first time ever.

"No," Lonegan whispered, still shaking his head, and then the old man held the bible out to him.

It pushed Lonegan backwards over a chair.

He caught himself on his hand, rolled into a standing position in the kitchen doorway. Never even spilled the cake.

"You've been using the oil," he said to the old man, touching his own hair to show.

The old man—William Jorgensson: a *he*, not an it—didn't understand, just kept leading with the Bible.

Lonegan smiled, shook his head no. Thanks, but no.

The old man breathed in sharp then, all at once, then out again, blood misting out now. Meaning it was almost over now, barbershop oil or no.

Again, he started making the creaking sound with his throat. Like he was trying to talk.

When he couldn't get it out, and Lonegan wouldn't take the Bible, the old man finally reached into his pocket, came out with a handful of broken wafers, stolen from the pan at church.

It was what Annie had said: her father bringing the church back to her, since she wouldn't go.

Lonegan held his hands away, his fingertips even, and stepped away again. Not that the wafers could get through boot leather. But still.

The Bible slapped the wooden floor.

"You old thief," Lonegan said.

The old man just stood there.

"What else you got in there, now?" Lonegan asked.

The old man narrowed his half-dead eyes, focused on his hand in his pocket, and came up with the bottle Lonegan had given him for free. It was empty.

Lonegan nodded about that, got the old man nodding too.

"That I can do something about, now," he said, and stepped long and wide around the old man, out the front door.

The heat was stifling, wonderful.

Lonegan balanced the cake just above his shoulder, unhooked the panel on the side of the buckboard. It slapped down, the mare spooking ahead a step or two, until the traces stopped her.

Lonegan glared at her, looked back to the house, then did it anyway, what he knew he didn't have to: palmed up the last two bottles of barbershop oil. They were pale blue in the sunlight, like a cat's eyes.

He stepped back into the living room, slapped the wall to let the old man know he was back.

The old man turned around slow, the soles of his boots scraping the wood floor the whole way.

"Here," Lonegan said, setting the two bottles down on the table, holding up the cake to show what they were in trade for.

The old man just stared, wasn't going to make it. His index finger twitching by his thigh, the nailbed stained blue.

"I'm sorry," Lonegan said. "For whatever that's worth."

By the time he'd pulled away, the old man had shuffled to the door, was just standing there.

"Give it six days," Lonegan said, touching his own hair to show what he meant, then laughed a nervous laugh, slapped the leather down on the mare's tender haunch.

Fucking Gultree.

He pushed out into the heat, was able to make himself wait all the way until dark for the cake. Because it was a celebration, he even sedated the mare, cut another flank steak off, packed it with poultice.

He'd forgot to collect any water, but then he'd forgot to collect all the jewelry and guns too.

There'd be more, though.

In places without women like Annie Jorgensson.

Lonegan wiped the last of the mare's grease from his mouth, pulled his chin hair down into a point, and pulled the cake plate into his lap, started fingering it in until he realized that he was just eating the sweet off the top, like his aunt had always warned him against. It needed to be balanced with the dry cake inside.

He cut a wedge out with his knife, balanced it into his mouth, and did it again and again, until something popped under his blade, deep in the cake.

It was a half a wafer.

Lonegan stared at it, stared at it some more. Tried to control his breathing, couldn't seem to.

Was it—was it from *this* Sunday's service, or from last?

Was what was in the old man's pocket been the whole take, or just part of it?

Lonegan's jaws slowed, then he gagged, threw up onto his chest, and looked all the way back to town, to the old man in the door, smiling now, lifting his Bible to show that he knew, that he'd known, that he'd been going to get religion into his daughter's life whether she wanted it or not.

Lonegan shook his head no, no, told the old man that—that, if she'd just waited to pull the trigger, he would have *told* her that it wasn't the poppy water. But then too was dead certain he could feel the wafer inside him, burrowing like a worm for his heart, his life.

He threw up again, but it was thin now, weak.

"…no," he said, the wet strings hanging from his chin. It didn't—it couldn't… it didn't happen *this* fast. Did it? Had it ever?

His fingers thick now, he sifted through the cake for another wafer, to see if he could tell which Sunday it had been from, but all the shards were too small, too broken up.

Annie. Goddamn you. *Which Sunday?*

But—but…

The oil, the barbershop oil. Hell yes. It slowed the wafers.

Lonegan stumbled up through the fire, scattering sparks, the cake plate shattering on a rock, and started falling towards the mare. To ride fast back to Gultree, back to the old man, those two blue bottles.

But the mare saw him coming, jerked her head away from the wagon wheel she was tied to.

The reins held. The spoke didn't.

She skittered back, still sluggish from what he'd dosed her with, and Lonegan nodded, made himself slow down. Held his hat out like there was going to be something in it this time, really, come on, old gal.

The mare opened her nostrils to the night, tasting it for oats, then turned her head sideways to watch Lonegan with one eye, then shied back when he stepped forward, shaking her mane in warning, flicking her tail like she was younger than her years, and when he took another step closer, leading with the hat, she ducked him, and in this way they danced for the rest of the night, her reins always just within reach, if he could just time his steps right. Or what he thought was his reach.

THE CREVASSE
DALE BAILEY AND NATHAN BALLINGRUD

Dale Bailey has published three novels, *The Fallen*, *House of Bones*, and *Sleeping Policemen* (with Jack Slay, Jr.). A fourth novel, *The Clearing* (also with Jack), is forthcoming. His short fiction—which has won the International Horror Guild Award and has been twice nominated for the Nebula Award—has been collected in *The Resurrection Man's Legacy and Other Stories*.

Nathan Ballingrud lives with his daughter just outside of Asheville, NC. His stories have appeared in *Inferno: New Tales of Terror and the Supernatural*, *The Del Rey Book of Science Fiction and Fantasy*, SCIFICTION, and the forthcoming *Naked City: New Tales of Urban Fantasy*. He recently won the Shirley Jackson Award for his short story "The Monsters of Heaven."

What he loved was the silence, the pristine clarity of the ice shelf: the purposeful breathing of the dogs straining against their traces, the hiss of the runners, the opalescent arc of the sky. Garner peered through shifting veils of snow at the endless sweep of glacial terrain before him, the wind gnawing at him, forcing him to reach up periodically and scrape at the thin crust of ice that clung to the edges of his facemask, the dry rasp of the fabric against his face reminding him that he was alive.

There were fourteen of them. Four men, one of them, Faber, strapped to the back of Garner's sledge, mostly unconscious, but occasionally surfacing out of the morphine depths to moan. Ten dogs, big Greenland huskies, gray and white. Two sledges. And the silence, scouring him of memory and desire, hollowing him out inside. It was what he'd come to Antarctica for.

And then, abruptly, the silence split open like a wound:

A thunderous crack, loud as lightning cleaving stone, shivered the ice, and the dogs of the lead sledge, maybe twenty-five yards ahead of Garner, erupted into panicky cries. Garner saw it happen: the lead sledge sloughed over—hurling Connelly into the snow—and plunged nose first through the ice, as though an enormous hand had reached up through the earth to snatch it under. Startled, he watched an instant longer. The wrecked sledge, jutting out of the earth like a broken stone, hurtled at him, closer, closer. Then time stuttered, leaping forward.

165

Garner flung one of the brakes out behind him. The hook skittered over the ice. Garner felt the jolt in his spine when it caught. Rope sang out behind him, arresting his momentum. But it wouldn't be enough.

Garner flung out a second brake, then another. The hooks snagged, jerking the sledge around and up on a single runner. For a moment Garner thought that it was going to roll, dragging the dogs along behind it. Then the airborne runner slammed back to earth and the sledge skidded to a stop in a glittering spray of ice.

Dogs boiled back into its shadow, howling and snapping. Ignoring them, Garner clambered free. He glanced back at Faber, still miraculously strapped to the travois, his face ashen, and then he pelted toward the wrecked sledge, dodging a minefield of spilled cargo: food and tents, cooking gear, his medical bag, disgorging a bright freight of tools and the few precious ampules of morphine McReady had been willing to spare, like a fan of scattered diamonds.

The wrecked sledge hung precariously, canted on a lip of ice above a black crevasse. As Garner stood there, it slipped an inch, and then another, dragged down by the weight of the dogs. He could hear them whining, claws scrabbling as they strained against harnesses drawn taut by the weight of Atka, the lead dog, dangling out of sight beyond the edge of the abyss.

Garner visualized him—thrashing against his tack in a black well as the jagged circle of grayish light above shrank away, inch by lurching inch—and he felt the pull of night inside himself, the age-old gravity of the dark. Then a hand closed around his ankle.

Bishop, clinging to the ice, a hand-slip away from tumbling into the crevasse himself: face blanched, eyes red rimmed inside his goggles.

"Shit," Garner said. "Here—"

He reached down, locked his hand around Bishop's wrist, and hauled him up, boots slipping. Momentum carried him over backwards, floundering in the snow as Bishop curled fetal beside him.

"You okay?"

"My ankle," he said through gritted teeth.

"Here, let me see."

"Not now. Connelly. What happened to Connelly?"

"He fell off—"

With a metallic screech, the sledge broke loose. It slid a foot, a foot and a half, and then it hung up. The dogs screamed. Garner had never heard a dog make a noise like that—he didn't know dogs *could* make a noise like that—and for a moment their blind, inarticulate terror swam through him. He thought again of Atka, dangling there, turning, feet clawing at the darkness, and he felt something stir inside him once again—

"Steady, man," Bishop said.

Garner drew in a long breath, icy air lacerating his lungs.

"You gotta be steady now, Doc," Bishop said. "You gotta go cut him loose."

"No—"

"We're gonna lose the sledge. And the rest of the team. That happens, we're all gonna die out here, okay? I'm busted up right now, I need you to do this thing—"

"What about Connell—"

"Not now, Doc. Listen to me. We don't have time. Okay?"

Bishop held his gaze. Garner tried to look away, could not. The other man's eyes fixed him.

"Okay," he said.

Garner stood and stumbled away. Went to his knees to dig through the wreckage. Flung aside a sack of rice, frozen in clumps, wrenched open a crate of flares—useless—shoved it aside, and dragged another one toward him. This time he was lucky: he dug out a coil of rope, a hammer, a handful of pitons. The sledge lurched on its lip of ice, the rear end swinging, setting off another round of whimpering.

"Hurry," Bishop said.

Garner drove the pitons deep into the permafrost and threaded the rope through their eyes, his hands stiff inside his gloves. Lashing the other end around his waist, he edged back onto the broken ice shelf. It shifted underneath him, creaking. The sledge shuddered, but held. Below him, beyond the moiling clump of dogs, he could see the leather trace leads, stretched taut across the jagged rim of the abyss.

He dropped back, letting rope out as he descended. The world fell away above him. Down and down, and then he was on his knees at the very edge of the shelf, the hot, rank stink of the dogs enveloping him. He used his teeth to loosen one glove. Working quickly against the icy assault of the elements, he fumbled his knife out of its sheath and pressed the blade to the first of the traces. He sawed at it until the leather separated with a snap.

Atka's weight shifted in the darkness below him, and the dog howled mournfully. Garner set to work on the second trace, felt it let go, everything—the sledge, the terrified dogs—slipping toward darkness. For a moment he thought the whole thing would go. But it held. He went to work on the third trace, gone loose now by some trick of tension. It too separated beneath his blade, and he once again felt Atka's weight shift in the well of darkness beneath him.

Garner peered into the blackness. He could see the dim blur of the dog, could feel its dumb terror welling up around him, and as he brought the blade to the final trace, a painstakingly erected dike gave way in his mind. Memory flooded through him: the feel of mangled flesh beneath his fingers, the distant *whump* of artillery, Elizabeth's drawn and somber face.

His fingers faltered. Tears blinded him. The sledge shifted above him as Atka thrashed in his harness. Still he hesitated.

The rope creaked under the strain of additional weight. Ice rained down around him. Garner looked up to see Connelly working his way hand over hand down the rope.

"Do it," Connelly grunted, his eyes like chips of flint. "Cut him loose."

Garner's fingers loosened around the hilt of the blade. He felt the tug of the dark at his feet, Atka whining.

"Give me the goddamn knife," Connelly said, wrenching it away, and together they clung there on the single narrow thread of gray rope, two men and one knife and the enormous gulf of the sky overhead as Connelly sawed savagely at the last of the traces. It held for a moment, and then, abruptly, it gave, loose ends curling back and away from the blade.

Atka fell howling into darkness.

They made camp.

The traces of the lead sledge had to be untangled and repaired, the dogs tended to, the weight redistributed to account for Atka's loss. While Connelly busied himself with these chores, Garner stabilized Faber—the blood had frozen to a black crust inside the makeshift splint Garner had applied yesterday, after the accident—and wrapped Bishop's ankle. These were automatic actions. Serving in France he'd learned the trick of letting his body work while his mind traveled to other places; it had been crucial to keeping his sanity during the war, when the people brought to him for treatment had been butchered by German submachine guns or burned and blistered by mustard gas. He worked to save those men, though it was hopeless work. Mankind had acquired an appetite for dying; doctors had become shepherds to the process. Surrounded by screams and spilled blood, he'd anchored himself to memories of his wife, Elizabeth: the warmth of her kitchen back home in Boston, and the warmth of her body too.

But all that was gone.

Now, when he let his mind wander, it went to dark places, and he found himself concentrating instead on the minutiae of these rote tasks like a first-year medical student. He cut a length of bandage and applied a compression wrap to Bishop's exposed ankle, covering both ankle and foot in careful figure-eights. He kept his mind in the moment, listening to the harsh labor of their lungs in the frigid air, to Connelly's chained fury as he worked at the traces, and to the muffled sounds of the dogs as they burrowed into the snow to rest.

And he listened, too, to Atka's distant cries, leaking from the crevasse like blood.

"Can't believe that dog's still alive," Bishop said, testing his ankle against his weight. He grimaced and sat down on a crate. "He's a tough old bastard."

Garner imagined Elizabeth's face, drawn tight with pain and determination, while he fought a war on the far side of the ocean. Was she afraid too, suspended over her own dark hollow? Did she cry out for him?

"Help me with this tent," Garner said.

They'd broken off from the main body of the expedition to bring Faber back to one of the supply depots on the Ross Ice Shelf, where Garner could care for him. They would wait there for the remainder of the expedition, which suited Garner just fine, but troubled both Bishop and Connelly, who had higher aspirations for their time here.

Nightfall was still a month away, but if they were going to camp here while they made repairs, they would need the tents to harvest warmth. Connelly approached as they drove pegs into the permafrost, his eyes impassive as they swept over Faber, still tied down to the travois, locked inside a morphine dream. He regarded Bishop's ankle and asked him how it was.

"It'll do," Bishop said. "It'll have to. How are the dogs?"

"We need to start figuring what we can do without," Connelly said. "We're gonna have to leave some stuff behind."

"We're only down one dog," Bishop said. "It shouldn't be too hard to compensate."

"We're down two. One of the swing dogs snapped her foreleg." He opened one of the bags lashed to the rear sledge, removing an Army-issue revolver. "So go ahead and figure what we don't need. I gotta tend to her." He tossed a contemptuous glance at Garner. "Don't worry, I won't ask *you* to do it."

Garner watched as Connelly approached the injured dog, lying away from the others in the snow. She licked obsessively at her broken leg. As Connelly approached she looked up at him and her tail wagged weakly. Connelly aimed the pistol and fired a bullet through her head. The shot made a flat, inconsequential sound, swallowed up by the vastness of the open plain.

Garner turned away, emotion surging through him with a surprising, disorienting energy. Bishop met his gaze and offered a rueful smile.

"Bad day," he said.

Still, Atka whimpered.

Garner lay wakeful, staring at the canvas, taut and smooth as the interior of an egg above him. Faber moaned, calling out after some fever phantom. Garner almost envied the man. Not the injury—a nasty compound fracture of the femur, the product of a bad step on the ice when he'd stepped outside the circle of tents to piss—but the sweet oblivion of the morphine doze.

In France, in the war, he'd known plenty of doctors who'd used the stuff to chase away the night haunts. He'd also seen the fevered agony of withdrawal. He had no wish to experience that, but he felt the opiate lure all the same. He'd felt it then, when he'd had thoughts of Elizabeth to sustain him. And he felt it now—stronger still—when he didn't.

Elizabeth had fallen victim to the greatest cosmic prank of all time, the flu that had swept across the world in the spring and summer of 1918, as if the bloody abattoir in the trenches hadn't been evidence enough of humanity's divine disfavor. That's what Elizabeth had called it in the last letter he'd ever had from her: God's judgment on a world gone mad. Garner had given up on God by then: he'd packed away the Bible Elizabeth had pressed upon him after a week in the field hospital, knowing that its paltry lies could bring him no comfort in the face of such horror, and it hadn't. Not then, and not later, when he'd come home to face Elizabeth's mute and barren grave. Garner had taken McReady's offer to accompany the expedition soon after, and though he'd stowed the Bible in his gear before he left, he hadn't opened it since and he wouldn't open it here, either, lying sleepless beside a man who might yet die because he'd had to take a piss—yet another grand cosmic joke—in a place so hellish and forsaken that even Elizabeth's God could find no purchase here.

There could be no God in such a place.

Just the relentless shriek of the wind tearing at the flimsy canvas, and the death-howl agony of the dog. Just emptiness, and the unyielding porcelain dome of the polar sky.

Garner sat up, breathing heavily.

Faber muttered under his breath. Garner leaned over the injured man, the stench of fever hot in his nostrils. He smoothed Faber's hair back from his forehead and studied the leg, swollen tight as a sausage inside the sealskin legging. Garner didn't like to think what he might see if he slit open that sausage to reveal the leg underneath: the viscous pit of the wound itself, crimson lines of sepsis twining around Faber's thigh like a malevolent vine as they climbed inexorably toward his heart.

Atka howled, a long rising cry that broke into pitiful yelps, died away, and renewed itself, like the shriek of sirens on the French front.

"Jesus," Garner whispered.

He fished a flask out of his pack and allowed himself a single swallow of whiskey. Then he sat in the dark, listening to the mournful lament of the dog, his mind filling with hospital images: the red splash of tissue in a steel tray, the enflamed wound of an amputation, the hand folding itself into an outraged fist as the arm fell away. He thought of Elizabeth, too, Elizabeth most of all, buried months before Garner had gotten back from Europe. And he thought of Connelly, that aggrieved look as he turned away to deal with the injured swing dog.

Don't worry, I won't ask you to do it.

Crouching in the low tent, Garner dressed. He shoved a flashlight into his jacket, shouldered aside the tent flap, and leaned into the wind tearing across the waste. The crevasse lay before him, rope still trailing through the pitons to dangle into the pit below.

Garner felt the pull of darkness. And Atka, screaming.

"Okay," he muttered. "All right, I'm coming."

Once again he lashed the rope around his waist. This time he didn't hesitate as he backed out onto the ledge of creaking ice. Hand over hand he went, backward and down, boots scuffing until he stepped into space and hung suspended in a well of shadow.

Panic seized him, the black certainty that nothing lay beneath him. The crevasse yawned under his feet, like a wedge of vacuum driven into the heart of the planet. Then, below him—ten feet? twenty?—Atka mewled, piteous as a freshly whelped pup, eyes squeezed shut against the light. Garner thought of the dog, curled in agony upon some shelf of subterranean ice, and began to lower himself into the pit, darkness rising to envelop him.

One heartbeat, then another and another and another, his breath diaphanous in the gloom, his boots scrabbling for solid ground. Scrabbling and finding it. Garner clung to the rope, testing the surface with his weight.

It held.

Garner took the flashlight from his jacket, and switched it on. Atka peered up at him, brown eyes iridescent with pain. The dog's legs twisted underneath it, and its tail wagged feebly. Blood glistened at its muzzle. As he moved closer, Garner saw that a dagger of bone had pierced its torso, unveiling the slick yellow gleam of subcutaneous fat and deeper still, half visible through tufts of coarse fur, the bloody pulse of viscera. And it had shat itself—Garner could smell it—a thin gruel congealing on the dank stone.

"Okay," he said. "Okay, Atka."

Kneeling, Garner caressed the dog. It growled and subsided, surrendering to his ministrations.

"Good boy, Atka," he whispered. "Settle down, boy."

Garner slid his knife free of its sheath, bent forward, and brought the blade to the dog's throat. Atka whimpered—"Shhh," Garner whispered—as he bore down with the edge, steeling himself against the thing he was about to do—

Something moved in the darkness beneath him: a leathery rasp, the echoing clatter of stone on stone, of loose pebbles tumbling into darkness. Atka whimpered again, legs twitching as he tried to shove himself back against the wall. Garner, startled, shoved the blade forward. Atka's neck unseamed itself in a welter of black arterial blood. The dog stiffened, shuddered once, and died—Garner watched its eyes dim in the space of a single heartbeat—and once again something shifted in the darkness at Garner's back. Garner scuttled backward, slamming his shoulders into the wall by Atka's corpse. He froze there, probing the darkness.

Then, when nothing came—had he imagined it? He must have imagined it—Garner aimed the flashlight light into the gloom. His breath caught in his throat. He shoved himself erect in amazement, the rope pooling at his feet.

Vast.

The place was vast: walls of naked stone climbing in cathedral arcs to the undersurface of the polar plain and a floor worn smooth as glass over long ages, stretching out before him until it dropped away into an abyss of darkness. Struck dumb with terror—or was it wonder?—Garner stumbled forward, the rope unspooling behind him until he drew up at the precipice, pointed the light into the shadows before him, and saw what it was that he had discovered.

A stairwell, cut seamlessly into the stone itself, and no human stairwell either: each riser fell away three feet or more, the stair itself winding endlessly into

fathomless depths of earth, down and down and down until it curved away
beyond the reach of his frail human light, and further still toward some awful
destination he scarcely dared imagine. Garner felt the lure and hunger of the
place singing in his bones. Something deep inside him, some mute inarticulate
longing, cried out in response, and before he knew it he found himself scrambling down the first riser and then another, the flashlight carving slices out of the
darkness to reveal a bas relief of inhuman creatures lunging at him in glimpses:
taloned feet and clawed hands and sinuous Medusa coils that seemed to writhe
about one another in the fitful and imperfect glare. And through it all the terrible summons of the place, drawing him down into the dark.

"Elizabeth—" he gasped, stumbling down another riser and another, until the
rope, forgotten, jerked taut about his waist. He looked up at the pale circle of
Connelly's face far above him.

"What the hell are you doing down there, Doc," Connelly shouted, his voice
thick with rage, and then, almost against his will, Garner found himself ascending once again into the light.

No sooner had he gained his footing than Connelly grabbed him by the collar and swung him to the ground. Garner scrabbled for purchase in the snow
but Connelly kicked him back down again, his blonde, bearded face contorted
in rage.

"You stupid son of a bitch! Do you care if we all die out here?"

"Get off me!"

"For a dog? For a goddamned *dog?*" Connelly tried to kick him again, but
Garner grabbed his foot and rolled, bringing the other man down on top of him.
The two of them grappled in the snow, their heavy coats and gloves making any
real damage all but impossible.

The flaps to one of the tents opened and Bishop limped out, his face a cari-
cature of alarm. He was buttoning his coat even as he approached. "Stop! *Stop
it right now!*"

Garner clambered to his feet, staggering backward a few steps. Connelly rose
to one knee, leaning over and panting. He pointed at Garner. "I found him in
the crevasse! He went down alone!"

Garner leaned against one of the packed sledges. He could feel Bishop watching him as tugged free a glove to poke at a tender spot on his face, but he didn't
look up.

"Is this true?"

"Of course it's true!" Connelly said, but Bishop waved him into silence.

Garner looked up at him, breath heaving in his lungs. "You've got to see it,"
he said. "My God, Bishop."

Bishop turned his gaze to the crevasse, where he saw the pitons and the rope
spilling into the darkness. "Oh, Doc," he said quietly.

"It's not a crevasse, Bishop. It's a stairwell."

Connelly strode toward Garner, jabbing his finger at him. "What? You lost your goddamned mind."

"Look for yourself!"

Bishop interposed himself between the two men. "*Enough!*" He turned to face Connelly. "Back off."

"But—"

"I said back off!"

Connelly peeled his lips back, then turned and stalked back toward the crevasse. He knelt by its edge and started hauling up the rope.

Bishop turned to Garner. "Explain yourself."

All at once, Garner's passion drained from him. He felt a wash of exhaustion. His muscles ached. How could he explain this to him? He could he explain this so that they'd understand? "Atka," he said simply, imploringly. "I could hear him."

A look of deep regret fell over Bishop's face. "Doc… Atka was a just a dog. We have to get Faber to the depot."

"I could still hear him."

"You have to pull yourself together. There are real lives at stake here, do you get that? Me and Connelly, we aren't doctors. Faber needs *you*."

"But—"

"Do you get that?"

"I… yeah. Yeah, I know."

"When you go down into places like that, especially by yourself, you're putting us all at risk. What are we gonna do without Doc, huh?"

This was not an argument Garner would win. Not this way. So he grabbed Bishop by the arm and led him toward the crevasse. "Look," he said.

Bishop wrenched his arm free, his face darkening. Connelly straightened, watching this exchange. "Don't put your hands on me, Doc," Bishop said.

Garner released him. "Bishop," he said. "Please."

Bishop paused a moment, then walked toward the opening. "All right."

Connelly exploded. "Oh for Christ's sake!"

"We're not going inside it," Bishop said, looking at them both. "I'm going to look, okay Doc? That's all you get."

Garner nodded. "Okay," he said. "Okay."

The two of them approached the edge of the crevasse. Closer, Garner felt it like a hook in his liver, tugging him down. It took an act of will to stop at the edge, to remain still and unshaken and look at these other two men as if his whole life did not hinge upon this moment.

"It's a stairwell," he said. His voice did not shake. His body did not move. "It's carved into the rock. It's got… designs of some kind."

Bishop peered down into the darkness for a long moment. "I don't see anything," he said at last.

"I'm telling you, it's *there!*" Garner stopped and gathered himself. He tried another tack. "This, this could be the scientific discovery of the century. You want to stick it to McReady? Let him plant his little flag. This is evidence of, of…" He trailed off. He didn't know what it was evidence of.

"We'll mark the location," Bishop said. "We'll come back. If what you say is true it's not going anywhere."

Garner switched on his flashlight. "Look," he said, and he threw it down.

The flashlight arced end over end, its white beam slicing through the darkness with a scalpel's clean efficiency, illuminating flashes of hewn rock and what might have been carvings or just natural irregularities. It clattered to a landing beside the corpse of the dog, casting in bright relief its open jaw and lolling tongue, and the black pool of blood beneath it.

Bishop looked for a moment, and shook his head. "God damn it, Doc," he said. "You're really straining my patience. Come on."

Bishop was about to turn away when Atka's body jerked once—Garner saw it —and then again, almost imperceptibly. Reaching out, Garner seized Bishop's sleeve. "What now, for Christ's—" the other man started to say, his voice harsh with annoyance. Then the body was yanked into the surrounding darkness so quickly it seemed as though it had vanished into thin air. Only its blood, a smeared trail into shadow, testified to its ever having been there at all. That, and the jostled flashlight, which rolled in a lazy half circle, its unobstructed light spearing first into empty darkness and then into smooth cold stone before settling at last on what might have been a carven, clawed foot. The beam flickered and went out.

"What the fuck…" Bishop said.

A scream erupted from the tent behind them.

Faber.

Garner broke into a clumsy run, high-stepping through the piled snow. The other men shouted behind him but their words were lost in the wind and in his own hard breathing. His body was moving according to its training but his mind was pinned like a writhing insect in the hole behind him, by the stark, burning image of what he had just seen. He was transported by fear and adrenaline and by something else, by some other emotion he had not felt in many years or perhaps ever in his life, some heart-filling glorious exaltation that threatened to snuff him out like a dying cinder.

Faber was sitting upright in the tent—it stank of sweat and urine and kerosene, eye-watering and sharp—his thick hair a dark corona around his head, his skin as pale as a cavefish. He was still trying to scream, but his voice had broken, and his utmost effort could now produce only a long, cracked wheeze, which seemed forced through his throat like steel wool. His leg stuck out of the blanket, still grossly swollen.

The warmth from the Nansen cooker was almost oppressive.

Garner dropped to his knees beside him and tried to ease him back down into his sleeping bag, but Faber resisted. He fixed his eyes on Garner, his painful wheeze trailing into silence. Hooking his fingers in Garner's collar, he pulled him close, so close that Garner could smell the sour taint of his breath.

"Faber, relax, relax!"

"It—" Faber's voice locked. He swallowed and tried again. "It laid an egg in me."

Bishop and Connelly crowded through the tent flap, and Garner felt suddenly hemmed in, overwhelmed by the heat and the stink and the steam rising in wisps from their clothes as they pushed closer, staring down at Faber.

"What's going on?" Bishop asked. "Is he all right?"

Faber eyed them wildly. Ignoring them, Garner placed his hands on Faber's cheeks and turned his head toward him. "Look at me, Faber. Look at me. What do you mean?"

Faber found a way to smile. "In my dream. It put my head inside its body, and it laid an egg in me."

Connelly said, "He's delirious. See what happens when you leave him alone?"

Garner fished an ampule of morphine out of his bag. Faber saw what he was doing and his body bucked.

"No!" he screamed, summoning his voice again. "No!" His leg thrashed out, knocking over the Nansen cooker. Cursing, Connelly dove at the overturned stove, but it was already too late. Kerosene splashed over the blankets and supplies, engulfing the tent in flames. The men moved in a sudden tangle of panic. Bishop stumbled back out of the tent and Connelly shoved Garner aside—Garner rolled over on his back and came to rest there—as he lunged for Faber's legs, dragging him backward. Screaming, Faber clutched at the ground to resist, but Connelly was too strong. A moment later, Faber was gone, dragging a smoldering rucksack with him.

Still inside the tent, Garner lay back, watching as the fire spread hungrily along the roof, dropping tongues of flame onto the ground, onto his own body. Garner closed his eyes as the heat gathered him up like a furnace-hearted lover.

What he felt, though, was not the fire's heat, but the cool breath of underground earth, the silence of the deep tomb buried beneath the ice shelf. The stairs descended before him, and at the bottom he heard a noise again: A woman's voice, calling for him. Wondering where he was.

Elizabeth, he called, his voice echoing off the stone. Are you there?

If only he'd gotten to see her, he thought. If only he'd gotten to bury her. To fill those beautiful eyes with dirt. To cover her in darkness.

Elizabeth, can you hear me?

Then Connelly's big arms enveloped him, and he felt the heat again, searing bands of pain around his legs and chest. It was like being wrapped in a star. "I ought to let you burn, you stupid son of a bitch," Connelly hissed, but he didn't. He lugged Garner outside—Garner opened his eyes in time to see the canvas part in front of him, like fiery curtains—and dumped him in the snow instead.

The pain went away, briefly, and Garner mourned its passing. He rolled over and lifted his head. Connelly stood over him, his face twisted in disgust. Behind him the tent flickered and burned like a dropped torch.

Faber's quavering voice hung over it all, rising and falling like the wind.

Connelly tossed an ampule and a syringe onto the ground by Garner. "Faber's leg's opened up again," he said. "Go and do your job."

Garner climbed slowly to his feet, feeling the skin on his chest and legs tighten. He'd been burned; he'd have to wait until he'd tended to Faber to find out how badly.

"And then help us pack up," Bishop called as he led the dogs to their harnesses, his voice harsh and strained. "We're getting the hell out of here."

By the time they reached the depot, Faber was dead. Connelly spat into the snow and turned away to unhitch the dogs, while Garner and Bishop went inside and started a fire. Bishop started water boiling for coffee. Garner unpacked their bedclothes and dressed the cots, moving gingerly. Once the place was warm enough he undressed and surveyed the burn damage. It would leave scars.

The next morning they wrapped Faber's body and packed it in an ice locker. After that they settled in to wait.

The ship would not return for a month yet, and though McReady's expedition was due back before then, the vagaries of Antarctic experience made that a tenuous proposition at best. In any case, they were stuck with each other for some time yet, and not even the generous stocks of the depot—a relative wealth of food and medical supplies, playing cards and books—could fully distract them from their grievances.

In the days that followed, Connelly managed to bank his anger at Garner, but it would not take much to set it off again; so Garner tried to keep a low profile. As with the trenches in France, corpses were easy to explain in Antarctica.

A couple of weeks into that empty expanse of time, while Connelly dozed on his cot and Bishop read through an old natural history magazine, Garner decided to risk broaching the subject of what had happened in the crevasse.

"You saw it," he said, quietly, so as not to wake Connelly.

Bishop took a moment to acknowledge that he'd heard him. Finally he tilted the magazine away, and sighed. "Saw what," he said.

"You know what."

Bishop shook his head. "No," he said. "I don't. I don't know what you're talking about."

"Something was there."

Bishop said nothing. He lifted the magazine again, but his eyes were still.

"Something was down there," Garner said.

"No there wasn't."

"It pulled Atka. I know you saw it."

Bishop refused to look at him. "This is an empty place," he said, after a long silence. "There's nothing here." He blinked, and turned a page in the magazine. "Nothing."

Garner leaned back onto his cot, looking at the ceiling.

Although the long Antarctic day had not yet finished, it was shading into dusk, the sun hovering over the horizon like a great boiling eye. It cast long shadows, and the lamp Bishop had lit to read by set them dancing. Garner watched them caper across the ceiling. Some time later, Bishop snuffed out the lamp and dragged the curtains over the windows, consigning them all to darkness. With it, Garner felt something like peace stir inside him. He let it move through him in waves, he felt it ebb and flow with each slow pulse of his heart.

A gust of wind scattered fine crystals of snow against the window, and he found himself wondering what the night would be like in this cold country. He imagined the sky dissolving to reveal the hard vault of stars, the galaxy turning above him like a cog in a vast, unknowable engine. And behind it all, the emptiness into which men hurled their prayers. It occurred to him that he could leave now, walk out into the long twilight and keep going until the earth opened beneath him and he found himself descending strange stairs, while the world around him broke silently into snow, and into night.

Garner closed his eyes.

THE LION'S DEN
STEVE DUFFY

Steve Duffy's stories have appeared in numerous magazines and anthologies in Europe and North America. 2010 sees the publication of two new collections of his short fiction, *The Moment Of Panic* (which includes the International Horror Guild award-winning tale, "The Rag-and-Bone Men") and *Tragic Life Stories*. He lives in North Wales.

It's so familiar now, that grainy digital footage of the lions' den. We've rerun it a hundred times, picked over it obsessively, advanced it frame by fuzzy frame. I'm sure all the experts, the psychologists, the security consultants that were brought in to analyse the clip (but who failed entirely in their glib attempts to explain it all away), feel in some way that they themselves experienced the whole thing. It's easy to forget that only a few people actually witnessed the incident first-hand, that Thursday afternoon in the late autumn of the last year of the old century. I was one of them. My colleagues and I saw it all first-hand. It gave us the edge on all the rest; we saw and heard and felt things no camera could catch, let alone one being operated by an overexcited amateur. But even we remain at a loss to explain exactly what happened...

Perhaps we're all trying too hard. Most people have written it off long since as fundamentally inexplicable—just one of those things. The boy was mad, they said, to do what he did: simple as that. But since when has madness been synonymous with simplicity? Granted, the incident was simple enough, on the face of it. Maybe it was precisely that simplicity which for some of us made the whole thing impossible, even then, to dismiss.

The zoo sits amongst quiet leafy suburbs, out where the city begins to lose interest in itself. Built in the 1960s, its enclosures are adequate—at a pinch—to the animals' needs, in terms of size and layout. Iron railings and concrete moats surround modest expanses of grassy slope and pruned-back leafless trees. An artificial river runs through the grounds, with an observation barge that sails on the hour, every hour; there are nocturamas for the insects, aviaries for the birds. On a day like that November day, a dull grey weekday nipped with the coming of winter, there will be only a handful of visitors. And I remember there were no school parties of screaming preteens, no coachloads of the elderly: only a handful of people wandering the broad tarmac paths between the enclosures, consulting their guides, adjusting the lenses on their cameras as the animals blinked listlessly back at them through the bars.

In the observation tower above the main block is the surveillance post, with its panoramic view across the whole of the compound. Further out, beyond the perimeter walls, the rooftops of a thousand bungalows, chimney-tops and satellite dishes peeking through the screens of quick-growing *leylandii*; beyond these, raw winter ground-mist on the plain, and the grey smudge of the distant city tower blocks. The view always depresses me, during my shifts in the tower. Maybe anyone who spends long enough around cages, whether as captive or keeper, will sooner or later feel the need for liberty, for transcendence; will at the very least catch himself gazing beyond the bars, meditating on the interconnected concepts of inside-outside. Reminding us where our duties lie, the CCTV cameras flick monotonously through their cycles of the main perimeter, pen to pen, avenue to avenue. Up in the God-seat we follow the sequence, indiscriminately surveilling animal and human, spectacle and spectator.

As familiar as some of the animals are the regulars, those people who visit the zoo so frequently as to become instantly recognisable to the security staff. We have nicknames for them, and in some instances their photos pinned up on the cork-board, with cautionary Post-It notes attached. It's our job to watch them and decide whether their interest in this or that animal goes beyond innocent curiosity; the endless enthralment of seeing a creature in its cage.

Inevitably, you see, a zoo will attract certain types of people, over and above its core visitor group. These range from the mostly harmless—the lonely and inadequate, the homeless, the community-care brigade—through to the more problematic types, the obsessives, the neurotics, and in extreme instances the dangerously, even suicidally unhinged. With the former, our job consists mostly of moving them on at closing time, rousing them if they try to sleep in the dark musty tunnels of the nocturama or the vivarium, making sure they don't present a nuisance to the staff or to other zoo users. With the latter, it can be very different.

Most identify with a particular animal, usually to the exclusion of all others. Often, it'll be monkeys, of which we have several species, or the great apes. They stand gripping the bars, watching as the simians dangle from their tyre swings or munch their way phlegmatically through buckets of bruised fruit. Occasionally, one will try to make contact: a hand will be thrust through the bars, and we need to be sure nothing is being passed that might be harmful, intentionally or otherwise. We took off one such woman a notepad and pencil; perhaps she expected the ape to communicate with her in some way or another, to provide some signifying rebus of his existence. On the pad she'd drawn herself, to a high degree of anatomical detail, in the pose of Leonardo's Universal Man. Above the self-portrait she'd scrawled the words *look monkey*. In the enclosure the ape sighed, settled back into his flaccid hairy old-man's pelt, scratched at his fleas with melancholy acceptance. Who knows? Perhaps he felt resentful that we'd confiscated the pad and pencil, denied him even this meagre opportunity for self-affirmation. They say an ape in the Paris zoo, given paintbrush and paper, once made a painting of the bars of his cage. But that's another matter entirely. We're keepers, first and foremost, not art critics. Before anything, it's our job to keep the animals out of harm's way.

Some people, you see, come armed with more than pencils. We've confiscated knives from people, air-rifles; apples with razor-blades stuck inside them, more than once. Out-and-out mutilators are pretty uncommon, thank god, but all zoo staff are perpetually on their guard against them. Why would anyone do a thing like that? It's well known that sadism presents early in life as a predilection for harming animals, but I've wondered sometimes: might there be a weird sort of jealousy mixed up with it too?

Consider for a moment the lot of your average zoo animal. They need no affirmation, know no doubt; existentially, they've got it cracked. Even without the identifying plaque in front of its enclosure, an ape is still an ape, unchallengeable in the fact of its apehood. No insecurity, no inadequacy to speak of outside the basic social dynamics of the group: the ranking ladder, who gets to mate with which females, who's in charge and who's not. And what have these sad sacks of humans got, the ones who mock and throw stones? Not even a plaque in front of their enclosure. Perhaps it's easier being a caged monkey then a caged man? But even so, it'd still be a pretty weak excuse. Just because an ape may have the existential edge on you is no reason to feed it a sandwich full of rat poison. We're always on the lookout for these suspect types, the vagrant ones, the loiterers, the sunken-eyed prowlers round cages and pens.

That day—that day and a thousand others, before and since—I was up in the God-seat, cycling through the CCTV feeds around the site. It was late in the afternoon; another two hours and we'd be closed. It hadn't been a particularly busy day, and there were fewer than thirty people spread out across the whole expanse of the zoo. A minibus-full of teenagers with Down's syndrome from a nearby sheltered-housing group; half-a-dozen students from the local college of art with folders and easels; two or three elderly couples; and a handful of unclassifiable adults. The kids were well-behaved enough for me not to worry about them getting up on top of walls or climbing fences, and the pensioners looked about ready to call it a day. I was concentrating on picking out the loners, the singletons.

And that's how I came to notice him on the CCTV: the boy, standing alongside the wall of the lion compound. He seemed young, not much older than a teenager, and at first I took him for one of the art students. But he had no sketchpad, no portfolio. As I looked, two or three of the students went past, and none of them acknowledged him, nor he them. I activated the manual override on the camera controls, and zoomed in on the boy.

He was facing slightly away from the camera, so I tried another angle from a different side of the compound. That didn't give me enough of a close-up. Back on the original camera, all I could make out was his clothing. He was wearing jeans and a camouflage jacket, and his sunbleached hair was hacked into a spiky straggling brush. *Come on, sonny,* I found myself muttering, *show yourself.* Obligingly he half-turned, and for the first time I got a look at his face.

Stubble, a scrappy sort of beard; but it's been a while now since stubble signified anything. He might have been sleeping rough, or he might have been a fashion model. It cut both ways. He was gaunt-looking, hollow-cheeked, but reasonably clean. His behaviour didn't strike me as particularly furtive, which went in his favour, but neither did he seem like one of those people who stand by the cage long enough to watch the animals do their tricks, then wander off in search of the cafeteria and the gift shop. I was sufficiently interested to keep the live camera on him, while at the same time spooling back through the last half-hour of lion-enclosure footage on the auxiliary monitor.

There he was. He'd hardly moved in all that time: as I glanced from the main monitor to the auxiliary, only the time-stamp on the latter showed up the difference. I was going to call it down on the walkie-talkie to one of the guards on the ground, but we were a man short that day anyway, so I decided to have a look myself. I handed over the control system to my colleague Graham Morris, told him where I was going and why, and picked up an on-charge walkie-talkie from the rack. I did briefly look at the firearms cabinet, where the guns and tranquilliser darts were kept, but decided against it. No sense in alarming anyone.

Clanking down the metal steps from the surveillance post I had three or four possibilities in mind concerning our mystery visitor, assuming that he wasn't some innocent sightseer who just happened to have a thing for lions. One, believe it or not, was drugs. I know it sounds ridiculous, not to say sick in the extreme, but we've had that problem in the past. A few years back one of our chimpanzees was slipped a dose of LSD, we think inside an apple. She went into an extended psychotic fugue, kept slamming her head into the bars till the vets had to put her down. That was radical by any standards: not particularly common, granted, but I hated to think what a tripping lion might do before we managed to sedate it.

Another (and you shouldn't get the wrong idea about this) was sex. Now I don't mean to suggest I thought the boy was going to try anything directly with a lion—though it's happened with most of the smaller mammals in the past, and at sea zoos practically all the time with porpoises and dolphins, so I'm told. There are all sorts of ways to get your jollies, and we've dragged our fair share of flashers and masturbators away from the railings, before and since. What all *that's* about I don't pretend to know, except that sex is at the bottom of so much, one way or another. When something goes wrong inside, then it's as likely to show up in a sexual context first as it is any other way, I suppose. But a lion… surely a lion would be a daunting enough proposition to make most people think twice?

Of course there was the animal-rights angle, which from what I'd seen on the CCTV seemed a distinct possibility. The boy did have that look of the zealot about him, I thought, as I swiped my smartcard through the security lock on the way out of the staff compound; a definite whiff of high ideals and crazy dreams. But then the timing was all wrong for an attempted release. Animal-rights activists tend (for obvious reasons) to hit a zoo at night, but since we'd beefed up our perimeter security with trip alarms and night vision, the Animal Liberation Front might find it a more tempting option to hide in the light, so to speak. Or it might not be a jailbreak, but a demonstration of some kind—though to whom he was planning to demonstrate, in an all but empty zoo, I couldn't quite imagine.

As I crossed the main piazza there was still another possibility in the back of my mind, grimmer than the others, probably the one which was worrying me the most. Every day someone out there comes to the end of his tether, decides he can't carry on any more, and starts looking for a really good method to end it all. How do you do it? Let me count the ways.

Pills: they make you vomit, before they do anything else. Plus, if you underestimate the dose you're apt to end up alive still, but hooked up in perpetuity to a dialysis machine, with maybe a really incapacitating stroke or two to boot. Gas stinks, and you need the nerve to stay put until the anoxia kicks in. Rope's tricky: if the drop's too short you'll choke slowly, and if it's too long, you'll decapitate yourself. Neither one of those outcomes is for the squeamish. Heights: well, lots of people have problems with heights at the best of times, and it's among the messiest and most traumatic of scenarios for the relicts, the discards, those you leave behind, the ones who have to identify you afterwards. Knives sting, and even the deepest cut can clot once you've passed out. Guns: would you believe the number of people who've held a firearm to their heads, pulled the trigger—and missed? Not missed entirely, of course; just missed enough to make sure they'll spend the rest of their lives in an IC ward being fed intravenously and turned each day to have their bedsores dressed. If they're lucky. Death's fraught with mistakes, and given the options, you might well decide it makes perfect sense to go down to the zoo, wait till it's not too busy and then let yourself down into the lions' den. Leave it to the experts, so to speak.

I'm not joking. The act has a sort of logic to it. The big cats are swift enough killers, as we've seen on a thousand wildlife documentaries, brief savage scuffles on the dusty Serengeti, and there is something about the act… I don't want to give the wrong impression here, but something almost approaching dignity. Some quality of fitness and distinction that's lacking in those other methods I've mentioned. Something gladiatorial, almost: a willingness to look death straight in the face. To look into its eyes, to feel its reeking carnivore's breath on your cheek…

But it's hell for us keepers. Once a big cat has tasted manflesh, it can never again be trusted. The line has been crossed: you know it, the beast knows it too, and you have to scrutinise every facet of its behavioural patterns around humans thereafter. If it shows the slightest deviation, there's only one thing for it. Hesitate, and you're lost. That's not a thing you'll hear for public consumption from the zoo authorities—they're far more likely to dole out the usual platitudes, there's no such thing as a maneater, there are only wild animals, doing what wild animals do, and our duty of care remains unchanged, blah blah—but believe me. In practice, the days of any such beast are numbered. As a keeper, someone who puts himself on the line with these creatures each day, you'd have to be either stupidly trusting, or just plain stupid, not to be aware of the situation, and ready to act upon it if necessary. I quickened my step almost unconsciously, skirting the artificial knoll where the baboons swarmed and barked to approach the lion enclosure from behind and slightly above where the boy had been standing.

There it was, a moated expanse of drab suburban veldt across the river; and there was the boy. I got out my field glasses and gave him the once-over. So far as I could tell, he seemed not to have moved. By now I wasn't thinking sex: half-an-hour is just too long for a compulsive masturbator to stay still, really. As far as animal rights went, he didn't appear to have either the equipment or the back-up for anything I could imagine a protestor would want to do. Violence was still at the back of my mind, as was self-destruction. I watched him through the glasses as he watched the lions, and the time wore on, another five, ten minutes. It was late in the afternoon now, and starting to get cold. You could smell the frost lying in wait behind autumn's mud and woodsmoke, and the first wisps of ground-mist were starting to rise along the riverbank. Before long Graham's voice would come over the tannoy, *the park is closing in twenty minutes, please make your way towards the main exit…*

Would the boy make his move before then? And what would it be? Above me the light sensors tripped in, and the bright white floods lit up along the broad avenues. Reflexively the boy looked up, then around him, as if startled out of his reverie. I decided it was time to go in closer. Casually, trying my best not to look like a policeman, I began to stroll down towards the lion enclosure, a couple of hundred yards off down the path.

I'd just reached the footbridge over the river when it all started to go off. The shrubs along the riverbank blocked my view of the compound for a moment. All I could see was a couple of the art students, pointing and shouting. I quickened my pace to jog on to the bridge, then broke into a flat-out run when I saw what was happening by the compound.

The boy was standing on the waist-high concrete wall, hauling himself up the railings. I shouted *no*, fumbled my walkie-talkie clear of its clip and gave the all-channel alert as I ran. We were going to need the tranquilliser darts, and quickly; or else medical support at best.

He was over the railings now, sliding out of sight down the concrete ramp into the moat. One of the students, a girl, was hanging over the wall, arms outstretched and yelling to him, but he took no notice.

I reached the compound just as he hit the bottom of the moat. All of us by the outer wall were shouting now, but I don't know whether he heard a thing. If he did, he showed no sign of responding. Instead, he straightened up from his crouch, and began to climb the opposite side.

Two or three other people had come over by now, drawn by the commotion. One of them owned a hand-held camcorder, and was filming continuously throughout what happened next. Looking at the film, this is what you see:

Jerks and blurs, then a wobbly balance as the autofocus kicks in. The boy has reached the top of the inner wall: he stands on the concrete lip a while before letting himself down into the compound proper. Nothing is hurried about him, nothing hesitant; he glances from side to side, almost expectantly: *where are they?*

They were there all right. Five in the pride: two males, one little more than a cub; three females, one of them pregnant. All of them in good condition, fit and active, a functioning pack. They have names, which we use when we have to in order to distinguish them, but I don't honestly see any point in naming a wild thing. It's a false sort of domesticity: it encourages you to project human motivations, human emotions on what's basically a natural born killer, pure and simple. Calling it "Simba" doesn't change its essential nature, or turn it into something out of Disney. It doesn't make it any more knowable, nor is it something you can shout out in times of crisis, like a dog's name. All any lion does that matters much can really be summed up under the most basic of headings. It eats, it sleeps, it procreates. Given the opportunity, it stalks and kills. And these lions weren't sleeping any more. All around the compound they were waking up and beginning to take notice, and they were getting ready to stalk.

You can see on the video; first one, then another comes into view, at the periphery of the screen. The big male, watching; and the most inquisitive of the females. The camera jumps around a lot—it's being operated by Mrs. Nora Bowen, sixty-three years old and growing more agitated by the minute—but you can make out the lions well enough. Three, four, five, here they all come. And the boy, stepping away from the retaining wall.

The condenser microphone on the camera is mostly picking up Mrs. Bowen, whose alarm and concern is immediately evident, and Mr. Bowen, who is alternately trying to get his wife to give him the camera and offering her technical instruction. Above their broad Lancashire accents you can just make out the sound of a man shouting in the distance. That's me.

I was at the lip of the moat, scrambling over: no time to get around to the proper entrance on the far side of the compound. Stay still, I was yelling; don't panic. (I suspect that whenever we tell someone not to panic, we're always partly talking to ourselves: I know I was.) Sliding inelegantly down the concrete, I lost sight of what was going on in the compound.

On the video, you can see what I was missing. Not much. Slowly and deliberately, the boy walks out into the middle of the flat grassy area, then stops. The lions are surrounding him in a rough semicircle. No escape.

Scrambling to the top of the inner moat wall—it's half the height of the outer, six feet as opposed to twelve—I knelt on the rim and took stock of the situation as best I could. I was now much closer to the boy, yards closer than Mrs. Bowen with her video camera. On the tape you can just about hear me calling—not yelling any more, I was too close to yell, it would have spooked the lions—calling to him to start walking backwards in my direction. Up on the wall, I could hear him. He was talking, but I couldn't understand anything that he said.

It wasn't any language I'd heard before. Thinking back now, it still sounds like the strangest mixture of sounds; but I can say with a degree of certainty that whatever it was, it wasn't gibberish. Peter Whelan, the first keeper to answer my emergency summons, thinks the boy was just making noises to mimic an animal, chatter and meaningless babble. The thing is, though, he hardly heard any of it, arriving as he did at the critical point in time when things began to get confused. I had a decent chance to listen to it, and it sounded to me structured, as if it carried significance and meaning.

What did the lions make of it? That's just another imponderable. They held their ground against the intrusion on to their territory, shifted their forepaws a little and gazed stonily at the intruder. The big male roared once, as if in warning, and some of the others were already growling, their heads low and watchful.

Slowly, still speaking to the lions in that same fluently hypnotic way, the boy began to undo the buttons on his jacket. He slipped it off, dropped it to one side, and then started on his shirt. Hello, here we go, I thought, glancing round distractedly for back-up: we've got an exhibitionist. For some reason, it was vitally important that the lions see his dangly bits. Stupid little sod. What is it with people, I asked myself helplessly. Couldn't they recognise a bad idea when they had one? Now it was up to me to stop him, or to pick up the bits when it was all over. "Get back here," I hissed. "Start walking backwards." I wonder if he even heard me.

He was taking his trousers off: I'd already spotted his desert boots, discarded at the bottom of the moat. In a few seconds he was naked under the floodlights, exposed to the pitiless scrutiny of the lions.

Beneath the panic that had impelled me across the moat I began to feel a deeper, more fundamental fear. *This isn't going to turn out well,* I told myself, wincing at the puniness of his skinny white body as he turned slightly, first one way, then the other, as if acknowledging each beast in turn. *This is going to be bad.* I'd never seen lions attacking a human before, not under these circumstances. I was fairly sure that was exactly what I was going to be seeing, any time now.

Again I glanced round for back-up. I could see Peter Whelan running at top speed over the brow of the hill near the baboon enclosure. He had a gun. I thought we were probably going to need it. I was horribly, miserably scared, because I could see already how this was going to end—the two of us, on the ground, trying to frighten off the lions, but there were only two of us, and there were five of them…

With a grunt Peter hit the bottom of the moat and scrambled up the other side to where I was. "Slowly," I warned him, hoisting him up alongside me. "Quiet. Don't get them any more wound up."

Though out of breath from his sprint, Peter understood the need for quiet. "Bloody hell, Jim," he panted, "this is a bad 'un."

"Went over a couple of minutes ago," I whispered back. "Then he got his kit off. What have you got?"

"Tranks," he said, unslinging his rifle, "and an airhorn." They run on compressed air, and sometimes come in useful for frightening a beast off. "Manoj is bringing the rest of the stuff."

"Right," I said. "I'm trying to get him to come back this way, but he isn't listening."

"What's he doing with his clothes off?" Peter frowned. "He's not trying it on, is he?"

"Not as yet," I told him. "Anyway, he doesn't seem that excited, does he?" This may seem not just distasteful, but irrelevant, but at least a hard-on would have been indicative of some sort of motive. As it was, another explainable scenario had gone out of the window, and we were still none the wiser as to his intentions.

"Actually, I wasn't looking, meself," whispered Peter, glancing over his shoulder. "Here's Manoj coming now."

Just then several things happened in quick succession. The boy's soft babbling had been gradually increasing in volume; now, it was loud enough to be picked up by the Bowens' camcorder mike. The tape's been played for a linguist from the nearby university: he said it didn't belong to any of the language groups he knew about, but was intrigued enough to request a copy of the tape. We had to tell him no. Too many outsiders have already seen it, and we don't want it ending up on the internet for the delectation of the clicktrance classes.

For a moment the boy's shouting distracted me from the arrival of Manoj, who'd just reached the other side of the moat, where the Bowens were. On the video you can see me glancing towards the camera, making first a shush gesture, then a hurry-up. Then, I turn back to the enclosure. On the audio, you can hear the boy, ranting away at the top of his voice, and the big male roaring. A moment of clarity on the tape catches him to perfection, head thrown back, no more than fifteen yards away from the boy.

"Give me the airhorn," I told Peter. "Take aim."

Peter raised the rifle to his shoulder. "Which one?" he said. "The big bastard?"

"Your call," I said. Under normal hunting circumstances, the females make the kill, but these circumstances were about as far from normal as you could imagine. It's the male's pleasure to ring-fence the pride from intruders, so my money was on the noisy alpha. But I had a nasty feeling that when one went, they'd all join in, and there was no way Peter could reload that fast. Maybe if he took the big fella first…

The boy was screaming himself hoarse by now; no trace of panic, but a commanding, almost exhortative tone, like a hellfire preacher at the climax of his sermon. He started jumping up and down, pumping his fists and stamping on the bare soil—that wasn't too preacherly a sight, I grant you, not in his state of undress. The lions surrounding him in their semicircle snarled and twitched their tails. My finger twitched on the trigger of the airhorn.

"Why doesn't he bloody shut it?" hissed Peter. "*Oy!*" Loud enough for the boy to hear him, under normal circumstances. Loud enough for the lions to react too, I thought. But none of them seemed to hear us, neither man nor beasts. They were too wrapped up in each other. We were fast approaching the moment of truth.

The next three things happened almost simultaneously. First, Manoj came clambering up the retaining wall of the moat, and we had to give him a hand, loaded down as he was with rifle and ammo—all live rounds, no tranquillizers.

Second, there was movement in the compound behind us. All of us—Peter, Manoj, and myself—looked up just in time to catch it. There was the boy, shrieking one last commandment to the evening sky, his breath condensing in the winter chill. And there were the lions, galvanised into life, up off their haunches and running at him. All five of them, all at once.

Peter tried to take the alpha male. He missed—we found the dart later, stuck into the ground. Manoj was just fumbling his rifle to his shoulder. I was blowing the airhorn in short sharp blasts, then just one long continuous hoot, feeling totally useless. Beside me, Manoj managed to get one shot off—again, a miss, which saved him a great deal of trouble later on—and then they were too close to the boy, practically on him already.

Then, in a sudden sparking fall of brilliance, all the floodlights round the compound shorted and went out.

To this day, we don't know the reason for that. The timing was too spot-on for it to have been coincidental, yet what could have caused it? On the video, everything goes dark, exaggeratedly so, darker than the time of day would strictly warrant, and then there's one brief explosion of light that floods out the whole screen. That's Mr. Bowen, alongside his wife, who's just remembered he has another camera, for stills. He presses the shutter release more or less by reflex, and the automatic flash kicks in.

Looking at his picture, you can see Peter and Manoj and me, up on the inner wall of the moat; I'm turning round to see why the lights have gone out. That's why I caught the flash full-on, which in turn is why I was functionally sightless for the next ten seconds or so. It's hard to make out anything inside the compound with the naked eye. Mr. Bowen's built-in flash was only good over a few yards, up close at parties, and it couldn't cut through the insidious dusk which had been gathering all the time, unnoticed under the floodlights. A digitally enhanced version of the photo brings out a little more detail: a blurred, indistinct heap, at just about the spot on which the boy was standing. They were all upon him.

Up on the wall, we could hear snarling and snapping and the thud of bodies on tight-packed soil, but we couldn't see anything of the boy. None of us could: I was squinting blind after taking the brunt of Mr. Bowen's flash, and the other two were still trying to adjust their vision after the floodlights went out. They both saw the lions fall upon him, and then he was lost beneath their colliding bodies, trapped under a rugby scrum of hot fur and strapping muscle. It wasn't until three or four minutes later, when the rest of the backup arrived with lanterns and a big mobile lighting rig we used for night photography, that we were able to get a proper look inside the compound. When we did, two things were immediately apparent.

The first thing was that the lions had dispersed back to their various areas of the compound. Our searching beams picked them up under trees, behind brush cover; we saw them snarl, bare their teeth at the intrusive shafts of light.

The other thing was more of an absence. Throughout all the compound, there was no trace whatsoever of the boy, alive or dead.

Not a sign. Later, back in the surveillance post, we ran all the CCTV from all over the zoo, and you never see him leave. It was probably because I spent more time than any of the others poring over the monitors that I came to realise something else, something equally weird; you never see him arrive. You see him going from compound to compound, on the way to the lions, but you never see him at the gate or outside, in the car park. No vehicle was left unaccounted-for, and he hadn't been on any of the coaches. I'd thought he was one of the art students. He wasn't.

All of this was after we'd searched the lion compound, thoroughly, all six of us. We closed down the zoo, got everybody out (after securing the video from Mr. & Mrs. Bowen), and we went through the whole compound, twice—once, quickly, by electric light, in the company of three extremely nervous policemen, and then a proper fingertip search the next morning. The lions were edgy throughout, irritable and jittery. They didn't like it any more than we did, and they needed watching. I don't think any of us had ever felt more vulnerable in the presence of the big cats than we did that evening, so soon after witnessing the beginning of a mauling incident.

But in a mauling incident you expect blood, and a carcass, and there was none—not even on the clothes. The compound was clean. There were some gnawed cow bones from the lions' last feedtime, and that was all. Nothing to suggest fresh predation. Nothing to suggest anybody had even been in there, except for the little pile of torn and tattered (but still unbloodied) clothing where the attack had taken place. We even went through their scat for the best part of a week, sifting the piles of acrid reeking carnivore stool for bone and tissue fragments. I suppose that was as good a way as any of demonstrating exactly where we were with the whole investigation. We just didn't have a clue.

So, back to the video evidence; back to the CCTV, and Mr. Bowen's photo. Long hours scouring the tapes, till we pieced together a narrative of the incident. The trouble was, it turned out to be one of those modern narratives, the open-ended kind where you're supposed to decide for yourself what the hell happened in the end. Art-house cinema of the most infuriating kind, with no climax, no release.

There's the boy, standing by the moat, climbing the wall. Here I come, just too late to stop him. There he is in the compound, stripped off and preaching his incomprehensible sermon to the lions. And then bang, out go the lights and all hell breaks loose. What I've told you is all we know, including the stuff you don't see on the video, my own impressions and sensations. And I defy you to make any more sense of it than we were able to at the time.

We were closed the next day and the Saturday as well, partly to do a proper search of the entire zoo, partly because we wanted to assess the behaviour of the lions. The search turned up nothing—I may as well tell you that straight away. As to the lions and their behaviour, that was a different matter, and a more troubling one. I'm not a qualified animal behaviourist, like Manoj; I am a zookeeper, though, which I think qualifies me as a high-ranking amateur. I know how big cats act: I know the rules of engagement, how to approach them, what signs to look out for. I know when to stand my ground, and when to run. It's hard-earned knowledge, and you come to rely on it. There are circumstances in which it's necessary to your survival, and you wouldn't want to get it wrong. And that Friday morning, when I was walking the lion compound with the other keepers, I felt something was wrong, even though we were doing everything right.

It would be stupid and incorrect to say that we never get nervous. A little nervousness around the carnivores is no bad thing, it stops you getting sloppy and keeps you alert. But that's fear of a known thing, a possibility comprehended. This was different. This was the feeling of not knowing what to be scared of. I felt—talking over things later we all felt—that there *were* signs out there, but we were missing them. Crucial signals, impacting directly on our safety and well-being, that we weren't picking up on because we couldn't recognise them. And even if we managed to spot them after all, would we understand them? I don't know. I felt as if the rules had been changed, and nobody had told us.

After a while it became actively unsettling, and I was very glad to get out. I remember the sky above the compound was black with starlings, one of those preposterously big flocks with thousands of birds wheeling and plummeting in perfect formation. Their hoarse raucous squawks filled the air as we left the enclosure. The lions padded back out of the holding area and congregated in the middle of the grassed area, watching us go. The male roared, once. Up on the hill, the baboons started up a racket of their own as if in answer. From all across the site, each animal seemed to join in the chorus. None of us keepers could think of anything to say.

And so the incident fizzled out. We'd managed to keep it out of the press, so there was no grief from that quarter. A local paper ran a brief story on an inside page the next day, but none of the nationals ever picked it up, nor the TV, which was just as well. I suppose some soap star broke up with her footballer boyfriend, or perhaps it was just the millennial ballyhoo waiting round the corner. The police kept an open case file on the incident, but seemed happy enough to drop it as soon as they could. There wasn't a lot in it for them, really. No missing person in the outside world to match up with our missing person inside the bars, if you see what I mean. I think they were treating it as petty trespass at best: no-one hurt and no victim, no real harm done, and no repercussions for anyone. And so the zoo settled back into its hibernatory winter peace and tranquillity… only not quite.

The first incident came just after New Year. This time, it's safe to say absolutely no-one was watching. I wasn't on duty that day, but I got the phone call around nine a.m.—could I come in straight away? It was urgent.

Up in the surveillance post that morning had been Graham. At the start of his shift, he'd been checking through the CCTV, going from compound to compound and along the avenues between. Everything was quiet. It was a dull rainy morning, and all the beasts were sheltering. Then, as the next camera clicked in, he got a shock. There was a lion loose outside the compound.

Unlike the previous incident, there's no permanent record of this. The system was in the middle of a refit, and no tape exists of what Graham saw that morning. However, he describes it consistently and straightforwardly, and his word is good enough for me. He saw a lion—a big male, but not *our* big male—out of the enclosure, padding up the path that led past the baboon enclosure.

As Graham caught sight of it, the lion looked up in the direction of the camera. As if it had seen him too, he said; as if the surveillance apparatus worked both ways. For a moment they looked at each other—"well, that was what it felt like," says Graham, somewhat embarrassedly. He's not a particularly imaginative man, so I don't believe that was a later embellishment of the truth. If he said it at all, it would have been because that was the impression he got. So they stared at one another, man and beast. After a long second or two the lion moved swiftly, out of shot and into the cover of some nearby bushes.

A dangerous animal out of its compound is automatically a grade-A emergency. Thankfully, the main gates wouldn't be open for another hour-and-a-half, but all timetables had gone out of the window now, of course. Immediately, Graham was on the walkie-talkies and the tannoy, ascertaining the whereabouts of every staff member. Once everyone was accounted for, he called the police. Next, he rang around all the other off-shift keepers, me included.

I arrived not long after the police. I showed them my accreditation (which mostly consisted of my uniform), and managed to attach myself to the first team to enter the park. I think they were glad to have me there. Though they looked every inch the television SWAT team with their flak jackets and SLRs, I could tell they were as nervous as hell. Overhead the helicopter was clattering in a circle around the perimeter. At least it drove the starlings away.

We were getting ready to enter through the main gates when the mobile phone of the co-ordinating officer rang. He answered it, listened briefly, and looked up. "Panic over," he said, unmistakable relief all over his rain-wet face. "It's back in its cage."

What had happened was, Graham had been checking the lion enclosure all the while, trying to ascertain which animal had got out. It might well have made a difference, since each beast has its own personality. Some can be easily cowed, and some are more prone to confrontation than others. The rain made things difficult. The pride were sheltering in and around the den, and it wasn't until Graham actually got in the Land Rover and went to check, that he was able to report back. Two males, three females, all present and correct.

We still searched the entire zoo, of course, although the search took place in an altogether more laid-back spirit than would otherwise have been the case. Unfortunately, the laid-backness didn't last, and before long we got the distinct impression that the police were a bit fed up with us. Bringing them all the way out to the suburbs on these false alarms—couldn't we run our own zoo properly, or what? They didn't exactly accuse us of wasting their time, but they came very close.

Graham took some flak, from zoo management as well as police, for sounding the alarm. I thought this was not just unfair but deeply, dangerously ignorant. What was he supposed to do? There was an animal outside its enclosure and running loose: a big predator, the biggest we had. All the protocols were in place for such an incident, and he'd had no choice but to follow them to the letter. Ah, but obviously you didn't check, they told him. Wouldn't it have been better if you'd checked? To which he could only point out, I did check, to the best of my ability—and besides, I saw what I saw. A lion, loose outside the compound. And then they would look at him, you know, in that *oh, really?* way, and Graham would have to bite his lip and try not to lose his temper.

Once the police had got back in their vans and cleared off, the rest of us keepers checked out the lion enclosure. There was no sign of an obvious breach of security. We looked in the bottom of the moat for scat, which you'd expect to find if one of the animals had been down there even temporarily. Twelve feet of more-or-less sheer concrete would be a formidable obstacle, after all. Nothing down there. No breaches of the fence around the back of the compound, either, so we were left with a variant on the same question that had troubled us the last time. How did it get out? And, come to that, how did it get back in again?

It had me beat. I believed Graham: how could I not? I trusted him absolutely. And for the next week I found myself lingering round the lion compound, just watching them, trying to work it out. That's how I saw their behaviour patterns had definitely changed. It hadn't just been a nervous reaction, that first morning after we lost the boy. You could see a real difference, if you knew what to look for. It wasn't the behaviour of beasts in a cage—nor, come to that, of uncaged beasts. It was something none of us had seen.

I asked Manoj, with his academic background in behavioural study, and he agreed. "It's not standard pack behaviour," he said, "it doesn't fit the captivity model, or any other model I've ever heard of. Over and above that—" he began, and stopped.

"It's bloody creepy," I finished, and he frowned at me. I don't think that was supposed to be part of the behavioural lexicon.

We didn't know it yet, but our troubles with the lions were only beginning. In the weeks and months that followed Graham's sighting, lions were spotted outside their compound on no less that five occasions—three times on CCTV, twice by keepers on foot. Concerning the former, we have tape of one such sighting. You can just about make out the unmistakable shape of the predator, moving through bushes around the edge of the zebra enclosure. This was the strangest of all, the one that completely defied all explanation. To be where it was when it was caught on camera, the lion would've had to escape its own compound, negotiate the moat and the twelve-foot wall and all that, pass—on a normal working day, with upwards of a hundred people on site—along the main thoroughfare of the zoo, and scale a ten-foot fence with spikes at the top. And it would have had to have done it all again, in reverse, to get back in the lions' den with the rest of its mates by the time Manoj and I arrived on the scene with our tranquiliser rifles. Because, as usual, we counted five lions in the compound by the time we got there.

On the tape, the zebras don't even seem to see the lion. There's no alarm, they don't go charging away to the far side of the compound. But as soon as they saw Manoj and me, they couldn't move fast enough. One glance, and they were gone, charging off in a rumble of hooves, leaving only a pile or two of steaming crap on the trampled grass. This was something we were getting used to by now. Even the friendliest beasts, the apes and the elephants, were starting to shy away from us, if not become actively hostile. This was odd—downright worrying, even—but it wasn't our biggest problem that spring.

The biggest problem was that we'd effectively lost any measure of control with regard to security in the most dangerous area of the whole zoo. Once you discounted (as you obviously had to) the notion that there was a stray lion, not a member of our pride, loose and roaming around the zoo, then you were left with the unpalatable fact that if one of ours did get out, then we'd have no way of distinguishing it from the phantom animal we were seeing on the CCTV. All our security compromised, in the worst possible way.

What were we supposed to do? Keep calling the police out on wild goose chases? We'd be like the boy who cried "wolf" once too often. Sooner or later, they wouldn't bother turning out; and who was to say that wouldn't be just the occasion they were needed? As a compromise measure, the management hired new guards—not experienced keepers, just untrained muscle from Group 4, really nothing more than glorified bouncers. They were supposed to patrol the avenues and walkways, with orders to call in anything out of the ordinary straight away. They were no use whatsoever; we might as well have saved our money. In fact, they were the proximate cause of our key fatality.

This was in April, an unseasonably hot spell towards the end of the month. I always used to like going about the grounds in springtime, the smells and sounds of nature reawakening from its winter hiatus, the blossom on the trees, the contentment of every animal at the return of sun and warmth. For the space of a week or so, I felt better walking my beat than I had since the turn of the year. It helped take my mind off things: not only the business with the lions, but now a problem with the new guards.

One or two of them had been seen behaving inappropriately round the animals. They'd been caught on CCTV hanging over the moats and throwing sweets, sometimes sticks and stones, cans of Coke, even. Some were actually taunting the animals through the bars of their cages. Stupid, loutish behaviour, the sort of thing we'd eject a member of the public for. By April, there was a significant undercurrent of hostility between the full-time staff and the temporaries. We were hardly even talking to each other, let alone co-operating fully and closely, as per the plan. That might have helped avoid the tragedy... but then again, didn't they bring it on themselves? Don't we all, in the last analysis?

It was late in the afternoon again, but the day had been warm and the sky was still filled with light. The last of the visitors had just left, and we'd locked down the outer compound. Peter and I were doing one last walk-through, checking there were no stragglers left behind, getting ready to put everything to bed. Usually this was my favourite time of day, in my favourite season. Under normal circumstances, I would have been relishing this stroll around the grounds. As it was, I was unaccountably nervous. Peter says he felt it too, and as I mentioned before, he's not an overly imaginative man.

There was something in the air—I think the animals sensed it too, because all over the site they were skittish, restless, unusually noisy. The gemsboks, when we passed by the antelope enclosure, were actually butting the fences. I got on the walkie-talkie to Manoj, up in the surveillance post, to get his opinion.

"I'll have a look," he said. "Stay on while I just get this... ah, you bloody thing. I hate these gadgets." I knew what he'd be doing: clicking through the various camera angles from the CCTV around the zoo till he got one that showed the antelopes. It sounded as if he was having a few technical problems. "Why don't they make these things—*oh, shit.*" Over the course of two words his entire tone changed. "Sam. Peter. You copy?"

"Yeah."

"Incident in progress, north side of the baboon enclosure. Two of the new guards, attack under way. Get over there right now. Stay on the line."

Again, it's captured on tape, but again there's a complication. Because it was spring, the blossom was out on the cherry trees that line the main avenue through the zoo. The blossom restricted the view of the baboon enclosure as seen from one of the CCTV cameras—the one, as luck would have it, through which Manoj was watching the developing incident. What he'd seen was this:

Two of the hired guards, standing by the wire mesh of the fence, making fun of the baboons. The leader of the troop, a powerful full-grown chacma, was practically in their faces, the other side of the chain-link. He was a grumpy, muscular specimen, a natural leader and a bully, not afraid to stamp his authority on the group, usually by means of his teeth. Manoj told me something he'd read about the species in an old and extremely politically incorrect text, something along the lines of: "A full-grown chacma is more than a match for two good dogs." This one, Manoj thought, would probably be more than a match for two stupid security men.

As he'd watched, one of the guards had actually jumped on to the fence and started rattling it, shaking it on its stanchions in imitation of a monkey, or so it looks on the tape. The other one had moved slightly to one side, obscured by the blossom of one of the nearby cherry trees. Like the other one, he was far too close to the fence.

Watching the tape, all you get is that there's some kind of commotion. The blossom stops you from seeing exactly what's happening, but you can see the reaction of the other guard. He drops down from the fence, and runs over to help his mate. You can also see the rest of the baboons stop hooting and grimacing, and watch. Just watch.

"That's the weird bit," Manoj said to me afterwards, the first time we looked through the VT together. "See the troop leader there?"

"He isn't doing anything," I said.

"Exactly." Manoj looked at me. "He's ceded authority to another animal."

I was confused. "Another member of the troop?"

"Not a chance," Manoj said decisively. "This boy? Never."

But it's true: you can see him standing back with the others, just watching, like us. After what seems like ages, but according to the timestamp on the tape is just over ten seconds, the guard falls back from the fence and into camera shot again.

Even on the tape you can see he's very badly messed up. The paramedics tried to save one of his eyes, I believe, but it was too late probably from the start. Most of the rest of his face he left inside the compound. Inside the cage, the baboons leap and cavort in a frenzy of excitement.

The other guard, who's dragged his wounded mate away from the fence and back on to the tarmac path, now lays him on the ground. Quite forgivably, he turns away for a moment to be sick before fumbling for his walkie-talkie. Then, something he sees away behind the cherry trees makes him stop what he's doing. He freezes for a second, and then he's off and running, disappearing out of shot.

God knows what he was running *from*, but he was heading towards us. We were on the far side of the zoo, sprinting flat out towards the baboon enclosure. Under normal circumstances we'd have met up near by the main block, and who knows? Things might have gone very differently for him—for all of us. As it was, he never got that far.

We could hear noise from all over the zoo by now: attack cries, hoarse belligerent roars and squawks and hoots that ranged across the whole spectrum of aggression. On bits and scraps of tape that follow the guard's progress along the main avenue, you can piece together what's happening. Each enclosure that he passes is filled with shrieking animals, pressed close to bars and fences. More than once the proximity of these malevolent creatures cause him to shy away, take evasive action. The chimps clinging to their chain-link fence scream and hurl excrement at him, and he trips and stumbles, but he's up on his feet and running again within a second.

He looks as if he's scared out of his wits. It would have been something to see what it was, back by the baboon enclosure, that put the fear of God up him that way. When he draws level with the elephants, lined up by the edge of their enclosure and trumpeting ferociously, it's their sheer bulk, I think, that sends him veering off in a different direction, off the main avenue and on to on of the side paths. This is the way to the nocturama, a tunnel sunk below ground level, home of the night creatures.

Manoj saw him sprinting down the brick-lined cutting that leads to the entrance to the tunnel. There's no CCTV inside there: it's too dark in the normal course of events. There's red-light illumination that lets you see the exhibits, but that's all. Only in an emergency are the normal bulbs switched on, from a switch-box by the entrance. And only later, long after it was of any practical use to us, did we remember that fact.

We were still running. From where we were, on the slightly higher ground, we could see the guard disappear into the cutting. What on earth was he was doing down there? Thumbing the walkie-talkie switch I panted, "Manoj?"

"Here."

"Why's he gone down the tunnel?"

"I don't know. *Wait*—" Manoj sounded rattled.

"What?"

"Did you see that? What's he doing with his clothes off?"

"What? Where?"

"… Never mind," directed Manoj. "The man that needs your help is over by the baboon compound. Leave that other now. Let him run around the place stark naked if he likes."

"But —"

But nothing. Already it was too late. From down in the nocturama we could hear the screams. The other guard had run into trouble.

Without thinking I changed course, ran down the slope towards the other entrance to the tunnel. Behind me Peter was arguing with Manoj on the walkie-talkie, but I only had ears for the screaming.

Please God, I was thinking as I ran, *for fuck's sake, no more bother. Just keep a lid on it until we can get these idiots out of here.* I don't know who I was praying to, if that was a prayer. It's not a thing I do. It must have been the screaming that got to me.

It came echoing out of the open-ended tunnel, so piercing and intense that as I drew level with the entrance I actually came to a stop, trying to remember what exactly we kept down there. Insects, bats, moths… nothing dangerous that I could bring to mind. Perhaps the bloke just had a thing about the dark, I told myself. Maybe he just got the fear. But I knew it was worse than that; every shred of instinct told me so. Fifteen years' experience in zoos, maybe. I suspect it was more like two million years' worth of evolutionary impulse.

The screaming stopped abruptly as I reached the head of the steps down into the tunnel. I thought I heard the sound of something running—I was going to say, footsteps, but it's as well to be exact. Something running, down in the dark.

I took one step down, and then another, then found myself unable to go any further. Coming up from that tunnel mouth was a stink like nothing I'd come across in all the years I'd spent around animals. I can hardly describe it, except to say that it reached deep into the ancestral parts of the brain, the centres of instinct and fear. It was stale and cloacal and rotten; it was the smell of must and decay, spoiled meat and sour animal piss. Rising through it like a basenote was the overpowering stink of blood.

Gagging at the stench, I took another few steps down into the tunnel. Peter caught up with me then, and it was easier with him there. We advanced down to the bottom of the steps, and into the nocturama. That stupid little prayer was running through my head still, like a mantra.

It was musty and mildewed and dripping down there. Green slime coated the plastic windows of the exhibits, and there was nowhere near enough light. We walked on into the dark, past moths measuring out the dimensions of their prisons, past fireflies flashing unintelligible signals. On the other side of the tunnel, the chiroptera: avid famished bats that swooped through the lightless recesses and clustered on the dead boughs of artificial trees. Predators and prey in the natural scheme of things. Now, they merely pressed closer to the glass and watched as we advanced.

On we went around the corner, where the stink was mounting. I'd slowed now to something less than walking pace. Had we been going any faster, we'd have fallen over it. It was hard to see in the semidark, but we could make out the shape clearly enough. A man, lying on his back. The red lightbulbs in the animal recesses made the blood seem almost transparent at first. Then Peter focussed his flashlight, and we saw what was left of him; which was not a lot.

Down in that sewer-smelling tunnel, trapped in such a narrow space with a thing like that... I wonder can you imagine how awful it was? Along the walls, the watching worm-lizards pressed greedily against the windows, tongues darting in and out of their cruel slits of mouths. And everywhere now, through all the length of the tunnel, the fierce reek of blood.

That was really the last straw, so far as the zoo was concerned. One guard dead in the tunnel, horribly mauled by some as yet unidentified predator. Another with the front half of his face chewed off: by a baboon, it was officially decided, though some responsible authorities, Manoj amongst them, begged to differ. These latter pointed out certain aspects of bite radius and attack pattern, and at the back of Manoj's mind—though it never really came up at the inquest—was the behaviour pattern of the other baboons in the enclosure, the temporary submissiveness of the troop leader.

Either way, we were doomed. The local council had been treating us like pariahs for god knows how long, even before the incident. We had animal-rights protestors crawling all over us at the best of times. Now, one man was dead and another maimed for life, and driven half crazy into the bargain. Wouldn't you be? It wasn't our fault, was all we could say in our defence: not that that cut any ice with the police. There was a full investigation, conducted of course in the hot moralistic glow of the media spotlight. That was hardly the best sort of publicity, as I'm sure you can imagine.

We were closed all through the Easter holidays, one of our busiest times, and then to cap it all the Health & Safety Directorate weighed in with their report. They delivered a damning assessment of our operation: among other things, they said the safety of the zoo was thoroughly and irretrievably compromised, that our security measures were demonstrably inadequate, and that we seemed to have no effective control over the movements of the animals, up to and including the most dangerous of the predators. In short, they had no option but to withdraw our public safety certificate, effective immediately.

That was it. In very short order, the council swung the axe, the board of directors resigned, and we were finished. Arrangements were made to flog off the assets and rehouse the animals in zoos around the country. Then the bulldozers would move in, the land would be sold for redevelopment, and a line would be drawn under the whole unfortunate affair. Which brings me more or less up to where we are right now.

These last few weeks and months before the closure have been the strangest of all. We run a skeleton staff—no need for security any more, not without visitors, no need to walk the compound more than once or twice a day. That's our excuse, anyway. The plain and simple fact is, we're scared now. The Health & Safety people were right, to that extent: we *have* lost our grip. Ever since the accident we've effectively lost track of how many animals there are in any given enclosure, at any given time. The most basic rule of zoo security has been breached, utterly and irrevocably it seems. Once darkness falls, animals are loose and roaming across the compound, and they run in strange new packs. It's no longer unusual to see big cats in with ungulates, or birds flocking across species. You'd expect a bloodbath every night, but it never happens.

By the same token, there have been no more attacks on humans since the killing of the guard, but still you can imagine how we feel. It's far from unusual for a keeper on the ground to see something on the path, ahead of him or behind him, towards the hours of dusk, or when mist and rain affect the visibility. At night, we basically cede control of the zoo; we have no choice. It's shameful—we can hardly look at each other sometimes—but it's also an oddly liberating thing to admit it. Peter feels the same way, Graham, even Manoj. After all we've seen, we can't be around these animals for long without getting the creeps.

You feel it at feeding times and during routine medical procedures. Even walking past the enclosures you sense it. A subtle, yet decisive change in the balance of our interaction; a shift in power. Though we're at least nominally free, able to leave at the end of our shifts and drive home to our empty houses in the suburbs, it's hard not to feel claustrophobic, imprisoned. The bars are there to protect us. Have we really come to depend on them so much? It's as if the beasts are the free ones, not us, not any more. As if some inconceivable insight has emancipated them, raised their consciousness to a level no one thought they'd ever reach. Those are Manoj's words, not mine. When he said it to me, just the other day, I asked him what he meant, and he threw up his hands in the air. "I don't know. I sound like a bloody swami, don't I?"

"You do, a bit," I said. We were up in the God-seat, watching the closed-circuit.

"Well, look at them," he said, indicating the lions on the monitor. "I'm keeping all the tapes, you know. I'm thinking of going back to university, doing my post-grad. I can use them for my thesis."

"Which will be?"

"I haven't got a title for it yet," he admitted. "This. All of this. How they've changed."

"That'll take some working-out," I said.

He nodded glumly. "Tell me about it," he sighed. It was as if the change came as a personal affront to him. "Breakdown of the old pack structures. Atypical response patterns in the presence of keepers and other humans. Complete lack of inter-species aggression. It's not natural."

"That can't be a permanent behavioural shift, though?" I wasn't having that. "We're not talking about the holy-rollers here, are we? And the lion shall lie down with the lamb?" As I said it, I remembered that evening by the lions' den. I'd thought the boy was a sacrificial lamb of his own appointing, another deluded Daniel driven crazy by too much Sunday school and animal-rights sermonising. Now, I didn't know what to think.

"I'm not sure it is a permanent shift, not in that sense, anyway. But suppose it isn't?" Manoj leaned back from the monitor, ran his hands through his thick black hair. "That's almost worse, if you think about it."

"How so?"

"Okay. We observe behavioural patterns in animals, which are the result of millions of years of evolutionary adaptation. Over the last three months, our animals here have demonstrated profound behavioural alterations, across all species, across all hierarchical relationships. Now, we either assume this change is a non-volitional response to external stimuli—that is, they used to behave *this* way, and now they behave *that* way, because there's something in the water, or they all had the same sort of brainstorm, or whatever—or else…"

"Or else?"

Manoj looked as if he was chewing a wasp. "Or else what we're seeing here is a volitional behaviour shift."

"You mean—they *decided* to do it?"

"They chose, yes. That would be the other alternative." I could see Manoj liked this option even less. "According to that scenario, what we're seeing here would be interpreted as possibly the first recorded instance of altruistic co-operation *across species* towards a common, mutually desirable goal—though what that might be, I have no idea. How could I? Now that sort of conceptualisation would require a level of self-awareness…" He broke off, lost in his own thoughts.

A movement on screen caught my eye. "Hang on—look there, at the lions. How many are there in those bushes?"

Manoj waved a hand in dismissal. "Don't bother," he said resignedly. "You can't keep track these days. Five, six. Who knows?"

It was true. It was a wilderness in there. Once, it had been a jungle, cut into manageable chunks and fenced in with steel and glass. We used to stand by the windows and listen to the racket, the bellows of frustration, the mournful shrieks and howls. What this new thing is… it's hard to say. More than anything, it feels like the calm before the storm.

We're aware of the consequences, even if we can't fully understand them. Soon, these animals with their strange new behaviours, their disconcerting calm and uncanny self-possession, will be crated up and shipped to a dozen zoos across Europe. What happens if they replicate these new memes in their new surroundings? What if they pass them on?

Over and above that, there's a world beyond the bars. The starlings flock each night in ever-growing numbers above the compound, roosting in the trees as the animals below stare unblinkingly upwards, as if towards the stars, the old bestiary of myths and legends in the sky. Maybe the ancient fables don't hold water any more. Maybe a change has come upon us, and nothing's safe in its cage.

LOTOPHAGI
EDWARD MORRIS

Edward Morris lives in Portland, Oregon where he lives and works with his muse, gallery artist Serena Blossom Appel.

Morris has published four novels: *There Was A Crooked Man*, *Arkadia*, *The Frank Principle*, and *Atlantis, 1999: A Memoir*. His short fiction and poetry has been published in *Murky Depths*, *Interzone*, *Arkham Tales*, *Helix*, *Mirage*, *Farrago's Wainscot* and other magazines and webzines. He is currently working on *Death Inc*, an online serial that is a prequel in his Crooked Man series.

When I wrote the following pages, or most of them, it was 2002. I lived in the woods, twenty miles from the nearest store, seven miles upland from the nearest mailbox, three miles from the nearest land-line telephone.

If you believe the stoners in Washington, there really are trolls in the Seattle steam-tunnels. The whole Northwest is legendary for the Americanized Yeti of the Sasquatch Nation. The filmic hoax of Bigfoot was no more or less than the Left Coast branch of the Alamagoosalum of New England, themselves mossy scions of the Midwestern Jackalope, kissing cousins of the Texan Chocolocco and Chupacabra, the far-branched family tree limb of the Jersey Devil...

And fuck you, too. There are forests where Man trying to protect the environment is utterly irrelevant. Those forests are the ones that people Don't Go In. Or if they do, not all of them makes it out.

Pandora was nineteen. Her parents told me she was nineteen. Then they slammed the door in my face. After that, I drove all night to the first strip club I found open at 8:00 a.m., and drank myself into a motel. Later Days, as we used to say at Aeolus Farm. Later Days, and better lays...

I went to the woods when I dropped out of college, down that miles-long potholy driveway where, as in the rest of the Willamette Region, enterprising land barons imported half the native flora from other worlds than this... I went to the mountains, to the old growth of the Cascade Range. I went to learn their ways.

I cast back my mind to 2002 and I'm right there, with flowers everywhere, flowers in Pandora's weird honey hair. I'm right there, in the stinky, grubby

201

shades of humanity bickering in tiny close quarters.

Bickering around all the parts of Outside that made it in to our little cultural reservation, in every hut and yurt, every hurt, wrapped in pillowcases and socks, the unnumbered poppets of Maya let loose to lay waste inside the wire, and eggs...

I went to the woods because I wished to die, to shuck off the last vestiges of civilization long before some stump-jumper found my bones. I went to the woods to abandon my origins and be claimed only by the loving arms of the forest mast, To slough off the life I squandered back in the city.

Back in that one-room palace on Burnside Boulevard, where the outsides of the windows were always black with soot. Back when I was still puzzled, waiting for a future that never happened, shoveling through Augean stables of horseshit just because someone told me there was a pony underneath.

Back in the ten seconds when I tried to begin again, and choked. Back in the darkness before Real Life.

I started looking for a village, that year, remembering stories from a Haitian girl I knew in school, about the Leaf Doctors who work for the Green Man, and protect the forest from all harm...

I think about the drowsy, rooty, mossy way any forest calls you to go to sleep in the daytime, find a bed of pine boughs and whatever else is handy, and get out of the light, get out of the day, root down into Mother Earth like a cicada, and *change*...

And what rough imago, all the while, slouching past your camera, turns its head at the flash of change, while the whales beach, and the seas leach ...

Sometimes, when you go looking for a village, what you find is the Island of the Lotus Eaters, like the one in The Odyssey *or* The Iliad *or whichever the fuck one it was we had to read back at Our Lady. In my foggy memory, on the bank of the stream, Mountain Grrl washed clothes on a flat rock and spun rumors out the needle-exchange of her summer wasp mouth and Liza Minelli nose, that Goo had warrants out for his arrest, or he was a sex offender or some dumb damn thing.*

She was the first of the droves to leave. She never said goodbye. I'm glad.

You see how *weird* I got out there? What it did to me now, when I try to explain what happened? You probably don't. Not yet.

But I'm the only one who made it off that co-op alive.

The last night. The last night I was there.

Comma, damn it.

My new California Grrl (twelve years my junior, with her silver eye shadow and big black spiral earrings and rather athletic ways of nearly killing her old man in bed) wants me to write about the last night at the Aeolus Co-Op Farm.

Sonia doesn't understand. I haven't explained much. Like why I was such a recluse, then, or how seventy people could just disappear and the cops not give a fuck. They were just dirty hippies, I want to tell her. They weren't people. Not to the law.

I remember lying on moldy sleeping bags, on my last night at the co-op. I remember dreaming about the face on the stone that Portland State University dragged out of the Columbia River down at Sauvie Island.

That round-eyed, inhuman face, neither condemning nor condoning, natural as a cloud. Impersonal, yet entirely predatory, in the cast of its filed teeth, the jut of its cannibal belly.

I remember seeing the Columbia Stone in the Portland Art Museum just last year, when I made myself go back for a friend's opening there. I remember having to go back to the hotel and take a Xanax. I remember wondering if there was ever human blood spilled across that great stone face.

I remember waking up throwing up. I haven't been back to the museum. I go to AA instead. It's big down here. It doesn't really help, but it gives me something else to look at…

I want to remember the way it got dark so quickly, even on the edge of the edge of Portland, after the November monsoons. We had every dwelling cold-proofed and rain-proofed, an activity that the summer months were *for*, by mutual consent and to the mutual way of thinking. (That part needed no infighting to accomplish, and fast.)

Every dwelling, too, had its own deadwood or peat fires going in the little scrounged stovepipe flues we had set up one to a room, made from fifty-gallon drums and spare parts. Waking up in the darkness there all those nights, I always felt as though I was eight again, sleeping over at my Gramma's, on the hide-a-bed in the living room by the old wood stove…

I remember the way it snowed a good foot or two both years I was there, weird for Oregon even in winter. AJ made some noises about climate change when he was trying to start up the old Willys Jeep we called Furthur. Furthur's radiator apparently suffered massive reflux at the onset of the first blizzards that fell hard upon the land, and took it by surprise.

I remember that AJ bought most of the weed I grew. I remember that he was all right. Italian, I think. He talked with an East Coast accent. Never said where he came from. But I remember him. I do…

I remember there were flowers breaking into bloom everywhere on Aeolus Farm that cold, cold spring the year after we incorporated, out at the edge of the Eighty-Second Avenue Miracle Mile toward Boring on the Springwater Electric Railway, out past the Rhodie-Gardens and golf courses, out where Portland starts to become Something Else.

Flowers everywhere, flowers on the violet-clad roof down below the tree, housing the longhouse structure that Big Scott, our token Polynesian, called the *falé*, where people slept most of the time. The *falé* smelled like sex and weed and was generally first-come first… whatever you were into, because it had the softest-built beds.

Aeolus was regularly hailed by the armchair anthropologists of the Downtown Weekly papers as an experiment in sustainability, since Deuce Longbow's family bought the land with that purpose and then traipsed away off to Tahiti to die of ingesting some unknown psychedelic, to hear wild-eyed Deuce (or Douche, as some of us came to know the titular oligarch of the collective) tell it.

Douche, of the mad composer hair, and the Gore-Tex clothes he wore until they stunk like rabid, rutting goat, like… Mountain Grrl. But I couldn't think about Mountain Grrl. That wasn't always her name, and she didn't always stink.

She used to bathe, like me, and wear weird oils like me, and wash her dreadies a few times a week to keep the bugs out. She was the farm's Chief Engineer, and I was their pet journalist. Everyone dug in their heels when we broke up. No one wanted to leave.

Deuce came down out of his ivory tree-sit tower pretty quick and put a whole new kink in that situation: Him. (The Frankenstein monster of a relationship that resulted when they got together almost put me off women for good, but Moth was no better.)

Deuce, of the big yompin Herman Survivor boots that steamed with pig manure from the two pot-bellied pigs that fertilized the back strawberry patches. (They stank about as much as the composting outhouses, which was barely at all.)

Deuce who kept up the sauna that a long ago "villager" named Jukka had dug into the side of the hill and made of fitted rock, and cob. Deuce, who liked bugs so much he almost socked me for killing a hornet when I was making the earthwork around the picking-garden.

He kept saying this word *Ahimsa, Ahimsa*. I kicked him in the balls, and down he went. Big Scott had to pull us apart and waddle us down the trail until we decided we were done. It felt like Deuce let him do it. Maybe he did.

Deuce was a touchy one. When I was first initiated onto that land, I saw his hypervigilance as a good thing. Like how he'd always finish people's sentences, and be right.

But after a while, I started to wonder. A lot. After a while, I started to hang wards around my hut, and sleep with a machete I made myself, one that I sharpened on a rock for one and one-half weeks. I counted. I waited. I hardly slept. I was getting out.

That machete got me out. I don't like to talk about that. Not even in Group, or at meetings. But I remember. Oh, I do…

"Didn't you used to be a Trustafarian?" I remember asking Moth, who was breaking up a big bag of marijuana buds and taking the seeds out before he left my hut with two dozen eggs' worth of ditch-weed. "Didn't you used to go to school? What the fuck are any of us even *doing*?"

Moodily, I chewed the strip of beef jerky almost forgotten in my right hand, looking at the waterlogged old Samuel R. Delany paperback I wasn't really reading since Moth interrupted me with his knock. Moth made a gesture with one small surgeon's hand that meant he was going to swat me, but he couldn't stop smiling.

I kept looking out the loophole window in the front door, thinking about his willing replacement Pandora, when we made sweet squeaky love in the milk shed and her hot, slithery cunt yanked my cock to shuddering orgasm in sinuous waves, greater and greater each time...

What was this? Every time I started thinking about real things, there'd be some intrusion like that... I had enough to do out here that I just stopped thinking, for longer and longer periods. But as the Poet said, the hook brought me back.

Like I was starting to know my place in the hunt. Like I was starting to become worthy to hunt, and eat, and feed on the lesser beasts that we could now herd...

Oh, my dreams were getting strange, and the thoughts in my own head ran far off course with no brain-mouth clutch in the way, sitting in the Delphic cave of my hut when I wasn't out chopping brush or sowing corn.

"... You know? Like, how people back in Maya," Moth used words like that like he was reading them from a book he held in his hands, and that irritating little smile never quit flipping up the corners of those big cock-sucking lips. "Civilization,whatever, they never mean it when they say How's It Going. They don't really fucking care. Do you?"

I shrugged. "Like sex and checks and special effects, child, it all depends on position and circumstance."

Moth frowned, his designer eyes that weren't contacts narrowing. "Eww. Meat." He was looking at the strip of beef jerky in my free hand. "You know that stuff rots for four years in your colon?"

I barely looked up. "Seems like you eat meat quite a bit." Moth blushed, and looked hurt. I knew I'd gotten to him. But I was getting really tired of the Come To Jesus meetings. About the only things he was good at were in bed. For some reason. But that, too, got old fast.

"Deuce... he told me once that he wanted to start a school for children and just... bend them to his will. And that if the aliens took over, he'd sign on with them." Moth's sea-blue eyes seemed to shine with their own light of fear. "And he was totally straight up. I was like 'Oh, haha, Deuce made a funny—'" The smile was instantly gone. "And he's just like, 'No. What you got to say?'"

But Moth left, too. Bound for Parts Unknown, Boring or Forest Grove or homeless on Hawthorne and singing for his supper, or maybe mumbled bones eaten cleaner than wolves could do, clutched by thumbs not quite thumbs...

But no one talked about that. At Aeolus we talked, talked, talked everything into the ground, ground, ground, in the weirdest, most stilted vocabulary-by-committee I ever heard. Except things like that. The things that were too terrifying.

It all seems like a dream now. Like someone else's summer job.

All I wanted was a hole in the ground to hide in, and a little time to think. I carved out my tiny chicken-coop of space from a sod hut and a hollow tree behind it, into a cozy outpost of words and images in the forest, drawing on home-stretched vellum and birch bark paper, writing the kind of poems I never thought I could.

Until four members of the co-op (and how that word looks like 'coop' to me even now) disappeared.

Read that again. Disappeared.

They didn't die, leave or get arrested. They just disappeared. Moth, Juice, Goo and Josh. Sounds like a goddamn band. All four of those heads just *vanished* the same spring, my second hiding out from everything I was hiding out from, doing everything I was doing, everything I would miss and still miss now…

Everyone had a theory. Everyone had a weapon. Everyone had a grudge, a pet beef, a sick hole shining through the set-up… which Aeolus was really starting to look like. But the bare fact was that we were being picked off by an unknown factor out in the middle of nowhere, and we couldn't call anyone. No one cared. We'd cut ourselves off from society, and now reaped our cry of Wolf.

There were a lot of malenky homeless tweakers denning in the blackberry brakes and living out of Burleigh trailers and mountain bikes by Johnson's Creek. Often, those wayfarers bashed each other bloody over a teener of meth or a half-rack of Pabst Blue Ribbon. We gave them food when they came by the farm, food and short shrift and very little else.

In pondering the Procrustean bandits of the Springwater Corridor, I feared the worst in my 20/20 rearview. Deuce stalled on getting the cops involved, though we were all residents of the land, and paid taxes from all the enterprises we had out there to keep ourselves from getting Waco'ed. (Hell, we had two sustainability grants from Mayor Katz, and one from the Governor!)

But Deuce kept whining through his black beard about our Rights, how the Cops would Take Away Our Rights, and we have Rights to do Something About It Ourselves, and We're Gonna Post A Watch, and the next night I heard Goo screaming All. Night. Long. Under the ground. All. Night. Long. And no one…

People started leaving in droves, and the ones that stayed were the bottom of the barrel. We all kept to ourselves, did what we had to do, bared our fangs and popped our claws. Me the most of all.

No one believed Cassandra, either, when she foretold wars, and rumors of wars. No one believes the cursed prophet who can't keep his nose out of the home brew, or his running mouth from running down everyone, himself the most of all. Blind Tiresias here didn't play well with others, you see. Blind Tiresias came to the land to forget.

I was drunk, and in a blackout for most of the afternoon. I was laid up drunk in my hut. I heard him screaming under the ground. I couldn't sleep, but didn't want to move. It makes me panic, when I get like that, when I *drink* like that, panic and lock up and I could *hear* Goo, I could *hear* him calling out for his Momma and praying to God the Father Son Anna Holy Ghost O My God I Am Heartily Sorry Fa Havin Offended Thee…

I tried to tell them, the next day, with predictable results. "Smoke a bowl," AJ told me. "You got the DT's. Take some ibuprofen from the First Aid kit in the *falé*. Shit, I'll cook youse a steak, if ya hang out for a minute. Yeah, pack that bowl up. And drink some water, like, *now*…"

I stood watch all night long, stoned and hooty owl-eyed, with A.J.'s bolt-action .30-06 laying across my knees. The woods were lovely, dark and deep, and I cursed every ROADWAY NOT IMPROVED sign down the chugging, thundering potholed way there over Foster Road and half the weird little side streets without a name in Multnomah County that shriek in fear at some incorporation date.

AJ took the Jeep into town once a week for provisions to trade weed or salvia or ten other herbs we grew down at the co-ops in Southeast and Sellwood. We had one computer that ran off a solar panel, and a Honda generator for this, that, and the other. With two whole gallons of gas. Go, Us.

I waited for the night to end, and drank coffee from a metal Goodwill percolator on a wood rack across the fire. (Big Scott made that rack. His oddly small hands had the feel for wood.)

Eventually, the sun rose and dispelled the vague, irrelevant mist of fear above the stream that wended through the farm.

Mountain Grrl never gave me a reason to want to stick around. Pandora did.

Pandora was a true crone-in-training, and I loved her. She went without a shirt when it was warm, and climbed around in the canopy trying to find the spots with the best echo to play this bamboo flute she had. That night was her six months' anniversary at Aeolus, and she still never ran out of surprises.

Behind us in my hut on the last night of that world, the Coleman lantern hissed out its firefly glow on the PGE wire-spool endtable. She brushed a shock of blonde dreadies out of her face and whaled out this Ziploc bag of weed that looked like a throw-pillow.

Her cerulean eyes sparkled. I could see a pack of rolling papers stuffed into the top, just beyond the yellow-and-blue-make-green of the seal.

"This is my headies, from before." she told me. "I was saving it." She reached for something in the front pocket of her too-long corduroy overalls. "'Cos this most definitely is a rainy day."

I looked toward the stretched canvas flap of the door. "Should I—" She rapidly shook her head, moving closer to me with her eyes on the seal of the bag.

One soft black anorak-clad shoulder brushed mine. She snagged the papers and peeled off two. "I still owe you, D.K."

I sat down on the mass of sleeping-bags and Army blankets that was the bed, goggling up at the tin ceiling, sealed with cedar pitch boiled from the sap of Large Marge, Moth's waggish name for the thickest tree whose trunk was the right corner of this room.

Pandora was incuriously bending up a massive joint with two of the papers. Eventually, she popped a match on one scrimshaw thumbnail, fired up the fireplace and passed it on down.

We hooked up off-and-on, Pandora and me. Out there, the usual bounds of a relationship were blown wide. We were all friends. She was her own woman. But I noticed every time anyone else got friendlier with her than the huggy sort of group mind would allow, they were gently but emphatically rebuffed. Things happen on their own clock in the woods.

I barely remember what we talked about while we got high. Before I knew it, we were giving each other shotguns, mouth-to-mouth hits of warm sweet smoke that ended the way a shotgun usually does between a boy and a girl, or one sex and some other thing…

I remember she roached the joint with less than a third to go in that round, and pushed me back onto the palette, murmuring: "I'm cold," as she peeled off her anorak and silenced me with another long, wet kiss.

I remember her sucking me off for what seemed like six hours of near-orgasm…

Then the air horns were screaming on all sides of us like Hell with the lid off—

(AJ brought them from an RV store when he first joined our little Ewok band, and rigged them to tripwires around the perimeter. If anyone or anything got too close, we'd hear a "WHEEEAAA—" and either go down and shut off the horn, or make ready. One or two of them played a solo sometimes when a varmint or a branch tripped the switch.)

—all screaming at once and we were UP! UP! UP! and charging out into A HIGH, ULULATING WARBLE THAT HOWLED DOWN FROM THE WOODS, LOUDER THAN THE AIR HORNS, *and no Person As I Understood the Definition Was Making That Sound, Yet The Throat Was Sentient…*

We could no longer deny Reality. Reality was colder than the fifth ring of Tibetan Hell. Reality was swirling, smacking branches and mad screams. Reality was dark, hunched shapes clambering and loping all around with glowing clubs and terrible purpose, clubbing villagers like baby seals.

Outside, AJ and Moth were fighting them off with crowbars. Moth had a hatchet, too. He didn't have it long, but he got it back fast right through the back of the neck.

AJ looked like a green ghost in a big Army field jacket with a hood, hanging with rattlesnake rattles and cowrie shells, long black hair in his face, nose sticking out like the cowcatcher of a locomotive. He still held a tallboy of hoarded beer in one hand.

Behind them were scared bangs and thumps from the two nearest huts. Someone threw a firecracker out the window, but its noise was lost in the wind. Green-black shapes clambered along, across, around the trunks, chittering like chimps. They were yanking on everything, trying to pull it all down.

"In the old days, in Africa," I heard Pandora say behind me in a very small voice, "They'd sacrifice one virgin a year to the Monkey God, so that the tree children, the leaf-doctors, would leave them alone for another year. But…"

Out in the clearing, AJ whirled right. I bellowed something. A big black claw that looked like a set of mossy lineman's spikes whickered down from an overhanging branch. AJ's tallboy of PBR disappeared. So did his hand at the wrist.

I got in front of Pandora, making myself into a human shield, and gestured for her to stay behind me. She did, but returned too quickly. "God damn it, I—" The spite in her eyes spoke tomes.

I waved her off, pulling the Velcro on my Leatherman and popping the big blade out. I was scared sober. Pandora put one hand on my shoulder. "I am perfectly capable of defending myself, you sexist p—"

My eyes suddenly grew to the size of fear itself. I put a hand over her mouth and gestured at the loop-hole in the door.

One of them was grinning down at us from the overhanging tree just outside. I could smell him. It didn't appear to be a social call.

Pandora reached in one overall pocket for her flute, a pale faery thing, delicate as a collarbone. "Shakespeare, college boy." she whispered. "For music hath charms to soothe the savage beast."

And right there, behind that door, she started in on a tune of her own composition, a thing of bright summer days and the weird butterflies that only live in the canopy, of wild imaginings and nothing in the way.

A lump grew in my throat, but died at the loop-hole… Pondering common ancestry and abandoned reactors, breathing through my mouth against the savage terrific stink…

Its face was swollen, toothless, mongoloid. The beard began at the eyes, patchy and straggly over pink, puckered radiation burns whose like I'd only ever seen on my father after weeks of visits to the Oncology lab.

Its hairy body and head were green, wound with symbiant moss. Those horrorshow claws were mirrored where it should have had toes, its legs as thick as young oaks, its eyes…

Human. Flatly, undeniably human.

"Where's *your* co-op?" I whispered to it, feeling insanity lifting me out of myself. The critter remained perfectly still, confused by the sound of the flute, looking like it was trying to remember something.

"How long you guys been out here? Is…" I swallowed. "Is anybody expecting you to come home any time soon?" I suddenly felt two inches tall, needing to back up and learn more, try again… And I knew that, even though Man's scent was planet-wide, the woods were very dark and deep indeed.

I should never have distracted it.

The next thing I remember after that was coming out of the blackout. Or whatever it was. When I hove out into the clearing, swaying three hundred and sixty degrees as I walked, a scream started trying to come out as I looked around.

There were lights, bobbing up and down, everywhere in the woods. Different fire, like fox-fire, like phosphorous. But phosphorous isn't *blue*...

Fungus-lights, something mucky gobbed on the ends of long clubs. Moth was standing in front of me, leading a line of slumped shadows that walked mostly on all fours. He looked strangely gray. There was dirt and cowshit on his face and hands, like he'd been digging for something. The seat of his Carhartt overalls was bloody.

Toward the back of the line, I saw Deuce, his black eyes hellishly alight, muttering to the shadows in low tones. Deuce, in his old green L.L. Bean coverall, with his wavy hair tied back in a ponytail, barking like the shadows, barking, barking with the shadows, egging them on...

Speaking their tongue. Then he looked straight at me, his voice the low, carrying sibilant hiss of a stage magician.

"My family's owned this land for a hundred and seventy-five years," he shrugged. "The Ancestors are like bears. Okay, smarter than the average. You just have to know when to talk to them. And when to feed—"

At that point, the lower half of him walked away from the upper with a splat/flap/SLAP and the thing that had leaned in leaned back up with the side of meat, the haunch, in its claws, and I just disconnected entirely, until—

I came out of it again. "Yeah, just like bears, all right," I agreed. I blinked twice, and found me there on the cold hill's side overlooking the sauna.

Across from me, Josh was running a hand through his graying crewcut. He must have just gotten off late shift down on the water front. He always biked the twenty miles back. Josh was a dock-walloper, and tough. You should have seen him bale hay.

I remember. I do.

"How did I get here," I said to Josh. It wasn't a question. He guffawed, his lined face looking very much like a younger version of the actor William H. Macy. He offered me a hand-blown glass pipe and a black Bic lighter.

"It's Alive," he said in his rolling TV-announcer voice. "What were you drinkin', dude, that apple-jack you were makin'?"

I nodded, having forgotten that everyone at Aeolus knew everything about everyone else, most of the time. Like the exuberant dogs he sometimes owned, Josh plowed on ahead with a big dopey smile, "Was it any good?"

I groaned. "I don't know. Tonight's all a blur. You know, this farm's over a thousand years old? There are parts of it that are really cool. It just needs some love. I heard it used to be a Funhouse. In Dante's time. It..."

"How long since you got a good night's sleep?" Josh asked me sagely.

"That's a good question." I had to think on it. "Something usually wakes me up. Either a dream to which I am fleeing, or without strength I come, and need to swim the hell up on out of there no matter what…"

I spun one hand, tired and starting to feel it, searching for words. Josh beat me to it. "Where the hell is everybody? I just got back."

I tried to tell him. I did. I can't remember what I said. Josh's eyes just kept getting bigger and bigger.

"We… We need to see about this," was all he said. Then he started rolling a cigarette fast.

The fire smelled great. There were coyotes yipping somewhere between Alpine and the horizon. The cowboy moon was a bleached, peeled, pickled skull.

The darkness beyond the lights of the farm looked two-dimensional, flat and featureless as the edge of the Known World in some Arthur C. Clarke nightmare at The End.

Except Clarke had too much hope to imagine the noises I could hear out past the edge of that darkness, too much faith in Evolution over Propitiation…

I passed him the pipe. Josh stayed my hand. "Finish that. I'm going to… see about this. You're fucked up, man, but… I'll be right back. Don't go any-where."

I waited five hours for Josh to come and reclaim his pipe. I counted the min-utes.

I found I could do that, in the dark, huddled around my smoky peat fire and ancient transistor radio spilling out KUFO heavy-metal and gabble into the night.

I had a box of old newspapers, and some *Reader's Digest* Condensed Books, scraps of notebook paper almost too used to use again. The fire kept going out, every couple of minutes.

I started burning old illusions of the soul, too. Some of them looked like my clothes. Some of them looked like my writings and drawings. Some of those were originals.

Then the lights were everywhere in the woods again. The lights, and the slouching shadows that you could *feel* staring at you, though they shuffled and brachiated on the other side of that black-gray 2-D void. Their laughter grew louder still, shaking the canopy. Vibrating the forest floor…

Overhead, the Western stars were a nightmarish acid trip too vast and inhu-man to fathom. Out there on the perimeter, there were too many stars, too many things to be careful of wishing for that might fall on you and knock you flat…

In the clearing, the shadows come and go. The Ancestors tie down their wriggling sacrifice, and take their good old time. I see it again. Again. Again. Until the day I die. And then I see it again. It happens again. I dream it Again.

The way I saw them last. Over my shoulder. When I fired the gun empty, threw the machete and ran through the jungle, with a twisted ankle and irretrievable pride, running, running, running like a little bitch. Again. They all do it again.

In the heat of the night, I heard Pandora scream, once. Then there was silence. The kind I didn't like…

And when I turned around again, that was the last time I drew breath as anything but a pillar of desiccated salt.

That was now for me, and this is then. There are gray streaks in my hair. I startle easily, and look so much like my Dad around the crow-tracked eyes that I forget I'm only 34.

I live on North Hollywood Boulevard now, in LA. It doesn't rain much here, or storm and blow and whack. I have to smoke hash to get to sleep. Sometimes I have to take stronger measures.

But by gods, I have central heating. And no trees anywhere. No places to hide. No… got to say it, no loop-holes.

I write hard speculative Science Fiction about far-flung worlds millions of years in the future. My books are the size of cinderblocks. Many trees die for me. Hopefully, one of them had the critter in it, the one that was leering at me and Pandora outside my door on the night I lost my mind, and at least one other vital organ.

It growled and puffed up like a baboon when I spoke, swung down on its strong back legs from the tree and punched right through my front door. Pandora was still screaming when he punched out the back wall with her slung over his shoulder.

They picked me up on the street in downtown Portland four days later, babbling. By then, I'd hurt myself quite badly, they said, and would have died.

The Forest Service never found my heart.

THE GAZE DOGS
OF NINE WATERFALL
KAARON WARREN

Kaaron Warren's first novel, *Slights* was published by Angry Robot Books in 2009. Her second, *Walking the Tree*, was launched in February 2010 and *Mistification*, came out later that year.

Her award-winning short fiction has appeared in *Poe*, *Paper Cities*, "Fantasy Magazine" and many other venues in Australia and around the world. Her story "Ghost Jail", which first appeared in *2012,* was reprinted in *The Apex Book of World SF* and "The Blue Stream", her second published story, was reprinted in *Dead Souls*. Warren lives in Canberra, Australia, with her family.

Rare dog breeds; people will kill for them. I've seen it. One stark-nosed curly haired terrier, over-doped and past all use. One ripped-off buyer, one cheating seller. I was just the go-between for that job. I shrank up small into the corner, squeezed my eyes shut, folded my ears over like a Puffin Dog, to keep the dust out.

I sniffed out a window, up and out, while the blood was still spilling. It was a lesson to me, early on, to always check the dog myself.

I called my client on his cell, confirming the details before taking the job.

"Ah, Rosie McDonald! I've heard good things about your husband."

I always have to prove myself. Woman in a man's world. I say I'm acting for my husband and I tell stories about how awful he is, just for the sympathy.

I'll bruise my own eye, not with make-up. Show up with an arm in a sling. "Some men don't like a woman who can do business," I say. "But he's good at what he does. An eye for detail. You need that when you're dealing dogs."

"I hear that. My friend is the one who was after a Lancashire Large. For his wife."

I remembered; the man had sent me pictures. Why would he send me pictures?

"He says it was a job well done. So you know what I'm after?"

"You're after a vampire dog. Very hard to locate. Nocturnal, you know? Skittish with light. My husband will need a lot of equipment."

"So you'll catch them in the day when they're asleep. I don't care about the money. I want one of those dogs."

"My husband is curious to know why you'd like one. It helps him in the process."

"Doesn't he talk?"

"He's not good with people. He's good at plenty, but not people."

"Anyway, about the dog: thing is, my son's not well. It's a blood thing. It's hard to explain even with a medical degree."

My ears ring when someone's lying to me. Even over the phone. I knew he was a doctor; I'd looked him up.

"What's your son's name?"

The silence was momentary, but enough to confirm my doubts there was a son. "Raphael," he said. "Sick little Raphael." He paused. "And I want to use the dog like a leech. You know? The blood-letting cure."

"So you just need the one?"

"Could he get more?"

"He could manage three, but your son…"

"Get me three," he said.

I thought, *Clinic. $5,000 a pop. Clients in the waiting room reading* Nature *magazine. All ready to have their toxins sucked out by a cute little vampire dog.* I decided to double my asking price, right there.

There are dogs rare because of the numbers. Some because of what they are or what they can do.

And some are rare because they are not always seen.

I remember every animal I've captured, but not all of my clients. I like to forget them. If I don't know their faces I can't remember their expressions or their intent.

The Calalburun. I travelled to Turkey for this puppy. Outside of their birthplace, they don't thrive, these dogs. There is something about the hunting in Turkey which is good for them. My client wanted this dog because it has a split nose. Entrancing to look at. Like two noses grown together.

The Puffin Dog, or Norwegian Lundehund. These dogs were close to extinction when a dog-lover discovered a group of them on a small island. He bred them up from five, then shared some with an enthusiast in America. Not long after that, the European dogs were wiped out, leaving the American dogs the last remaining.

The American sent a breeding pair and some pups back to Europe, not long before her own dogs were wiped out. From those four there are now about a thousand.

The dogs were bred to hunt Puffins. They are so flexible (because they sometimes needed to crawl through caves to hunt) that the back of their head can touch their spine. As a breed, though, they don't absorb nutrients well, so they die easily and die young. We have a network, the other dealers and I. Our clients want different things at different times so we help each other out. My associate in Europe knew of four Puffin Dogs.

It's not up to me to ponder why people keep these cripples alive. Animal protection around the world doesn't like it much; I just heard that the English RSPCA no longer supports Crufts Dog Show because they say there are too many disabled dogs being bred and shown. Dogs like the Cavalier King Charles Spaniel, whose skull is too small for its brain. And a lot of boxer dogs are prone to epilepsy, and some bulldogs are unable to mate, or are unable to give birth unassisted.

It's looks over health. But humans? Same, same.

The Basenji is a dog which yodels. My client liked the sound and wanted to be yodelled to. I don't know how that worked out.

Tea cup dogs aren't registered and are so fragile and nervous they need to be carried everywhere. Some say this is the breeders' way of selling off runts.

Then there's the other dogs. The Black Dogs, Yellow Dogs, the Sulphurous Beast, the Wide-Eyed Hound, the Wisht Hound, and the Hateful Thing. The Gabriel Hound.

I've never been asked to catch one of these, nor have I seen one, but godawful stories are told.

The only known habitat of the vampire dog is the island of Viti Levu, Fiji. I'd never been there but I'd heard others talk of the rich pickings. I did as much groundwork as I could over the phone, then visited the client to get a look at him and pick up the money. No paper trail. I wore tight jeans with a tear across the ass and a pink button up shirt.

He was ordinary; they usually are. The ones with a lot of money are always confident but this one seemed overly so. Stolen riches, I wondered. The ones who get rich by stealing think they can get away with everything. Two heads taller then me, he wore a tight blue T-shirt, blank. A rare thing; most people like to plaster jokes on their chests. He didn't shake my hand but looked behind me for the real person, my husband.

"I'm sorry, my husband was taken ill. He's told me exactly what I need to do, though," I said.

The client put his hand on my shoulder and squeezed. "He's lucky he's got someone reliable to do his dirty work," the guy said.

He gave me a glass of orange soda as if I were a child. That's fine; making money is making money.

I told him we'd found some dogs, but not for sale. They'd have to be caught and that would take a lot more.

"Whatever... Look, I've got a place to keep them."

He showed me into his backyard, where he had dug a deep hole. Damp. The sides smooth, slippery with mud. One push and I'd be in there.

I stepped back from the edge.

"So, four dogs?" he said. "Ask your husband if he can get me four vampire dogs."

"I will check."

It was a year since my husband Joe had his spine bitten half out by a glandular-affected bull dog, and all he could do was nod, nod, nod. Bobble head, I'd call him if I were a cruel person. I had him in an old people's home where people called him young man and used his tight fists to hold playing cards. When I visit, his eyes follow me adoringly, as if he were a puppy.

My real hunting partner was my sister-in-law Gina. She's an animal psychologist. An animal psychic, too, but we don't talk about that much. I pretend I don't believe in it, but I rely on the woman's instincts.

The job wouldn't be easy, but it never is in the world of the rare breed.

My bank account full, our husband and brother safe with a good stock of peppermints, Gina and I boarded a flight for Nadi, Fiji. Ten hours from LA, long enough to read a book, snooze, maybe meet a dog-lover or two. We transferred to the Suva flight, a plane so small I thought a child could fly it. They gave us fake orange juice and then the flight was done. I listened to people talk, about local politics, gossip. I listened for clues, because you never know when you'll hear the right word.

Gina rested. She was keen to come to Fiji, thinking of deserted islands, sand, fruit juice with vodka.

The heat as we stepped off the plane was like a blanket had been thrown over our heads. I couldn't breathe in it and my whole body steamed sweat. It was busy but not crazy, and you weren't attacked by cabbies looking for business, porters, jewellery sellers. I got a lot of smiles and nods.

We took a cab which would not have passed inspection in New York and he drove us to our hotel, on Suva Bay. There were stray dogs everywhere, flaccid, unhealthy looking things. The females had teats to the ground, the pups were mangy and unsteady. They didn't seem aggressive, though. Too hot, perhaps. I bought some cut pineapple from a man at the side of the road and I ate it standing there, the juice dripping off my chin and pooling at my feet. I bought another piece, and another, and then he didn't have any change so I gave him twenty dollars. Gina couldn't eat; she said the dogs put her off. That there was too much sickness.

I didn't sleep well. I felt slick with all the coconut milk I'd had with dinner; with the fish, with the greens, with the dessert. And new noises in a place keep me awake, or they enter my dreams in strange ways.

I got up as the sun rose and swam some laps. The water was warm, almost like bath water, and I had the pool to myself.

After breakfast, Gina and I took a taxi out to the latest sighting of vampire dogs, a farm two hours drive inland. I like to let the locals drive. They know where they're going and I can absorb the landscape and listen while they tell me stories.

The foliage thickened as we drove, dark leaves waving heavily in what seemed to me a still day. The road was muddy so I had to be patient; driving through puddles at speed can get you bogged. A couple of trucks passed us. Smallish covered vehicles with the stoutest workers in the back. They waved and smiled at me and I knew that four of them could lift our car out of the mud if we got stuck.

The trucks swerved and tilted and I thought that only faith was keeping them on the road.

The farm fielded dairy cows and taro. It seemed prosperous; there was a letter box rather than an old juice bottle, and white painted rocks lined the path.

There was no phone here, so I hadn't been able to call ahead. Usually I'd gain permission to enter, but that could take weeks, and I wanted to get on with the job.

I told the taxi driver to wait. A fetid smell filled the car; rotting flesh.

"Oh, Jesus," Gina said. "I think I'll wait, too."

I saw a pile of dead animals at the side of a dilapidated shed; a cow, a cat, two mongooses. They could've been there since the attack a week ago.

"Well, wait there," I told Gina. "I'll call you if I need you."

Breathing through my mouth, I walked to the pile. I could see bite marks on the cow and all the animals appeared to be bloodless, sunken.

"You are who?" I heard. An old Fijian woman, wearing a faded green T-shirt that said, 'Nurses know better' pointed at me. She looked startled. They didn't see many white people out here.

"You from the *Fiji Times*?" she said. "We already talked to them."

I considered for a moment how best to get the information. She seemed suspicious of the newsmakers, tired of them.

"No, I'm from the SPCA. I'm here to inspect the animals and see if we can help you with some money. If there is a person hurting the animals, we need to find that person and punish them."

"It's not a person. It is the vampire dogs. I saw them with my own eyes."

"This was done by dogs?"

She nodded. "A pack of them. They come out of there barking and yelping with hunger, and they run here and there sucking their food out of any creature they find. They travel a long way sometimes, for new blood."

"So they live in the hills?" I thought she'd pointed at the mountains in the background. When she nodded, I realised my mistake. I should have said, "Where do they live?"

It was too late now; she knew what she thought I wanted to hear.

"They live in the hills."

"Doesn't anyone try to stop them?"

"They don't stop good. They are hot to the touch and if you get too near you might burn up."

"Shooting?"

"No guns. Who has a gun these days?"

"What about a club, or a spear? What about a cane knife? What I mean is, can they be killed?"

"Of course they can be killed. They're dogs, not ghosts."

"Do they bite people?"

She nodded. "If they can get close enough."

"Have they killed anyone? Or turned anyone into a vampire?"

She laughed, a big, belching laugh which brought tears to her eyes. "A person can't turn into a vampire dog! If they bite you, you clean out the wound so it doesn't go nasty. That's all. If they suck for long enough you'll die. But you clean it out and it's okay."

"So what did they look like?"

She stared at me.

"Were they big dogs or small?" I measured with my hand, up and down until she grunted; knee high.

"Fur? What colour fur?"

"No fur. Just skin. Blue skin. Loose and wrinkly."

"Ears? What were their ears like?"

She held her fingers up to her head. "Like this."

"And they latched onto your animals and sucked their blood?"

"Yes. I didn't know at first. I thought they were just biting. I tried to shoo them. I took a big stick and poked them. Their bellies. I could hear something sloshing away in there."

She shivered. "Then one of them lifted its head and I saw how red its teeth were. And the teeth were sharp, two rows top and bottom, so many teeth. I ran inside to get my husband but he had too much *kava*. He wouldn't even sit up."

"Can I see what they did?" I said. The woman looked at me.

"You want to see the dead ones? The *bokola*?"

"I do. It might help your claim."

"My claim?"

"You know, the SPCA." I walked back to the shed.

Their bellies had been ripped out and devoured and the blood drained, she said.

There were bite marks, purplish, all over their backs and legs, as if the attacking dogs were seeking a good spot.

The insects and the birds had worked on the ears and other soft bits.

I took a stick to shift them around a bit.

"The dogs will come for those *bokola*. You leave them alone." She waved at the pile of corpses.

"The dogs?"

"Clean-up dogs. First the vampires, then the clean-up. Their yellow master sends them."

"Yellow master?" She shook her head, squeezed her eyes shut. Taboo subject.

"You wouldn't eat this meat? It seems a waste."

"The vampire dogs leave a taste behind," the woman told me. "A *kamikamica* taste the other animals like. One of the men in my village cooked and ate one of those cows. He said it made him feel very good but now he smells of cowhide. He can't get the smell off himself."

"Are any of your animals left alive?"

The woman shook her head. "Not the bitten ones. They didn't touch them all, though."

"Can I see the others?" I would look for signs of disease, something to explain the sudden death. I wanted to be sure I was in the right place.

One cow was up against the back wall of the house, leaning close to catch the shade. There was a sheen of sweat on my body. I could feel it drip down my back.

"*Kata kata*," the woman said, pointing to the cow. "She is very hot."

It looked all right, apart from that.

I could get no more out of her.

Gina was sweating in the taxi. It was a hot day, but she felt the heat of the cow as well. "Any luck?" she said.

"Some. There's a few local taboos I'll need to get through to get the info we need, though."

"Ask him," she said, pointing at the driver. "He's Hindu."

Our taxi driver said, "I could have saved you the journey. No Fijian will talk about that. We Hindus know about those dogs."

He told us the vampire dogs lived at the bottom of Ciwa Waidekeulu. "*Thiwa Why Ndeke Ulu*," he said. Nine Waterfall. In the rainforest twenty minutes from where we were staying.

"She said something about a yellow master?"

"A great yellow dog that is worse than the worst man you've ever met."

I didn't tell him I'd met some bad men.

"You should keep away from him. He can give great boons to the successful, but there is no one successful. No one can defeat the yellow dog. Those who fail will vanish, as if they have never been." He stopped at a jetty, where some children sold us roti filled with a soft, sweet potato curry. Very, very good.

The girl who cleaned my room was not chatty at first, but I wanted to ask her questions. She answered most of them happily once I gave her a can of Coke. "Where do I park near Ciwa Waidekeulu? How do I ask the Chief for permission to enter? Is there fresh water?"

When I asked her if she knew if the vampire dogs were down there, she went back to her housework, cleaning an already-spotless bench. "These are not creatures to be captured," she said. "They should be poisoned." To distract me, she told me that her neighbours had five dogs, every last one of them a mongrel, barking all night and scaring her children. I know what I'd do if I were her. The council here puts out notices of dog poisonings, *Keep Your Dogs In While We Kill The Strays*, so all she'd have to do is let their dogs out while the cull was happening. Those dogs'd be happy to run; she said they used to leap the fence, tearing their guts, until her neighbour built his fence higher. They're desperate to get out.

The council does a good job with the poisoning, she told me, but not so good with the clean up. Bloated bodies line the streets, float down the river, clog the drains.

They don't understand about repercussions, and that things don't just go away.

My doctor client was pleased with the progress when I called him. "So, when will you go in?"

With the land taboo, I needed permission from the local chief or risk trouble. This took time. Most didn't want to discuss the vampire dogs, or the yellow dog king; he was forbidden, also. "It may be a couple of weeks. Depends on how I manage to deal with the locals."

"Surely a man would manage better," he said. "I know your husband doesn't like to talk, but most men will listen to a man better. Maybe I should send someone else."

"Listen," I told him, hoping to win him back, "I've heard they run with this Fat Cock of a dog. Have you heard that? People have seen the vampire dogs drop sheep hearts at this yellow dog's feet. He tossed the heart up like it was a ball, snapped it up."

The man smacked his lips. I could hear it over the phone. "I've got a place for him, if you catch him as well."

"If you pay us, we'll get him. There are no bonus dogs."

"Check with your husband on that."

I thought of the slimy black hole he'd dug.

"They say that if you take a piece of him, good things will come your way. People don't like to talk about him. He's taboo."

"They just don't want anyone else taking a piece of him."

We moved to a new hotel set amongst the rain forest. The walls were dark green in patches, the smell of mould strong, but it was pretty with birdsong and close to the waterfalls which meant we could make an early start.

We ate in their open air restaurant, fried fish, more coconut milk, Greek meatballs. Gina didn't like mosquito repellent, thinking it clogged her pores with chemicals, so she was eaten alive by them.

"Have you called Joe?" she asked me over banana custard.

"Have you?" We smiled at each other; wife and sister ignoring him, back home and alone.

"We should call him. Does he know what we're doing?"

"I told him, but you know how he is." She was a good sister, visiting him weekly, reading to him, taking him treats he chewed but didn't seem to enjoy.

We drank too much Fijian beer and we danced around the snooker table, using the cues as microphones. No one seemed bothered, least of all the waiters.

The next morning, we called a cab to drop us at the top of the waterfall. You couldn't drive down any further. In the car park, souvenir sellers sat listlessly, their day's takings a few coins that jangled in their pockets. Their faces marked with lines, boils on their shins, they leaned back and stared as we gathered our things together.

"I have shells," one boy said.

"No turtles," Gina said, flipping her head at him to show how disgusting that trade was to her.

"Not turtles. Beetles. The size of a turtle."

He held up the shell to her. There was a smell about it, almost like an office smell; cleaning fluids, correcting fluids, coffee brewed too long. The shell was metallic grey and marbled with black lines. Claws out the side, small, odd, clutching snipers. I had seen, had eaten, prawns with claws like this. Bluish and fleshy, I felt like I was eating a sea monster.

"From the Third waterfall," the seller said. "All the other creatures moved up when the dogs moved into Nine Waterfall."

I'm in the right place, I thought. "So there are dogs in the waterfall?"

"Vampire dogs. They only come out for food. They live way down."

An older vendor hissed at him. "Don't scare the nice ladies. They don't believe in vampire dogs."

"You'd be surprised what I believe in," Gina said. She touched one finger to the man's throat. "I believe that you have a secret not even your wife knows. If she learns of it, she will take your children away."

"No."

"Yes." She gave the boy money for one of the shells and opened her large bag to place it inside.

He said, "You watch out for yellow dog. If you sacrifice a part of him you'll never be hungry again. But if you fail you will die on the spot and no one will know you ever lived. If you take the right bit you will never be lonely again."

I didn't know that I wanted a companion for life.

As we walked, I said, "How did you know he had a secret?"

"All men have secrets."

The first waterfall was overhung by flowering trees. It was a very popular picnic site. Although it took twenty minutes to reach, Indian women were there with huge pots and pans, cooking roti and warming dhal while the men and children swam. I trailed my hand in the water; very cool, not the pleasant body temperature water of the islands, but a refreshing briskness.

Birdsong here was high and pretty. More birds than I'd seen elsewhere: broadbills, honey-eaters, crimson and masked parrots, and velvet doves. Safe here, perhaps. The ground was soft and writhing with worms. The children collected them for bait, although the fish were sparse. Down below, the children told us, were fish big enough to feed a family of ten for a week. They liked human bait, so men would dangle their toes in. I guessed they were teasing us about this. The path to the second waterfall was well-trodden. The bridge to the second waterfall had been built with good, treated timber, and seemed sturdy.

The waterfall fell quietly here. It was a gentler place. Only the fishermen sat by the water's edge; children and women not welcome. The fish were so thick in the water they could barely move. The fishermen didn't bother with lines; they reached in and grabbed what they wanted.

Gina breathed heavily.

"Do you want to slow down a bit? I don't think we should dawdle, but we can slow down," I said.

"It's not that. It's the fish. I don't usually get anything from fish, but I guess there's so many of them. I'm finding it hard to breathe."

The men stood up to let us past.

"There are a lot of fish," I said. Sometimes the obvious is the only thing to say. "Where do they come from?" I asked one of the men. "There are so few up there." I pointed up to the first waterfall.

"They come from underground. The centre of the earth. They are already cooked when we catch them, from the heat inside."

He cut one open to demonstrate and it was true; inside was white, fluffy, warm flesh. He gestured it at me and I took a piece. Gina refused. The meat was delicate and sweet and I knew I would seek without finding it wherever else I went in the world.

"American?" the man said.

"New Zealand," Gina lied.

"Ah, Kiwi!" he said. "Sister!" They liked the New Zealanders better than Australians and Americans because of closer distance, and because they shared a migratory path. Gina could put on any accent; it was like she absorbed the vowel sounds.

I could have stayed at the second waterfall but we had a job to do, and Gina found the place claustrophobic.

"It's only going to get worse," I said. "The trees will close in on us and the sky will vanish."

She grunted. Sometimes, I think, she found me very stupid and shallow. She liked me better than almost anybody else did, but sometimes even she rolled her eyes at me.

The third waterfall was small. There was a thick buzz of insects over it. I hoped not mosquitoes; I'd had dengue fever once before and did not want hemorrhagic fever. I stopped to slather repellent on, strong stuff which repelled people as well.

The ground was covered with small, green-shelled cockroaches. They were not bothered by us and I could ignore them. The ones on the tree trunks bothered me more. At first I thought they were bark, but then one moved. It was as big as my head and I couldn't tell how many legs. It had a jaw which seemed to click, and a tail like a scorpion which it kept coiled.

"I wouldn't touch one," Gina said.

"Really? Is that a vision you had?"

"No. They just look nasty," and we shared a small laugh. We often shared moments like that, even at Joe's bedside.

Gina stumbled on a tree root the size of a man's thigh.

"You need to keep your eyes down," I said. "Downcast. Modest. Can you do that?"

"Can you?"

"Not really."

"Joe always liked 'em feisty."

Gina's breath came heavy now and her cheeks reddened.

"It's going to be tough walking back up."

"It always is. I don't even know why you're dragging me along. You could manage this alone."

"You know I need you to gauge the mood. That's why."

"Still. I'd rather not be here."

"I'll pay you well. You know that."

"It's not the money, Rosie. It's what we're doing. Every time I come out with you it feels like we're going against nature. Like we're siding with the wrong people."

"You didn't meet the client. He's a nice guy. Wants to save his kid."

"Of course he does, Rosie. You keep telling yourself that."

I didn't like that; I've been able to read people since I was twelve, when it became necessary. Gina's sarcasm always confused me, though.

At the fourth waterfall, we found huge, stinking mushrooms, which seemed to turn to face us.

Vines hung from the trees, thick enough we had to push them aside to walk through. They were covered with a sticky substance. I'd seen this stuff before, used as rope, to tie bundles. You needed a bush knife to cut it. I'd realised within a day of being here you should never be without a bush knife and I'd bought one at the local shop. I cut a dozen vines, then coiled them around my waist.

Gina nodded. "Very practical." She was over her moment, which was good.

Hard to work as a team with someone who didn't want to be there.

What did we see at the fifth waterfall? The path here was very narrow. We had to walk one foot in front of the other, jungle fashion, models showing off.

There were no vines here. The water was taken by one huge fish, the size of a Smart car. The surface of the water was covered with roe and I wondered where the mate was. Another underground channel? It would have to be a big one. It would be big but confining. It would hold the mate maybe like my husband was held by his injury. But I'm happy with him that way. He can't interfere with my business. Can't tell me how to do things.

At the sixth waterfall, we saw our first dog. It was very small and had no legs. Born that way? It lay in the pathway unmoving, and when I nudged it, I realised it was dead.

Gina clutched my arm. Her icy fingers hurt and I could feel the cold through my layers of clothing.

"Graveyard," she said. "This is their graveyard."

The surface of the sixth pool was thick with belly-up fish. At the base of the trees, dead insects like autumn leaves raked into a pile.

And one dead dog. I wondered why there weren't more.

"He has passed through the veil," Gina said, as if she were saying a prayer. "We should bury him."

"We could take him home to the client. He already has a hole dug in his back-yard. He's kind of excited at the idea of keeping dogs there."

Is there a name for a person who takes pleasure in the confinement of others?

We reached the seventh waterfall.

We heard yapping, and I stiffened. I opened my bag and put my hand on a dog collar, ready. Gina stopped, closed her eyes.

"Puppies," she said. "Hungry."

"What sort?"

Gina shook her head. We walked on, through a dense short tunnel of wet leaves.

At the edge of the seventh waterfall there was a cluster of small brown dogs. Their tongues lapped the water (small fish, I thought) and when we approached, the dogs lifted their heads, widened their eyes and stared.

"Gaze dogs," I said.

These were gaze dogs like I'd never seen before. Huge eyes. Reminded me of the spaniel with the brain too big.

"Let's rest here, let them get used to us," Gina said.

I glanced at my watch. We were making good time; assuming we caught a vampire dog with little trouble, we could easily make it back up by the sunfall.

"Five minutes."

We leaned against a moss-covered rock. Very soft, damp, with a smell of underground.

The gaze dogs came over and sniffled at us. One of the puppies had deep red furrows on its back; dragging teethmarks. I had seen this sort of thing after dog fights, dog attacks. Another had a deep dent in its side, filled with dark red scab and small yellow pustules. Close up, we could see most of the dogs were damaged in some way.

"Food supply?" Gina said.

I shuddered. Not much worried me, but these dogs were awful to look at.

One very small dog nuzzled my shoe, whimpering. I picked it up; it was light, weak. I tucked it into my jacket front. Gina smiled at me. 'You're not so tough!'

"Study purposes." I put four more in there; they snuggled up and went to sleep.

She seemed blurry to me; it was darker than before. Surely the sun wasn't further away. We hadn't walked that far. My legs ached as if I had been hiking for days.

At the eighth waterfall we found the vampire dogs. Big, gazing eyes, unblinking, watching every move we made. The dogs looked hungry, ribs showing, stomachs concaved.

"They move fast," Gina whispered, her eyes closed. "They move like the waterfall."

The dogs abruptly swarmed forward and knocked me down. Had their teeth into me in a second, maybe two.

The feeling of them on me, their cold, wet paws heavy into my flesh, but the heat of them, the fiery touch of their skin, their sharp teeth, was so shocking I couldn't think for a moment; then I pulled a puppy from my jacket and threw it.

Their teeth already at work, the dogs saw the brown flash and followed it.

They moved so fast I could still see fur when they were gone.

I threw another puppy and another vampire dog peeled off with a howl. The first puppy was almost drained, its body flatter, as if the vampires sucked out muscle, too.

"Quick," Gina said. "Quick." She had tears in her eyes, feeling the pain of the puppies, their deaths, in her veins.

I threw a third puppy and we ran down, away from them. We should have run up, but they filled the path that way.

I needed a place to unpack my bag, pull out the things I'd need to drop three of them. Or four.

We heard a huffing noise like an old man coughing up a lifetime. We were close to the base and the air was so hard to breathe we both panted. Gina looked at me. "It must be the alpha. The yellow dog."

It seemed to me she stopped breathing for a moment.

"We could try to take a piece of him. We'd never be lonely again, if we did that."

The vampire dogs growled at us, wanting more puppies. The last two were right against my belly; I couldn't reach them easily and I didn't want to.

"I don't want to see the ninth waterfall," Gina said. I shook my head. If the vampire dogs were this powerful, how strong would their alpha be?

"It's okay. I'm ready now. I'll take three of them down quietly; the others won't even notice. Then we'll have to kick our way out."

She nodded.

We turned around and he was waiting. That dog.

He was crippled and pitiful but still powerful. His tail, his ears and his toes had been cut off by somebody brave. Chunks of flesh were gone from his side. People using him as sacrifice for gain.

Gina was impressive; I could see she was in pain. Was she feeling the yellow dog's pain? She was quiet with it, small grunts. She walked towards him.

The closer she got to the dog the worse it seemed to get. "I want to lay hands on him, give him comfort," Gina said.

The dog was the ugliest I've ever seen. Of all the strays that've crossed my path here, this one was the most aggressive. This dog would make a frightening man, I thought. A man I couldn't control. Drool streamed down his chin.

He sat slouched, rolled against his lower back. Even sitting he reached to my waist.

All four legs were sprawled. He reminded me of an almost-drunk young man, wanting a woman for the night and willing to forgo that last drink, those last ten drinks, to achieve one. Sprawled against the bar, legs wide, making the kind of display men can.

His fur was the colour of piss, that golden colour you don't want to look at too hard, and splotched with mud, grease, and something darker.

One ear was half bitten off. The other seemed to stand straight up, unmoving, like a badly made wooden prosthetic.

One lip was split, I think; it seemed blurry at this distance.

He licked his balls. And his dog's lipstick stuck out, fully twelve centimetres, long, pink and waving.

Thousands of unwanted puppies in there.

He wasn't threatening; I felt sorry for him. He was like a big boy with the reputation of being a bully, who has never hurt anyone.

But when we got close to the yellow dog I realised he was perfect, no bits missing. An illusion to seduce us to come closer. Gina stepped right up to him.

"Gina! Come back!" but she wouldn't.

"If I comfort him, he will send me a companion. A lifetime companion," she said.

"Come live with me!" I said. "We'll take some gaze pups, rescue them. We'll live okay."

He reared back on his hind legs and his huge skull seemed to reach the trees.

He lifted his great paw high.

Around our feet, the vampire dogs gathered. I grabbed one, syringe at the ready. Another. I sedated them and shoved them in my carry bag.

The yellow dog pinned Gina with his paws. The vampire dogs surrounded him, a thick blue snarling band around him.

I threw my last two gaze dog pups at them but they snapped at them too quickly. I had no gun. I picked up three rocks and threw one, hard. Pretended it was a baseball and it was three balls, two strikes.

The vampire dogs swatted the rock away as if it were a dandelion. I threw another, and the last, stepping closer each time.

And the yellow dog had his teeth at Gina's throat. I ran forward, thinking only to tear her away, at least drag her away from his teeth.

The vampire dogs were all over me, biting my eyes, my ears, my lips.

I managed to throw them off, though perhaps they let me.

The yellow dog sat crouched, his mouth covered with blood. At his paws, I thought I saw hair, but I wondered: *what human has been down here? Who else but me would come this far?*

I backed away. Two sleeping vampire dogs in my bag made no noise and emitted no odour; I was getting away with it. They watched me go, their tongues pink and wet. The yellow dog; again, from afar he looked kindly. A dear old faithful dog. I took two more vampire dogs down, simple knock out stuff in a needle, and I put them in my bag. A soft blanket waited there; no need to damage the goods.

I picked up another gaze dog pup as I walked. This one had a gouge in his back, but his fur was pale brown, the colour of milk chocolate. He licked me. I put him down my jacket, then picked up another for a companion.

It took me hours to reach the top. Time did not seem to pass, though. Unless I'd lost a whole day. When I reached second waterfall, there were the same fishermen. And the families at the first waterfall, swimming, cooking and eating as if there was no horror below them. They all waved at me but none offered me food or drink.

The souvenir salesmen were there at the top. "Shells?" they said. "Buy a shell. No sale for a week, you know. No sale. You will be the first." I didn't want a shell; they came from the insects I'd seen below and didn't want to be reminded of them.

I called a cabbie to take me to my hotel. I spent another day, finalising arrangements for getting the dogs home (you just need to know who to call) then I checked out of my room.

The doctor was happier than I'd thought he'd be. Only two dogs had survived, but they were fit and healthy and happily sucked the blood out of the live chicken he provided them.

"You were right; you work well alone," he said. "You should dump that husband of yours. You can manage alone."

I'd just come from visiting Joe and his dry-eyed gaze, his flaccid fingers, seemed deader than ever. The nurses praised me up, glad there was somebody for him. "Oh, you're so good," they said. "So patient and loyal. He has no one else." Neither do I, I told them.

A month or so later, the doctor called me. He wanted to show me the dogs; prove he was looking after them properly.

A young woman dressed in crisp white answered the door.

"Come in!" she said.

"You know who I am?"

Leading me through the house, she gave me a small wink. "Of course."

I wasn't sure I liked that.

She led me outside to the backyard; it was different. He'd tiled the hole and it was now a fish pond. The yard was neater, and lounge chairs and what looked like a bar were placed in a circle. Six people sat in the armchairs, reading magazines, sipping long drinks.

"He didn't tell me there was a party."

"Take a seat. The doctor will be with you shortly," the young woman said. Three of the guests looked at their watches as if waiting for an appointment.

I studied them. They were not a well group. Quiet and pale, all of them spoke slowly and lifted their glasses gently as if in pain or lacking strength. But they all had expensive shoes. Gold jewellery worn with ease. The doctor had some wealthy friends.

They made me want to leap up, jump around, show off my health.

The young woman came back and called a name. An elderly woman stood up.

"Thank you, nurse," she said. It all clicked in then; I'd been right. The doctor was charging these people dearly for treatment.

It was an hour before he dealt with his patients and called me in.

The vampire dogs rested on soft blankets. They were bloated, their eyes rolling. They could barely lift their heads. Bleeding-therapy was profitably back, even if leeches were out.

"You see my dogs are doing well."

"And so are you, I take it. How's your son?"

He laughed. "You know there's no son."

The doctor gave me another drink. His head didn't bobble. We drank vodka together, watching the vampire dogs prowl his yard, and a therapist would say my self-loathing led me to sleep with him.

I crawled out of his bed at 2 or 3 a.m., home to my gaze dogs. They were healing well and liked to chew my couch. They jumped up at me, licking and yapping, and the three of us sat on the floor, waiting for the next call to come in.

DEAD LOSS
CAROLE JOHNSTONE

Carole Johnstone is originally from Scotland and now lives in north Essex, England. Her short stories have been published in *Black Static* and several anthologies including *Voices*, *Grants Pass* and *Dead Souls*, and the forthcoming *Catastrophia* and *Close Encounters of the Urban Kind*. Her first novella, *Frenzy*, was recently published. Her website can be found at www.carolejohnstone. com

They had made good time, at least. These days, Lachlan took his luck wherever he could find it, and a three-knot south-westerly in a cloudless January sky was just that. Never mind that the cod always waited for the kind of storm that gave Lachlan palpitations. *The Relict* was only two days out of port. They weren't fishing yet.

He had never much aspired to be a fisherman, but had come last in a stoically long line of them. Years spent at sea with his father had instilled in him both knowledge and a cast-iron stomach that only the old stalwarts could better. He could cast and haul, clean and gut. He could sense a storm over the horizon and the contents of a net haul by the creak of winch and drum. But he had no love for any of it. Not fishing, not boats. And never the sea.

"Blackhall, get yer arse astern and see to the bloody floats. I'm no paying ye to stare at the fuckin' sky, laddie!"

The skipper was just a head and a muscled arm thrust out of the small window of the forward wheelhouse, but Lachlan moved quickly towards the working deck, where the rest of the five-man crew were already examining the net and its warps. *The Relict's* first-mate, a weather-beaten casualty of the North Sea named Irvine, eyed Lachlan's approach with something near to kind contempt.

"Best no' get on the wrong side ae Gibson this early on, pal. He only took ye on at all because ye were first on Peterheid dock."

This was Lachlan's first trip on *The Relict*. It was his first crew job on the high sea. He had spent his entire career onboard the pelagic fleets that hugged the Scottish coast. But demand for herring and mackerel had dropped, while deep-sea cod rarely fell out of favour, despite decreased quotas. And as much as Lachlan might resent it, getting a place aboard *The Relict* had been a lucky break for him.

The first in a very long time.

They finally dropped anchor close to the Continental Shelf Boundary with Norway. Here, the sea was black and uneasy, its swells frilled with white foam. Lachlan looked to the sky as they prepared to cast. It was slate grey and hung heavy with cloud. A low winter sun occasionally blinded in watery refractions. He hoped that the cod would be merciful. All that empty sea with no land to orientate it was a little too unnerving. A little too alien.

The Relict was a stern trawler, its single net set and hauled behind two weighted otter boards attached to towing warps. While Irvine operated the net drum and winches close to the gantry, Lachlan helped feed the vast net, its floats and *cookie* weights over the ramp and stern, trying not to look much beyond their own pocket of dark sea. The wind picked up as the last of the net disappeared, the heavy otter boards following. Lachlan suffered an uncommon lurch of nausea as the twin towing warps sunk down under the viscid surface.

Irvine's grin was wide and mostly toothless. He slapped a thick hand against Lachlan's shoulder, shaking his stomach further loose of its moorings.

"Welcome to the Devil's Hole, Lackey."

Lachlan let what was swiftly becoming a tired joke pass, if only because the location rang a bell inside those reluctant archives long planted inside his head. "Christ, no-one told me we were—"

Irvine's weathered face set like cement. "This is a God-fearin' boat, son. Only the skipper's allowed tae curse Him and ye kens it!"

The loudest chuckle came from a crew-hand named Robert MacKenzie. MacKenzie was the kind of career deckhand that Lachlan would have gone out of his way to avoid on dry land; the kind that pissed away his pay and took it out on hapless *lubbers* at pub closing. He worked the iceboxes and trawl doors alongside his equally amenable brother. Lachlan had no clue what *his* name was. They were Bert and Ernie on *The Relict*. The other crewman: a perpetually silent, bearded man carrying maybe fifty pounds too many, had been christened Bob. Clearly there were more important things to do aboard *The Relict* than waste imagination. Like casting net and gear more than 130 fathoms down into one of the most notorious trenches within the North Sea.

"Ye're no midwater trawlin' now, Lackey," Bert grinned. "Skipper says he's seen a bloody great shoal ae cod on the sonar, we drop the trawl tae the bottom and haul 'em in."

When the engines started again, Lachlan hid his startled jump in a loud cough. Cold wind slapped his hair against his face, scratching his eyes. The deck vibrated under his feet in a nasty hum. The boat's engines momentarily stalled, then roared louder, taking up the slack. The Gilson winches groaned, and the drum drew the warps tight. They began to pull.

Lachlan hated bottom-trawling. Hated the very idea of it: of a vast weighted net dragged over rock and corpse and wreck. There were too many obstacles—too many perils waiting deep down where they could never be seen. Waiting to snag or stall. Waiting to sink.

At five a.m. they started bringing the net in. Aside from their tiny island of light, the world was dark and formless. The expectant gulls and gannets invisibly flocked and dived, their caws loud and unwieldy. The wind whipped around their heads, creating wailing echoes around the wheelhouse, and railing against the gantry and aerial mast above their heads. Lachlan again suffered under the weight of a foreboding that was as lethargic as it was certain. The beginnings of a downpour spattered hard against his oilskins, as Irvine signalled the winding of the net drum with a warning shout.

Slowly, the towing warps reappeared, dragging the otter boars behind. The smell of the sea grew stronger, as if they had dredged its bed clean: salt, fish, and something else—an odour that was as earthy as it was alien.

Standing close to the stern doors, Lachlan helped secure the weighted ground line at the net's beginning, while Bob took care of the foot rope's luminous floats. As the winch gears strained and groaned, the funnel-like mouth of the net gradually narrowed towards the tight-meshed cod end. After a brief struggle, Ernie released the trawl-end knot, and the catch was finally spewed onto the deck.

Not one word was uttered as they stared down at their haul. It neither squirmed nor skittered, nor sought silver-grey purchase in sucking mouths and flapping gills. It wasn't alive. And it wasn't cod.

"What the hell is this?" In the harsh spotlight, Gibson's florid face appeared almost comical in its slow confusion. "Ernie, take the fuckin' wheel." The skipper elbowed Lachlan aside as he hunkered down close to the deck, his eyes wary. "What the hell is this?"

Bert had plucked one from the deck, and was holding it at arm's length with an ugly grimace. "Maybes they're bullheads, Skipper. They sure *look* a wee bit like bullheads."

"Ye ever seen a bullhead or rockfish this fuckin' big, Bert?" Gibson replied, baring his teeth. "'Cause in twenty-five years at sea, I fuckin' haven't."

Lachlan could only bring himself to prod at one with his boot. He understood Bert's inference. Like the bullhead, they were blotched brown and red, with a large head and long-spined body. But there the similarity ended. Beyond a flat, moon-shaped carapace, there stretched a jointed body lined with pinched claws that terminated in a tapering tail with a long spike at its end. They were better than a foot long.

That queer sliding dread scratched at Lachlan's neck again, and he patted it down with slick gloves. In death, the creatures had curled inward like foetuses, each body plate crunched tight at one end and splayed wide at the other, like the jointed plastic snake he had terrorised his sister with for years. Their ribbed claws twitched in slow spasm. Between larger compound eyes, they displayed six smaller orbs arranged in opposing triangles. Lachlan could see his shadow in them.

When he caught sight of Bob picking up another, Lachlan kicked the one on the end of his boot away. It made a nasty, *weighty* sound as it slid back towards the opened trawl doors. "Don't touch their spines!"

Gibson shot him a well practiced look of scorn. "Ye tellin' me Lackey senior seen one ae these bastards afore, eh?"

Lachlan, mollified by the fact that both Bert and Bob had instantly dropped their own specimens back onto the deck at his shout, found that he was able to meet Gibson's furious gaze. "They look like sea scorpions to me, Skipper."

"Oh aye? Ye think ye're the only one wi' a wee bit knowledge ae marine biology, Lackey, eh?" Gibson kicked one of the larger creatures along the deck with another curse. It connected with the base of the trawl gantry with a sickening crack. "Sea fuckin' scorpions were around afore even fishes. They were over six foot long, Lackey." He slapped wet hair behind his ears as he strode towards starboard. "Christ knows, I've dredged up moor peat and mammoth teeth afore now; one officious little prick down the Maritime Museum bought some lumps ae crap off me five year ago, calling 'em *Paleolithic huntin' artefacts*, but I ken a big fuckin' ugly fish from an extinct arthropod, eejit." He thrust a finger back towards their dead haul. "And that ain't fuckin' prehistoric. That's non-viable fuckin' by-catch, laddie."

As much as five uncomfortable minutes passed in relative silence: the crew looking to one another or to their catch, while Gibson still stood inside the shelter deck staring out into the choppy sea. Lachlan realised that their winged scavengers had disappeared, leaving behind only the shouted roar of a Force 6—perhaps now closer to 7—and the slow rumble of *The Relict*'s engine. Finally Gibson turned back to the stern.

"Bert, open the hatch and put the fuckers on ice. Maybes some other officious little prick'll pay good money to stick 'em on pins in a display case. And there's what looks like two score coley and haddock still in the cod end—get 'em on ice first. Might earn us a half pint each if we're lucky." He ambled back towards the wheelhouse with another muttered curse. "These fuckin' *bottom-rollers* and their rockhoppers ploughin' up the bed like butchers. We're the ones have the fishery quotas and grief, while those big bastards unearth fuck knows what, and take home five hundred grand hauls."

The rain began in earnest as Bob lifted clear the central hatch above the hold and clambered down its ladder.

"Think the skipper's a wee bit pissed at you," Bert grinned, his ill-humour recovered, even if his eyes still betrayed their unease.

Lachlan didn't answer. Pulling on rubber gloves, he tossed the dead bodies into the muted space below, his heart beating too slowly, his breath the colour of winter. He didn't look at Bert, and he didn't look at *them*. He lifted and tossed until his back screamed and his joints seized. Like the gulls before it, his sense of foreboding had vanished—to be replaced by a quickening fear as formless and dazzling as a sun's reflection against choppy sea.

The storm winds grew wilder throughout the day, confining the crew to quarters. They didn't cast the net again. Taking advantage of the unexpected reprieve, they took to their bunks well before sunset, and even Lachlan surrendered easily to sleep.

He was awoken from a nightmare of abyssal night into another just as dark, his arms flailing wildly where he had been floundering in long, endless gullets of rock and sulphurous cloud—chased deeper still by monsters. Monsters crouched in black never touched by sun.

"What the fuck?"

Bob's voice came to him as if from too great a distance, until Lachlan climbed higher out of sleep and heard the sound again. A low metallic thud towards the stern. And then another.

"Lachlan? What the shit is that?"

Lachlan jumped down from his cot on unsteady legs. "Could be a mako."

Bob got out of his own bunk, his generous belly all but obscuring Silver Surfer boxers. "A mako?"

Another thud sounded amidships, perhaps as little as ten feet aft. It reverberated along the hull, and Lachlan balked under an assault of sudden claustrophobia that momentarily had him longing for the freezing, rain-swept deck above.

Bob's eyes were frightened white spheres. "I've heard of one mako this far out, Lachlan, but not *three*."

When another thud hit hard against the hull directly ahead of him, Lachlan actually cringed away as if he expected the metal to buckle against it. In the following silence, his breath whistled through his teeth as he stepped tentatively closer, pressing his ear against the cold metal.

For one moment, all he could hear was the hum of the engine and the far off roar of the swell many feet above them. And then another thud sounded forward, close to the bow. His heart got going again after a few lost beats, and he managed to keep his ear close, steadying himself against the flat of his palms. He could hear something else under those thuds, something quieter and somehow worse. It reminded him of nails drawn slowly down a chalkboard. He thought of twitching claws and tapering tails that terminated in long spikes. They were trying to find a way in. Lachlan stumbled backward before crashing into the lower bunk.

Bob hauled him back onto his feet. "Not *five*—" His head swivelled wildly back towards the stern, his fingers nipping at Lachlan's arms. "Six! Jesus Christ. What *is* that?"

Lachlan shook his head once, twice. His heart jack-hammered against his ribcage. "I don't know."

The next morning dawned clear and calm. They ate a breakfast of salted porridge and thick coffee in silence. After the second mug, Gibson cleared his throat too loudly. "We've moved into Viking sector. There's another shadow out towards

Silver Pit. In one hour we'll drop the net." He stood up and headed back towards the galley. "Get the gear ready."

A framed motto hung above the exit from the fore cabin, and Lachlan glanced up at it seconds before the North Sea wind tore every other thought from his head. *Whatever's for ye won't go by ye.* As if it had a choice, caught in the dragging maw of a two hundred foot wide trawler net.

Icy rain returned as they set the gear. The winch gears strained and groaned. Banter was loud and too obviously forced. Lachlan watched the *cookies* sink and the floats disappear, their luminous pink swiftly overwhelmed by black. *The Relict*'s engine stalled and protested before taking up the slack. The net drum drew the warps tight. They began to trawl.

Around lunchtime, Lachlan found Gibson hunched over his haphazardly stationed monitors in the wheelhouse, an extinguished and soggy roll-up pinched tight between his lips.

"Skipper? You want a brew?"

Gibson turned eyes that were too startled towards him, and Lachlan looked away until he heard the skipper clear his throat. "Come here, laddie. Come and have a look at this."

Amid a bewildering plethora of electronics—gear controls and hydraulic monitoring consoles, trawl sensors and satellite navigation screens—Lachlan better recognised the black sonar grid and its sweeping circumference of green. Less than one hundred yards beyond their stern, it highlighted a vast hourglass shape in neon relief.

"Is that or is that no' a shoal ae fuckin' cod?"

Lachlan eyed the shadow with the dubiety of someone as familiar with cod as he was with the confidence of a trawler boat's skipper. "It could be."

Gibson's forehead ploughed new furrows. "Come on, boy, yer father was the best fisherman I ever kenned." He stabbed at the monitor with a finger that trembled. "Is that or is that no' a shoal ae fuckin' cod?"

The radio burst into static life, startling them both.

"This is the Met Office shipping forecast, issued on behalf of the Maritime and Coastguard Agency, at 1300 on Friday 15 January. There are warnings of gales in Biscay, Sole, Rockall, Hebrides and Malin. Fisher, Cromarty, Forth, Tyne and Dogger: Southwest 4 or 5, backing south 5 or 6, veering west 6 to 7 later in Forth and Tyne. Forties, Viking, and North Utsire: storm warning. Easterly 7 to gale 9, occasionally severe gale 10, becoming cyclonic later. Rough or very rough. Rain, sleet, and poor visibility."

Lachlan swallowed down a wave of bile as his stomach rode another swell. He turned back to the exit in an effort to pretend that he hadn't seen the same weakness in the captain's eyes. "Whatever it is, Skipper, we've trawled it. It's already ours."

They began winching in the net mid afternoon, a half-hearted smurry of sleet and rain hampering their already slow progress. This time the hydraulics screamed in protest as the warps wound backwards over the net drum. When the drum suddenly stalled, the warps stuck fast just above the otter board line, white smoke rising from their grinding efforts.

"We're *hung down!*" Irvine bellowed, whilst exacerbating *The Relict*'s screams by hauling back and forth upon the gears of the Gilson winches. Despite their previous catch and the growing storm, despite their very literal bumps in the night, every deckhand—Lachlan included—ran to the stern doors and began manually winding in the net and the first of its pink floats. The net was worth thousands. If it truly *was* snagged on the bottom, they stood to lose a lot more than just the price of another haul.

Gibson came up behind Lachlan, his curses loud and panicked. "Ernie, take the fuckin' wheel." He glanced up at the stern gantry. "Quit ridin' the gears, Irvine. Gi'e it some slack, then haul back fast on the hydraulics." He shoved hard against Lachlan, and breathed hot against his ear. "You some kind of Jonah, Lackey, eh? In twenty-five years at sea, I've never—"

"We're tippin' stern, Skipper!" Bert suddenly roared, stumbling away from the open trawl doors before grasping fast to a *cookie* along what little foot rope had made it back onboard.

"Shit!" Lachlan slid down the slick deck towards the ramp and its open trawl doors, missing the dark space between them only through a contrary lurch of the boat's hull. Sandwiched between Gibson and Bob, and now looking down upon the dark roiling sea just below the stern, Lachlan found himself remembering the final moments of Rose and Jack aboard the *Titanic*. His self-conscious chuckle sounded too much like a scream.

"Skipper, we need to lose the gear!" Irvine shouted from far away.

Sleet battered icy bullets against Lachlan's face, blurring his vision as *The Relict* rode high on a swell before plummeting too deep and too wet. Salt water momentarily washed out his gaping mouth, and then they were riding high again. The winches screamed—and the stern dropped like a stone. Towards dark, and the abyss of Lachlan's nightmares. Towards the vast hourglass shape caught inside their net. Bert gave an inhuman scream as he suddenly spun out into dark, white-speckled space, arms flailing.

"Cut us loose, Irvine!" Gibson screamed in Lachlan's ear. "Cut us loose!"

They managed to salvage the otter boards and the main drag of the towing warps. Aside from Bert MacKenzie, they had lost the net and its potential haul, bridle, foot rope and ground line. *The Relict*'s engine sputtered as feebly as its hydraulics. Grey smoke filtered up from the engine room. As the predicted Force 10 raged around their bow, *The Relict*'s crew lolled exhausted inside its fore cabin.

"It was a fuckin' rock."

Lachlan glanced at the skipper's face. It was ashen and slack. The wet lips that clamped down on his roll-up trembled.

While Irvine rode the swell above them and Ernie saw to the struggling engine, Bob, Gibson and Lackey pushed uneaten stovies around their plates in the galley. The wind howled, and the engine struggled. Crockery and pans rattled hard inside their locked confines.

"When will the tow reach us?"

Gibson turned blazing eyes upon Bob, who shrunk backwards in his seat as if the skipper had struck him.

"What the fuck are ye askin' *me* for? Can ye hear that out there, eh? It's called a fuckin' storm, Bob. There's sixty knot winds, sleet, and zero fuckin' visibility. I ken that the Port Authority boys are fuckin' saints an' all that, but even they wouldnae be stupid enough to leave Peterheid now."

Lachlan pushed up from the booth with a curse. He tossed his plate into the metal sink, where it shattered too loudly. A strange warmth tingled down his arms and legs, not unlike the first shot of rum after a long trip. Stalking towards his quarters, he threw Gibson the very best scowl that he could muster. "It wasn't a *fuckin'* rock, and you know it. And it wasn't cod."

That night there were no more thuds against the hull, no more drawn-out scratches. Lachlan stared impotently up into darkness, imagining the rust bubbles and rivets less than two feet above his head—and then the howling, rain-slick deck beyond. He slept for maybe a little over an hour, keeping one palm always flat against the cold hull. He knew that they were still out there. Waiting to find another way in.

They went back on deck a little after six a.m. The rising sun cast orange fingers over a now settled sea, while the working boards sparkled white over patchy brown. Flurries of snow caught upon Lachlan's eyelashes as he stood behind Irvine's rigid shoulder, and he blinked them away. The wind tickled hair against his temples. His nose ran while his fingers stung and pulsed. He had forgotten his gloves. He noticed none of it.

As far as the eye could see, there floated bodies. Huge collections of herring and whiting mixed with bottom-feeders like eel and halibut, flounder and roughy. Invertebrates—shellfish, crabs and pink-frilled anemones—filled the spaces between them like iced flowers on a cake. There were *thousands* of them, from every zone of the sea. From sunlight, through twilight, and down to dark. A grey-brown carpet that stretched beyond even the widening horizon, rocked by the swell and buffeted by the growing breeze.

"Jesus."

Lachlan didn't know who said it, but he agreed. There was nothing else to say. When Gibson slammed shut the wheelhouse door, every one of them jumped.

"Christ, what the fuck is this now?"

Lachlan was no longer fooled by the skipper's indignant fury. Gibson was terrified, and dangerously so—the kind of terrified that got people killed, where otherwise they might have lived to tell a bad tale. Lachlan had been happy to put his fate in Gibson's hands while they had been fighting sea swells and trawling the bottom, but this was different. Gibson was old school and too stuck in his own beliefs to ever want to see past them.

"We need to get out of here, Gibson. The storm's broken."

Gibson's mouth set into a thin, tight line. He didn't look towards the sea again. "We need a tow. Do ye have any idea how much fuckin' fuel we've already—"

Irvine's lips suddenly curled over his few teeth in an ugly grimace of their own. "We have lost a man, Gibson! And ye want tae quibble over fuel?" He reached a trembling arm starboard. "There are *things* down there! Ye ken that just as well as any ae us. *Big* fuckin' things, Gibson." The first-mate's voice cracked and dropped to a whisper. "And all ae this…this slaughter…it's for us. Ye ken that too."

"They've been following us since we caught those sea scorpions."

Gibson found a better target in Lachlan, and rounded on him, eyes blazing. The sweat was running off his nose and chin in thin rivers. "They're no' sea fuckin' scorpions, alright? Do ye lot hear yerselves? Ye ken what ye're sayin' don't ye? That out there is what—yon ugly, dead bastards' mummys and daddys, eh?" Now breathing so hard that the veins in his neck stood out in purple cords, Gibson spun on his heel and made for the wheelhouse. "There's another Force 10 comin' up from Forties and Cromarty. We stay put and we wait for our tow." He wrenched open the wheelhouse door with a shaky curse, and tried to throw them one last glare of contempt. "Have a fuckin' word wi' yerselves."

When Ernie suddenly banged open the central hatch, Lachlan let escape a guttural cry and stumbled backwards into Irvine. Ernie's grin was hollow and far from apologetic. Black shadows pulled in around his eyes. Balanced on the narrow ladder, he hauled the first icebox over his shoulder and threw it onto the deck, where it slid fast over a bank of ice and came to rest close to the now redundant gantry. Another swiftly followed it.

"They want 'em, they can fuckin' have 'em."

None of them looked at the lifeless bodies floating on the sea, any more than they did the dead creatures in their hands as they threw them back. When the last of them were gone, icy wet air whistled through Lachlan's lungs and stung his throat. Until then, he hadn't even realised that he had been holding his breath.

Bob screamed high and wild when a thud sounded directly under the stern doors. Irvine grasped hold of Lachlan for balance when another came, and then another—shaking the boards under their feet, reverberating rings of assaulted metal and rivet. The fourth was a concentrated effort—and far more effective. Lachlan skidded on a patch of frozen snow as something rammed hard against the keel below the stern doors, rocking the boat enough to lay Irvine out flat and wrench a second scream from Bob.

An icebox slid along the deck, slamming into Lachlan's ankle as *The Relict* righted itself in a low roll. *Coley 15#* had been scrawled on its polystyrene lid.

When he looked back towards the open hatch, Ernie grinned again, another two boxes balanced high on his shoulders. Small, unhealthy spots of colour had appeared at his cheekbones. "Gi'e 'em all ae it. All ae it!"

The next blow dislodged a sheet of ice close to a stack of *cookies*. Lachlan watched the ice slip and slide, battering itself against the round, steel balls until there was nothing of it left, save wet timber smears and powder. He closed his eyes. Another much closer banging stalled Lachlan's heart again, until he realised that Irvine had begun throwing his fists against the wheelhouse door.

"The bastard's locked himself in! Gibson! Open this door!"

Lachlan hoisted up the first box of coley, struggled back to starboard, and began hurling the fish into the sea. Their slick, cold skin slipped through his fingers and he swallowed bile. This time he looked down.

All around *The Relict* there had opened up a space of dark water perhaps as much as ten feet wide. Apart from the dead coley, not one of the floating bodies came close to penetrating this space, and when Lachlan tried to see down beyond the black and the boat's slick reflection, he saw only himself: a small, round head peering out of its besieged castle. But they were down there. He didn't need to see them to know that; didn't need to *feel* them as they rammed harder and faster under his feet. They were down there alright. And a few handfuls of dead fish weren't about to make them go away.

And then came a sound like a traffic collision—a terrific roar followed by shattered, grinding metal and debris. *Screams*. Lachlan's stomach lurched up and away as his world became suddenly inverted. Vertigo held back his own screams as he fell down, down towards that corridor of black. He hit the water too hard and too fast. Pain shot up through his calves and thighs. His groin and pelvis prickled as if hot, and he drew in lungfuls of saltwater as he sank like a stone. Recovering from its near capsize, *The Relict* rolled too low, casting Lachlan further into shadow and wrenching a scream from his sea-clogged throat.

Cold dark silence filled his head. The abyss of his nightmares felt very near. When he imagined that he felt something bump against his thigh, he recoiled backward in an agitated mass of bubbles and flailing limbs, his fist colliding with *The Relict*'s rough hull in a muted thump.

They were here. Sinking lower into cold shadow, Lachlan's heartbeat quickened inside his ears. The air that escaped the corners of his mouth tickled his cheeks and hairline. The sun was an ephemeral suggestion of gold too far above him.

He recoiled again when something glanced off his shoulder, and then he grasped fast to the rope and pulled. It tugged briefly back in reply and returned to slack. Cold crept inside his skin like thousands of fine needles, while his lungs burned as if on fire. He couldn't haul himself up; he likely couldn't even hang on while others did the pulling for him. But still he couldn't let go.

They came out of the darkness like a rushing mob: flashing white limbs and scales, snapping claws and spines—the smallest of them still easily the size of an adult crocodile. They circled around him, jostling for space, pushing against one another with long-reaching webbed paddles. Under water, those disjointed segments of armour plating appeared almost graceful, winding and unwinding with fluid ease, flicking spiked tails towards him. Taunting him. Their venomous spines quivered and lengthened. Those clustered, unblinking eyes fixed fast to his own.

Lachlan had no more horror left in him. His lungs screamed as they moved in closer, blocking out the light that filtered from above with almost exquisite indolence. They touched his flaccid skin, puncturing his flesh.

Despite his pain, his terror, Lachlan fought to hold onto consciousness. Even as his sight crept darker at its edges like burning paper, his eyes never left the flat, ringed carapaces; the writhing, tapering tails; the ridged claws that opened and closed, opened and closed. The round, crowded spheres of liquid black. These ancient resurrections had been no more interested in their dead juveniles than they had been in the coley. *They* were not the bottom-feeders, the scourge of the sea floor. But they were perhaps its new champions.

As the last of the light disappeared, plunging Lachlan into darkness, and biting, searing, *tearing* agony, he clung to the rope even after all coherence had left him. Dangled like the bait that he had always been.

STRAPPADO
LAIRD BARRON

Laird Barron's work has appeared in such publications as *The Magazine of Fantasy & Science Fiction, SCIFICTION, Inferno: New Tales of Terror and the Supernatural, Poe: 19 New Tales Inspired by Edgar Allan Poe*, and *The Del Rey Book of Science Fiction and Fantasy*. It has also been reprinted in numerous year's best anthologies. His debut collection, *The Imago Sequence & Other Stories*, was the winner of the inaugural Shirley Jackson Award. A second collection, *Occultation*, is forthcoming from Night Shade Books. Barron is an expatriate Alaskan currently at large in Washington State.

Kenshi Suzuki and Swayne Harris had a chance reunion at a bathhouse in an Indian tourist town. It had been five or six years since their previous Malta liaison, a cocktail party at the British consulate that segued into a branding iron hot affair. They'd spent a long weekend of day cruises to the cyclopean ruins on Gozo, nightclubbing at the elite hotels and casinos, and booze-drenched marathon sex before the dissolution of their respective junkets swept them back to New York and London in a storm of tears and bitter farewells. For Kenshi, the emotional hangover lasted through desolate summer and into a melancholy autumn. And even now, when elegant, thunderously handsome Swayne materialized from the crowd on the balcony like the Ghost of Christmas Past—!

Kenshi wore a black suit; sleek and polished as a seal or a banker. He swept his single lock of gelled black hair to the left, like a gothic teardrop. His skin was sallow and dewlapped at his neck, and soft at his belly and beneath his Italian leather belt. He'd been a swimmer once, earnestly meant to return to his collegiate form, but hadn't yet braced for the exhaustion of such an endeavor. He preferred to float in hotel pools while dreaming of his supple youth, once so exotic in the suburbs of white bread Connecticut. Everyone but his grandparents (who never fully acclimated to their transplantation to the West) called him Ken. A naturalized U.S. citizen, he spoke meager Japanese, knew next to zero about the history or the culture and had visited Tokyo a grand total of three times. In short, he privately acknowledged his unworthiness to lay claim to his blood heritage and thus lived a life of minor, yet persistent regret.

Swayne wore a cream colored suit of a cut most popular with the royalty of

242 — LAIRD BARRON

South American plantations. *It's in style anywhere I go*, he explained later as they undressed one another in Kenshi's suite at the Golden Scale. Swayne's complexion was dark, like fired clay. His slightly sinister brows and waxed imperial lent him the appearance of a Christian devil.

In the seam between the electric shock of their reunion and resultant delirium fugue of violent coupling, Kenshi had an instant to doubt the old magic before the question was utterly obliterated. And if he'd forgotten Swayne's sly, wry demeanor, his faith was restored when the dark man rolled to face the ceiling, dragged on their shared cigarette and said, "Of all the bathhouses in all the cities of the world…."

Kenshi cheerfully declared him a bastard and snatched back the cigarette. The room was strewn with their clothes. A vase of lilies lay capsized and water funneled from severed stems over the edge of the table. He caught droplets in his free hand and rubbed them and the semen into the slick flesh of his chest and belly. He breathed heavily.

"How'd you swing this place all to yourself?" Swayne said. "Big promotion?"

"A couple of my colleagues got pulled off the project and didn't make the trip. You?"

"Business, with unexpected pleasure, thank you. The museum sent me to look at a collection—estate sale. Paintings and whatnot. I fly back on Friday, unless I find something extraordinary, which is doubtful. Mostly rubbish, I'm afraid." Swayne rose and stretched. Rich, gold-red light dappled the curtains, banded and bronzed him with tiger stripes.

The suite's western exposure gave them a last look at the sun as it faded to black. Below their lofty vantage, slums and crooked dirt streets and the labyrinthine wharfs in the shallow, blood-warm harbor were mercifully obscured by thickening tropical darkness. Farther along the main avenue and atop the ancient terraced hillsides was a huge, baroque seventeenth-century-monastery, much photographed for feature films, and farther still, the scattered manors and villas of the lime nabobs, their walled estates demarcated by kliegs and floodlights. Tourism pumped the lifeblood of the settlement. They came for the monastery, of course, and only a few kilometers off was a wildlife preserve. Tour buses ran daily and guides entertained foreigners with local folklore and promises of tigers, a number of which roamed the high grass plains. Kenshi had gone on his first day, hated the ripe, florid smell of the jungle, the heat, and the sullen men with rifles who patrolled the electrified perimeter fence in halftracks. The locals wore knives in their belts, even the urbane guide with the Oxford accent, and it left Kenshi feeling shriveled and helpless, at the mercy of the hatefully smiling multitudes.

Here, in the dusty, grimy heart of town, some eighty kilometers down the coast from grand old Mumbai, when the oil lamps and electric lamps fizzed alight, link by link in a vast, convoluted chain, it was only bright enough to help the muggers and cutthroats see what they were doing.

"City of romance," Swayne said with eminent sarcasm. He opened the door to the terrace and stood naked at the rail. There were a few tourists on their verandas and at their windows. Laughter and pop music and the stench of the sea carried on the lethargic breeze as it snaked through the room. The hotel occupied the exact center of a semicircle of relatively modernized blocks—the chamber of commerce's concession to appeasing Westerners' paranoia of marauding gangs and vicious muggers. Still, three streets over was the Third World, as Kenshi's colleagues referred to it while they swilled whiskey and goggled at turbans and sarongs and at the Buddhists in their orange robes. It was enough to make him ashamed of his continent, to pine for his father's homeland, until he realized the Japanese were scarcely more civilized as guests.

"The only hotel with air conditioning and you go out there. You'll be arrested if you don't put something on!" Kenshi finally dragged himself upright and collected his pants. "Let's go to the discothèque."

"The American place? I'd rather not. Asshole tourists swarm there like bees to honey. I was in the cantina a bit earlier and got stuck near a bunch of Hollywood types whooping it up at the bar. Probably come to scout the area or shoot the monastery. All they could talk about is picking up on 'European broads.'"

Kenshi laughed. "Those are the guys I'm traveling with. Yeah, they're scouting locations. And they're all married, too."

"Wankers. Hell with the disco."

"No, there's another spot—a hole in the wall I heard about from a friend. A local."

"Eh, probably a seedy little bucket of blood. I'm in, then!"

Kenshi rang his contact, one Rashid Obi, an assistant to an executive producer at a local firm that cranked out several dozen Bollywood films every year. Rashid gave directions and promised to meet them at the club in forty-five minutes. Or, if they were nervous to travel the streets alone, he could escort them…. Kenshi laughed, somewhat halfheartedly, and assured his acquaintance there was no need for such coddling. He would've preferred Rashid's company, but knew Swayne was belligerently fearless regarding forays into foreign environments. His lover was an adventurer and hard bitten in his own charming fashion. Certainly Swayne would mock him for his timidity and charge ahead regardless. So, Kenshi stifled his misgivings and led the way.

The discothèque was a quarter mile from the hotel and buried in a misshapen block of stone houses and empty shops. They found it mostly by accident after stumbling around several narrow alleys that reeked of urine and the powerful miasma of curry that seeped from open apartment windows. The entry arch was low and narrow and blackened from soot and antiquity. The name of the club had been painted into the worn plaster, illegible now from erosion and neglect. Kerosene lamps guttered in inset sconces and shadows gathered in droves. A speaker dangled from a cornice and projected scratchy sitar music. Two Indian men sat on a stone bench. They wore baggy, lemon shirts and disco slacks likely purchased from the black market outlets in a local bazaar. They shared the stem of the hookah at their sandaled feet. Neither appeared interested in the arrival of the Westerners.

"Oh my God! It's an opium den!" Swayne said and squeezed Kenshi's buttock. "Going native, are we, dear?"

Kenshi blushed and knocked his hand aside. He'd smoked half a joint with a dorm mate in college and that was the extent of his experimentation with recreational drugs. He favored a nice, dry white wine and the occasional import beer, preferably Sapporo.

The darkness of the alley followed them inside. The interior lay in shadow, except for the bar, which glowed from a strip along its edge like the bioluminescent tentacle of a deep sea creature, and motes of gold and red and purple passing across the bottles from a rotating glitter ball above the tiny square of dance floor wedged in the corner. The sitar music issued from a beat box and was much louder than it had been outside. Patrons were jammed into the little rickety tables and along the bar. The air was sharp with sweat and exhaled liquor fumes.

Rashid emerged from the shadows and caught Kenshi's arm above the elbow in the overly familiar manner of his countrymen. He was shorter than Kenshi and slender to the point of well-heeled emaciation. He stood so close Kenshi breathed deeply of his cologne, the styling gel in his short, tightly coiled hair. He introduced the small man from Delhi to a mildly bemused Swayne. Soon Rashid vigorously shepherded them into an alcove where a group of Europeans crowded together around three circular tables laden with beer bottles and shot glasses and fuming ashtrays heaped with the butts of cigarettes.

Rashid presented Swayne and Kenshi to the evening's co-host, one Luis Guzman, an elderly Argentinean who'd lived abroad for nearly three decades in quasi political exile. Guzman was the public relations guru for a profoundly large international advertising conglomerate, which in turn influenced, or owned outright the companies represented by the various guests he'd assembled at the discothèque.

Kenshi's feet ached, so he wedged in next to a reedy blonde Netherlander, a weather reporter for some big market, he gathered as sporadic introductions were made. Her hands bled ink from a mosaic of nightclub stamps, the kind that didn't easily wash off, so like rings in a tree, it was possible to estimate she'd been partying hard for several nights. This impression was confirmed when she confided that she'd gone a bit wild during her group's whirlwind tour of Bangkok, Mumbai and this "village" in the space of days. She laughed at him from the side of her mouth, gaped fishily with her left eye, a Picasso girl, and pressed her bony thigh against him. She'd been drinking boleros, and lots of them, he noted. *What goes down must come up*, he thought and was sorry for whomever she eventually leeched onto tonight.

The Viking gentleman looming across from them certainly vied for her attention, what with his lascivious grimaces and bellowing jocularity, but she appeared content to ignore him while trading glances with the small, hirsute Slav to the Viking's left and occasionally brushing Kenshi's forearm as they shared an ashtray. He soon discovered Hendrika the weathergirl worked for the Viking, Andersen, chief comptroller and inveterate buffoon. The Slav was actually a native of Minsk named Fedor; Fedor managed distribution for a major vodka label and possessed some mysterious bit of history with Hendrika. Kenshi idly wondered if he'd been her pimp while she toiled through college. A job was a job was a job (until she found the job of her dreams) to a certain subset of European woman, and men too, as he'd been pleased to discover during his many travels. In turn, Hendrika briefly introduced Kenshi to the French Contingent of software designers—Francoise, Jean Michelle, and Claude; the German photographer Victor and his assistant Nina, and Raul, a Spanish advertising consultant. They extended lukewarm handshakes and one of them bought him a glass of bourbon, which he didn't want but politely accepted. Then, everyone resumed roaring, disjointed conversations and ignored him completely.

Good old Swayne got along swimmingly, of course. He'd discarded his white suit for an orange blazer, black shirt and slacks and Kenshi noted with equal measures of satisfaction and jealousy that all heads swiveled to follow the boisterous Englishman. Within moments he'd shaken hands with all and sundry and been inducted by the club of international debauchers as a member in good standing. That the man didn't even speak a second language was no impediment—he vaulted such barriers by shamelessly enlisting necessary translations from whoever happened to be within earshot. Kenshi glumly thought his friend would've made one hell of an American.

Presently Swayne returned from his confab with Rashid and Guzman and exclaimed, "We've been invited to the exhibition. A *Van Iblis!*" Swayne seemed genuinely enthused, his meticulously cultivated cynicism blasted to smithereens in an instant. Kenshi barely made him out over the crossfire between Andersen and Hendrika and the other American, Walther. Walther was fat and bellicose, a colonial barbarian dressed for civilized company. His shirt was untucked, his tie an open noose. Kenshi hadn't caught what the fellow did for a living, however Walther put whiskey after whiskey away with the vigor of a man accustomed to lavish expense accounts. He sneered at Kenshi on the occasions their eyes met.

Kenshi told Swayne he'd never heard of Van Iblis.

"It's a pseudonym," Swayne said. "Like Kilroy, Or Alan Smithee. He, or she, is a guerilla. Not welcome in the U.K.; *persona non grata* in the free world you might say." When Kenshi asked why Van Iblis wasn't welcome in Britain, Swayne grinned. "Because the shit he pulls off violates a few laws here and there. Unauthorized installations, libelous materials, health code violations. Explosions!" Industry insiders suspected Van Iblis was actually comprised of a significant number of member artists and exceedingly wealthy patrons. Such an infrastructure seemed the only logical explanation for the success of these brazen exhibitions and their participants' elusiveness.

It developed that Guzman had brought his eclectic coterie to this part of the country after sniffing a rumor of an impending Van Iblis show and as luck would have it, tonight was the night. Guzman's contacts had provided him with a hand scrawled map to the rendezvous, and a password. A password! It was all extraordinarily titillating.

Swayne dialed up a slideshow on his cell and handed it over. Kenshi remembered the news stories once he saw the image of the three homeless men who'd volunteered to be crucified on faux satellite dishes. Yes, that had caused a sensation, although the winos survived relatively intact. None of them knew enough to expose the identity of his temporary employers. Another series of slides displayed the infamous pigs' blood carpet bombing of the Viet Nam War Memorial from a blimp that then exploded in midair like a Roman candle. Then the so called "corpse art" in Mexico, Amsterdam and elsewhere. Similar to the other guerilla installations, these exhibits popped up in random venues in any of a dozen countries after the mildest and most surreptitious of advance rumors and retreated underground within hours. Of small comfort to scandalized authorities was the fact the corpse sculptures, while utterly macabre, were allegedly comprised of volunteers with terminal illnesses who'd donated their bodies to science, or rather, art. Nonetheless, at the sight of grimly posed seniors in antiquated bathing suits, a bloated, eyeless Santa in a coonskin cap, the tri-headed ice-cream vendor and his chalk-faced Siamese children, Kenshi wrinkled his lip and pushed the phone at Swayne. "No, I think I'll skip this one, whatever it is, thank you very much."

"You are such a wet blanket, Swayne said. "Come on, love. I've been dying to witness a Van Iblis show since, well forever. I'll be the envy of every art dilettante from Birmingham to Timbuktu!"

Kenshi made polite yet firm noises of denial. Swayne leaned very close; his hot breath tickled Kenshi's ear. He stroked Kenshi's cock through the tight fabric of his designer pants. Congruently, albeit obliviously, Hendrika continued to rub his thigh. Kenshi choked on his drink and finally consented to accompany Swayne on his stupid side trek, would've promised anything to spare himself this agonizing embarrassment. A lifetime in the suburbs had taught him to eschew public displays of affection, much less submit to a drunken mauling by another man in a foreign country not particularly noted for its tolerance.

He finished his drink in miserable silence and awaited the inevitable.

They crowded aboard Guzman's two Day-Glo rental vans and drove inland. There were no signs to point the way and the road was narrow and deserted. Kenshi's head grew thick and heavy on his neck and he closed his eyes and didn't open them until the tires made new sounds as they left paved road for a dirt track and his companions gently bumped their legs and arms against his own.

It wasn't much farther.

Daylight peeled back the layers of night and deposited them near a collection of prefabricated warehouse modules and storage sheds. The modules were relatively modern, yet already cloaked in moss and threaded with coils of vine. Each was enormous and had been adjoined to its siblings via additions and corrugated tin walkways. The property sat near the water, a dreary, fog-shrouded expanse surrounded by drainage ditches and marshes and a jungle of creepers and banyan trees.

Six or seven dilapidated panel trucks were parked on the outskirts; 1970s Fords imported from distant USA, their white frames scorched and shot with rust. Battered insignia on the door panels marked them as one-time property of the ministry of the interior. Alongside the trucks, an equally antiquated, although apparently functional, bulldozer squatted in the high grass; a dull red model one would expect to see abandoned in a rural American pasture. To the left of the bulldozer was a deep, freshly ploughed trench surmounted by plastic barrels, unsealed fifty-five gallon drums and various wooden boxes, much of this half concealed by canvas tarps. Guzman commented that the owners of the land were in the embryonic stage of prepping for large scale development—perhaps a hotel. Power lines and septic systems were in the offing.

Kenshi couldn't imagine who in the hell could possibly think building a hotel in a swamp represented a wise business investment.

Guzman and Rashid's groups climbed from the vans and congregated, faces slack and bruised by hangovers, jet lag, and burgeoning unease. What had seemed a lark in the cozy confines of the disco became a more ominous prospect as each took stock and realized he or she hadn't a bloody clue as to north or south, or up and down, for that matter. Gnats came at them in quick, sniping swarms, and several people cursed when they lost shoes to the soft, wet earth. Black and white chickens scratched in the weedy ruts.

A handful of Indians dressed in formal wear grimly waited under a pavilion to serve a buffet. None of them smiled or offered any greeting. They mumbled amongst themselves and loaded plates of honeydew slices and crepes and poured glasses of champagne with disconsolate expressions. A Victrola played an eerie Hindu-flavored melody. The scene reminded Kenshi of a funeral reception. Someone, perhaps Walther, muttered nervously, and the sentiment of general misgiving palpably intensified.

"Hey, this is kinda spooky," Hendrika stage-whispered to her friend Fedor. Oddly enough, that cracked everybody up and tensions loosened.

Guzman and Rashid approached a couple of young, drably attired Indian men who were scattering corn from gunny sacks to the chickens, and started a conversation. After they'd talked for a few minutes, Guzman announced the exhibition would open in about half an hour and all present were welcome to enjoy the buffet and stretch their legs. Andersen, Swayne, and the French software team headed for the pavilion and mosquito netting.

Meanwhile, Fedor fetched sampler bottles of vodka supplied by his company and passed them around. Kenshi surprised himself by accepting one. His throat had parched during the drive and he welcomed the excuse to slip away from Hendrika whose orbit had yet again swung her all too close to him.

He strolled off a bit from the others, swiping at the relentless bugs and wishing he'd thought to wear that rather dashing panama hat he'd "borrowed" from a lover on location in the Everglades during a sweltering July shoot. His stroll carried him behind a metal shed overgrown with banyan vines. A rotting wooden addition abutted the sloppy edge of a pond or lagoon; it was impossible to know because of the cloying mist. He lit a cigarette. The porch was cluttered with disintegrating crates and rudimentary gardening tools. Gingerly lifting the edge of a tarp slimy with moss, he discovered a quantity of new plastic barrels. Hydrochloric Acid, CORROSIVE! and a red skull and crossbones warned of hazardous contents. He quickly snatched back his hand and moved away lest his cigarette trigger a calamity worthy of a Darwin Award.

"Uh, yeah—good idea, Sulu. Splash that crap on you and your face will melt like glue." Walther had sneaked up behind him. The man drained his mini vodka bottle and tossed it into the bushes. He drew another bottle from the pocket of his sweat-stained dress shirt and had a pull. The humidity was awful here; it pressed down in a smothering blanket. His hair lay in sticky clumps and his face was shiny and red. He breathed heavily, laboring as if the brief walk from the van had led up several flights of stairs.

Kenshi stared at him considering and discarding a series of snappy retorts. "Asshole," he finally said under his breath. He flicked his cigarette butt toward the scummy water and edged around Walther and made for the vans.

Walther laughed. "Jap fag," he said. The fat man unzipped and began pissing off the end of the porch.

"I'm not even fucking Japanese, you idiot," Kenshi said over his shoulder. No good, he realized; the tremor in his voice, the quickening of his shuffle betrayed his cowardice in the face of adversity. This instinctive recoil from trouble, the resultant wave of self-loathing and bitter recriminations was as it ever had been with Kenshi. Swayne would've smashed the jerk's face.

Plucking the thought from the air, Walther called, "Don't go tell your Limey boyfriend on me!"

Guzman gathered everyone into a huddle as Kenshi approached. He stood on the running board of a van and explained the three rules regarding their impending tour of the exhibition: no touching, no souvenirs, no pictures. "Mr. Vasilov will come around and secure all cell phones, cameras and recorders. Don't worry, your personal effects will be returned as soon as the tour concludes. Thank you for your cooperation."

Fedor dumped the remaining limes and pears from a hotel gift basket and came around and confiscated the proscribed items. Beyond a few exaggerated sighs, no one really protested; the prohibition of cameras and recording devices at galleries and exclusive viewings was commonplace. Certainly, this being Van Iblis and the epitome of scofflaw art, there could be no surprise regarding such rules.

At the appointed time the warehouse doors rattled and slid aside and a blond man in a paper suit emerged and beckoned them to ascend the ramp. He was large, nearly the girth of Andersen the Viking, and wore elbow length rubber gloves and black galoshes. A black balaclava covered the lower half of his face. The party filed up the gangway in pairs, Guzman and Fedor at the fore. Kenshi and Swayne were the next to last. Kenshi watched the others become swiftly dissolving shadows backlit as they were by a bank of humming fluorescent lamps. He thought of cattle and slaughter pens and fingered his passport in its wallet on a string around his neck. Swayne squeezed his arm.

Once the group had entered, five more men, also clothed in paper suits and balaclavas, shut the heavy doors behind them with a clang that caused Kenshi's flesh to twitch. He sickly noted these five wore machetes on their belts. Blood rushed to his head in a breaker of dizziness and nausea. The reek of alcohol sweat and body odor tickled his gorge. The flickering light washed over his companions, reflected in their black eyes, made their faces pale and strange and curiously lifeless, as if he'd been suddenly trapped with brilliantly sculpted automatons. He understood then that they too had spotted the machetes. Mouths hung open in moist exclamations of apprehension and dread and the inevitable thrill derived from the alchemy of these emotions. Yet another man, similarly garbed as his compatriots, wheeled forth a tripod mounted Panaflex motion picture camera and began shooting the scene.

The floor creaked under their gathered weight. Insulating foam paneled the walls. Every window was covered in black plastic. There were two narrow openings at the far end of the entry area; red paint outlined the first opening, blue paint the second. The openings let into what appeared to be darkened spaces, their gloom reinforced by translucent curtains of thick plastic similar to the kind that compartmentalized meat lockers.

"You will strip," the blonde man said in flat, accented English.

Kenshi's testicles retracted, although a calmness settled over his mind. He dimly acknowledged this as the animal recognition of its confinement in a trap, the inevitability of what must ultimately occur. Yet, one of this fractious group would argue, surely Walther the boor, or obstreperous Andersen, definitely and assuredly Swayne. But none protested, none resisted the command, all were docile. One of the anonymous men near the entrance took out his machete and held it casually at his waist. Wordlessly, avoiding eye contact with each other, Kenshi's fellow travelers began to remove their clothes and arrange them neatly, or not so much, as the case might've been, in piles on the floor. The blond instructed them to form columns and face the opposite wall. The entire affair possessed the quality of a lucid dream, a not-happening in the real world sequence of events. Hendrika was crying, he noted before she turned away and presented him with her thin backside, a bony ridge of spine, spare haunches. She'd drained white.

Kenshi stood between oddly subdued Swayne and one of the Frenchmen. He was acutely anxious regarding his sagging breasts, the immensity of his scarred and stretched belly, his general flaccidity, and almost chuckled at the absurdity of it all.

When the group had assembled with their backs to him, the blond man briskly explained the guests would be randomly approached and tapped on the shoulder. The designated guests would turn and proceed into the exhibit chambers by twos. Questions? None were forthcoming. After a lengthy pause it commenced. Beginning with Guzman and Fedor, each of them were gradually and steadily ushered out of sight with perhaps a minute between pairings. The plastic curtains swished and crackled with their passage. Kenshi waited his turn and stared at the curdled yellow foam on the walls.

The tap on the shoulder came and he had sunk so far into himself it was only then he registered everyone else had gone. The group comprised an uneven number, so he was odd man out. Abruptly, techno music blared and snarled from hidden speakers, and beneath the eardrum shattering syncopation, a shrill, screeching like the keening of a beast or the howl of a circular saw chewing wood.

"Well, friend," said the blond, raising his voice to overcome the music, "you may choose."

Kenshi found it difficult to walk a straight line. He staggered and pushed through the curtain of the blue door into darkness. There was a long corridor and at its end another sheet of plastic that let in pale light. He shoved aside the curtain and had a moment of sick vertigo upon realizing there were no stairs. He cried out and toppled, arms waving, and flopped the eight or so feet into a pit of gravel. His leg broke on impact, but he didn't notice until later. The sun filled his vision with white. He thrashed in the gravel, dug furrows with elbows and heels and screamed soundlessly because the air had been driven from his lungs. A shadow leaned over him and brutally gripped his hair and clamped his face with what felt like a wet cloth. The cloth went into his nose, his mouth, choked him.

The cloth tasted of death.

Thanks to a series of tips, authorities found him three weeks later in the closet of an abandoned house on the fringes of Bangalore. Re-creating events, and comparing these to the experiences of those others who were discovered at different locations but in similar circumstances, it was determined he'd been pacified with drugs unto a stupor. His leg was infected and he'd lost a terrible amount of weight. The doctors predicted scars, physical and otherwise.

There'd been police interviews; FBI, CIA, NSA. Kenshi answered and answered and they eventually let him go, let him get to work blocking it, erasing it to the extent erasing it was possible. He avoided news reports, refused the sporadic interviews, made a concentrated effort to learn nothing of the aftermath, although he suspected scant evidence remained, anyway. He took a leave of absence and cocooned himself.

Kenshi remembered nothing after the blue door and he was thankful.

Months after their second and last reunion, Swayne rang him at home and asked if he wanted to meet for cocktails. Swayne was in New York for an auction, would be around over the weekend, and wondered if Kenshi was doing all right, if he was surviving. This was before Kenshi began to lie awake in the dark of each new evening, disconnected from the cold pulse of the world outside the womb of his apartment, his hotel room, the cabs of his endless stream of rental cars. He dreamed the same dream; a recurring nightmare of acid-filled barrels knocked like dominoes into a trench, the grumbling exertions of a red bulldozer pushing in the dirt.

I've seen the tape, Swayne said through a blizzard of static.

Kenshi said nothing. He breathed, in and out. Starless, the black ceiling swung above him, it rushed to and fro, in and out like the heartbeat of the black Atlantic tapping and slapping at old crumbling seawalls, not far from his own four thin walls.

I've seen it, Swayne said. After another long pause, he said, *Say something, Ken.*

What?

It does exist. Van Iblis made sure copies were circulated to the press, but naturally the story was killed. Too awful, you know? I got one by post a few weeks ago. A reporter friend smuggled it out of a precinct in Canada. The goddamned obscenity is everywhere. And I didn't have the balls to look. Yesterday, finally.

That's why you called. Kenshi trembled. He suddenly wanted to know. Dread nearly overwhelmed him. He considered hanging up, chopping off Swayne's distorted voice. He thought he might vomit there, supine in bed, and drown.

Yeah. We were the show. The red door people were the real show, I guess. God help us, Ken. Ever heard of a Palestinian hanging? Dangled from your wrists, cinder blocks tied to your ankles? That's what the bastards started with. When they were done, while the people were still alive...." Swayne stopped there, or his next words were swallowed by the static surf.

Of course, Van Iblis made a film. No need for Swayne to illuminate him on that score, to open him up again. Kenshi thought about the empty barrels near the trench. He thought about what Walther said to him behind the shed that day.

I don't even know why I picked blue, mate, Swayne said.

He said to Swayne, *Don't ever fucking call me again.* He disconnected and dropped the phone on the floor and waited for it to ring again. When it didn't, he slipped into unconsciousness.

One day his copy arrived in a plain envelope via anonymous sender. He put the disk on the sidewalk outside of his building and methodically crushed it under the heel of his wingtip. The doorman watched the whole episode and smiled indulgently, exactly as one does to placate the insane.

Kenshi smiled in return and went into his apartment and ran a bath. He slashed his wrists with the broken edge of a credit card. Not deep enough; he bled everywhere and was forced to hire a service to steam the carpets. He never again wore short sleeve shirts.

Nonetheless, he'd tried. There was comfort in trying.

Kenshi returned to the Indian port town on company business a few years later. Models were being flown in from Mumbai and Kolkata for a photo shoot near the old monastery. The ladies wouldn't arrive for another day and he had time to burn. He hired a taxi and went looking for the Van Iblis site.

The field wasn't difficult to find. Developers had drained the swamp and built a hotel on the site, as advertised. They'd hacked away nearby wilderness and plopped down high-rise condos, two restaurants and a casino. The driver dropped him at the Ivory Tiger, a glitzy, towering edifice. The lobby was marble and brass and the staff a pleasant chocolate mahogany, all of whom dressed smartly, smiled perfectly white smiles and spoke flawless English.

He stayed in a tenth floor suite, kept the blinds drawn, the phone unplugged, the lights off. Lying naked across crisp, snow-cool sheets was to float disembodied through a great silent darkness. A handsome businessman, a fellow American, in fact, had bought him a white wine in the lounge; a sweet talker, that one, but Kenshi retired alone. He didn't get many erections these days and those that came ended in humiliating fashion. Drifting through insoluble night was safer.

In the morning, he ate breakfast and smoked a few cigarettes and had his first drink of the day. He was amazed how much he drank anymore and how little effect it had on him. After breakfast he walked around the hotel grounds, which were very much a garden, and stopped at the tennis courts. No one was playing; thunderclouds massed and the air smelled of rain. By his estimation, the tennis courts were near to, if not directly atop the old field. Drainage grates were embedded at regular intervals and he went to his knees and pressed the side of his head against one until the cold metal flattened his ear. He listened to water rushing through subterranean depths. Water fell through deep, hollow spaces and echoed, ever more faintly. And, perhaps, borne through yards of pipe and clay and gravel that hold, some say, fragments and frequencies of the past, drifted whispery strains of laughter, Victrola music.

He caught himself speculating about who else went through the blue door, the exit to the world of the living, and smothered this line of conjecture with the bribe of more drinks at the bar, more sex from this day on, more whatever it might take to stifle such thoughts forever. He was happier thinking Hendrika went back to her weather job once the emotional trauma subsided, that Andersen the Viking was ever in pursuit of her dubious virtue, that the Frenchmen and the German photographer had returned to their busy, busy lives. And Rashid....

Blue door. Red door. They might be anywhere.

The sky cracked and rain poured forth.

Kenshi curled into a tight ball, chin to chest and closed his eyes. Swayne kissed his mouth and they were crushingly intertwined. Acid sluiced over them in a wave, then the lid clanged home over the rim of the barrel and closed them in.

THE LAMMAS WORM
NINA ALLAN

Nina Allan's fiction has been published regularly in magazines such as *Black Static*, *Interzone*, and *Midnight Street*, and her first collection of stories, *A Thread of Truth*, was published in 2008. Her story "Angelus" won the Aeon Award in 2007. She lives and works in London.

Lammas Worm: *manifestation, sometimes corporeal, of the spirit of daemonic potency. See also Lammas, Lammas Tide, Lammas Eve, Gule of August, Spirit of First Birth.*
(Taken from *A Fabulous History of England*, John Scobie Press 1881.)

The girl's name was Leonie Pickering. Someone had labelled her like a parcel, scrawling her name in square black capitals on the back of an old cereal packet then fastening it around her neck with a piece of string. There was no return address. She was wearing a yellow dress, soiled at the back with what looked like mud, or perhaps excrement.

Her features were odd. I don't mean deformed, just strangely put together. Her skull was elongated, like the artists' impressions of the Neanderthal people who used to roam the earth before modern man came along and made such a mess of things. There was a small ridge on her forehead, just above her eyebrows. Her eyes were a liquid black. Her frizzy dark hair looked a mass of tangles, matted together at the back like a piece of old carpet. She seemed not to have a clue where she was.

It was early on a Sunday morning, well before nine, and there wasn't very much on the roads. We had played a ground in Marlborough the night before and our next stop was Cirencester. Most of the wagons were already there. I was bringing up the rear with Rudy Shyler and Piet van Aspen. Rudy was taking it slowly because his engine had developed a knock and I was taking it slowly because I always tended to end up driving with Piet. Piet was moving at a snail's pace, as usual, because that was the fastest his decrepit old jalopy would go. Rudy braked so suddenly I almost went into the back of him. *Steady on, Rudy,* I thought. *What the hell do you think you're doing?* Then I saw the kid. She was standing at the edge of the road, staring out into the traffic like a dummy in a shop window. I hooted to warn Piet to slow down then pulled over on to the verge. As I switched off the ignition I saw Rudy jump down from his cab. He went straight up to the girl and put out his hand to her, the way you might do with a frightened animal. The girl's lips drew back from her teeth in a kind of snarl. She looked like an angry baboon.

She was tiny, no more than five feet tall. *Shit*, I thought. *She'll have his hand off if he's not careful*. I opened the door to get down.

"What's going on?" said Mae. She had been dozing in the seat beside me. Her blue eyes had a misty, faraway look, as if she were still half in a dream.

"Just some kid," I said. "A runaway, I think. I'm going to help Rudy before he does something stupid. You stay here."

I wasn't in the habit of telling Mae what to do but for some reason the girl made me nervous. Mae leaned forward and peered through the windscreen.

"She doesn't look like a runaway to me. I reckon she's been dumped there."

"Perhaps," I said. I was sure she was right. I jumped down from the cab and went over to where Rudy was standing. Up close the girl seemed even smaller, and so skinny she looked half-starved. Rudy towered over her like a full-grown grizzly on its way to the hunting grounds. Rudy was a gentle giant, daft as a brush, but the kid wasn't to know that and I supposed she was terrified.

"Back off a bit," I said to him. "Give her some room."

I noticed that she had no shoes on. Her feet were bony and narrow, with high, graceful arches, the feet of a ballet girl. Her toes were long, more like fingers than ordinary toes. I put out my hand as Rudy had done, hoping to show the girl that I meant no harm.

"Are you hurt?" I said. "Can we give you a lift somewhere?"

The girl's lips pulled back in another snarl and I caught a glimpse of uneven, yellow teeth. A second later she was flying right at me. I leapt instinctively to one side, my mind seething with visions of those crooked yellow incisors gouging into my flesh. She raced straight by me and underneath Rudy's trailer, going flat like a rat under a grain store and tucking herself in behind one of the wheels.

"Well that's our morning cancelled," said Rudy. "Anybody fancy a cup of tea?"

I swore quietly to myself. I had visions of us stuck there for hours, trying to tempt the girl back out on to the roadside so we could drive on. Eventually I supposed we would have to call the police. I imagined them forcing the girl out with a cattle prod and then carting her off somewhere in the back of a panda car. I didn't like the idea of that. I rested my hand on the wheel-hub and bent down, hoping to see better, but there was just the rusty, diesel-smelling underside of Rudy's wagon and the humped dark unmoving shape I knew was the girl.

"What's happened? Has Rudy got a flat?"

Piet's voice made me jump sky high. In all the fussing over the girl I had forgotten all about him.

"No such luck," said Rudy. "We've gone and got ourselves a luggage louse."

Luggage louse was an old company expression for stowaway. Piet edged closer to the trailer, toddling down the bank with that rolling, sideways walk of his. The grass was long and slippery and I was afraid he was about to go flying.

"Let me see," he said. "Perhaps I can help."

Privately I thought the sight of Piet might only make her more frightened, but I stepped back from the wagon, giving up my space by the wheel. I watched Piet peering into the shadowy darkness, wondering what he would make of it all. He had on his old jeans, and one of the brightly-coloured paisley shirts he liked to wear, a diminutive figure, shorter by a number of inches than the runaway girl.

"Come on," he said. "Don't be afraid."

Piet was about forty then, although like many dwarfs he had an ageless quality. His whole lower body was stunted, and in addition to this he had spina bifida. Mostly he could get about all right but from time to time he was in a lot of pain. The curvature of his spine meant that he carried his head a little to one side. With his well-shaped mouth and high cheekbones his face was strikingly handsome. He had iridescent violet-coloured eyes. The public loved him, not just for the freakish contrast between his noble head and mangled body, but for his broad cockney accent, his dandyish clothes and his passion for gambling. Many people seemed to assume that a carnival was not a carnival if there wasn't a resident dwarf somewhere around, and Piet was the kind of dwarf they wanted to see.

Officially he was in charge of the funhouse. Unofficially he ran poker games into the small hours, relieving the local card kings of large sums of money. He had been with us for longer than anyone could remember. He never talked about his life before the company and none of the stories about him seemed to join up. My father told me that Piet had Dutch grandparents and that he had spent his childhood on one of the Rotterdam barges. But Vaska Malahniuk's wife Marnie told me that was all nonsense, that Piet had grown up in a children's home attached to the London Hospital in Whitechapel. The Malahniuks were both aerialistes. They had been very close to my father before he retired.

"Piet never knew his parents at all," said Marnie. "Although I think he had a sister he was very fond of."

"What was she like?" I asked her. I was endlessly curious about Piet. The idea that someone could erase their past and walk into a new life was fascinating to me.

"I couldn't tell you, love, I never knew her. I think she died when Piet was still in the home."

It was often difficult to tell what Piet was thinking. I guess he had grown so used to hiding his feelings that in a way he was always performing, even when he wasn't on stage. But I swear I saw something go off in him at the sight of Leonie Pickering, some sort of inner explosion. He became incredibly still, and a light came into his eyes, the same as when he knew he was about to win an important hand at cards. Something must have happened in her too, or at least she seemed less afraid of him than she had been of Rudy and me, because suddenly she raised her head and began inching forward. As she emerged into the light she put a hand up to push back her hair. The hand was filthy like the rest of her, but the fingers were long and delicate, finely-made. Some of her fingernails were broken, as if she had been scrabbling on the underside of a coffin lid.

Gradually she straightened up, her black eyes never leaving Piet's face. The scrap of cardboard with her name on it was still fastened about her neck.

"It's all right," said Piet, very softly. "Would you like to have a ride with me in my van?"

Slowly he reached out his hand, and incredibly the girl took it, her long fingers wrapping themselves around Piet's short stubby ones like vine suckers around a beanpole. She looked down at the ground then, as if giving herself up to his charge. Piet set off back towards his trailer, leading the girl step by step along the verge as if she were a blind woman. Her dress flapped in the warm July breeze like a creased yellow flag.

"Bloody hell," said Rudy. "What do you reckon?"

"What I reckon is we're late already," I said. "Let's get back on the road."

I swung myself into the cab and started the engine. I was aware that Mae was eager to talk but I drove the rest of the way in silence. I couldn't get what had happened out of my mind. As we lined up to enter the ground it occurred to me that Leonie Pickering, in her smallness and her vulnerability, might well have reminded Piet of his dead sister.

Cirencester was a good pitch, the ground adjoining one of the main roads into the town and with views of the Cotswold Hills in the distance. I parked the trailer then left Mae to sort out our stuff while I went to help Vaska and Rudy with the marquees. I forgot about Piet for a while, though later on when I caught sight of old Jones doing his site inspection I thought it best to go and tell him about our strange visitor. Jones's real name was Diccory Bellever and in his heyday and before he put on all the weight he was famous all over Europe as an escapologist and wire walker. The name Jones came from Davy Jones's Locker, and the near-miss Jones had had in his twenties when one of his routines had gone wrong and he sank to the bottom of the Solent wrapped in half a hundredweight of chains.

"Can she do anything?" he said. "I mean, can she work?"

"I don't know," I said. "I doubt it. She's just a kid."

Jones sighed. "You know how I feel about carrying dead wood, Marek. And the last thing we need is the cops on our backs if she's run off from somewhere. How old do you think she is?"

"About fifteen," I said. "I didn't really get a proper look at her." Actually I thought she was younger, but I didn't want Jones blowing a fuse.

"Can you handle this for me, Marek? God knows I've got enough on my plate." Jones sighed again, and folded his sinewy, still-muscular arms around the vast barrel of his stomach.

"Don't worry," I said. "I'll have a word with Piet, see how the land lies." I wandered around the outfield for a bit then ambled over to Piet's trailer. There was no sign of Piet but I could smell cooking so I guessed he was inside making supper. The girl was sitting on the trailer steps under the awning. She was wearing one of Piet's vests and a pair of his corduroys. The trousers were too short for her and the shirt too big. The armholes gaped open, revealing the hollows of her armpits, matted with tawny hair, and her saucer-sized adolescent breasts. In front of her was a deep-sided bowl containing a generous helping of Boston beans and the paprika-seasoned potato cakes that were Piet's speciality. She was shovelling beans into her mouth with a spoon, her head bent low and her hair almost dragging in the food. She looked up at my approach and put both arms around the bowl as if she were afraid I might try and take it away from her. There was a crusting of potato on her upper lip.

A moment later Piet appeared in the doorway. He had a tea towel tied around his waist, and was holding a potato masher.

"Mark," he said. I am Marek Platonov, the knife thrower. My father, Grigor Platonov, was a champion fire eater. Mae and Piet have always called me Mark. "Would you like some latkes? There's plenty to go round."

"No thanks, Piet," I said. 'I'm having my supper later with Mae."

I wondered how Piet had managed to persuade the girl to remove the filthy yellow dress she had been wearing. Once when we were both drunk I asked Piet what he did for sex. He told me there was a woman he saw in London from time to time. I had assumed he meant a prostitute. Now I wondered if he saw this girl as her replacement. The idea worried me but I didn't see what I could do about it. I chatted with Piet for a while then went to get changed. By the time I arrived backstage Marina was already there.

"You're late," she said. "What's all this about a runaway?"

Marina Kraicek and I are astrological twins. We were born on the same night but to different mothers, just fifteen minutes apart. We were inseparable as children and spent most of our teenage years thinking we were in love, but things don't always turn out the way you plan. Marina met Tolley and then I met Mae. Things were difficult for a while, but I don't think either of us ever considered breaking up our act. We had a connection on stage that was close to telepathic. You don't throw something like that away. What you do is bury the past the best you can.

"Just some weird kid," I said. "Piet's looking after her."

She gave me a look, as if she suspected me of trying to hide something. I shrugged my shoulders in a silent denial and then it was time for us to go on.

It was a full house and a good crowd, and I was soon lost in the danger and the excitement of the strange craft that earned me my living. When I got back to the trailer I found Mae already in bed. She was reading *The Aspen Papers*. I could never understand Mae's addiction to Henry James. I had tried reading him, for her sake, but had found his writing turgid and deeply dull.

"In bed with another man again, I see," I said.

"Oh, Henry's the perfect gentleman," she said, smiling up at me. "All we ever do is sit and talk."

I took the book from her hands and laid it aside. She was wearing a white slip of some silky material that clung to her breasts and pooled in her lap like spilled milk. I undressed quickly and lay down beside her.

We slept where we lay, in the warmth and salt-stickiness of our lovemaking. I woke once in the night, and pulled the sheet up over us. Mae's hair lay scattered across the pillow, turned silver by the moonlight creeping in between the curtains. In the instant before I fell asleep again I glimpsed in my mind the face of Leonie Pickering, her narrow lips drawn back from her discoloured teeth.

After Cirencester came Stroud, then Tetbury and Malmesbury and Frome. Each time we arrived at a new ground the girl would jump down from the cab and run about like a child that disliked being shut indoors. She made no attempt to help us set up, but would sidle up to us as we worked, standing at a short distance with her hands behind her back as if we were some fascinating new species of animal and she was afraid she might scare us away. It was unnerving at first but we soon grew used to it. For the first couple of days she was silent, then suddenly she wouldn't shut up, though it was sometimes difficult to make out what she was saying. Every now and then something would startle her and she would dash to find Piet. She seemed devoted to Piet, yet sometimes she teased him, pulling faces behind his back. Once I saw her dart out from behind some bushes and begin jeering at him in her high excited sing-song voice, cupping her hands around her mouth to make a loud hailer.

"Come on, Piet-Piet, you old slowcoach, you old monster!"

She leapt up on the fence, gripping the top bar with those extraordinary long toes of hers. She seemed light as a feather, with all the natural balance and poise of a trained wire walker. The spikes of her elbows cut "v" shapes in the clear July air, and her top rode up, exposing a stripe of her flat dirt-brown stomach. I felt a rush of desire in spite of myself. Most of the time she gave me the creeps.

Piet bought her things, clothes mostly, but also the bright, gaudy trinkets she seemed to have a passion for: silver-backed brushes and mirrors, gilt snuffboxes, crystal animals. Some of the things, I could tell, were actually quite valuable. Leonie guarded them jealously, counting and recounting them, glowering from under her eyebrows at anyone who came too near.

Piet called her "the kid" or "the hoodlum," and tried to make light of his attachment to her. He insisted she'd had a tough life and deserved a bit of care and attention, but within a matter of days it was obvious not just to me but to everyone else that he was in love with her.

"The girl is something special, Mark," he said to me. "She has talent. Just you wait and see."

I dismissed his words, believing they were just another aspect of his infatuation, but in fact he turned out to be right. Leonie Pickering was special. She possessed the kind of talent you see once in a lifetime. She reminded each of us, in her way, of who we were.

She reminded me of my father, and my father's father, of the days when circus had really meant something. In the years before the war, when my grandfather was still performing, people would save for weeks to get a ticket to see him and talk about what they had seen for years to come. Leonie gave me a window on that world. Sometimes I still dream about what I saw.

It was midweek, a Wednesday, and we were pitched up at Shepton Mallet. There was no matinee that day, so I decided to take advantage of the fine summer weather and go for a walk. On my way up the hill I caught sight of Milena, Marina's sister, practising her bareback riding in one of the fields. She had used some yellow rope to rough out a circle, and her two horses, Gideon and Gilgamesh, were cantering around it in opposite directions. Milena was standing on Gilgamesh's back, her bare feet dusty with rosin. As the two horses passed each other she leapt in the air and somersaulted down on to the back of Gideon. Neither horse so much as broke his stride.

Milena was a tall girl, much taller than Marina, with the flat-chested, well-muscled build of the professional gymnast. She was five years older than Marina and I and because of that she had always seemed distant from us. On that day she was wearing a pair of snagged ballet hose and an old running vest but she was still incredible to watch. She had worked with horses all her life, yet I could never help being impressed by her control over them, especially since Gideon and Gilgamesh were big horses, rangy and full of mettle, with the narrow muzzle and intelligent eyes of the true Arab thoroughbred.

I stood and watched them, leaning against the gate with my eyes half closed against the glare of the sun. Suddenly I saw Leonie entering the field on horseback through a gap in the hedge. She was riding Pierrot, one of the two skewbald ponies that the twins used to pull their glass carriage. As I watched she stood up on the horse's back, bent backwards and then went into a handstand. She was wearing a halter top and yellow shorts, the thin material pulled tight across her buttocks. The soles of her feet flashed white as plovers against the sky.

She made a whooping noise, somersaulting off the horse's back and landing on her feet in the grass. Milena called out to her and Leonie responded excitedly, but they were too far away for me to hear what they were saying. I realised Milena must have been training the girl. Just then Milena caught sight of me. She sprinted towards me across the field, her long legs lithe as a deer's.

"Oh Marek, you mustn't spoil things. This was meant to be a surprise." She leaned on the gate, resting her chin on her hands, smelling faintly of horses and dry bracken. Golden freckles dusted the top parts of her cheeks.

"How long has she been doing this?" I said.

"Only a week. But she's a natural. I've never known anything like it."

We both turned to look at her then. Leonie stood with her arms around the horse's neck, her face resting against his withers. She seemed to be breathing him in. Pierrot whickered with pleasure, slapping flies away from his hindquarters with his tail.

"I won't say anything," I said. And I didn't, not even to Mae, although I wanted to. I didn't have to keep the secret long. Five days later at Yeovil, Leonie's act was added to the bill.

At first she was just a warm-up for Milena. She didn't do anything too complicated, just a couple of turns of the ring and some basic tumbles. But what a carnival audience wants mostly is spectacle, the sense that they are seeing something extraordinary and preferably freakish. With her small size and her long toes Leonie Pickering was an immediate success. She wore a tiny sequined leotard and Pierrot wore a plume of pink ostrich feathers. Old Jones came down to watch, prepared to be furious, but he changed his tune quickly enough when he heard the applause.

For a while Milena seemed happy to regard Leonie as her protégée. But soon things began to change. Leonie's stunts became more daring and her act quickly became the main draw in the show. By the time we played the Goth festival at Whitby I think Milena hated Leonie. Even worse, she had begun to show her age.

On the last night we got a fire going and Rudy organised his usual pig roast. Piet had some kind of stomach bug and had gone to bed early. He had seemed uncommonly tired in recent weeks. The girl left her things strewn about the trailer and made no attempt to clear up after herself. Piet was forever cleaning or preparing more food. I began to grow concerned about him. I knew that Piet, like many dwarfs, had a dicky heart.

"Oh nonsense," he said when I suggested he should get Leonie to help out more. "You're only young once." His violet eyes had their faraway look. His veins stood out in blue knots on the backs of his hands.

Leonie sat close to the fire. She gorged herself on meat, sitting hunched over a pile of spare ribs with the juice running down her chin as if she hadn't eaten for a week. Yet she had eaten most of a chicken at lunchtime, I had seen Piet cook it for her. No matter how much she ate she never seemed to put on weight. It was as if she had a tapeworm inside her. Once she had finished she slipped away, disappearing into the darkness. She never stayed anywhere long if Piet wasn't there.

I watched her leave, then after a few minutes I followed her. We were camped in a field set back from the clifftop, high above the town. Once away from the fire it was bitterly cold. There was no moon and it was very dark, but I could just about see Leonie as she hurried along. I moved quickly to close the distance between us then reached out and grabbed her by the elbow. She was wearing an old anorak, something of Piet's. My fingers slithered on the down-filled plastic. She let out a scream but I quickly stopped her mouth with my other hand.

"It's all right," I said. "It's just Mark."

I took my hand away from her mouth. Her teeth were chattering with cold or perhaps it was fright. I pulled her towards me and unzipped her coat. I was already hard. She seemed to weigh nothing at all.

I gripped her head between my hands and forced my mouth down on hers, opening her lips with my tongue. Her flesh was cold. My first taste of her was sour, the tart acidity of unripe apples. But there was something behind it, a clogged stickiness, as if I were gulping mud, and in my nostrils the foetid odour of spoiled meat.

She was clinging to me eagerly. I pushed her away, wiping at my mouth with the sleeve of my coat.

"What's wrong with you?" I said. "Are you sick?"

Leonie laughed then pulled her coat tightly about her and scampered away.

I was horrified at what I had done, that Leonie might tell Piet or even Mae. I couldn't understand what had come over me. I wondered if whatever disease she had might turn out to be catching.

I never looked forward to winter. It was then that I worried most about the future. Sitting in a Dalston laundrette on a Sunday afternoon while freezing February rain lashed the pavement outside I would start to think of my father's last years in a static caravan on the Isle of Sheppey and wondering what would happen when I lost my touch.

I tended to go for long walks. When I became particularly restless I would get on a train and just go somewhere, calling Mae later from some down-at-heel boarding house in Lowestoft or Aberystwyth, telling her I would be back the following day.

It must have been hell to live with, and that winter was particularly bad. I felt constantly on edge, as if there were some urgent unfinished business I had to attend to. I lay awake into the small hours, Mae soundly asleep beside me, endlessly reliving those few brief violent moments on the cliff.

Piet always spent his winters in Norfolk, and this time Leonie had gone with him. I had last seen Piet in the service station on the Peterborough ring road where we had stopped off for a final breakfast before going our various ways. Leonie had stayed behind in the van. She seemed to have a dislike of public places. As I watched Piet heading for the A47 turn-off for Wisbech I couldn't help asking myself how he and Leonie would occupy the long winter months.

"Do you think they'll be all right?" Mae said.

"He'll look after her, don't worry," I said, and we had left it at that. I had avoided Leonie since Whitby, but now more than ever I wanted to know the truth about her, who she was and where she had come from. The obsession did not fade with time as I hoped it would. Instead it seemed to grow stronger and in the end I grew sick of myself. I told Mae I needed to get out of London.

"I'm going stir crazy," I said. "It's only for a couple of days."

She smiled at me sadly. I hated leaving her, but I did it anyway. I packed an overnight bag and hitched a lift in a Ford Sierra. I was in Cirencester before nightfall.

I remembered the town as bustling, almost festive, but the arrival of winter had made it turn in on itself and I barely recognised it. The streets seemed dour and stark, the stone cottages huddled like beggars, the outlying fields where we had set up our tents reduced to a grubby wet pastureland. I booked into a bed and breakfast on the Gloucester Road. In spite of the dreariness of the weather and of the place I felt curiously exhilarated. I realised how rarely I had the chance to be alone.

I slept better than I had in weeks and woke up refreshed. I was eager to explore the town. It was not the tourist sites I was interested in, the Norman arch or St. John's church or the fine old buildings on Castle Street, but the corner newsagents and garage forecourts, the rows of terraced cottages with their untidy back gardens, the anonymous outskirts. I knew it was crazy but I couldn't help myself. I wanted to see where Leonie might have lived.

I walked for a couple of hours. The houses I passed were mostly well-kept and respectable-looking and I quickly began to resent them for it. My eyes fastened keenly on any sign of dereliction or dilapidation: a rotting shed on an overgrown allotment, the torn mesh on a line of empty rabbit pens, a broken pane of glass, replaced with cardboard, in the window of an abandoned Morris Minor. Through the gaping doorways of old tractor barns I caught glimpses of rusting machinery. On a low-slung washing line outside a mouldering farmhouse a yellow dress flapped wetly in the chilly air. I kept feeling I was being watched, yet in all the time I was walking I hardly laid eyes on a soul. Finally it began to rain. There was nothing for it but to head back into town.

The library was housed in a modern building, which had recently undergone a refurbishment. As well as the main lending library there was a reference section, where you could consult a selection of more specialised textbooks, or use one of the library's PCs. I paid for an hour and logged on. I typed *Leonie Pickering* into the search bar, but none of the results it generated seemed even remotely relevant. I did a search for local papers, and discovered that the main newspaper for the Cirencester area was the *Wilts and Gloucestershire Standard*. I clicked on the tab marked archive, then went back a full twelve months. I felt frustrated at first, with so much information to sift through, but I became engrossed in spite of myself and quickly became sidetracked. The articles were mundane but they had the compulsive quality of any good soap opera. I was halfway through a story about the neighbourhood war that erupted over a dog-stealing incident when the name *Pickering* leapt out at me from the opposite page.

It seemed that in the May of the year before a local man called Wilfred Pickering had been taken into custody for the murder of his grandson Eric Quayle. According to the newspaper report the boy was less than a month old when he died and he had been in the care of his grandfather at the time.

A later report said that Wilfred Pickering had been acquitted. The report carried a photograph of Pickering leaving the courthouse together with a woman the paper claimed was Willis Quayle, Pickering's twenty-nine-year old daughter and the mother of Eric Quayle. The picture was out of focus, and the two people in it were facing away from the camera. They could have been anyone.

I carried on searching, typing in *Wilfred Pickering* and *Eric Quayle* and even *Pickering murder*, but all I managed to find were the same two articles in slightly different versions in other newspapers, plus one further photograph of Willis Quayle. She had on the same belted mackintosh she had been wearing in the other photograph and I guessed that both pictures had been taken at the time of the court hearing. The photographer had made an attempt to get her in close up, but she had turned her head at the last moment, blurring her features.

I was no further forward. I considered paying for more time on the computer but decided against it. It was late in the afternoon and I had had enough. For all I knew the Wilfred Pickering in the articles was a complete red herring. Pickering was a common enough name, after all. I closed down all my searches and called it a day.

Outside it had stopped raining but it was beginning to get dark and the wind had turned bitingly cold. I was also extremely hungry and I realised I hadn't eaten since breakfast. I headed back towards the old part of town, where I knew most of the eating places were bound to be concentrated. I went into the first pub I came to, a place called the Dog and Soldier. It was a narrow-fronted, dark red building with small windows and did not look particularly inviting but I wasn't in the mood for hunting around. Once inside though I was pleasantly surprised. The place was cheerful and deceptively spacious, a warren of side rooms and alcoves extending a long way back from the street. There was a log fire burning, and a television set in one corner tuned to a football match. I heard relaxed laughter and the chink of glasses. The clock above the bar was showing half-past five.

I ordered a pint and the chicken casserole from the bar menu then went to sit down. I felt suddenly very tired. I tried watching the football but couldn't summon up much enthusiasm for it. I wished I had something to read. Then I noticed there was a small bookcase just to the right of the television. The top shelf was stacked with magazines, *Woman's Own* and *House and Garden* and *What Car*, the same as you might find in a dentist's waiting room. On the lower shelves there were some paperback spy thrillers and crime novels, also a clutch of guide books and town histories, most of them long out of date. None of them appealed to me. I flicked through the pages of one or two of the spy stories, trying to rouse an interest, but it all seemed too involved, too much of an effort, and eventually I settled on one of the guide books, a dusty red hardback called *Gloucestershire Myths and Legends*. The boards were cracked, and the book smelled as if it had spent a long time in someone's attic, but the chapters were short and I thought I could probably read through one or two of them while I waited for my food to arrive.

The book was not what I had expected. I had prepared myself for something po-faced and old-fashioned, but the prose was clear and direct and the stories themselves were compelling. There was one about a primary school teacher who turned out to be a distant relation of the Pied Piper of Hamelin, and another where the inhabitants of a village got together and burned one of their neighbours as a witch. I supposed the book was meant as a gimmick, the kind of joke travelogue that was either funny or unsettling depending on the state of your nerves. It certainly kept me entertained. There was one story that was particularly gruesome about a giant mythical land leech called the Lammas Worm. The book claimed that some of the more isolated communities in the steep wooded valleys around Stow had built a cult around it, that they kidnapped local girls and offered them to the worms in a kind of debased marriage ceremony. The offspring the girls gave birth to were monsters, a man-worm hybrid of low intelligence and rapacious appetite. The girls themselves had to be slaughtered, not so much to conceal the crimes of the cult as to assuage the agony and madness that followed in the wake of what they had suffered.

I laughed nervously to myself as I read this, and I jumped in my seat when the barman brought my food. The Dog and Soldier was evidently a popular place to go for an early supper, and I was glad to be surrounded by other people. Just as I was clearing my own plate the barman delivered two steaming platters of fish and chips to the men at the table next to me. The men were both large, with callused hands and ruddy complexions. They ate steadily and with intense concentration, as if they were engaged in some arduous professional task. They finished their food at the exact same moment, then sat back in their seats, their beer bellies resting comfortably on their knees. One of them began setting up a game of chequers.

"I see they finally caught up with that Pickering lunatic," said one of them.

"I don't read the *Standard*," said the other. "Not since that new bloke took over the sports page. It's really gone downhill since then."

"They say he drowned that kid in a bucket like a new-born puppy. Deformed, they say it was, not properly a child at all. That's why he drowned it, at least that's what Pickering says. Says he wanted to put it out of its misery. But you can't believe everything you read though, can you? Not the way the papers are these days."

"I suppose that's what you get for fecking your own daughter."

The two of them began to laugh, a soft, companionable chuckle that rocked them back on their chairs and hid their eyes in the flesh of their faces like currants in dough. A wave of heat and nausea rushed over me, a sensation so intense that I wondered if there had been something wrong with the food I had just eaten. The two draughts players seemed to shimmer before me like a mirage. Their conversation had already begun to take on an edge of the surreal. I turned away from them so that I could put *Gloucestershire Myths and Legends* back on its shelf, and when I looked at them again they were so deeply engrossed in their draughts game it was as if they had never spoken.

When I reached for my beer I found my hand was shaking, and my sweaty fingers left visible prints on the glass. In spite of the log fire and the massed body heat of the many drinkers standing around the bar my teeth had begun to chatter. There was a sharp, dry tickling at the back of my throat, as if someone had given it a prod with one of my knives. I realised with a kind of dazed relief that the sickness and dread I was experiencing had nothing to do with the chicken casserole or the book of horror stories or even the prurient gossip of the two draughts players. I was simply going down with a cold.

I paid for my food and left. As I walked through the darkened streets the cold symptoms intensified and by the time I got back to the guesthouse I was ready to drop. I didn't often catch colds but when I did they always laid me up badly. When I woke the next morning my throat was burning and my nose was blocked with mucus. All I wanted was to turn on my side and go back to sleep, but somehow I managed to get myself moving. I knew that no matter how rough I was feeling I didn't want to spend another night alone in Cirencester. I bought some aspirin from a local chemist, swallowed three tablets straight off and set off on foot towards the bypass.

I was lucky that day. In less than ten minutes I caught a ride from a frozen foods haulier who let me sleep in the back of his van all the way to Potter's Bar. I was home before it got dark. Mae was so preoccupied with feeding me chicken soup and dosing me with more aspirin that she didn't ask me a single question about my trip.

I did my best to forget what had happened, to put it all down to a kind of fugue state brought on by the 'flu virus. But sometimes I would hear again the quietly contemptuous laughter of the two red-nosed draughts players, remember the book with its dented covers, and a feeling of panic would creep over me. I drowned the panic in tedium; the blank grey stasis of those days in late February and early March that normally left me tense as a wire now soothed me with their sameness, their repetition. Once I was fit again I found work on a building site and later in a canning factory. In the evenings I sat on the sofa with Mae in front of the gas fire and read detective stories. Around midnight we went to bed and made love. Gradually I realised that I was happy, that I was glad it was just Mae and me. I wanted things to stay the way they were. I saw the approach of the start of the season with something like dread.

On the weekend of the spring equinox we gathered as usual at Stevenage for the off. When I first saw Leonie I hardly recognised her. Her frizzy hair was combed smooth, and there was a dash of vermilion lipstick on her mouth. Her jeans and T-shirt were spotless and most extraordinary of all she was wearing shoes. She smiled at me, and I could not tell if that smile was meant as invitation or mockery. I felt like shaking her. It was as if the peace of the last two months had never been.

"Mark!" Piet came hurrying across to where we were standing on the outfield, moving with that lopsided, twisting gait of his that always reminded me of a brandy bottle rolling downhill. Normally he might have greeted me with a high five, or by punching me playfully in the stomach, but on this occasion he put both arms around my waist and hugged me close, as if he had not seen me for many years.

He raised his head then and looked at me and I saw his violet eyes were shining with a kind of dumb elation. He kept tugging at my shirt cuff, and I realised he was trying to show me something.

"We've got something to tell you," he said. "We got married last week."

He thrust out his hand, eagerly displaying the gold band. I saw then that Leonie was wearing a ring also, a matching band in the same yellow gold but narrow as wire.

"They had to make it specially," Piet said. "They didn't have anything small enough to fit her." He took her hand and bent forward to kiss the ring. Leonie's painted lips twitched in a half smile.

"Silly old monster," she said quietly. She touched the back of his hair with her other hand then wandered off to where Rudy Shyler was getting ready to load the ponies. She laid her face against Pierrot's neck then nuzzled him behind the ear. She stood for a while, watching Rudy fill up the haynets, then went inside Piet's trailer and closed the door.

"She's pregnant," Piet said suddenly. His face filled up with a kind of earnest tenderness. I stammered my congratulations. I felt my stomach curdle and a chill went through me, as if cold hands had reached inside me and given my intestines a squeeze.

Once we were on the road I told Mae the news.

"I think it's wonderful," she said. "Piet is one of the angels. If anyone can help that girl it's him."

She glanced across at me as if fully expecting me to agree with her, but I said nothing and kept my eyes on the road. I hoped she was right, but I doubted it. In my heart I already believed that Leonie Pickering was beyond help, but I could not explain that to Mae. I was afraid that if I tried she would think I had gone insane.

I watched Leonie like a hawk. I was waiting for a sign, I suppose, something I could use to prove what she really was. My suspicions disturbed me so profoundly they kept me awake at night. And yet my sexual desire for her only seemed to grow more intense. Sometimes when I made love to Mae I found myself imagining Leonie's tiny, bud-like breasts, her brittle clavicle, the ripe green stench of her. I imagined myself battering her so hard with my body that it broke her bones. I would come so violently then that it was like having a piece of me torn away. Sometimes there were tears on my cheeks. I would lie in Mae's arms, my breath coming in heavy gasps while she stroked my hair. Eventually I would fall asleep, waking the next morning to a bad headache, as if I had been drinking heavily the night before.

We had three full houses at Cambridge, and Leonie's picture was in the local paper.

"You're going to be famous, my sweetheart," Piet said to her. "We'll have to start keeping a scrapbook."

He seemed thrilled with the photograph, and carried it with him everywhere.

"Aren't you worried about her performing?" I asked him. I hoped he would know what I meant without my having to mention the pregnancy directly. He beamed like a schoolboy who had just been awarded a gold star for some improbable feat, a record-breaking tap dance, maybe, and shook his head.

"She knows what she's doing, you only have to look at her. She'll know when it's time to stop."

I had to suppose he was right. We played Northampton and Rugby and Warwick, Coventry and Leamington and Worcester, then headed south towards Great Malvern and Tewkesbury. Leonie performed every night and usually did the matinees too. Her act, as daring as ever, had become even more ambitious, her movements so quick and light you could almost believe she was weightless. I saw her do things that Milena had never attempted, not even when she was in her prime. Leonie loved being in the spotlight and she relished applause, wolfing it down the same way she wolfed her food. In the down times she was oddly withdrawn. When she was not rehearsing she spent most of her time with Corinne Cooley, who ran the insect circus. Corinne was part Chinese, with long black braids that reached down to the ground. She was very fat and ponderous in her movements, and always reminded me of the giant African land snails that had long been a favourite feature of her act. She would have made three of Leonie. But Leonie seemed calm in her presence, and although they were physical opposites their friendship seemed to benefit them both.

I dreaded our return to Cirencester; I was convinced that the place was unlucky. On the evening we arrived there I tried to work out my anxiety in rehearsal. I had to practise without Marina. She had injured her arm the week before and so I had to re-jig most of our routine. The tension in me worked in my favour and I was throwing well, but even so my heart was not in it. Piet must have been anxious too, because I couldn't get rid of him. He stood and watched me, congratulating me on every throw, even the easy ones, until I finally gave in and asked him what was on his mind.

"Do you think I should talk to her?" he said at once. "Try and explain where we are?"

"I think it's best we don't make a thing of it,' I said. 'Just carry on as normal. It's no big deal."

I was trying to reassure myself as much as him. In all our months on the road

Leonie had displayed no curiosity about the towns we visited or the distances we travelled. Time seemed to have no meaning for her beyond the immediate moment. She was like an animal in this way. I looked across at her, sitting with Corinne on the back steps of Corinne's caravan looking at fashion magazines. She seemed perfectly calm and happy. It never occurred to me that the trouble might come from outside.

No one saw the boy arrive. It was a beautiful evening, warm and filled with the scents of wood smoke and dry grass. Rudy and Vaska had a quoits match going and I remember hearing the twins' accordion. Leonie's scream came out of the blue. It was a dreadful sound, high and drilling. I thought at first it was one of the horses.

He was skinny as a daddy-long-legs, his narrow, pointed chin shiny with acne, the back of his jeans jacket stained heavily with what looked like machine oil. His right cheek was horribly scarred, the hardened tissue bunching out of his face like some kind of cancerous growth. I had seen a similar injury once before, in a lion tamer who had been mauled by one of his cats.

His feet were bare. I noticed with slow astonishment his toes: long, almost prehensile, the same as Leonie's.

Leonie was backed up to the door of Corinne's caravan, pressing her hands to her face. Corinne stood off to one side in a slew of magazines. Her black, pinprick eyes looked completely blank.

"I knew you'd come back," said the youth. "Dad's been asking."

His voice was unpleasantly nasal and for some reason I felt certain his clothes were squirming with lice. He darted forward and grabbed Leonie by the arm, moving with unnatural speed. Leonie screamed again and then bit his arm, shaking her head from side to side like a dog with a bone.

"Get off me you cow!" The youth shrieked with pain and tried to pull his arm away but this only seemed to make Leonie hang on tighter. She thrashed out wildly with her tiny fists, raining down blows on his chest and lower abdomen. I dived in behind her and locked my arms about her waist, trying to pull her backwards and away. It was the first time I had touched her since Whitby. Her body was stiff as a rail and she reeked of fear. As I struggled to restrain her Vaska and Rudy came dashing over and laid hold of the bawling youth on either side. By our joint efforts we managed to separate them. The youth clutched at his injured arm and blood flowed down between his fingers in bright rivulets. He tried to turn on Rudy but Rudy was triple his weight and twice his height. It was really no contest. Rudy locked his fingers into his hair and tugged it, forcing the boy's face up towards him.

"You can see you're not wanted, son, so bugger off. If we catch you round here again we'll feed you to the blooming lions."

Someone laughed, Tolley, I think. Rudy and Vaska marched the boy as far as the road and turned him loose, giving him a push and a shove by way of encouragement. I saw him standing there, a dishevelled stick figure, his long arms trailing. He should have been pathetic, comical even, but something about him made all the hairs rise up on the back of my neck.

"I'll tell Dad what you did, you dirty bitch,' he screamed. 'Don't think you've heard the last of this."

He turned then and ran, his bare feet slapping the concrete. I was left holding Leonie. Her body had relaxed a little but she was shaking so hard it was difficult to keep hold of her. Her dress was glued to her back with sweat, and gradually I realised that the acrid stench boiling off her was not just body odour and that she had wet herself. There was a damp patch on the ground between her feet.

It was then that Piet appeared, his chest heaving from the effort of running. Leonie moaned at the sight of him and threw herself into his arms. They huddled together like frightened puppies. The rest of us stood around awkwardly, not knowing quite what to do.

"Who was that?" Piet said to her at last. "What was it that frightened you, sweetheart?" He stroked her head, his pudgy fingers smoothing her ruffled hair. I saw his gold ring flash, catching the last of the evening sunlight.

"Aaron," Leonie stammered. "He's my brother."

Leonie didn't perform that night, but for the rest of us it was business as usual, *the show must go on*, as the saying goes. I was exhausted by the end, but I still lay awake for some time, my ears alert to every sound. When I finally fell asleep I slept like the dead. When I woke the next morning my head felt muzzy and sore. I washed and dressed then went outside. I saw Piet at once, standing at the edge of the ground and looking down towards the town. I walked over and stood beside him.

"How is she?" I asked.

"Much better," he said. "But I've told Jones she's not going on tonight. It's too much of a risk, with that bastard around. Especially in her condition."

I nodded in agreement, though I felt more than ever embarrassed and dis-quieted by the mention of Leonie's pregnancy. She was still not showing at all, and I could not help remembering that when I grabbed hold of her the evening before her belly had been as hard and flat as a child's.

"Tell Mae I've gone into town," I said at last. "I need to stretch my legs. I'll be back in an hour."

I think I had some insane idea of returning to the Dog and Soldier, of hunt-ing down the two red-nosed draughts players and demanding they tell me what they knew about the Pickerings. It wasn't until I reached the High Street that I realised that all the pubs would still be closed. I wandered aimlessly through the streets for a while, trying to gather my thoughts. Once I thought I saw Aaron Pickering, slipping away from me between the houses, but as soon as I set off in pursuit he disappeared.

There was no more sign of him that day or the following morning. We packed up and set off for Stroud. Leonie stayed in the trailer, and I did not see her again until five days later, when we arrived at Melksham. I was shocked at the state of her. Her hair was a mess, and her skin had a greyish cast, as if she were sickening for something. The worst thing was that all her natural grace seemed to have left her. There was a clumsiness in the way she walked, and she held her arms awkwardly, slightly away from her body, as if her sides were painful or bruised.

I thought her circus days were over but I was wrong about that. She didn't perform at Melksham but at Frome she went on for the matinee. I watched her go into the ring, half-convinced she would fall and injure herself, but once she was in front of the audience her clumsiness seemed to evaporate. Her performance was tight and spotless and appeared to be completely secure. The crowd were mainly schoolchildren and they gave her a standing ovation. As I turned to go backstage I overheard one little girl speaking excitedly to her teacher.

"Is that lady real?" she said. "Or did they make her up out of computers?"

"Of course she's real, Janey," said the teacher, a pretty young woman with shiny light chestnut-brown hair. "You can smell her from here. Here, you've got some chocolate on your chin."

The teacher leaned over and dabbed at the girl's face with a large white handkerchief. Her glossy hair swung forward like a bell. The child's pale eyes glimmered in the shadows like blue crystals.

Leonie did not appear in the main performance and I assumed she had spent the evening resting in the trailer. But later as I returned to the van I saw a dark shape moving swiftly between the wagons. I thought at first it was a fox or a stray dog on the lookout for food, but suddenly it made a dash for Piet's trailer and I saw that it was Leonie. For a moment she looked straight at me, her tiny face pale in the security lights, her black eyes hard and glittering as jewels. I took a single step towards her, but she went inside the van, disappearing so suddenly it was as if she had melted through the door. I wondered where she had been. She never usually went far without Piet.

"She's seeing him, I know she is," Piet said to me a day or two later. We were at Warminster by then, and the summer was ripening, the fields around the camp heavy with corn. I thought at first Piet was talking about some love rival, some lad she had met in the town. When I realised he meant her brother I knew at once it made a hideous kind of sense. The thought that Aaron Pickering had been with us ever since Cirencester, shadowing us, spying on us, perhaps even stowing away in our wagons, filled me with horror. I told Piet he must have got it wrong.

"She can't stand the guy," I said. "You saw what she was like."

I didn't tell him that I had already been a witness to one of Leonie's midnight escapades, but from that moment on I saw Aaron Pickering everywhere, or imagined I did, and my thoughts dwelt on him constantly. He disturbed and repulsed me, as an infected wound repulses, or a seething mass of maggots on a garbage heap. I couldn't get him out of my mind.

We continued travelling south and west. The nights were hot and humid, the trailer was like an oven. In Yeovil the dashboard thermometer reached a high of thirty-four degrees. I lay sleeplessly in bed beside Mae, making futile attempts to get more comfortable. From the very far distance came the rumble of thunder, but it was a dry sound, like an old man coughing, and did nothing to dispel the heat of the day. I lay twisted in the sheet, my mind turning in exhausted circles. I thought Mae was asleep. When she spoke to me out of the darkness I jumped a mile.

"I know there's something wrong, Mark. I wish you would tell me."

"It's nothing," I said. "It's this heat, that's all. I can't sleep."

I laid my hand in the small of her back. I wanted to make love to her but my thoughts and the sweltering heat had sapped my strength.

"I think we should talk," she said. "I know there's something." Her voice was heavy and slurred. A couple of minutes later we were both asleep.

We were awakened by Leonie screaming. There was the crash of breaking glass and then, unbelievably, a burst of wild laughter. Mae started to get out of bed but I told her to stay where she was. I threw on a pair of jeans and raced outside.

The door to Piet's trailer stood wide open, and as I ran towards it I saw a man emerge. He was completely naked, his scrawny body white against the surrounding darkness. He started down the trailer steps but then tripped and fell headlong. In the light from Piet's old carriage lantern I saw that it was Aaron Pickering. His back was a mass of scars, as if he had been beaten on repeated occasions with a nylon rope or a cat o' nine tails. As he picked himself up off the ground I saw that his groin had been shaved. His penis hung stunted and flaccid like a limp white worm.

Our eyes met and he grinned. Then he was on his feet and racing away. I was after him in a moment but he had a head start on me and unlike Pickering I wasn't used to running in bare feet. It was clear to me almost at once that I wasn't going to catch him. I stood at the edge of the ground, breathing in painful gasps and trying to work out which way he had gone. In the light of the single streetlamp the road was empty. It was as if the youth had simply vanished into thin air.

At that moment there was a flash of lightning so bright it was as if daylight had momentarily been restored. The thunderclap that accompanied it was loud enough to make me cover my ears. There was a moment of complete hiatus, as if the universe itself had paused for breath, and then the heavens opened. It was as if the rain of many months had been saved and stored precisely for this moment. I was saturated in an instant, the torrent coming down so hard I could almost imagine I was standing under a waterfall. The ground gave up its heat with a hissing sigh.

It was a moment of insanity, of joy. I felt flooded with an intense vitality, a kind of pagan exhilaration. My skin prickled and my heart rate increased. The smell of wet grass was intoxicating. It was as if every cell in my body stood rampant, confirming its allegiance to the earth.

I wanted to run and shriek, to roll in the bracken, to give myself up to the night.

It was only the sight of Piet that stopped me, that brought me back to myself. He had tried to run after Aaron Pickering but had fallen down. He lay on the soaking ground, his violet eyes overrunning with rain and helpless tears.

"I woke up and he was there in the bed with us," he wept. "He was lying on top of her. I threw the water glass at him. I didn't know what else to do."

He tried to get to his feet but couldn't get any purchase on the slippery ground. He was still crying, and his tiny body was beginning to shake with cold. I knew that Piet's lungs were not of the normal capacity, that colds and chills were more dangerous for him than for other people.

"We can worry about all that later," I said. "Let's just get you out of this rain."

Some of the others had appeared by this time but I waved them away. I didn't want to have to talk about what I had seen. I caught Piet under the arms and lifted him up. He was surprisingly heavy. I supported him towards his trailer but when we got there we found the door locked and all the curtains drawn. I rattled the door handle and called Leonie's name but the noise of the rain drowned everything out. I toyed with the idea of fetching my hacksaw and cutting my way in but decided that would probably make things worse.

"She's had a bad scare," I said to Piet. "Let's give her some time to calm down. Come over to our place, at least until the morning. You need a change of clothes, for a start."

I looked down at him and for the first time I noticed he was still in his pyjamas. By the time I got him back to our trailer Mae already had the kettle on. She gave Piet some towels to dry himself and found an old dressing gown of mine for him to put on. I took the cushions off the sofa and made up the foldaway bed.

"Try not to dwell on things," I said to Piet. "You'll see her in the morning."

He hadn't spoken a word since his outburst about Pickering. He looked more miserable than I had ever seen him, shrunken somehow, and it was not just that my burgundy dressing gown was way too big for him. It was as if the stuff that made him Piet was leaching away.

Mae hung his sopping clothes over the drier in the bathroom and made him a cup of sweet tea. Once we were sure he was asleep we went back to bed.

"Has that boy gone for good, do you think?" Mae said. Her soft features were drawn tight with anxiety, and suddenly I had a raindrop-bright memory of the first time I saw her, all by herself, hanging around the entrance to the funhouse and eating a chocolate ice cream. I had known I was in love with her before we exchanged so much as a single word.

"I don't know," I said at last. She seemed better after that. Perhaps it was because she knew I was no longer lying to her.

The next day dawned bright and clear, with that particular apple-crisp freshness that only comes in the wake of a summer storm. The sky was high and infinite and blue.

Piet's trailer was as quiet as death. I wondered if Leonie had escaped in the night somehow, but I didn't like to say as much to Piet. I left him with Mae while I went and did my morning practice with Marina. We worked in silence for a while, going over the routines we intended to use in that evening's performance, then suddenly Marina turned to face me. She still had a knife in her hand, one of the antique Savitskas that had belonged to my father. She was in her tracksuit bottoms, with her hair pulled back from her face in a black bandeau.

"What's been going on with Piet?" she said. "What have you done? I bloody well want to know."

Her eyes flashed, sharp as the knife, yet what I read in them was hurt, for whatever secrets she thought I was keeping from her, for the summer as it passed its zenith, for the way our lives had diverged, long ago and inexplicably, the way a road does when it suddenly splits in two.

"I've done nothing," I said. "I don't know what you're talking about." I bowed my head, refusing to meet her eyes.

If I get free of this it's over, I thought suddenly. I felt heartsick and somehow in peril, and I knew then that I was finished with the company. It was as if, peering through the dust-streaked windscreen of my old trailer, I had unexpectedly glimpsed the shape of another life.

The day passed in a kind of dream, the sun arcing across the sky like a blow torch slowly cutting through a steel bulkhead. When it got to five o'clock and there was still no movement from Piet's trailer I had a quiet chat with Vaska and we decided we would have to break in. I used the hacksaw to cut around the lock then eased my hand through the hole and opened the door from inside. The drawn curtains had created a dingy semi-darkness, and there was a bad smell, a cross between rancid butter and rotten vegetables. Except for the faint buzzing of a fly trapped in the narrow corridor between the curtain and the window glass the place was eerily silent. I looked cautiously about, prepared to find squalor and chaos, but there was just Piet's living room, with the ancient Ultrabrite television in the corner and the reproduction Audubon bird prints on the walls. There was a half-finished cup of coffee on the draining board in the kitchen but apart from that it was spotless. I left the bedroom until last. The sheets were torn back from the bed, and I saw shards of glass glittering like tiny daggers on the carpet, the remnants, I supposed, of the broken water glass. The rancid smell was far stronger. The room appeared as empty as the others but I knew it was not. Somehow I could sense her presence, tugging away at my being like the pull of a tiny fish at the end of a line. Or perhaps it's just hindsight that makes me think this. Most likely it was just that I refused to believe she had escaped without my knowing.

"What shall we do?" said Vaska. "She's gone."

Silently I shook my head, willing him to be quiet. I knelt down and peered under the bed but there was nothing there. Then I crossed to the wardrobe and opened the door.

Leonie was crouched inside, folded so tightly into the narrow space that my first confused impression was that this was not Leonie herself but some clever imitation, a shopkeeper's mannequin made to look exactly like her. She was hugging her knees, the tiny face upturned, a white blank space in the greenish forest of paisley shirts and velvet jackets. She was holding something of Piet's, a lemon-coloured silk waistcoat, clutching it between her fingers as if for support. She had on some brief garment, a slip or camisole, stained in patches with a dark viscous substance that looked like treacle.

The rancid smell was close to overpowering.

My heart was knocking in my chest like a hammer on stone. I seemed to hover above myself, observing my own actions with a rapt curiosity as if I might be tested on them later. I had a sudden and poignant memory of a children's quiz programme that Marina and I used to watch on BBC1, where they showed a panel of young contestants a short piece of film and then asked them questions about it: *how many boys were on the bus? What colour was the headmaster's car? Which hand was holding the gun?*

We had always enjoyed that programme. I was still thinking about it when Leonie unfurled her limbs and came out of the wardrobe, shooting between my legs like a spider passing through a crack in the wall. I could not believe the speed with which it happened. One minute I was looking right at her, the next there was just the wardrobe's velvety interior, the terrible smell, the cacophonous jangle of wire coat hangers.

"Catch her!" I yelled. I heard Vaska roar uncomprehendingly behind me but it was already too late. I bolted past him, striking my elbow painfully against the door handle. I saw Leonie ahead of me, in the square, cupboard-like space between the kitchen and the tiny bathroom. I lunged at her, grabbing at the back of her camisole, but the material slipped through my fingers. She flung herself out through the door of the trailer, which foolishly I had not thought to close.

She ran hunched over as if protecting her stomach then staggered and went down on all fours. Her hands were splayed, her outstretched fingers clawing the dirt. The crowd drew back, parting before her as if she were not the girl they had sheltered and worked with for more than a year, not her at all, but some other creature, dangerous and diseased. The bright daylight made her garment transparent, and as she righted herself again I saw that she was naked beneath it, the narrow hips and child's breasts, the dark tuft of hair between her legs were all clearly visible. Her belly, once so flat, seemed to have become enormous overnight. It swung before her, quivering grotesquely, like the stomach of a famine victim distended by poisonous fluids. Her pale skin was criss-crossed with blue, the veins pulsing in her flesh like living wires. She looked back at me once, her face blank with terror, as if it was not me she saw but some vision of hell. Then she gathered herself and ran on, making for the ragged copse of beeches at the edge of the field.

I went after her at top speed, yelled out for Vaska to follow. At the back of everything, as if from some far distance, I could hear Piet crying Leonie's name, like a drowning man miles from the shore and calling for help.

We kept looking for several hours, tracking back and forth through the fields and copses and the small tracts of woodland in the immediate vicinity of the camp but in the end it began to get dark and we had to stop. As we retraced out steps to the wagons I caught sight of something white glimmering in the grass. It was a scrap of cloth from Leonie's camisole. Part of me did not like to touch it, but I picked it up anyway. As soon as it got light Rudy joined us and we carried on with the search. I had hardly slept a wink all night, kept awake by the helpless, agonised sound of Piet's weeping.

It was Rudy that found her. She was lying in a shallow ditch at the edge of a small stand of sycamores, half in and half out of one of the old poacher's shacks that were common in the area, as a hiding place for illegal snares or simply as a protection from the rain. An obvious place, really. I don't know how we had missed it the night before.

She lay with her face to the ground and half covered in leaves. Her legs were drawn up under her, the filthy smock torn almost in two. The tops of her thighs were slathered with congealed blood and some other substance, a greenish-yellow mucus that stank like bile. I knew without having to touch her that she was dead.

"Where's the child?" said Vaska, stupidly.

"Goodness knows," I mumbled. "A fox must have taken it, I suppose."

I don't know if they saw what I saw, the narrow track through the leaves where something had dragged itself free of Leonie's body and crawled away. The leaves had been pushed aside, revealing the brown earth beneath, and over it a silvery encrustation, transparent and brittle as ice, some kind of solidified slime. It crackled when I touched it, breaking into glistening pieces like spun sugar.

I moved about noisily, kicking up twigs and leaves, covering up the traces as quickly as I could.

"Are we going to call the police?" said Rudy.

"Are you mad?" I said. "They'll keep us here for weeks."

We walked back across the fields. None of us spoke. The sun was up by then, and I realised it was the first day of August, Lammas day. My grandmother Dmitra used to say that any child born on Lammas day was a sign of good fortune for the whole community, but she was funny that way, a great believer in old proverbs and superstitious rituals. My father always insisted it was a lot of nonsense, and that I shouldn't believe a word of it.

Piet became ill soon afterwards, and seemed to go downhill very quickly. Someone came to take him away, a stocky, rather taciturn man with a Dutch accent who claimed he was Piet's older brother. We heard later that Piet had died in a hospital in Amsterdam, of complications following a heart attack.

I thought how strange it was, that Piet had had a family that cared about him after all. It made all the years I had known him seem unreal, as if his time with us had been a fantasy of his own making, a kind of dream-projection, and all the time he was somewhere else, living another kind of life entirely.

I worked on until the end of the season. I thought at first that I would not be able to do that, but actually it came easily. People said I was *on fire*, and I would smile at that, and think of my father. I gave everything those last few months, with a kind of desperate joy, and it seemed as if nothing could go wrong for me, that I could not make a mistake, the kind of perfection that only comes when you no longer care.

I told no one about my plans, but I think Marina guessed. We went weeks at a time without speaking, though we performed together as well as ever.

On a freezing January morning Mae and I left our old life behind. I drove the trailer to a campsite in Leigh-on-Sea, where I had booked a berth for the rest of the winter. It would give us some time to think, if nothing else.

Mae settled quickly. She signed on to a computing course at the local college and soon got a job as a receptionist at a private clinic that specialised in cosmetic surgery. I teased her about it at first, but she said she liked it, she liked hearing people's stories, that in some strange way it reminded her of the company.

For a while I earned money as I had always done in the off season, working on building sites and in factory compounds, getting by but without any particular aim for the future. In the end I took up a new trade as a sales rep for a pharmaceuticals firm. It was Mae, in fact, who found me the job. I thought at first that I would hate it, but I quickly learned that there was an art to selling potions, a kind of alchemical magic that I grew increasingly fascinated by and that I suppose reminded me also of the company. It also gave me the freedom to travel, and I found there was enough of my old life in my new one to keep me satisfied.

My usual patch was the Home Counties, the old fortress towns of the south coast, the rural hinterland of Kent and Essex, the outer suburbs of South East London, but occasionally something came up that would take me a bit further afield. About eighteen months after I started working as a rep the chap who did the South West fell off a ladder whilst painting a window and broke his arm. He was off work for a couple of months, and his beat was temporarily split between me and one of the others. It meant a lot of extra driving but I didn't mind. It was late July when I happened to drive through Yeovil. I had no calls to make there but it had been a packed day, made more tiring by the heat, and I decided it was as good a place for a rest stop as any. I enquired at several bed and breakfasts only to find there were no vacancies. I hadn't realised I would have such trouble in finding a room. Yeovil was not on the coast, and even in high summer it was usually a quiet backwater.

Eventually a pub landlord took pity on me and let me sleep in his own spare room for a nominal fee.

"What's going on?" I asked him. "Why are you so booked up?"

"It always gets like this when the carnival's in town," he said. "It's the Lammas fair. But you're not from around here, are you, so you weren't to know."

I ate a meal in the pub, and afterwards I set out walking across the fields. It was a perfect summer evening, the sky high and transparent, the sun setting behind the trees in an amethyst haze. I found the place easily, as if my feet still carried a memory from the time before. I was expecting the old shack to have been taken down, or blown down, but it was still there, its boards a little more warped and weathered but otherwise it looked the same. As I approached I saw that the lower branches of the trees had been hung with ribbons and paper decorations, stars and lanterns and other, more mysterious shapes. The walls of the shack had been chalked all over with a series of symbols, or letters in a foreign alphabet I did not recognise. In the doorway of the hut an assortment of food had been laid out on some squares of rush matting: summer berries and plantains, three golden plaited loaves of Lammas bread.

It was a still place, but somehow not quiet, and I was anxious to leave. As I turned away something bright and shiny caught my eye. I reached out my hand, grasping at the empty air, and found myself holding a small glass ornament. It was star-shaped, about the size of a fifty pence piece, and had been tied to a twig with a piece of nylon thread. I brought it closer to look at it properly, and it was only then I saw what was embedded at its heart. It was a small grub, or insect, with a long, segmented putty-coloured body and six multi-jointed amber-coloured legs. Its legs were flung out to either side, as if it had died while trying to escape.

I had never seen anything like it before, and did not wish to again. I left the glass star where it was, and hurried away.

TECHNICOLOR
JOHN LANGAN

John Langan is the author of *Mr. Gaunt and Other Uneasy Encounters* (Prime 2008) and *House of Windows* (Night Shade 2009). His stories have appeared in *The Magazine of Fantasy & Science Fiction*. He lives in upstate New York with his wife and son.

Langan says: When I was a college freshman, my English class read a selection of Poe's stories, including "The Masque of the Red Death." For "The Masque," the Professor gave us the assignment of figuring out what we thought the meaning to the story's elaborate color schema was. He spent an entire class writing our responses on the board, comparing our answers. At the end of class, we asked him what he thought. He smiled and said, "I don't know."

Here's another attempt at an answer.

Come on, say it out loud with me: "And Darkness and Decay and the Red Death held illimitable dominion over all." Look at that sentence. Who says Edgar Allan Poe was a lousy stylist? Thirteen words—good number for a horror story, right? Although it's not so much a story as a masque. Yes, it's about a masque, but it is a masque, too. Of course, you all know what a masque is. If you didn't, you looked it up in your dictionaries, because that's what you do in a senior seminar. Anyone?

No, not a play, not exactly. Yes? Good, okay, "masquerade" is one sense of the word, a ball whose guests attend in costume. Anyone else?

Yes, very nice, nicely put. The masque does begin in the sixteenth century. It's the entertainment of the elite, and originally, it's a combination of pantomime and dance. Pantomime? Right—think "mime." The idea is to perform without words, gesturally, to let the movements of your body tell the story. You do that, and you dance, and there's your show. Later on, there's dialogue and other additions, but I think it's this older sense of the word the story intends. Remember that tall, silent figure at the end.

I'm sorry? Yes, good point. The two kinds of masque converge.

Back to that sentence, though. Twenty-two syllables that break almost perfectly in half, ten and twelve, "And Darkness and Decay and the Red Death" and "held illimitable dominion over all." A group of short words, one and two syllables each, takes you through the first part of the sentence, then they give way to these long, almost luxurious words, "illimitable dominion." The rhythm—you see how complex it is? You ride along on these short words, bouncing up and down, alliterating from one "d" to the next, and suddenly you're mired in those Latinate polysyllables. All the momentum goes out of your reading; there's just enough time for the final pair of words, which are short, which is good, and you're done.

Wait, just let me—no, all right, what was it you wanted to say?

Exactly, yes, you took the words out of my mouth. The sentence does what the story does, carries you along through the revelry until you run smack-dab into that tall figure in the funeral clothes. Great job.

One more observation about the sentence, then I promise it's on to the story itself. I know you want to talk about Prospero's castle, all those colored rooms. Before we do, however, the four "d"'s. We've mentioned already, there are a lot of "d" sounds in these thirteen words. They thread through the line, help tie it together. They also draw our attention to four words in particular. The first three are easy to recognize: they're capitalized, as well. Darkness, Decay, Death. The fourth? Right, dominion. Anyone want to take a stab at why they're capitalized?

Yes? Well…okay, sure it makes them into proper nouns. Can you take that a step farther? What kind of proper nouns does it make them? What's happened to the Red Death in the story? It's gone from an infection you can't see to a tall figure wandering around the party. Personification, good. Darkness, Decay, (the Red) Death: the sentence personifies them; they're its trinity, its unholy trinity, so to speak. And this godhead holds dominion, what the dictionary defines as "sovereign authority" over all. Not only the prince's castle, not only the world of the story, but all, you and me.

In fact, in a weird sort of way, this is the story of the incarnation of one of the persons of this awful trinity.

All right, moving on, now. How about those rooms? Actually, how about the building those rooms are in, first? I've been calling it a castle, but it isn't, is it? It's "castellated," which is to say, castle-like, but it's an abbey, a monastery. I suppose it makes sense to want to wait out the Red Death in a place like an abbey. After all, it's both removed from the rest of society and well-fortified. And we shouldn't be too hard on the prince and his followers for retreating there. It's not the first time this has happened, in literature or life. Anyone read *The Decameron*? Boccaccio? It's a collection of one hundred stories told by ten people, five women and five men, who have sequestered themselves in, I'm pretty sure it's a convent, to wait out the plague ravaging Florence. The Black Death, that one.

If you consider that the place in which we find the seven rooms is a monastery, a place where men are supposed to withdraw from this world to meditate on the next, its rooms appear even stranger. What's the set-up? Seven rooms, yes, thank you, I believe I just said that. Running east to west, good. In a straight line? No. There's a sharp turn every twenty or thirty yards, so that you can see only one room at a time. So long as they follow that east to west course, you can lay the rooms out in any form you like. I favor steps, like the ones that lead the condemned man to the chopping block, but that's just me.

Hang on, hang on, we'll get to the colors in a second. We need to stay with the design of the rooms for a little longer. Not everybody gets this the first time through. There are a pair of windows, Gothic windows, which means what? That they're long and pointed at the top. The windows are opposite one another, and they look out on, anybody? Not exactly: a chandelier hangs down from the ceiling. It is a kind of light, though. No, a candelabra holds candles. Anyone else? A brazier, yes, there's a brazier sitting on a tripod outside either window. They're, how would you describe a brazier? Like a big metal cup, a bowl, that you fill with some kind of fuel and ignite. Wood, charcoal, oil. To be honest, I'm not as interested in the braziers as I am in where they're located. Outside the windows, right, but where outside the windows? Maybe I should say, What is outside the windows? Corridors, yes, there are corridors to either side of the rooms, and it's along these that the braziers are stationed. Just like our classroom. Not the tripods, of course, and I guess what's outside our windows is more a gallery than a corridor, since it's open to the parking lot on the other side. All right, all right, so I'm stretching a bit, here, but have you noticed, the room has seven windows? One for each color in Prospero's Abbey. Go ahead, count them.

So here we are in this strange abbey, one that has a crazy zig-zag suite of rooms with corridors running beside them. You could chalk the location's details up to anti-Catholic sentiment; there are critics who have argued that anti-Catholic prejudice is the secret engine driving Gothic literature. No, I don't buy it, not in this case. Sure, there are stained-glass windows, but they're basically tinted glass. There's none of the iconography you'd expect if this were anti-Catholic propaganda, no statues or paintings. All we have is that enormous clock in the last room, the mother of all grandfather clocks. Wait a minute...

What about those colors, then? Each of the seven rooms is decorated in a single color that matches the stained glass of its windows. From east to west, we go from blue to purple to green to orange to white to violet to—to the last room, where there's a slight change. The windows are red, but the room itself is done in black. There seems to be some significance to the color sequence, but what that is—well, this is why we have literature professors, right? (No snickering.) Not to mention, literature students. I've read through your responses to the homework assignment, and there were a few interesting ideas as to what those colors might mean. Of course, most of you connected them to times of the day, blue as dawn, black as night, the colors in between morning, noon, early afternoon, that kind of thing. Given the east-west layout, it makes a certain amount of sense. A few more of you picked up on that connection to time in a slightly different way, and related the colors to times of the year, or the stages in a person's life. In the process, some clever arguments were made. Clever, but not, I'm afraid, too convincing.

What! What's wrong! What is it! Are you all—oh, them. Oh for God's sake. When you screamed like that, I thought—I don't know what I thought. I thought I'd need a new pair of trousers. Those are a couple of graduate students I've enlisted to help me with a little presentation I'll be putting up shortly. Yes, I can understand how the masks could startle you. They're just generic white masks; I think they found them downtown somewhere. It was their idea: once I told them what story we would be discussing, they immediately hit on wearing the masks. To tell the truth, I half-expected they'd show up sporting the heads of enormous fanged monsters. Those are relatively benign.

Yes, I suppose they do resemble the face the Red Death assumes for its costume. No blood splattered on them, though.

If I could have your attention up here, again. Pay no attention to that man behind the curtain. Where was I? Your homework, yes, thank you. Right, right. Let's see… oh—I know. A couple of you read the colors in more original ways. I made a note of them somewhere—here they are. One person interpreted the colors as different states of mind, beginning with blue as tranquil and ending with black as despair, with stops for jealousy—green, naturally—and passion—white, as in white-hot—along the way. Someone else made the case for the colors as, let me make sure I have the phrasing right, "phases of being."

Actually, that last one's not bad. Although the writer could be less obtuse; clarity, people, academic writing needs to be clear. Anyway, the gist of the writer's argument is that each color is supposed to take you through a different state of existence, blue at one end of the spectrum representing innocence, black at the other representing death. Death as a state of being, that's… provocative. Which is not to say it's correct, but it's headed in the right direction.

I know, I know: Which is? The answer requires some explanation. Scratch that. It requires a boatload of explanation. That's why I have Tweedledee and Tweedledum setting up outside. (Don't look! They're almost done.) It's also why I lowered the screen behind me for the first time this semester. There are some images I want to show you, and they're best seen in as much detail as possible. If I can remember what the Media Center people told me… click this… then this…

Voila!

Matthew Brady's *Portrait* of Edgar, taken 1848, his last full year alive. It's the best-known picture of him; were I to ask you to visualize him, this is what your minds' eyes would see. That forehead, that marble expanse—yes, his hair does make the top of his head look misshapen, truncated. As far as I know, it wasn't. The eyes—I suppose everyone comments on the eyes, slightly shadowed under those brows, the lids lowered just enough to suggest a certain detachment, even dreaminess. It's the mouth I notice, how it tilts up ever-so-slightly at the right corner. It's hard to see; you have to look closely. A strange mixture of arrogance, even contempt, and something else, something that might be humor, albeit of the bitter variety. It wouldn't be that much of a challenge to suggest colors for the picture, but somehow, black and white is more fitting, isn't it? Odd, considering how much color there is in the fiction. I've often thought all those old Roger Corman adaptations, the ones Vincent Price starred in—whatever their other faults, one thing they got exactly right was Technicolor, which was the perfect way to film these stories, just saturate the screen with the most vibrant colors you could find.

I begin with the *Portrait* as a reminder. This is the man. His hand scraped the pen across the paper, brought the story we've been discussing into existence word by word. Not creation *ex nihilo*, out of nothing, creation… if my Latin were better, or existent, I'd have a fancier way to say out of the self, or out of the depths of the self, or—hey—out of the depth that is the self.

Moving on to our next portrait… Anyone?

I'm impressed. Not many people know this picture. Look closely, though. See it?

That's right: it isn't a painting. It's a photograph that's been tweaked to resemble a painting. The portrait it imitates is a posthumous representation of Virginia Clemm, Edgar's sweetheart and child bride. The girl in the photo? She'll be happy you called her a girl. That's my wife, Anna. Yes, I'm married. Why is that so hard to believe? We met many years ago, in a kingdom by the sea. From? "Annabel Lee," good. No, just Anna; although we did meet in the King of the Sea Arcade, on the Jersey shore. Seriously. She is slightly younger than I am. Four years, thank you very much. You people. For Halloween one year, we dressed up as Edgar and Virginia—pretty much from the start, it's been a running joke between us. In her case, the resemblance is striking.

As it so happened, yes we did attend a masquerade as the happy couple. That was where this photo was taken. One of the other guests was a professional photographer. I arranged the shot; he took it, then used a program on his computer to transform it into a painting. The guy was quite pleased with it; apparently it's on his website. I'm showing it to you because… well, because I want to. There's probably a connection I could draw between masquerade, the suppression of one identity in order to invoke and inhabit another, that displacement, and the events of our story, but that's putting the cart about a mile before the horse. She'll like that you thought she was a girl, though; that'll make her night. Those were her cookies, by the way. Are there any left? Not even the sugar cookies? Figures.

Okay, image number three. If you can name this one, you get an "A" for the class and an autographed picture of the Pope. Put your hand down, you don't know. How about the rest of you?

Just us crickets…

It's just as well; I don't have that picture of the Pope anymore. This gentleman is Prosper Vauglais. Or so he claimed. There's a lot about this guy no one's exactly sure of, like when he was born, or where, or when and where he died. He showed up in Paris in the late eighteen-teens and caused something of a stir. For one winter, he appeared at several of the less reputable *salons* and a couple of the, I wouldn't go so far as to say more reputable—maybe less disreputable ones.

His "deal?" His deal, as you put it, was that he claimed to have been among the quarter of a million soldiers under Napoleon Bonaparte's personal command when, in June of 1812, the Emperor decided to invade Russia. Some of you may remember from your European history classes, this was a very bad idea. The worst. Roughly a tenth of Napoleon's forces survived the campaign; I want to say the number who limped back into France was something like twenty-two thousand. In and of itself, being a member of that group is nothing to sneeze at. For Vauglais, though, it was only the beginning. During the more-or-less running battles the French army fought as it retreated from what had been Moscow, Vauglais was separated from his fellows, struck on the head by a Cossack's sword and left for dead in a snow bank. When he came to, he was alone, and a storm had blown up. Prosper had no idea where he was; he assumed still Russia, which wasn't too encouraging. Any Russian peasants or what have you who came across French soldiers, even those trying to surrender, tended to hack them to death with farm implements first and ask questions later. So when Prosper strikes out in what he hopes is the approximate direction of France, he isn't what you'd call terribly optimistic.

Nor is his pessimism misplaced. Within a day, he's lost, frozen and starving, wandering around the inside of a blizzard like you read about, white-out conditions, shrieking wind, unbearable cold. The blow to his head isn't helping matters, either. His vision keeps going in and out of focus. Sometimes he feels so nauseated he can barely stand, let alone continue walking. Once in a while, he'll see a light shining in the window of a farmhouse, but he gives these a wide berth. Another day, and he'll be closer to death than he was even at the worst battles he saw—than he was when that saber connected with his skull. His skin, which has been numb since not long after he started his trek, has gone from pale to white to this kind of blue-gray, and it's hardened, as if there's a crust of ice on it. He can't feel his pulse through it. His breath, which had been venting from his nose and mouth in long white clouds, seems to have slowed to a trickle, if that. He can't see anything; although, with the storm continuing around him, maybe that isn't so strange. He's not cold anymore—or, it's not that he isn't cold so much as it is that the cold isn't torturing him the way it was. At some point, the cold moved inside him, took up residence just beneath his heart, and once that happened, that transition was accomplished, the temperature outside became of much less concern.

There's a moment—while Vauglais is staggering around like you do when you're trying to walk in knee-high snow without snowshoes, pulling each foot free, swiveling it forward, crashing it through the snow in front of you, then repeating the process with your other foot—there's a moment when he realizes he's dead. He isn't sure when it happened. Some time in the last day or so. It isn't that he thinks he's in some kind of afterlife, that he's wandering around a frozen hell. No, he knows he's still stuck somewhere in western Russia. It's just that, now he's dead. He isn't sure why he hasn't stopped moving. He considers doing so, giving his body a chance to catch up to his apprehension of it, but decides against it. For one thing, he isn't sure it would work, and suppose while he's standing in place, waiting to fall over, someone finds him, one of those peasants, or a group of Russian soldiers? Granted, if he's already dead, they can't hurt him, but the prospect of being cut to pieces while still conscious is rather horrifying. And for another thing, Prosper isn't ready to quit walking. So he keeps moving forward. Dimly, the way you might hear a noise when you're fast asleep, he's aware that he isn't particularly upset at finding himself dead and yet moving, but after recent events, maybe that isn't so surprising.

Time passes; how much, he can't say. The blizzard doesn't lift, but it thins, enough for Vauglais to make out trees, evergreens. He's in a forest, a pretty dense one, from what he can see, which may explain why the storm has lessened. The trees are—there's something odd about the trees. For as close together as they are, they seem to be in almost perfect rows, running away into the snow on either side of him. In and of itself, maybe that isn't strange. Could be, he's wandered into some kind of huge formal garden. But there's more to it. When he looks at any particular tree, he sees, not so much bark and needles as black, black lines like the strokes of a paintbrush, or the scratches of a pen, forming the approximation of an evergreen. It's as if he's seeing a sketch of a tree, an artist's estimate. The black lines appear to be moving, almost too quickly for him to notice; it's as if he's witnessing them being drawn and re-drawn. Prosper has a sudden vision of himself from high above, a small, dark spot in the midst of long rows of black on white, a stray bit of punctuation loose among the lines of an unimaginable text.

Eventually, Vauglais reaches the edge of the forest. Ahead, there's a building, the title to this page he's been traversing. The blizzard has kicked up again, so he can't see much, but he has the impression of a long, low structure, possibly stone. It could be a stable, could be something else. Although there are no religious symbols evident, Prosper has an intuition the place is a monastery. He should turn right or left, avoid the building—the Russian clergy haven't taken any more kindly to the French invaders than the Russian people—instead, he raises one stiff leg and strikes off towards it. It isn't that he's compelled to do so, that he's in the grip of a power that he can't resist, or that he's decided to embrace the inevitable, surrender to death. He isn't even especially curious about the stone structure. Forward is just a way to go, and he does.

As he draws closer, Vauglais notices that the building isn't becoming any easier to distinguish. If anything, it's more indistinct, harder to make out. If the trees behind him were rough drawing, this place is little more than a scribble, a jumble of lines whose form is as much in the eye of the beholder as anything. When a figure in a heavy coat and hat separates from the structure and begins to trudge in his direction, it's as if a piece of the place has broken off. Prosper can't see the man's face, all of which except the eyes is hidden by the folds of a heavy scarf, but he lifts one mittened hand and gestures for Vauglais to follow him inside, which the Frenchman does.

And…no one knows what happens next.

What do I mean? I'm sorry: wasn't I speaking English? No one knows what happened inside the stone monastery. Prosper writes a fairly detailed account of the events leading up to that point, which is where the story I'm telling you comes from, but when the narrative reaches this moment, it breaks off with Vauglais's declaration that he's told us as much as he can. End of story.

All right, yes, there are hints of what took place during the five years he was at the Abbey. That was what he called the building, the Abbey. Every so often, Prosper would allude to his experiences in it, and sometimes, someone would note his remarks in a letter or diary. From combing through these kinds of documents, it's possible to assemble and collate Vauglais's comments into a glimpse of his life with the Fraternity. Again, his name. There were maybe seven of them, or seven after he arrived, or there were supposed to be seven. He referred to "Brother Red," once; to "The White Brother" at another time. Were the others named Blue, Purple, Green, Orange, and Violet? We can't say; although, as an assumption, it isn't completely unreasonable. They spent their days in pursuit of something Vauglais called The Great Work; he also referred to it as The Transumption. This seems to have involved generous amounts of quiet meditation combined with the study of certain religious texts—Prosper doesn't name them, but they may have included some Gnostic writings.

The Gnostics? I don't suppose you would have heard of them. How many of you actually got to church? As I feared. What would Sr. Mary Mary say? The Gnostics were a religious sect who sprang up around the same time as the early Christians. I guess they would have described themselves as the true Christians, the ones who understood what Jesus' teachings were really about. They shared sacred writings with the more orthodox Christians, but they had their own books, too. They were all about *gnosis*, knowledge, especially of the self. For them, the secret to what lay outside the self was what lay inside the self. The physical world was evil, a wellspring of illusions and delusions. Gnostics tended to retreat to the desert, lead lives of contemplation. Unlike the mainstream Christians, they weren't much on formal organization; that, and the fact that those Christians did everything in their power to shunt the Gnostics and their teachings to the margins and beyond, branding some of their ideas as heretical, helps explain why they pretty much vanished from the religious scene.

"Pretty much," though, isn't the same thing as "completely." (I know: such precise, scientific terminology.) Once in a while, Gnostic ideas would resurface, usually in the writings of some fringe figure or another. Rumors persist of Gnostic secret societies, occasionally as part of established groups like the Jesuits or the Masons. Which begs the question, Was Vauglais's Fraternity one of these societies, a kind of order of Gnostic monks? The answer to which is—

Right: no one knows. There's no record of any official, which is to say, Russian Orthodox religious establishment: no monastery, no church, in the general vicinity of where we think Prosper was. Of course, a bunch of Gnostic monastics would hardly constitute anything resembling an official body, and so might very well fly under the radar. That said, the lack of proof against something does not count as evidence for it.

That's true. He could have been making the whole thing up.

Transumption? It's a term from classical rhetoric. It refers to the elision of a chain of associations. Sorry—sometimes I like to watch your heads explode. Let's say you're writing your epic poem about the fall of Troy, and you describe one of the Trojans being felled by an arrow. Let's say that arrow was made from the wood of a tree in a sacred grove; let's say, too, that that grove was planted by Hercules, who scattered some acorns there by accident. Now let's say that, when your Trojan hero sinks to the ground, drowning in his own blood, one of his friends shouts, "Curse the careless hand of Hercules!" That statement is an example of transumption. You've jumped from one link in a chain of associations back several. Make sense?

Yes, well, what does a figure of speech have to do with what was going on inside that Abbey?

Oh wait—hold on for a moment. My two assistants are done with their set up. Let me give them a signal... Five more minutes? All right, good, yes. I have no idea if they understood me. Graduate students.

Don't worry about what's on the windows. Yes, yes, those are lamps. Can I have your attention up here, please? Thank you. Let me worry about Campus Security. Or my masked friends out there will.

Okay—let's skip ahead a little. We were talking about The Transumption, a.k.a. The Great Work. There's nothing in his other references to the Abbey that offers any clue as to what he may have meant by it. However, there is an event that may shed some light on things.

It occurs in Paris, towards the end of February. An especially fierce winter scours the streets, sends people scurrying from the shelter of one building to another. Snow piles on top of snow, all of it turning dirty gray. Where there isn't snow, there's ice, inches thick in places. The sky is gray, the sun a pale blur that puts in a token appearance for a few hours a day. Out into this glacial landscape, Prosper leads half a dozen men and women from one of the city's less-disreputable *salons*. Their destination, the catacombs, the long tunnels that run under Paris. They're quite old, the catacombs. In some places, the walls are stacked with bones, from when they were used as a huge ossuary. (That's a place to hold the bones of the dead.) They're also fairly crowded, full of beggars, the poor, searching for shelter from the ravages of the season. Vauglais has to take his party deep underground before they can find a location that's suitably empty. It's a kind of side-chamber, roughly circular, lined with shelves full of skull piled on skull. The skulls make a clicking sound, from the rats shuffling through them. Oh yes, there are plenty of rats down here.

Prosper fetches seven skulls off the shelves and piles them in the center of the room. He opens a large flask he's carried with him, and pours its contents over the bones. It's lamp oil, which he immediately ignites with his torch. He sets the torch down, and gathers the members of the *salon* around the skulls. They join hands.

It does sound as if he's leading a séance, doesn't it? The only difference is, he isn't asking the men and women with him to think of a beloved one who's passed beyond. Nor does he request they focus on a famous ghost. Instead, Vauglais tells them to look at the flames licking the bones in front of them. Study those flames, he says, watch them as they trace the contours of the skulls. Follow the flames over the cheeks, around the eyes, up the brows. Gaze into those eyes, into the emptiness inside the fire. Fall through the flames; fall into that blackness.

He's hypnotizing them, of course—Mesmerizing would be the more histori-cally-accurate term. Under the sway of his voice, the members of the *salon* enter a kind of vacancy. They're still conscious—well, they're still perceiving, still aware of that heap of bones burning in front of them, the heavy odor of the oil, the quiet roar of the flames—but their sense of their selves, the accumulation of memory and inclination that defines each from the other, is gone.

Now Prosper is telling them to think of something new. Picture the flesh that used to clothe these skulls, he says. Warm and smooth, flushed with life. Look closely—it glows, doesn't it? It shines with its living. Watch! watch—it's dying. It's growing cold, pale. The glow, that dim light floating at the very limit of the skin—it's changing, drifting up, losing its radiance. See—there!—ah, it's dead. Cool as a cut of meat. Gray. The light is gone. Or is it? Is that another light? Yes, yes it is; but it is not the one we have watched dissipate. This is a darker glow. Indigo, that most elusive of the rainbow's hues. It curls over the dull skin like fog, and the flesh opens for it, first in little cracks, then in long windows, and then in wide doorways. As the skin peels away, the light thickens, until it is as if the bone is submerged in a bath of indigo. The light is not done moving; it pours into the air above the skull, over all the skulls. Dark light is rising from them, twisting up in thick streams that seek each other, that wrap around one another, that braid a shape. It is the form of a man, a tall man dressed in black robes, his face void as a corpse's, his head crowned with black flame—

Afterwards, when the half-dozen members of the *salon* compare notes, none of them can agree on what, if anything, they saw while under Vauglais's sway. One of them insists that nothing appeared. Three admit to what might have been a cloud of smoke, or a trick of the light. Of the remaining pair, one states flat-out that she saw the Devil. The other balks at any statement more elaborate than, "Monsieur Vauglais has shown me terrible joy." Whatever they do or don't see, it doesn't last very long. The oil Prosper doused the skulls with has been consumed. The fire dies away; darkness rushes in to fill the gap. The trance in which Vauglais has held the *salon* breaks. There's a sound like wind rushing, then quiet.

A month after that expedition, Prosper disappeared from Paris. He had attempted to lead that same *salon* back into the catacombs for a second—well, whatever you'd call what he'd done. A summoning? (But what was he summoning?) Not surprisingly, the men and women of the *salon* declined his request. In a huff, Vauglais left them and tried to insert himself into a couple of even-less-disreputable *salons*, attempting to use gossip about his former associates as his price of admission. But either the secrets he knew weren't juicy enough—possible, but I suspect unlikely—or those other *salons* had heard about his underground investigations and decided they preferred the comfort of their drawing rooms. Then one of the men from that original *salon* raised questions about Prosper's military service—he claimed to have found a sailor who swore that he and Vauglais had been on an extended debauch in Morocco at the very time he was supposed to have been marching towards Moscow. That's the problem with being the flavor of the month: before you know it, the calendar's turned, and no one can remember what they found so appealing about you in the first place. In short order, there's talk about an official inquiry into Prosper's service record—probably more rumor than fact, but it's enough for Vauglais, and he departs Paris for parts unknown. No one sees him leave, just as no one saw him arrive. In the weeks that follow, there are reports of Prosper in Libya, Madagascar, but they don't disturb a single eyebrow. Years—decades later, when Gauguin's in Tahiti, he'll hear a story about a strange white man who came to the island a long time ago and vanished into its interior, and Vauglais's name will occur to him, but you can't even call that a legend. It's… a momentary association. Prosper Vauglais vanishes.

Well, not all of him. That's right: there's the account he wrote of his discovery of the Abbey.

I beg your pardon? Dead? Oh, right, yes. It's interesting—apparently, Prosper permitted a physician connected to the first *salon* he frequented to conduct a pretty thorough examination of him. According to Dr. Zumachin, Vauglais's skin was stubbornly pallid. No matter how much the doctor pinched or slapped it, Prosper's flesh remained the same gray-white. Not only that, it was cold, cold and hard, as if it were packed with ice. Although Vauglais had to inhale in order to speak, his regular respiration was so slight as to be undetectable. It wouldn't fog the doctor's pocket mirror. And try as Zumachin might, he could not locate a pulse.

Sure, Prosper could have paid him off; aside from his part in this story, there isn't that much information on the good doctor. For what it's worth, most of the people who met Vauglais commented on his skin, its pallor, and, if they touched it, its coldness. No one else noted his breathing, or lack thereof, but a couple of the members of that last *salon* described him as extraordinarily still.

Okay, back to that book. Actually, wait. Before we do, let me bring this up on the screen…

I know—talk about something completely different. No, it's not a Rorschach test. It does look like it, though, doesn't it? Now if my friends outside will oblige me… and there we go. Amazing what a sheet of blue plastic and a high-power lamp can do. We might as well be in the east room of Prospero's Abbey.

Yes, the blue light makes it appear deeper—it transforms it from ink-spill to opening. Prosper calls it "*La Bouche*," the Mouth. Some mouth, eh?

That's where the design comes from, Vauglais's book. The year after his disappearance, a small Parisian press whose biggest claim to fame was its unauthorized edition of the Marquis de Sade's *Justine* publishes Prosper's *L'Histoire de Mes Aventures dans L'Etendu Russe*, which translates something like, "The History of My Adventures in the Russian," either "Wilderness" or "Vastness." Not that anyone calls it by its title. The publisher, one Denis Prebend, binds Vauglais's essay between covers the color of a bruise after three or four days. Yes, that sickly, yellowy-green. Of course that's what catches everyone's attention, not the less-than-inspired title, and it isn't long before customers are asking for "*le livre verte*," the green book. It's funny—it's one of those books that no one will admit to reading, but that goes through ten printings the first year after it appears.

Some of those copies do find their way across the Atlantic, very good. In fact, within a couple of months of its publication, there are at least three pirated translations of the green book circulating the booksellers of London, and a month after that, they're available in Boston, New York, and Baltimore.

To return to the book itself for a moment—after that frustrating ending, there's a blank page, which is followed by seven more pages, each showing a separate design. What's above me on the screen is the first of them. The rest—well, let's not get ahead of ourselves. Suffice it to say, the initial verdict was that something had gone awry in the printing process, with the result that the *bouche* had become *bouché*, cloudy. A few scholars have even gone so far as to attempt to reconstruct what Prosper's original images must have been. Prebend, though—the publisher—swore that he'd presented the book exactly as he had been instructed.

For those of us familiar with abstract art, I doubt there's any great difficulty in seeing the black blot on the screen as a mouth. The effect—there used to be these books; they were full of what looked like random designs. If you held them the right distance from your face and let your eyes relax, almost to the point of going cross-eyed, all of sudden, a picture would leap out of the page at you. You know what I'm talking about? Good. I don't know what the name for that effect is, but it's the nearest analogue I can come up with for what happens when you look at the Mouth under blue light—except that the image doesn't jump forward so much as sink back. The way it recedes—it's as if it extends, not just through the screen, or the wall behind it, but beyond all that, to the very substratum of things.

To tell the truth, I have no idea what's responsible for the effect. If you find this impressive, however…

Look at that: a new image and a fresh color. How's that for coordination? Good work, nameless minions. Vauglais named this "*Le Gardien*," the Guardian. What's that? I suppose you could make an octopus out of it; although aren't there a few too many tentacles? True, it's close enough; it's certainly more octopus than squid. Do you notice… right. The tentacles, loops, whatever we call them, appear to be moving. Focus on any one in particular, and it stands still—but you can see movement out of the corner of your eye, can't you? Try to take in the whole, and you swear its arms are performing an intricate dance.

So the Mouth leads to the Guardian, which is waving its appendages in front of…

That green is bright after the purple, isn't it? Voila "*Le Récif*," the Reef. Makes sense, a cuttlefish protecting a reef. I don't know: it's angular enough. Person-ally, I suspect this one is based on some kind of pun or word play. "*Récif*" is one letter away from "*récit*," story, and this reef comes to us as the result of a story; in some weird way, the reef may be the story. I realize that doesn't make any sense; I'm still working through it.

This image is a bit different from the previous two. Anyone notice how?

Exactly: instead of the picture appearing to move, the light itself seems to—I like your word, "shimmer." You could believe we're gazing through water. It's—not hypnotic, that's too strong, but it is soothing. Don't you think?

I'll take your yawn as a "yes." Very nice. What a way to preface a question. All right, all right. What is it that's keeping you awake?

Isn't it obvious? Apparently not.

Yes! Edgar read Prosper's book!

When. The best evidence is sometime in the early eighteen-thirties, after he'd relocated to Baltimore. He mentions hearing about the green book from one of his fellow cadets at West Point, but he doesn't secure his own copy until he literally stumbles upon one in a bookshop near Baltimore's inner harbor. He wrote a fairly amusing account of it in a letter to Virginia. The store was this long, narrow space located halfway down an alley; its shelves were stuffed past capacity with all sizes of books jammed together with no regard for their subject. Occasionally, one of the shelves would disgorge its contents without warning. If you were underneath or to the side of it, you ran the risk of substantial injury. Not to mention, the single aisle snaking into the shop's recesses was occupied at irregular intervals by stacks of books that looked as if a strong sneeze would send them tumbling down.

It's as he's attempting to maneuver around an especially tall tower of books, simultaneously trying to avoid jostling a nearby shelf, that Edgar's foot catches on a single volume he hadn't seen, sending him—and all books in the immediate vicinity—to the floor. There's a huge puff of dust; half a dozen books essentially disintegrate. Edgar's sense of humor is such that he appreciates the comic aspect of a poet—as he styled himself—buried beneath a deluge of books. However, he insists on excavating the book that undid him.

The copy of Vauglais's essay he found was a fourth translation that had been done by a Boston publisher hoping to cash in on the popularity of the other editions. Unfortunately for him, the edition took longer to prepare than he'd anticipated—his translator was a Harvard professor who insisted on translating Prosper as accurately as he could. This meant an English version of Vauglais's essay that was a model of fidelity to the original French, but that wasn't ready until Prosper's story was last week's news. The publisher went ahead with what he titled *The Green Book of M. Prosper Vauglais* anyway, but he pretty much lost his shirt over the whole thing.

Edgar was so struck at having fallen over this book that he bought it on the spot. He spent the next couple of days reading and re-reading it, puzzling over its contents. As we've seen in "The Gold Bug" and "The Purloined Letter," this was a guy who liked a puzzle. He spent a good deal of time on the seven designs at the back of the book, convinced that their significance was right in front of him.

Speaking of those pictures, let's have another one. Assistants, if you please—

Hey, it's Halloween! Isn't that what you associate orange with? And especially an orange like this—this is the sun spilling the last of its late light, right before all the gaudier colors, the violets and pinks, splash out. You don't think of orange as dark, do you? I know I don't. Yet it is, isn't it? Is it the darkest of the bright colors? To be sure, it's difficult to distinguish the design at its center; the orange is filmy, translucent. There are a few too many curves for it to be the symbol for infinity; at least, I think there are. I want to say I see a pair of snakes wrapped around one another, but the coils don't connect in quite the right way. Vauglais's name for this was "*Le Coeur,*" the Heart, and also the Core, as well as the Height or the Depth, depending on usage. Obviously, we're cycling through the seven rooms from "The Masque of the Red Death;" obviously, too, I'm arguing that Edgar takes their colors from Prosper's book. In that schema, orange is at the center, three colors to either side of it; in that sense, we have reached the heart, the core, the height or the depth. Of course, that core obscures the other one—or maybe not.

While you try to decide, let's return to Edgar. It's an overstatement to say that Vauglais obsesses him. When his initial attempt at deciphering the designs fails, he puts the book aside. Remember, he's a working writer at a time when the American economy really won't support one—especially one with Edgar's predilections—so there are always more things to be written in the effort to keep the wolf a safe distance from the door. Not to mention, he's falling in love with the girl who will become his wife. At odd moments over the next decade, though, he retrieves Prosper's essay and spends a few hours poring over it. He stares at its images until they're grooved into the folds of his brain. During one long afternoon in 1840, he's sitting with the book open to the Mouth, a glass of water on the table to his right. The sunlight streaming in the windows splinters on the water glass, throwing a rainbow across the page in front of him. The arc of the images that's under the blue strip of the bow looks different; it's as if that portion of the paper has sunk into the book—behind the book. A missing and apparently lost piece of the puzzle snaps into place, and Edgar starts up from the table, knocking over his chair in the process. He races through the house, searching for a piece of blue glass. The best he can do is a heavy blue jug, which he almost drops in his excitement. He returns to the book, angles the jug to catch the light, and watches as the Mouth opens. He doesn't waste any time staring at it; shifting the jug to his right hand, he flips to the next image with his left, positions the glass jug over the Guardian, and… nothing. For a moment, he's afraid he's imagined the whole thing, had an especially vivid waking dream. But when he pages back to the Mouth and directs the blue light onto it, it clearly recedes. Edgar wonders if the effect he's observed is unique to the first image, then his eye lights on the glass of water, still casting its rainbow. He sets the jug on the floor, turns the page, and slides the book closer to the glass.

That's how Edgar spends the rest of the afternoon, matching the designs in the back of Vauglais's book to the colors that activate them. The first four come relatively quickly; the last three take longer. Once he has all seven, Edgar re-reads Prosper's essay and reproaches himself as a dunce for not having hit on the colors sooner. It's all there in Vauglais's prose, he declares, plain as day. (He's being much too hard on himself. I've read the green book a dozen times and I have yet to find the passage where Prosper hints at the colors.)

How about a look at the most difficult designs? Gentlemen, if you please…

There's nothing there. I know—that's what I said, the first time I saw the fifth image. "*Le Silence*," the Silence. Compared to the designs that precede it, this one is so faint as to be barely detectable. And when you shine a bright, white light onto it, it practically disappears. There is something in there, though; you have to stare at it for a while. Moreso than with the previous images, what you see here varies dramatically from viewer to viewer.

Edgar never records his response to the Silence, which is a pity. Having cracked the secret of Vauglais's designs, he studies the essay more carefully, attempting to discern the use to which the images were to be put, the nature of Prosper's Great Work, his Transumption. (There's that word again. I never clarified its meaning vis à vis Vauglais's ideas, did I?) The following year, when Edgar sits down to write "The Masque of the Red Death," it is in no small part as an answer to the question of what Prosper was up to. That answer shares features with some of the stories he had written prior to his 1840 revelation; although, interestingly, they came after he had obtained his copy of the green book.

From the looks on your faces, I'd say you've seen what the Silence contains. I don't suppose anyone wants to share?

I'll take that as a "No." It's all right: what you find there can be rather… disconcerting.

We're almost at the end of our little display. What do you say we proceed to number six? Here we go…

Violet's such a nice color, isn't it? You have to admit, some of those other colors are pretty intense. Not this one, though; even the image—"*L'Arbre*," the Tree—looks more or less like a collection of lines trying to be a tree. Granted, if you study the design, you'll notice that each individual line seems to fade and then re-inscribe itself, but compared to the effect of the previous image, this is fairly benign. Does it remind you of anything? Anything we were discussing, say, in the last hour or so?

Oh never mind, I'll just tell you. Remember those trees Vauglais saw outside the Abbey? Remember the way that, when he tried to focus on any of them, he saw a mass of black lines? Hmmm. Maybe there's more to this pleasant design than we'd thought. Maybe it's, not the key to all this, but the key trope, or figure.

I know: which means what, exactly? Let's return to Edgar's story. You have a group of people who are sequestered together, made to disguise their outer identities, encouraged to debauch themselves, to abandon their inner identities, all the while passing from one end of this color schema to the other. They put their selves aside, become a massive blank, a kind of psychic space. That opening allows what is otherwise an abstraction, a personification, to change states, to manifest itself physically. Of course, the Red Death doesn't appear of its own volition; it's called into being by Prince Prospero, who can't stop thinking about the reason he's retreated into his abbey.

This is what happened—what started to happen to the members of the *salon* Prosper took into the Parisian catacombs. He attempted to implement what he'd learned during his years at the Abbey, what he first had perceived through the snow twirling in front of his eyes in that Russian forest. To manipulate—to mold—to…

Suppose that the real—what we take to be the real—imagine that world outside the self, all this out here, is like a kind of writing. We write it together; we're continuously writing it together, onto the surface of things, the paper, as it were. It isn't something we do consciously, or that we exercise any conscious control over. We might glimpse it in moments of extremity, as Vauglais did, but that's about as close to it as most of us will come. What if, though, what if it were possible to do something more than simply look? What if you could clear a space on that paper and write something *else*? What might you bring into being?

Edgar tries to find out. Long after "The Masque," which is as much caution as it is field guide, he decides to apply Prosper's ideas for real. He does so during that famous lost week at the end of his life, that gap in the biographical record that has prompted so much speculation. Since Virginia succumbed to tuberculosis some two years prior, Edgar's been on a long downward slide, a protracted effort at joining his beloved wife. You know, extensive forests have been harvested for the production of critical studies of Edgar's "bizarre" relationship with Virginia; rarely, if ever, does it occur to anyone that Edgar and Virginia might honestly have been in love, and that the difference in their ages might have been incidental.

Yet what is that final couple of years but a man grieving himself to death? Yes, Edgar approaches other women about possible marriage, but why do you think none of those proposals work out?

Not only is Edgar actively chasing his death, paddling furiously towards it on a river of alcohol; little known to him, death has noticed his pursuit, and responded by planting a black seed deep within his brain, a gift that is blossoming into a tumor. Most biographers have remained ignorant of this disease, but years after his death, Edgar's body is exhumed—it doesn't matter why; given who Edgar was, of course this was going to happen to him. During the examination of his remains, it's noted that his brain is shrunken and hard. Anyone who knows about these things will tell you that the brain is one of the first organs to decay, which means that what those investigators found rattling around old Edgar's cranium would not have been petrified gray matter. Cancer, however, is a much more durable beast; long after it's killed you, a tumor hangs around to testify to its crime. Your guess is as good as mine when it comes to how long he'd had it, but by the time I'm talking about, Edgar is in a pretty bad way. He's having trouble controlling the movements of his body, his speech; half the time he seems drunk, he's stone cold sober.

There's something else. Increasingly, wherever he turns his gaze, whatever he looks at flickers, and instead of, say, an orange resting on a plate, he sees a jumble of black lines approximating a sphere on a circle. It takes him longer to recall Vauglais's experience in that Russian forest than you'd expect; the cancer, no doubt, devouring his memory. Sometimes the confusion of lines that's replaced the streetlamp in front of him is itself replaced by blankness, by an absence that registers as a dull white space in the middle of things. It's as if a painter took a palette knife and scraped the oils from a portion of their picture until all that remained was the canvas, slightly stained. At first, Edgar thinks there's something wrong with his vision; when he understands what he's experiencing, he speculates that the blank might be the result of his eyes' inability to endure their own perception, that he might be undergoing some degree of what we would call hysterical blindness. As he's continued to see that whiteness, though, he's realized that he isn't seeing less, but more. He's seeing through to the surface those black lines are written on.

In the days immediately prior to his disappearance, Edgar's perception undergoes one final change. For the slightest instant after that space has uncovered itself to him, something appears on it, a figure—a woman. Virginia, yes, as he saw her last, ravaged by tuberculosis, skeletally thin, dark hair in disarray, mouth and chin scarlet with the blood she'd hacked out of her lungs. She appears barefoot, wrapped in a shroud stained with dirt. Almost before he sees her, she's gone, her place taken by whatever he'd been looking at to begin with.

Is it any surprise that, presented with this dull white surface, Edgar should fill it with Virginia? Her death has polarized him; she's the lodestone that draws his thoughts irresistibly in her direction. With each glimpse of her he has, Edgar apprehends that he's standing at the threshold of what could be an extraordinary chance. Although he's discovered the secret of Prosper's designs, discerned the nature of the Great Work, never once has it occurred to him that he might put that knowledge to use. Maybe he hasn't really believed in it; maybe he's suspected that, underneath it all, the effect of the various colors on Vauglais's designs is some type of clever optical illusion. Now, though, now that there's the possibility of gaining his beloved back—

Edgar spends that last week sequestered in a room in a boarding house a few streets up from that alley where he tripped over Prosper's book. He's arranged for his meals to be left outside his door; half the time, however, he leaves them untouched, and even when he takes the dishes into his room, he eats the bare minimum to sustain him. About midway through his stay, the landlady, a Mrs. Foster, catches sight of him as he withdraws into his room. His face is flushed, his skin slick with sweat, his clothes disheveled; he might be in the grip of a fever whose fingers are tightening around him with each degree it climbs. As his door closes, Mrs. Foster considers running up to it and demanding to speak to this man. The last thing she wants is for her boarding house to be known as a den of sickness. She has taken two steps forward when she stops, turns, and bolts downstairs as if the Devil himself were tugging her apron strings. For the remainder of the time this lodger is in his room, she will send one of the serving girls to deliver his meals, no matter their protests. Once the room stands unoccupied, she will direct a pair of those same girls to remove its contents—including the cheap bed—carry them out back, and burn them until nothing remains but a heap of ashes. The empty room is closed, locked, and removed from use for the rest of her time running that house, some twenty-two years.

I know: what did she see? What could she have seen, with the door shut? Perhaps it wasn't what she saw; perhaps it was what she felt: the surface of things yielding, peeling away to what was beneath, beyond—the strain of a will struggling to score its vision onto that surface—the waver of the brick and mortar, of the very air around her, as it strained against this newness coming into being. How would the body respond to what could only register as a profound wrongness? Panic, you have to imagine, maybe accompanied by sudden nausea, a fear so intense as to guarantee a lifetime's aversion to anything associated with its cause.

Had she opened that door, though, what sight would have confronted her? What would we see?

Nothing much—at least, that's likely to have been our initial response. Edgar seated on the narrow bed, staring at the wall opposite him. Depending on which day it was, we would have noticed his shirt and pants looking more or less clean. Like Mrs. Foster, we would have remarked his flushed face, the sweat soaking his shirt; we would have heard his breathing, deep and hoarse. We might have caught his lips moving, might have guessed he was repeating Virginia's name over and over again, but been unable to say for sure. Were we to guess he was in a trance, caught in an opium dream, aside from the complete and total lack of opium-related paraphernalia, we could be forgiven.

If we were to remain in that room with him—if we could stand the same sensation that sent Mrs. Foster running—it wouldn't take us long to turn our eyes in the direction of Edgar's stare. His first day there, we wouldn't have noticed much if anything out of the ordinary. Maybe we would have wondered if the patch of bricks he was so focused on didn't look just the slightest shade paler than its surroundings, before dismissing it as a trick of the light. Return two, three days later, and we would find that what we had attributed to mid-afternoon light blanching already-faded masonry is a phenomenon of an entirely different order. Those bricks are blinking in and out of sight. One moment, there's a worn red rectangle, the next, there isn't. What takes its place is difficult to say, because it's back almost as fast as it was gone; although, after its return, the brick looks a bit less solid…less certain, you might say. Ragged around the edges, though not in any way you could put words to. All over that stretch of wall, bricks are going and coming and going. It almost looks as if some kind of code is spelling itself out using the stuff of Edgar's wall as its pen and paper.

Were we to find ourselves in that same room, studying that same spot, a day later, we would be startled to discover a small area of the wall, four bricks up, four down, vanished. Where it was—let's call what's there—or what isn't there—white. To tell the truth, it's difficult to look at that spot—the eye glances away automatically, the way it does from a bright light. Should you try to force the issue, tears dilute your vision.

Return to Edgar's room over the next twenty-four hours, and you would find that gap exponentially larger—from four bricks by four bricks to sixteen by sixteen, then from sixteen by sixteen to—basically, the entire wall. Standing in the doorway, you would have to raise your hand, shield your eyes from the dull whiteness in front of you. Blink furiously, squint, and you might distinguish Edgar in his familiar position, staring straight into that blank. Strain your gaze through the narrowest opening your fingers can make, and for the half a second until your head jerks to the side, you see a figure, deep within the white. Later, at a safe remove from Edgar's room, you may attempt to reconstruct that form, make sense of your less-than-momentary vision. All you'll be able to retrieve, however, is a pair of impressions, the one of something coalescing, like smoke filling up a jar, the other of thinness, like a child's stick-drawing grown life-sized. For the next several months, not only your dreams, but your waking hours will be plagued by what you saw between your fingers. Working late at night, you will be overwhelmed by the sense that whatever you saw in that room is standing just outside the cone of light your lamp throws. Unable to help yourself, you'll reach for the shade, tilt it back, and find… nothing, your bookcases. Yet the sensation won't pass; although you can read the spines of the hardcovers ranked on your bookshelves, your skin won't stop bristling at what you can't see there.

What about Edgar, though? What image do his eyes find at the heart of that space? I suppose we should ask, What image of Virginia?

It—she changes. She's thirteen, wearing the modest dress she married him in. She's nine, wide-eyed as she listens to him reciting his poetry to her mother and her. She's dead, wrapped in a white shroud. So much concentration is required to pierce through to the undersurface in the first place—and then there's the matter of maintaining the aperture—that it's difficult to find, let alone summon, the energy necessary to focus on a single image of Virginia. So the figure in front of him brushes a lock of dark hair out of her eyes, then giggles in a child's high-pitched tones, then coughs and sprays scarlet blood over her lips and chin. Her mouth is pursed in thought; she turns to a knock on the front door; she thrashes in the heat of the disease that is consuming her. The more time that passes, the more Edgar struggles to keep his memories of his late wife separate from one another. She's nine, standing beside her mother, wound in her burial cloth. She's in her coffin, laughing merrily. She's saying she takes him as her lawful husband, her mouth smeared with blood.

Edgar can't help himself—he's written, and read, too many stories about exactly this kind of situation for him not to be aware of all the ways it could go hideously wrong. Of course, the moment such a possibility occurs to him, it's manifest in front of him. You know how it is: the harder you try to keep a pink elephant out of your thoughts, the more that animal cavorts center-stage. Virginia is obscured by white linen smeared with mud; where her mouth is, the shroud is red. Virginia is naked, her skin drawn to her skeleton, her hair loose and floating around her head as if she's under water. Virginia is wearing the dress she was buried in, the garment and the pale flesh beneath it opened by rats. Her eyes—or the sockets that used to cradle them—are full of her death, of all she has seen as she was dragged out of the light down into the dark.

With each new monstrous image of his wife, Edgar strives not to panic. He bends what is left of his will toward summoning Virginia as she was at sixteen, when they held a second, public wedding. For an instant, she's there, holding out her hand to him with that simple grace she's displayed as long as he's known her—and then she's gone, replaced by a figure whose black eyes have seen the silent halls of the dead, whose ruined mouth has tasted delicacies unknown this side of the grave. This image does not flicker; it does not yield to other, happier pictures. Instead, it grows more solid, more definite. It takes a step towards Edgar, who is frantic, his heart thudding in his chest, his mouth dry. He's trying to stop the process, trying to close the door he's spent so much time and effort prying open, to erase what he's written on that blankness. The figure takes another step forwards, and already, is at the edge of the opening. His attempts at stopping it are useless—what he's started has accrued sufficient momentum for it to continue regardless of him. His lips are still repeating, "Virginia."

When the—we might as well say, when Virginia places one gray foot onto the floor of Edgar's room, a kind of ripple runs through the entire room, as if every last bit of it is registering the intrusion. How Edgar wishes he could look away as she crosses the floor to him. In a far corner of his brain that is capable of such judgments, he knows that this is the price for his *hubris*—really, it's almost depressingly formulaic. He could almost accept the irony if he did not have to watch those hands dragging their nails back and forth over one another, leaving the skin hanging in pale strips; if he could avoid the sight of whatever is seething in the folds of the bosom of her dress; if he could shut his eyes to that mouth and its dark contents as they descend to his. But he can't; he cannot turn away from his Proserpine as she rejoins him at last.

Four days prior to his death, Edgar is found on the street, delirious, barely-conscious. He never recovers. Right at the end, he rallies long enough to dictate a highly-abbreviated version of the story I've told you to a Methodist minister, who finds what he records so disturbing he sews it into the binding of the family Bible, where it will remain concealed for a century and a half.

As for what Edgar called forth—she walks out of our narrative and is not seen again.

It's a crazy story. It makes the events of Vauglais's life seem almost reasonable in comparison. If you were so inclined, I suppose you could ascribe Edgar's experience in that rented room to an extreme form of auto-hypnosis which, combined with the stress on his body from his drinking and the brain tumor, precipitates a fatal collapse. In which case, the story I've told you is little more than an elaborate symptom. It's the kind of reading a literary critic prefers; it keep the more… outré elements safely quarantined within the writer's psyche.

Suppose, though, suppose. Suppose that all this insanity I've been feeding you isn't a quaint example of early-nineteenth-century pseudoscience. Suppose that its interest extends well beyond any insights it might offer in interpreting "The Masque of the Red Death." Suppose—let's say the catastrophe that overtakes Edgar is the result of—we could call it poor planning. Had he paid closer attention to the details of Prosper's history, especially to that sojourn in the catacombs, he would have recognized the difficulty—to the point of impossibility—of making his attempt alone. Granted, he was desperate. But there was a reason Vauglais took the members of his *salon* underground with him—to use as a source of power, a battery, as it were. They provided the energy; he directed it. Edgar's story is a testament to what must have been a tremendous—an almost unearthly will. In the end, though, it wasn't enough.

Of course, how could he have brought together a sufficient number of individuals, and where? By the close of his life, he wasn't the most popular of fellows. Not to mention, he would have needed to expose the members of this hypothetical group to Prosper's designs and their corresponding colors.

Speaking of which: pleasant as this violet has been, what do you say we proceed to the *piece de resistance*? Faceless lackeys, on my mark—

Ahh. I don't usually talk about these things, but you have no idea how much trouble this final color combination gave me. I mean, red and black gives you dark red, right? Right, except that for the design to achieve its full effect, putting up a dark red light won't do. You need red layered over black—and a true black light, not ultraviolet. The result, though—I'm sure you'll agree, it was worth sweating over. It's like a picture painted in red on a black canvas, wouldn't you say? And look what it does for the final image. It seems to be reaching right out of the screen for you, doesn't it? Strictly speaking, Vauglais's name for it, "*Le Dessous*," the Underneath, isn't quite grammatical French, but we needn't worry ourselves over such details. There are times I think another name would be more appropriate: the Maw, perhaps, and then there are moments I find the Underneath perfect. You can see why I might lean towards calling it a mouth—the Cave would do, as well—except that the perspective's all wrong. If this is a mouth, or a cave, we aren't looking into it; we're already inside, looking out.

Back to Edgar. As we've said, even had he succeeded in gathering a group to assist him in his pursuit, he would have had to find a way to introduce them to Prosper's images and their colors. If he could have, he would have... reoriented them, their minds, the channels of their thoughts. Vauglais's designs would have brought them closer to where they needed to be; they would have made available certain dormant faculties within his associates.

Even that would have left him with challenges, to be sure. Mesmerism, hypnosis, as Prosper himself discovered, is a delicate affair, one subject to such external variables as running out of lamp oil too soon. It would have been better if he could have employed some type of pharmacological agent, something that would have deposited them into a more useful state, something sufficiently concentrated to be delivered via a few bites of an innocuous food—a cookie, say, whose sweetness would mask any unpleasant taste, and which he could cajole his assistants to sample by claiming that his wife had baked them.

Then, if Edgar had been able to keep this group distracted while the cookies did their work—perhaps by talking to them about his writing—about the genesis of one of his stories, say, "The Masque of the Red Death"—if he had managed this far, he might have been in a position to make something happen, to perform the Great Work.

There's just one more thing, and that's the object for which Edgar would have put himself to all this supposed trouble: Virginia. I like to think I'm as romantic as the next guy, but honestly—you have the opportunity to rescript reality, and the best you can come up with is returning your dead wife to you? Talk about a failure to grasp the possibilities...

What's strange—and frustrating—is that it's all right there in "The Masque," in Edgar's own words. The whole idea of the Great Work, of Transumption, is to draw one of the powers that our constant, collective writing of the real consigns to abstraction across the barrier into physicality. Ideally, one of the members of that trinity Edgar named so well, Darkness and Decay and the Red Death, those who hold illimitable dominion over all. The goal is to accomplish something momentous, to shake the world to its foundations, not play out some hackneyed romantic fantasy. That was what Vauglais was up to, trying to draw into form the force that strips the flesh from our bones, that crumbles those bones to dust.

No matter. Edgar's mistake still has its uses as a distraction, and a lesson. Not that it'll do any of you much good. By now, I suspect few of you can hear what I'm saying, let alone understand it. I'd like to tell you the name of what I stirred into that cookie dough, but it's rather lengthy and wouldn't do you much good, anyway. I'd also like to tell you it won't leave you permanently impaired, but that wouldn't exactly be true. One of the consequences of its efficacy, I fear. If it's any consolation, I doubt most of you will survive what's about to follow. By my reckoning, the power I'm about to bring into our midst will require a good deal of... sustenance in order to establish a more permanent foothold here. I suspect this is of even less consolation, but I do regret this aspect of the plan I'm enacting. It's just—once you come into possession of such knowledge, how can you not make use—full use of it?

You see, I'm starting at the top. Or at the beginning—before the beginning, really, before light burst across the perfect formlessness that was everything. I'm starting with Darkness, with something that was already so old at that moment of creation that it had long forgotten its identity. I plan to restore it. I will give myself to it for a guide, let it envelop me and consume you and run out from here in a flood that will wash this world away. I will give to Darkness a dominion more complete than it has known since it was split asunder.

Look—in the air—can you see it?

For Fiona

HONORABLE MENTIONS

Atkins, Peter "The Mystery," *Spook City.*
Barron, Laird "Catch Hell," *Lovecraft Unbound.*
Berman, Steve "Kinder," *Phantom.*
Bestwick, Simon "Never Say Goodbye," *Pictures of the Dark.*
Bestwick, Simon "The Proving Ground," *Pictures of the Dark.*
Bestwick, Simon "Red Light," *Pictures of the Dark.*
Black, Holly "The Boy Who Cried Wolf," *Troll's Eye View.*
Bodard, Aliette de "The Lonely Heart," *Black Static 9.*
Clark, Simon "Mine," *Exotic Gothic 3.*
Clark, Simon "Our Lord of Quarters," *Hellbound Hearts.*
Clarke, Roz "Haunt-Type Experience," *Black Static 9.*
Dowling, Terry "Two Steps Along the River," *Exotic Gothic 3.*
Evenson, Brian "Second Boy," *Unsaid 4.*
Evenson, Brian "Windeye," *Pen America 11: Make Believe.*
Finch, Paul "Lives Less Ordinary," *Bare Bone 11.*
Gaiman, Neil "Feminine Endings," *Four Letter Word: Original Love Letters.*
Gleason, William "The Hanged Man," *Analog* October.
Goss, Theodora "The Puma," *Apex Magazine* March.
Houarner, Gerard "The Mule," *A Blood of Killers.*
Hughes, Lee "Turn the Crank," *Cern Zoo*
Irwin, Sharon "Begin with Water," *Dead Souls.*
Jones, Stephen Graham "The Ones That Got Away," *Phantom.*
Kelly, Michael "The Woods," *Tesseracts Thirteen.*
Kiernan, Caitlín R. "Galápagos," *Eclipse Three.*
Kosmatka, Ted & Poore, Michael "Blood Dauber," *Asimov's SF* Oct/Nov.
Lane, Joel "Face Down," *The Terrible Changes.*
Langan, John " The Wide, Carnivorous Sky," (novella) *By Blood We Live.*
Link, Kelly "The Cinderella Game," *Troll's Eye View.*
Lukyanenko, Sergei "Foxtrot at High Noon," *By Blood We Live.*
Nickle, David "The Radejastians," *Tesseracts Thirteen.*
Oliver, Reggie "Baskerville's Midgets," *Madder Mysteries.*
Richards, Tony "Birchiam Peer, " *British Invasion.*
Schaller, Eric "The Sparrow Mumbler," *New Genre 6.*
Siemienowicz, Miranda "Penthouse," *Overland 195.*

Strantzas, Simon "A Seed on Barren Ground," *Cold to the Touch.*
Tem, Steve Rasnic "The Cabinet Child," *Phantom.*
Thomas, Ben "The Man with the Myriad Scars," *Weird Tales 352.*
Totton, Sarah "Flatrock Sunners," *Black Static 12.*
Unsworth, Simon Kurt "Mami Wata," *Exotic Gothic 3.*
Valente, Catherynne M. "A Delicate Architecture," *Troll's Eye View.*
Williams, Conrad "Slitten Gorge," *British Invasion.*
Yolen, Jane and Stemple, Adam "Little Red," *Firebirds Soaring.*

COPYRIGHT PAGE

Night Shade Books Is an Independent Publisher of Quality SF, Fantasy and Horror

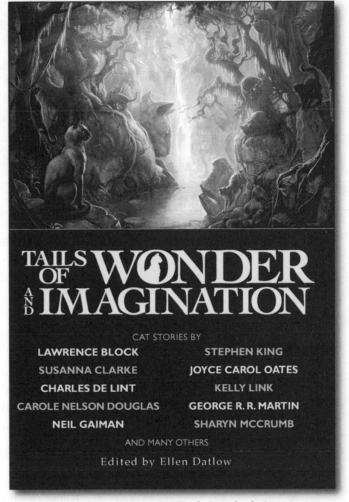

TAILS OF WONDER AND IMAGINATION

CAT STORIES BY

LAWRENCE BLOCK   STEPHEN KING

SUSANNA CLARKE   JOYCE CAROL OATES

CHARLES DE LINT   KELLY LINK

CAROLE NELSON DOUGLAS   GEORGE R. R. MARTIN

NEIL GAIMAN   SHARYN MCCRUMB

AND MANY OTHERS

Edited by Ellen Datlow

ISBN 978-1-59780-170-6, Trade Paperback; $15.95

What is it about the cat that captivates the creative imagination? No other creature has inspired so many authors to take pen to page. Mystery, horror, science fiction, and fantasy stories have all been written about cats.

From legendary editor Ellen Datlow comes *Tails of Wonder and Imagination*, showcasing forty cat tales by some of today's most popular authors. With uncollected stories by Stephen King, Tanith Lee, Peter S. Beagle, and Theodora Goss, and a previously unpublished story by Susanna Clarke, plus feline-centric fiction by Neil Gaiman, Kelly Link, George R. R. Martin, Lucius Shepard, Joyce Carol Oates, Graham Joyce, and many others.

Tails of Wonder and Imagination features more than 200,000 words of stories in which cats are heroes and stories in which they're villains; people transformed into cats, cats transformed into people. And yes, even a few cute cats.

Ellen Datlow has been editing short science fiction, fantasy, and horror for almost thirty years. She was co-editor of *The Year's Best Fantasy and Horror* for twenty-one years and currently edits *The Best Horror of the Year*. She has edited or co-edited many other anthologies, most recently *The Coyote Road* and *Troll's Eye View* (with Terri Windling), *Inferno, Poe: 19 New Tales Inspired by Edgar Allan Poe, Lovecraft Unbound, Digital Domains: A Decade of Science Fiction and Fantasy,* and *Darkness: Two Decades of Modern Horror.*

Forthcoming are *The Best Horror of the Year, Volume 3, Haunted Legends* (with Nick Mamatas), *Naked City: New Tales of Urban Fantasy, The Beastly Bride,* and *Teeth* (the latter two with Terri Windling).

She has won multiple awards for her editing, including the World Fantasy, Locus, Hugo, International Horror Guild, Shirley Jackson, and Stoker Awards. She was named recipient of the 2007 Karl Edward Wagner Award for "outstanding contribution to the genre."

For more information, visit her website at www.datlow.com.